The Road to
Pemberley

The Road to
Pemberley

An Anthology *of* New Pride and Prejudice Stories

Edited by
Marsha Altman

Ulysses Press

Published in the United States by
Ulysses Press
P.O. Box 3440
Berkeley, CA 94703
www.ulyssespress.com

ISBN: 978-1-56975-934-9
Library of Congress Catalog Number 2011922510

Acquisitions Editor: Keith Riegert
Managing Editor: Claire Chun
Editor: Kathy Kaiser
Proofreaders: Abigail Reser, Lauren Harrison
Production: Judith Metzener
Cover design: what!design @ whatweb.com
Cover photo: detail of *Mr. and Mrs. Thomas Coltman* by Joseph Wright of Derby
    (1734–1797) © National Gallery, London / Art Resource, NY

Printed in Canada by Transcontinental Printing

10 9 8 7 6 5 4 3 2 1

Distributed by Publishers Group West

Table of Contents

❧ **Introduction** 7
BY MARSHA ALTMAN

❧ **The Pemberley Ball** 11
BY REGINA JEFFERS

❧ **But He Turned Out Very Wild** 80
BY SARAH A. HOYT

❧ **A Long, Strange Trip** 107
BY ELLEN GELERMAN

❧ **An Ink-Stained Year** 122
BY VALERIE T. JACKSON

❧ **The Potential of Kitty Bennet** 181
BY JESSICA KELLER

❧ **A Good Vintage Whine** 228
BY TESS QUINN

❧ **Georgiana's Voice** 254
BY J. H. THOMPSON

❧ **Secrets in the Shade** 331
BY BILL FRIESEMA

❧ **A View from the Valet** 382
BY NACIE MACKEY

❧ *Beneath the Greenwood Trees* 412
BY MARILOU MARTINEAU

❧ *Father of the Bride* 457
BY LEWIS WHELCHEL

❧ *Pride and Prejudice Abridged* 482
BY MARSHA ALTMAN

❧ *Acknowledgments* 488

Introduction

Congratulations! If you have purchased this book, you are now a member of an active culture, if you were not in fact one already: the culture of Jane Austen's writing. Recently, it has been particularly prolific, leading to the creation of this anthology to highlight some of the best short fiction drawn from literally thousands of stories written in the style of Jane Austen over the past twenty years, most of them in the last five.

This is not by any means a new social phenomenon. The first known spin-off of Jane Austen's work was published in 1913. Sybil G. Brinton's *Old Friends and New Fancies* sought to continue the adventures of characters from all six of Jane Austen's published novels in one book. Its commercial success is unknown, as very few editions of Brinton's book existed until it was reprinted in 1998, well after it had, like Austen's own work, fallen into the public domain.

The second spin-off was the vastly superior *Pemberley Shades* by Dorothy Bonavia-Hunt, which focused exclusively on the characters from *Pride and Prejudice*. This too went out of print except for a brief publication in the 1970s, and was revived again in 2007 by Laughing Man Publications, a press I created for the express purpose of republishing *Pemberley Shades*. The book's unavailability had made it the stuff of legends. After the text was digitalized, other publishers have done their own reprintings to return the novel to the public conversation.

The first wave of the real revival of Austen-inspired fiction began in 1995, when the BBC miniseries of *Pride and Prejudice* aired.

This time, aspiring authors had a friend called the Internet, and this friend could connect them to thousands and then millions of people who might be interested in reading their work for the cost of the modem and a small monthly fee. This was also when the technology for digital printing improved enough to make print-on-demand books possible; this took the publisher out of the equation and made self-publishing available to people other than the very rich. Such self-published Jane Austen novels made their appearance on the market in 1997 and 1998, while short-form fiction found its way onto organized online forums like *The Republic of Pemberley* and *The Derbyshire Writer's Guild*. This surge lasted a few years, then the enthusiasm retreated to the most loyal and dedicated fans.

When the second wave arrived with the big-screen adaptation of *Pride and Prejudice*, publishers were better prepared, and a good deal of previously self-published Jane Austen books were scooped up by traditional presses and republished. The Internet now spawned countless websites (a slight exaggeration—you actually *can* count the number of Austen sites in existence) and opportunities for writers.

Which is where I come in (because I am clearly the most important person here, not Jane Austen). When I saw the *Pride and Prejudice* movie in 2005, I was not unfamiliar with the story, having read the book in 1999 and seen the miniseries a few years after that. But while I simply liked previous incarnations, I was at a time in my life when, for some reason, Austen's words—or more accurately, Elizabeth and Darcy's—spoke to me as they have to countless (this time it is not an exaggeration) readers and viewers since the novel was first published in 1813. The presence of other Austen-inspired fiction by amateur—and some not very amateur—writers encouraged me to dip my pen into this type of historical fiction wholly unreserved (as the original draft of my first novel on Fanfiction.net makes obvious). Three years and ten manuscripts later, I had a book deal, a pile of *Pride and Prejudice* books on my shelf, and more English history tomes than is feasible for someone with an apartment in Manhattan.

I have never shied away from using the term "fan fiction" (or "fanfic") to describe what it is we are reading here. It is a precise technical term: fiction written by fans of an original work. Since entering the publishing world, never have I seen so many euphemisms for the obvious: sequels, spin-offs, inspirations, retellings, reinventings, and "paraliterature."

The last I encountered in a rather brusque manner. After my first book deal and my graduation from City College of New York with a Master of Fine Arts in Creative Writing, I made the traditional Austen pilgrimage to England, visiting the house where she did most of her writing in Chawton, her grave in Winchester, and the estate that probably served as the inspiration for Pemberley (and was in fact used for exterior shots in the 2005 movie), Chatsworth House. Most of the places I visited sought to cash in on the craze with every bit of paraphernalia possible, which is why I own a key chain with Jane Austen's image on one side and the opening line to *Pride and Prejudice* on the other, and a feathered pen that came in a package with an oil picture that is labeled as Mr. Darcy (but is obviously the likeness of Colin Firth).

At one of these locations, I pointed out the presence of some books on the shelf of the gift shop. "Oh, you've got fanfic! I love this stuff. You know, my own book—"

"It's not fan fiction!" the person working the register said, waving a finger in my direction. "It's *paraliterature*. We only sell books that are retellings from Darcy's point of view. The sequel stuff is junk!"

The technicalities of how this line was drawn eluded me, as one of the novels on the shelf featured a piece of *paraliterature* in which Darcy, Lord Byron, and several servants engaged in a well-written omnisexual orgy, but the implication was that that was somehow better than my little post-novel story and Jane Austen would be more approving of its existence. I decided not to mention this, as the mood was already confrontational and I still had things to buy in the shop.

Anyway, here's some fan fiction. Enjoy!

Marsha Altman
New York, New York, 2011

The Pemberley Ball
BY REGINA JEFFERS

Regina Jeffers is the author of several Jane Austen adaptations including *Darcy's Passions*, *Darcy's Temptation*, *Vampire Darcy's Desire*, *The Phantom of Pemberley* and *Captain Wentworth's Persuasion*. She considers herself a Janeite and spends her free time with the Jane Austen Society of North America and AustenAuthors.com. A teacher for nearly forty years in the public school systems of three different states, Jeffers is a Time Warner Star Teacher Award winner, a Martha Holden Jennings Scholar, a Columbus Educator Award winner, and a guest panelist for the Smithsonian. She's served on various national educational committees and is often sought as a media literacy consultant. Her first Regency romance, *The Scandal of Lady Eleanor*, was released in March 2011 by Ulysses Press.

In writing "The Pemberley Ball," Jeffers decided to stay with the originally proposed theme of this anthology, Elizabeth and Darcy's first year of marriage and the challenges they might face individually and together.

❧◈❧

Part 1

Yes.

She had said yes. She would be his. Forever. After a year of piercing heartache, Elizabeth Bennet had accepted his proposal, and where winter had once held sway in Darcy's heart, springtime now filled it. Although he had been loath to admit it, Elizabeth had fascinated him from the beginning—fascinated him more than anyone else ever had.

Yet Darcy had at first scarcely allowed her to be pretty; he had looked at her without admiration at the Meryton assembly; and when they next met, he looked at her only to criticize. But no sooner had he made it clear to himself and his friends that Elizabeth had hardly a good feature than he realized that her dark eyes were uncommonly intelligent. "Eyes that could haunt a man's sleep," he told himself as he checked his cravat in the mirror.

"I beg your pardon, sir," his valet said and looked up from brushing Darcy's jacket.

Darcy smiled. "It is nothing, Mr. Jordan—just thinking aloud."

In the mirror, Darcy watched the man—who had served him for fifteen years—roll his eyes. Darcy understood perfectly. Less than a week earlier, he had been an outsider—an observer of life, never a participant. He had fought valiantly to maintain his distance, keeping his friends and acquaintances to a minimum. Years ago, he had learned his lesson the hard way. Darcy's most trusted friend had betrayed him on every level. Even now, as his fists closed tightly at his side, he could taste the bitterness. Yet despite the fact that his brain had warned him to be wary, he had chosen to place his trust in another—Elizabeth Bennet.

Her acceptance had given him the hope that things could be different. Elizabeth brought warmth and naturalness and a bit of defi-

12

ance; but there was vulnerability also. She had bravely withstood Caroline Bingley's barbs while devotedly nursing her sister. She had verbally fenced with the paragon of haughtiness that was his aunt, Lady Catherine, and had come away unscathed. Despite Darcy's best efforts to resist Elizabeth, she made him laugh.

"Your coat, sir." Mr. Jordan held the jacket as Darcy slipped his arms through and allowed the valet to straighten the seams across his shoulders.

"Thank you, Mr. Jordan." Darcy tugged easily on his cuffs to set the line. "I will be at Longbourn for the supper hour." It was his first meal with the Bennets as Elizabeth's betrothed, and he pronounced his evening's entertainment more so to solidify the event's reality in his mind than to keep his valet informed.

Again, the amused twitch of Jordan's lips told Darcy that his man understood how Darcy's life had changed. "Very good, sir."

He realized that his servants had waited for him to choose a bride—to bring a mistress to Pemberley. Now he was to marry Elizabeth and take her to his ancestral home. In the fullness of time, they would set up a nursery. He knew now that only Elizabeth— with her loving nature, her common sense, and her *goodness*—could be the mother of his children. "Turn down the bed, and lay out my things, and then you may be excused for the evening. Upon my return, I will undress myself." Darcy accepted a handkerchief from Mr. Jordan.

"As you wish, Mr. Darcy."

Darcy's heart swelled with happiness as he sat beside Elizabeth at the Longbourn table. The most recent time he had dined with the Bennets, her mother had placed him as far away from Elizabeth as the table would allow. He had spent the meal on one side of Mrs.

Bennet. Such a situation had given pleasure to neither of them, and he certainly had not appeared to advantage. Whenever he and Elizabeth's mother had spoken to each other, Darcy could not abandon his formal tone. Tonight, *ungraciousness* would not describe him.

"The venison is excellent, Mrs. Bennet," he announced. The way the Bennets talked over one another made him wish for a quiet meal at Pemberley. He relished such meals, which he currently shared with his sister, and he looked forward to sharing them with Elizabeth. Picturing Elizabeth at his table was a recurring daydream.

Elizabeth gave him the smallest of smiles, and his heart jumped. There had been a time when he prayed for such moments, and now they were his to cherish.

Mrs. Bennet preened with his praise and then returned her attention to her eldest daughter and Mr. Bingley. This pleased Darcy; that left him to converse with Mr. Bennet and Elizabeth, the true intellects at the table. Unwilling to lose his favorite daughter, Mr. Bennet had originally not welcomed Darcy's courtship of Elizabeth, but Mr. Bennet had subsequently accepted Elizabeth's assurance of her regard for Darcy.

"Elizabeth tells me that you are considering investing in railroads, Mr. Darcy."

Mr. Bennet sipped his wine, but Darcy observed the man's eyebrows rise mockingly. "It appears prudent to become a partner while the companies are forming. I am considering a small company catering to Derbyshire's needs, taking products to Liverpool for shipment to the Americas and north toward Manchester and the factories. The cities draw workers from the estates. It would be a way to save my father's legacy."

Surprisingly, Mr. Bennet's expression changed to one of respect. "Well, Lizzy. It appears that your young man has a head for business."

Elizabeth looked lovingly at her father, tears pricking the corners of her eyes. "Yes, Papa." Then she smiled. "It is a happy situation. Mr. Darcy shall not bore me with inane chatter at the breakfast table. He has, I fear, quite a good mind," she said playfully. And although she spoke kindly of him, Darcy flinched. Being teased, even kindly, still hurt him as if were twelve years old once again.

Back at Netherfield, Darcy had always enjoyed engaging Elizabeth in what he fondly called verbal swordplay, but somehow this felt different, and his tone came out sharper than he intended. "I pride myself on being well read." Darcy had responded automatically, and he waited for the "attack," but it did not come. Instead, Elizabeth looked questioningly at him. Darcy gave his head a little shake, telling her not to ask. Then he turned to her father, "Mr. Bennet, what might you tell me of Miss Elizabeth's childhood? I will need plenty of stories for our friends if I am to brighten the long winters of Derbyshire."

Throughout the rest of the meal, Mr. Bennet—with occasional comments from his wife or one of Elizabeth's sisters—regaled Darcy with tales of a young Elizabeth's exploits. Everything that he had ever considered that he knew of her changed somehow. He discovered the source of Elizabeth's self-deprecation lay in Mrs. Bennet's continual praise of her eldest and her youngest. He now understood why Mary Bennet sought refuge in her music, and the immature Kitty in her interest in fashion. Each girl claimed her own niche, and Elizabeth's strengths rested in less stereotypically feminine accomplishments. She possessed a pleasing voice, but Elizabeth did not play the pianoforte exceptionally well, nor was her needlework beyond being adequate. She was not gifted in languages nor did she paint tables, cover screens, or net purses.

Elizabeth owned a quick wit, and she used it as her defense against being found wanting. "Follies and nonsense, whims and inconsistencies, do divert me, and I laugh at them whenever I can," she had said one evening at Netherfield, when Caroline Bingley had insisted on Elizabeth's walking about the room with her. Now, despite thoroughly enjoying the flush of pink coloring her skin, Darcy considered how many of Elizabeth's earlier escapades might appear quite mortifying to her in their retellings. It seemed that many of her embarrassing moments had come at her own hand. She often acted impulsively. Although he understood why she used her daring as a diversion, he could not help but wonder if Elizabeth would not be happier if known for her merits, rather than her mistakes. *But negative attention is still attention,* he told himself.

◆◆◆

"I suppose my mother forgets that I, too, have a wedding to plan," Elizabeth said softly beside him. They sat together in a Longbourn drawing room. As was typical, after the evening meal, Mr. Bennet had retreated to his study to read. Kitty examined the latest fashion plates, and Mary practiced her music. Mrs. Bennet had demanded that Jane Bennet and Bingley join her in the sitting room to finalize plans for their wedding breakfast. So although others remained in the room, he and Elizabeth might as well have been alone.

Darcy was not sure whether she had meant for him to overhear her muttering. With a deep sigh, Elizabeth turned to him. "It is abhorrent of me to complain after all your ministrations on my sister's behalf. Forgive me, Mr. Darcy."

Darcy watched carefully, expecting Elizabeth to turn her moment of envy into another disparagement of her own failings, but she did no such thing. Evidently, this was a private moment: Elizabeth would show him a face that spoke the truth: Her mother's preference bruised his future wife's feelings. "I would forgive you

16

anything, Elizabeth, if we could move beyond your calling me Mr. Darcy. Could you not call me by my given name?"

She smiled broadly. "You wish for me to call you Fitzwilliam? I would enjoy that, sir."

"Then say it, Elizabeth," he whispered hoarsely—his breathing suddenly constricted. Her eyes mesmerized him. The effect she had on him always took Darcy by surprise.

Elizabeth leaned in closer, unaware of what she did to his composure. "Fitzwilliam, have I told you how happy I am to become your wife?" she murmured softly.

Desire shot through Darcy. He had planned to kiss her this evening—had actually dreamed how it would be. His finger now traced a line from her temple to her chin. "You, my dearest, loveliest Elizabeth, do not know how long I have waited for you to say so."

Realizing their impropriety, Elizabeth blushed and leaned away from him. "May we speak of the wedding, sir?"

Darcy sighed but he said evenly, "Of course, Miss Elizabeth. What do you wish to settle?"

Elizabeth turned to him again. "We must agree on the ceremony's date. Do you favor a long engagement?"

Darcy straightened his shoulders, a posture he automatically adopted when completing business transactions; and, after all, among his society, marriage was a business. "I have waited to claim you for a year. I must admit that I am of the persuasion to finalize that claim as soon as possible, but I am not insensitive to the fact that this is a greater change for you. You must leave your home and family behind to start a new life with me. And although I wish to have you on Pemberley's staircase when I return from my trips, I will understand if you insist on a longer waiting period."

Elizabeth blushed again. "You have thought of me with you at Pemberley, Fitzwilliam?" she asked sweetly.

Darcy smiled. "You would be shocked, Elizabeth, at how often each day you enter my mind."

"How often?" she prompted.

"Too often," he growled quietly. "And in too many ways." Then he was silent, willing away his arousal with a mental recitation of multiplication tables.

"Oh!" she said and gasped. A long pause followed. Elizabeth glanced at Kitty, who was sketching a fashionable dress pattern. "Except for my father, I do not believe anyone here will realize I am gone," she murmured. Her face was sad for a moment, and then she turned to Darcy with a smile. "A shorter engagement seems advisable," she said with more confidence. "Mr. Bingley tells me that the North Road can be hazardous in winter. If we are to Derbyshire, it would be judicious to do so sooner rather than later."

"Mr. Bingley is correct. Derbyshire winters can be cruel. Plus, I would wish to celebrate the holidays at Pemberley. Georgiana and I have spent the past few Christmases in London. It is my dream to take you to my home and for you to share it with my sister. With your acceptance, I will instruct Mrs. Reynolds to open up the house for a winter ball. We have not held one at Pemberley for more than a decade. I can introduce my new wife—the estate's new mistress—to my close family and friends."

Darcy saw Elizabeth's look of apprehension, although she tried to hide it. "Then after the calling of the banns…how much longer after that?" she thought aloud.

Darcy's lips curved upward. "If it were my choice, the very next day after the third calling."

"My sister and Mr. Bingley have chosen the Monday after our third Sunday for their date. Do you wish for a double wedding, Mr. Darcy?"

He frowned. "I had not considered a double wedding, nor had I foreseen our final banns would be called so close to Miss Bennet's chosen day." His voice took on an encouraging tone. "Despite my close association with Bingley, I would not be pleased to share the day of our joining with his and Miss Bennet's. I would rather have you, not your sister, be the center of attention in your first hours as my wife."

Elizabeth expelled a sigh of relief. "Thank you, Fitzwilliam," she whispered, "for understanding. I love Jane, but the day I become Mrs. Darcy is not a day I would want to share with another."

"Then a week after the final calling," he declared. "That is a month from this Sunday. Is that sufficient time, Elizabeth?"

"It is perfect, Fitzwilliam. The first week of November," she said wistfully.

<hr />

"Your hat, Mr. Darcy," Elizabeth said teasingly as she clung to his arm.

"Walk me out," he said softly. He caught her hand and tugged Elizabeth along behind him. As soon as they were away from the lights of Longbourn's windows, Darcy pulled her into his embrace.

"Fitzwilliam," she said and giggled. But she willingly leaned against him, resting her head on Darcy's chest. He wrapped his greatcoat about her, both to keep her warm and to keep her in his embrace.

He bent his head to speak into her ear. "Elizabeth," he rasped, "it is my intention to kiss you." He felt her stiffen. "If you do not want this, then you should return to the house immediately." Darcy waited for her decision. When she remained in his arms, he felt exhilaration. Elizabeth would accept his kiss. He lifted her chin and lowered his mouth to hers.

He kept one arm about her to steady her. With his other hand, Darcy cupped her chin, tilting her head gently upward. Elizabeth was an innocent and he took his time. He brushed his lips across hers before adding some pressure. He skimmed his tongue along her lip's line, and she opened for him. Even then, Darcy did not deepen the kiss—just enjoyed the possibility. After a few moments, he reluctantly removed his lips from hers. "You are delicious," he whispered.

Elizabeth clung to his coat's lapels, but she breathed the words, "So are you."

Darcy recognized her blush's heat as he bent to kiss the tip of her nose. "We will take my curricle and see some of the countryside tomorrow," he declared.

"Orders, Mr. Darcy?" she taunted as she released her hold and prepared to move away.

He slid his hands down Elizabeth's arms, capturing her hands in his. Darcy chuckled. "My dear, our relationship is new. Of course, you will not object if I issue orders. It is only after we marry that you will voice your opposition."

Elizabeth stepped back. "Have you learned nothing of my nature, Mr. Darcy? There is a stubbornness about me that the will of others cannot quash. With every attempt to intimidate me, my courage always rises."

Darcy laughed warmly. "Now *there* is the Elizabeth Bennet who has plagued my every waking moment for a year." He caught her hand again and led Elizabeth to where his horse stood waiting. "I will call for you at ten."

"Yes, Fitzwilliam," she said a little too sweetly to be sincere. "I shall be anticipating it."

Darcy kissed her forehead. "Good evening, Elizabeth. I, too, will anticipate the day and hour."

She sat quietly beside him as Darcy deftly worked the reins to turn the curricle toward Oakham Mount. They had walked there the day after his second proposal, but Darcy had seen nothing but the woman he loved. Today, he had hoped to actually take in the Hertfordshire countryside, spend time with Elizabeth, and maybe steal another kiss. "Have I offered you an offense, Elizabeth?" Ten minutes had passed since she had spoken.

Elizabeth looked reluctantly at him as Darcy slowed the horse to an easy walk. "No, sir," she said and gulped.

He brought the animal to a halt and turned to her, before availing himself of her hand and removing her glove. Elizabeth looked away when he began to trace circles on her palm. "Elizabeth, I can count on these pretty fingers how many sentences you have spoken to me today. Can you not trust me with your thoughts?"

"Trust?" she echoed softly as he raised her chin to see her eyes clearly.

"Do you wish for me to return you to Longbourn?" Darcy watched as a flash of recognition crossed her face. "Is that it, sweetheart? You did not want to accompany me today?"

Elizabeth flinched when he reached for her cheek. "Not exactly."

Darcy returned her hand to her lap. "Then tell me exactly. I will not be angry, no matter what it is."

"We...we have not been...been alone like this before," she confessed.

"Like what?" he encouraged. "Did you think I had plans to seduce you?" Frustration played through his tone.

Elizabeth stifled a sob. "No."

"Sweetheart, you must tell me what disturbs you. I will not look at you, and you may look away if you wish, but I would hear what brings you sorrow." He turned to face forward.

Silence—broken only by a bird's call and a rabbit's race through the underbrush. Finally, she cleared her throat. "Yesterday evening...when I returned to the house...my mother had observed our embrace." Elizabeth paused again, but Darcy forced himself to look straight head. He had given his word. "My mother chastised me for my behavior and wondered aloud if my so-called wantonness was the source of your proposal."

Darcy mumbled a curse. "I apologize if my action has brought you humiliation," he said through gritted teeth. "Did you object to my kiss? Did it make you uncomfortable?"

"No." Her face flamed. "I enjoyed it."

How her family treated Elizabeth incensed him. "I will not live my life by the standards established by others." Mrs. Bennet, Darcy reflected, had shut the barn door after the horse escaped. If she had exercised some control over her youngest, he would not have been forced to lay out several thousand pounds to entice George Wickham to marry Lydia Bennet. "We are engaged and an expression of our affection is natural." Without looking at her, he picked up Elizabeth's hand and brought it to his lips. "I will not demand more of you than what you are comfortable with. But we must spend time alone, Elizabeth. How else are we to really get to know each other? At Pemberley, we must be of one mind on how to keep the estate successful. And we have an obligation to an heir. Both of those require that we become familiar with each other prior to exchanging vows. I hope that we can consult with each other—act as partners in running our estate and raising our family."

Elizabeth sucked in a sharp breath. "You wish your wife to be your partner also?"

"I do. I could have chosen a woman as Pemberley's mistress long ago, but I needed something more than a pretty figure. I am not saying that your figure is lacking! But your mind is impressive, too, owing in part to your extensive reading. When I speak of railroads or crop rotation, your eyes do not glaze over, nor do you simply nod. You challenge, and you puzzle, and you demand."

"I see." Elizabeth was silent a moment. "You appreciate me for who I am, Fitzwilliam."

"I do."

She looked at him broodingly. "I shall speak to my father. Perhaps he can persuade my mother to curb her tongue," she announced.

"And if he cannot?"

"I shall ignore her remarks. In a month, you will be my husband."

They had left the carriage behind, making the last part of the summit's climb on foot. "I love the view from here," Elizabeth said, turning in circles, taking it all in. Darcy's watched her with pleasure. "See." She pointed off to the left. "Past that second tree line is the steepled roof of Netherfield." Darcy's eyes followed her arm's line as he stepped behind her. "And that patchwork field is part of Sir William Lucas's land." Elizabeth shifted to stand closer when Darcy snaked his arms about her waist and kissed the nape of her neck. He heard the quick intake of her breath. "And...and over there...to the right, one can see Longbourn's entrance."

"All I see is your beauty," Darcy whispered. "I did not see these sights when we visited this overlook most recently." He kissed behind her ear. "I suspect we will need to be married many years before I will see Longbourn's entrance from this point."

Elizabeth turned in his arms. "I never realized, Mr. Darcy, that you were capable of sweet courtship words," she teased, sliding her arms about his waist.

One eyebrow rose. "You think me capable of only mundane or scholarly conversation, Miss Bennet?"

Elizabeth laid her cheek against his chest. "No." She shook her head slightly. "No, Fitzwilliam. There was a time that I would have said so, but not now. Your letter's genuine adieus and then our time at Pemberley showed me otherwise. I was foolish to have so misjudged you." She sighed deeply and closed her eyes.

Darcy grasped her to himself more tightly. "Elizabeth, you have no idea how right this feels."

"Yes, I do." She moved closer as Darcy lowered his head for a kiss.

"We should return to Longbourn, Elizabeth!" he called as she skittered ahead of him, turning down another pathway.

She smiled joyously. "You must see this, Fitzwilliam. Please. Really, you must."

"No," he asserted. "It is past the hour that we agreed to return. Mr. Bingley and I are to call on the vicar today."

Elizabeth walked backward along the trail, teasingly motioning for him to follow. "My family is accustomed to my being late, and Mr. Bingley will not complain about more time with Jane."

Darcy folded his arms across his chest and gave her his sternest look. "I insist, Elizabeth. Do not play games today." The controlled cadences of his voice indicated his irritation.

"Games?" Her voice lost its playfulness. "It is not a game, Fitzwilliam. When I wish to share something important with you, it is not a game. Not an hour ago, you declared that in our life together we would be partners. You asked to know more of me, but at your first chance to do so, you shun the opportunity."

"I have a responsibility to Bingley, and I gave my word to your father that we would return before the afternoon meal."

She shook her head, willing his words away. "I absolve you of fault for my tardiness. Return to Longbourn and your appointments. I shall find my own way."

"Elizabeth, be reasonable," he pleaded. "I will not leave you alone. A gentleman would never do so."

She laughed but it was a bitter sound. "Have no worry, Mr. Darcy. As you so eloquently expressed at Rosings, my connections make me inferior. I am not a lady. You have recognized the degradation of your association with me. Of my family obstacles." Tears stung her eyes. Elizabeth turned on her heel and strode away.

"Be that way!" he shouted to her retreating form. Frustrated, he returned to the waiting carriage. "If she thinks that I will chase after her," he growled under his breath, "she has another think coming."

***

Elizabeth rushed forward, desperate to put space between her and the most infuriating man that she had ever known. Thoughts of him—of his demanding tone—spurred her on. She had expected pangs of anguish, but only annoyance arrived. Ignoring her tears, she broke into a run.

***

Darcy sat, impatiently waiting for her return. *What if that trail is not a dead end?* he asked himself. *Then I am sitting here, making an even bigger fool of myself.* Reluctantly, he stepped to the ground. Taking a deep breath to regain his composure, he started off at a leisurely pace along the trail Elizabeth had followed. He would not run after her. Elizabeth was quite capable of handling the uneven terrain and the encroaching foliage, which narrowed the path. But then the path became even narrower. *Is this even passable?* he wondered as he pushed a low-hanging branch aside.

Then he saw her, standing perfectly still. Her back to him. Instantly, he regretted their argument. She had acted impetuously, but that was no reason that they should argue. "Elizabeth," he said softly, stepping into the small clearing.

She refused to acknowledge him. Her anger, obviously, remained.

"I am sorry that we had words. I was insensitive to what you tried to tell me." He edged forward. She remained eerily still. Darcy circled to her side. "Please, Elizabeth, can you not forgive me? We should be celebrating our happiness."

By now, he was in a position to see her profile. Dried tear tracks showed, but something else remained. Fear. Pure fear. Carefully, he examined her whole body. Every nerve was on alert. "What is it, sweetheart?" But her answer never came. Elizabeth did not even breathe. Then he saw it. Darcy swallowed his own fear. "Do not move!" he rasped.

Part 2

Her right foot rested at an awkward angle in a rabbit's hole. That was a problem, but not the crisis that had sent his blood racing. "Elizabeth," he whispered, "I will get you out of this."

She did not respond, but he saw hope flicker in her eyes.

"Sweetheart, without moving your foot, I need for you to loosen your cloak's hook. I cannot chance that your garment will catch one of the snakes against your leg." She had stepped into a hibernating nest of adders. He could see three moving slowly about her half boot. Their backs' brown zigzag patterns and their large heads clearly identified their species. "Can you do that for me?"

She barely breathed, but he heard her nevertheless. "I am frightened."

"I know, love." He slowly removed his greatcoat, draping it over a nearby branch. "But I cannot do this alone. Together, we are invincible. Unfasten the cloak, and hold it until I tell you to let it drop. Do you understand?"

Elizabeth gave the slightest nod and then slowly lifted her arms. When her hands stilled, Darcy inched forward. "When I tell you to do so, drop the cloak from your shoulders. It will cover the two by the hole's opening." Darcy inhaled slowly. "I will jerk you free before the one by your boot strikes." Darcy edged within inches of her. "I love you, Elizabeth," he whispered. "On three, you will drop the cloak. One. Two. Three."

Darcy saw it all in slow motion. The dark blue cloak slithered from her shoulders, covering the two smaller adders on her left as he tossed Elizabeth over his shoulder. The snake resting on her boot's toe fell back into the hole, but Darcy had not seen the fourth one hidden under her skirt's hem. When it struck his Hessian boots, the impact surprised him, but he did not pause to inspect the damage. Ignoring the brambles tearing at his jacket, he ran some fifteen meters along the path before he stopped suddenly and clutched Elizabeth to him. "Tell me you are well!" he demanded as his hands traced her face and arms. "Did it strike you? The adder?" he pleaded.

Elizabeth sobbed, but other than a few scratches on her face, he saw no wounds. "Your legs?" he begged. "Did the adder strike your legs?" he ground out the words.

"No," she wept. "You saved me." Elizabeth collapsed against him, and Darcy gulped for air.

"My God!" His hands shook as he stroked her back. "I could have lost you."

"I am sorry," she moaned. "I was silly. Oh, God, Fitzwilliam, I am sorry."

Darcy wiped her tears away with his thumbs. "As long as you are unhurt." He kissed her forehead and cuddled her again. After a few minutes, Darcy moved a bit away from her. "Stay here. Let me retrieve my coat and your wrap."

"Leave the cloak." Elizabeth looked warily down the trail, as if she expected an army of snakes to have followed them.

Darcy examined her face closely. "Are you sure?"

"I cannot bear it, Fitzwilliam. I would feel as if the snakes crawled on me." She shivered.

Darcy nodded. "I will retrieve the cloak, and you can donate it to someone in need. I will buy you a new one as a wedding gift." He strode away. Seconds later, he returned, placing his coat over her shoulders. "Can you walk?"

"I am not sure. I turned my ankle."

Before scooping her into his arms, Darcy draped the cloak over a bush. "You will allow me to tend to my future wife," he announced as he carried Elizabeth along the trail.

She laced her arms about his neck and kissed Darcy's cheek. "I could become accustomed to such luxuries, Mr. Darcy."

"If this is what it takes to keep you safe, then I will gladly persevere." He lifted her into the curricle's seat. "May I have a kiss for my efforts?" He cupped her chin in his large palm.

"If that is what it takes to keep you happy, then I will gladly persevere." She leaned forward to touch his waiting lips with hers.

Darcy winked at her. "That it is, my love." Then he disappeared into the underbrush to retrieve her cloak, which he folded carefully and stuffed in the small trunk under the curricle's seat. "Let me take you home."

———

"You were lucky," Charles Bingley observed as he examined the mark on Darcy's boot. "It did not penetrate the leather." They had called on the local vicar to make arrangements for their separate ceremonies. Now, they relaxed together in Bingley's study.

Charles and Jane Bennet were both part of Mr. Pinncatch's congregation. The man would call their banns two more times before their ceremony. "Mrs. Bennet must be beside herself to have three daughters married within such a short time," the vicar had observed as he recorded Darcy's information in his official records.

"I imagine the lady is quite content." Darcy would tolerate Mrs. Bennet for Elizabeth's sake, but he held little respect for the woman—even less so now that he had seen firsthand how the lady slighted her middle daughters, especially Elizabeth.

"You will request the banns called in your home parish, Mr. Darcy?" Pinncatch inquired.

Darcy brought their business to a close. "I will inform Mr. Bradford, but I will purchase a common license. I do not expect to return to Derbyshire before the date Miss Elizabeth has chosen for our joining. It may be difficult to provide the necessary paperwork for your records before the ceremony."

"Either way is acceptable, sir. I cannot imagine anyone would object to your marrying Miss Elizabeth." Darcy could think of several: Charles's sister, Caroline Bingley, and Darcy's aunt, Lady Catherine, were among them.

"Of course," he assured the vicar. "Miss Elizabeth is above reproach." But even as he said the words, something had nagged at him.

"Miss Elizabeth must have been terribly frightened."

Bingley's words brought Darcy back to their conversation. "I will have to teach my young bride about the consequences of impetuous actions," he observed.

Bingley's surprise showed. "Surely, Darcy, you do not place the blame of today's near disaster on Miss Elizabeth's shoulders?"

Darcy looked at Bingley narrowly as he sipped his brandy. "And why should I not? Despite my insistence that we had given our word to return to Longbourn, Elizabeth set off on her own. She is fortunate that I refused her demand to leave her to her own devices."

Bingley swirled the brandy in his glass. "I would not have denied her in the first place."

"Really?" Darcy's eyebrow rose. He longed to share Pemberley with Elizabeth, but he would not allow her to control him.

Bingley smiled calmly. "Really. Miss Elizabeth is young, and maybe a bit unpredictable, but she possesses what you most require. You need an heir, and the lady is young enough to bear you healthy children. And instead of saying that she acts before she thinks, I, personally, prefer to think of Miss Jane Bennet's sister as a young woman with a zest for life. Is not her energy what attracted you to the lady originally?"

Darcy paused before answering. "I am not sure what attraction the lady held."

"You will enjoy the Meryton bonfire," Elizabeth said as she snuggled against Darcy's shoulder. They shared a carriage with Bingley and Miss Bennet. Darcy had sent his large coach to London to bring Georgiana and Mrs. Annesley, his sister's companion, to Netherfield. He needed reinforcements. Bingley's youngest sister would descend on his friend's estate on Tuesday, just in time to put a damper on Darcy's enjoyment of the wedding of his old friend and Miss Jane Bennet. At least, with Georgiana in residence, Darcy could feign seeing to his sister's needs.

"It celebrates the village's founding," Jane Bennet explained.

Bingley caught his fiancée's hand. "I do not recall a bonfire last year. Did I miss it somehow?"

"The weather right after Michaelmas was so wet. Everything had to be postponed, and then finally it was canceled," Elizabeth explained.

"Ah. Now I understand."

"Sometime we will have to join the Bonfire Night in York," Darcy added. "The best bonfire toffee I have ever eaten."

"So what shall we see tonight?" Bingley asked good-naturedly.

"Lots of food...and people—" Jane began.

"And dancing," Elizabeth interrupted.

"Dancing in a village square?" Darcy snarled.

"I swear, Fitzwilliam, must you find everything repugnant?" she blurted.

Resentfully, Darcy said, "I am aware that you enjoy dancing more than I do."

Elizabeth eased away, realizing that she had stirred his ire. "I spoke out of line, Mr. Darcy," she said apologetically.

Darcy should have accepted her apology, but he was slow to forgive. This was their second tiff in less than four days, and, unbidden, questions formed in his mind. Would they always snipe at each other? Were their personalities too different? *I hope not*, he told himself.

———

The evening seemed colder than the temperature. Elizabeth remained by his side, but they showed no affection. It was as he wished, but it felt wrong. He preferred Elizabeth on his arm, so that he could cup her hand with his free one. "I gave your cloak to Mr. Pinncatch to pass on to a needy soul. I have asked Georgiana to bring you a new one from town."

Elizabeth glanced down at the plain brown wool that she wore. She had borrowed it, an old one of Charlotte's, from Lady Lucas. "I thank you, sir. It is kind of you, although I do not deserve it."

"Of course, you deserve it. As my wife, you will order a whole new wardrobe," he assured her.

Elizabeth blushed, but she managed to say, "I have apologized more in the past few days than I have in the past several years. And I suppose I must offer my sincere regrets again. Although I have experienced Pemberley's grandeur, I had not thought so much of the differences in our styles of life." Glancing around to assure privacy, she looked up at him. "If you have questions of our suitability, Mr. Darcy, you must not feel compelled to maintain our engagement."

Darcy caught her elbow and directed Elizabeth away from the milling crowd. He could not believe what she had just said: She did not want to marry him. "First, Miss Elizabeth, a gentleman never breaks an engagement. If I did, you would be ruined socially."

"Not as much as if I canceled the ceremony," she asserted.

Darcy frowned. His heart raced uncontrollably. "You have actually considered this?" A cold, sick feeling gripped him.

Elizabeth's eyes dropped, and she clutched her hands before her. "It is not my desire, sir. Yet I cannot help but feel that I am a disappointment to you. That the reality of me—of my life—of my family—is more difficult than you had expected."

Darcy thought a moment before he spoke. "Elizabeth, I have eight years on you, and where you have known a certain freedom, I have known nothing but duty and responsibility and name. We are products of our upbringings, but does that mean we should not be together? As a couple, our differences will make us stronger, not weaker. I have no desire to end our engagement. I pray that you feel the same." He waited impatiently for Elizabeth's response.

"I chose you, Mr. Darcy. Not your wealth. Not your estate. Not your family name or prestige."

"And I chose you, Miss Elizabeth, above all others," he said evenly.

As he stared into her eyes, he recognized her apprehension, and Darcy resolved to protect and love her. Only when Bingley came to ask Elizabeth to join the others in the Founders' Day dance did Darcy release her.

When Elizabeth had suggested that they end their engagement, his secret "sensible" response had been to agree, but then his heart screamed, *You cannot let her go!* And for a moment, he could not breathe. A strange spasm had clutched his heart and had shaken him to his core. With her, Darcy had left his sane, rational self behind. When Elizabeth had spoken of terminating their betrothal, Darcy had wanted to drop to his knees to beg her to change her mind.

Elizabeth joined the party revelers, but her mind remained on Darcy. She had gambled with her future when she asked if he wished to call off the engagement. Fitzwilliam Darcy was a complicated man, and Elizabeth was not sure she could be a fit wife for him. He needed so much. At one time, she had thought of him as proud and not much more, but she had erred. Darcy was so much more.

Earlier, she had argued with her mirrored reflection. "Mr. Darcy's wealth has not brought him contentment. Therefore, he needs me." She drew in a shuddering breath. "A good man rests beneath that austere exterior, but how do I reach him? I will not allow anyone to hurt him—even myself. I will step away first."

"Come, Miss Elizabeth," Bingley's words brought her attention to the roaring fire. The town residents would lock hands and dance around the flames in a cross between a Spanish fandango and a Scottish reel. Using a strathspey traveling step and a slide, the inner circle would move clockwise, and the outer one counterclockwise. Elizabeth caught Bingley's hand on her right and that of Bryson Lucas, Charlotte Collins's oldest brother, on her left. With a laugh, she stepped into the dance.

⋅✦⋅

Darcy watched Elizabeth. Earlier, she had taken his words as an insinuation that he found her clothing unsuitable for his future wife, and, of course, she had taken offense. Yet, as usual, he had not explained himself accurately. In reality, he had only thought of finally having the right to dress her in the finest silks. Elizabeth in satin and lace. Her beautiful face was so expressive.

When he held her, Darcy felt alive in ways that he could not explain, even to himself. He sometimes thought that if he could hold Elizabeth all day and all night, then his world would right itself. He was, he knew, exceptionally privileged. But life brought disappointment, and sometimes grief, and often disillusionment. His life was not simple. And he was rarely carefree; he took matters seriously. From the time of reaching his maturity, Darcy had carried the weight of Pemberley on his shoulders. As a brother, a landlord, and an estate master, so many people's happiness was in his guardianship. So much power. So much responsibility. So much loneliness.

He ought to join her—take Elizabeth's hand and weave a crazy side step around an open fire. But he would not—could not—live life that freely. He was Fitzwilliam Darcy of Pemberley. He had to maintain the pretense. Traces of numbness had descended over him when Elizabeth had said the words aloud, the ones he most feared. The fear that no one could love him—the man, not the pose. He had thought he had found such a woman in Elizabeth Bennet, but how was he to know for sure? Since his early youth, he had never shown anyone, other than Georgiana, the real Fitzwilliam Darcy. Would he forever have to be only the master of Pemberley? Could he not just be Will again? He tried to make eye contact with Elizabeth, but she danced and laughed and made merry with her family and friends. She had left him behind.

As he watched, Elizabeth turned suddenly to Bingley and caught his right hand with hers. Pulling slightly away from each other, they circled around a central axis and stepped through. She half skipped and half danced by Darcy before catching her sister's left hand. She began to make her way down the line of surprised dancers, who laughed and soon followed, copying her spontaneous allemande.

Darcy looked on with amusement as Elizabeth, having made a complete ring of the rest of her group, shrugged her shoulders when she met Bryson Lucas. The boy, possibly sixteen years old, caught both her hands, and they revolved as partners, turning tightly in a close circle. Elizabeth leaned back and laughed, her eyes bright. Darcy wished that he could truly make her happy. He wanted that more than anything.

Hearing the music coming to an end, he turned to retrieve Elizabeth's borrowed cloak from the cloakroom. He picked up the offending item and once again thought of the one he had asked Georgiana to bring with her to Netherfield. He had seen it on display when he escorted his sister along Bond Street. His instant thought was *Elizabeth*. This occurred weeks before he returned to Hertfordshire—when he still thought it hopeless—this love he felt. Yet, he reflected as he made his way through the Founders' Day crowd, he had known immediately that the cloak was made for Elizabeth Bennet.

Then he heard it. Elizabeth's scream rang out above the noise of the crowd. When he turned, at first, Darcy could not find her among the others, who covered their faces in shock. Then Elizabeth burst through the throng and ran toward the village center. To his horror, fire snaked up the back of her dress.

"No!" he yelled as he accelerated to reach her. "Do not run!" he called, but Elizabeth either did not hear or did not understand. She ran harder, trying to escape the flames.

Darcy ground out each step, lengthening his stride, and as he closed the distance, he prayed that he could reach her in time. "Lizzy!" he bellowed. Thankfully, her steps stuttered, and Darcy dove for her, taking her down with him, covering her with the same brown wool cloak he had disdained earlier. Grateful now to be holding it, he encircled her with his arms and rolled Elizabeth across the ground as he protected her face in his shoulder.

Finally, he released her. Scrambling to his knees, Darcy patted her legs and back with the burned cloak before he rolled her over. "Tell me you are well," he pleaded as he pushed the loose hair from her face. Before she could respond, Darcy clutched her to him. Then he rocked her in his arms. Fear drained from him as he held her. "Oh, my God, Elizabeth," he said. "Oh, darling."

She sobbed and clung to him. "Thank you," she said shakily.

Bingley and Jane made their way through the onlookers. Jane stroked her sister's hair, but Darcy refused to release Elizabeth. "Lizzy, are you burned?" Jane asked.

Elizabeth shook her head, and Darcy reached to cover her exposed leg. "Let us take you home," he whispered. "Bingley, would you bring the carriage around?"

"Certainly, Darcy." Bingley moved away quickly.

"Miss Bennet, might your sister use your cloak until we reach the coach?"

Jane nodded and hurried to retrieve her wrap. Although many onlookers remained, Darcy whispered to his intended, "Tell me the truth. Are you burned? Your legs? Anywhere?"

She looked up at him. "Maybe...a bit on my calf."

"Is that all?"

She nodded and buried her face in his cravat. "You saved me again."

Darcy swallowed hard. "I do not object to seeing to your safety, but I could do without the fear coursing through me." He helped her up. "Should we summon a physician?"

"I would hate to draw Dr. Potier from the festivities." She took the handkerchief that he offered and wiped her face.

"Maybe it would be better if the gentleman saw to your needs before we returned to Longbourn," he suggested.

Elizabeth gave him a half smile. "If you insist, sir."

Darcy breathed easier. "What? No argument?" he teased.

"I believe you have earned an evening away from my sharp tongue."

Jane returned with her cloak. "Here, Lizzy," she said as she wrapped it about Elizabeth's shoulders.

"Miss Elizabeth?" a voice came behind them. "I apologize. My hand slipped." Bryson Lucas was pale with horror.

"It is fine, Bryson," she assured him. "It was not your fault."

Darcy touched the boy's shoulder. "How about finding Dr. Potier for Miss Elizabeth? Tell him to meet us at his office."

"Right away, sir." The boy pushed his way through the crowd.

"I have her, Miss Bennet." Darcy caught Elizabeth's arm to support her weight. "Why do you not join Bingley in the coach. I will see to Elizabeth."

"It is as if it were made for you," Georgiana Darcy said as Elizabeth modeled the new cloak.

Darcy looked on, agreeing silently with his sister's sentiments. He had known how the cloak's color would emphasize the green of Elizabeth's hazel eyes. The fur-trimmed hood and wood toggle clasps picked up the mahogany highlights of her hair.

"Do you like it, Fitzwilliam?" Elizabeth asked as she turned slowly for his review.

He smiled seductively. "Absolutely. Georgiana has an astute eye for fashion."

Georgiana's face reflected her happiness. She and Darcy had called at Longbourn so that she could renew her acquaintance with Elizabeth. In Lambton, Georgiana had taken an instant liking to Elizabeth Bennet, and Miss Elizabeth's unexpected withdrawal due to pressing family business had come as a disappointment. "I am far from fashion conscious, Brother. Do not tease me," the girl warned charmingly. Then she handed Elizabeth another small package. "This one is from me. Welcome to the family, Miss Elizabeth."

"Oh, you should not have!" she gasped but took the bundle wrapped in brown paper and loosened the string. New leather gloves, the exact color of the cloak's trim, were revealed. "They are perfect, Miss Darcy." Tears misted Elizabeth's eyes.

"Please." The girl took both of Elizabeth's hands in hers. "You must call me Georgiana. We are to be sisters. May I call you Elizabeth?"

Elizabeth smiled brightly and then gave Georgiana a spontaneous hug. "Of course, you may call me Elizabeth. I am so pleased that you will be part of my new family. Leaving all my dear sisters behind will be a sorrow to me. We shall be close friends, Georgiana."

Darcy breathed a sigh of relief. It had been his wish from the beginning for Elizabeth and Georgiana to be friends. His sister had suffered too many years on her own. He had tried to be available for her, but with a twelve-year difference in age, Darcy often felt more like Georgiana's father than her brother. Elizabeth was but four years Georgiana's senior. He motioned to the chairs so they might spend time together. "How is your leg today?" he asked when they were settled.

"A bit sore, but it shall heal." Elizabeth poured tea. "Thank you, sir."

Georgiana said, "It was such a shock." The girl shook her head. "I could not believe it when Fitzwilliam told me what happened. You were so fortunate."

"Good fortune comes in the form of your brother," Elizabeth said evenly.

He accepted a cup of tea. "Miss Elizabeth has had an unusual week. I pray that such unusualness is not repeated." A slight grimace crossed Elizabeth's face.

Elizabeth turned the conversation to Georgiana's current studies and trip from London. Then the other unmarried Bennet sisters—all of whom still lived at Longbourn—returned, chattering and with flushed cheeks, from a walk. Elizabeth introduced Georgiana to Jane, Mary, and Kitty. Happily, Fitzwilliam's sister and Kitty became friendly quickly, as Kitty asked Georgiana's advice on Kitty's latest design. Even Mary took the time to share her music.

"I have never seen my sister converse so readily with strangers," Darcy noted as he and Elizabeth sat together in the drawing room. Although the door remained open, no one thought to chaperone them. He had captured her hand.

"Miss Darcy has probably never been in a house full of girls, all about her own age. Georgiana knows music and art and fashion, but the girls in the Bennet household know what it means to be a sister. It will do Miss Darcy well to be among other young women," Elizabeth assured him.

Darcy doubted that Georgiana would learn anything of merit from Elizabeth's younger sisters. Mary lacked any social skills, and Kitty was silly. Darcy would prefer that Georgiana associate with Miss Jane Bennet or Elizabeth—and even his betrothed had conducted herself poorly of late. "My sister has been sheltered, but I would not say it has been to Georgiana's deficit. She shall make a gentleman a fine wife when she makes her come out."

"You think to bring Miss Darcy out soon?"

"I do."

Elizabeth paused. "As your wife, shall I be involved?"

"Most certainly. As Mrs. Darcy, you will give Georgiana credibility," he assured her.

Elizabeth bit her bottom lip. "How might I do that, Fitzwilliam? As you have pointed out previously, I am not a pillar of society. I grieve for providing you moments of concern, but I would know true remorse if I did something that reflected poorly on Georgiana."

Despite his conscience telling him not to criticize, he said softly, "Then perhaps we need to reexamine some of your actions of late."

Although she did not raise her voice, Elizabeth's face displayed her instant anger. "I held the belief, sir, that you had fallen in love with me because you admired my liveliness. Is that not what you told me only a fortnight ago?"

"Actually, I said that I admired you for the liveliness of your mind," he modified.

"And I insisted that you were always noble and just, and that in your heart you thoroughly despised the persons who so assiduously courted you, and you, sir, never corrected me."

Darcy stiffened. It was to be another argument. "Did I not praise your affectionate behavior to Miss Bennet while she lay ill at Netherfield?"

"Yes, I placed my good qualities under your protection, as I recall." She turned her back on him. "I told you that you had my permission to exaggerate my good qualities as much as possible. I did not realize at the time that my caring for Jane was my only quality of merit worth recognizing."

A shiver ran down his spine. "And you were to find occasions for teasing and quarreling with me as often as you deemed necessary. Is this how our life is to be, Elizabeth? Sniping at each other over minor details?"

Part 3

Where do we go from here? Darcy asked himself. Neither Darcy nor Elizabeth enjoyed what their relationship had become, and, as was his nature, Darcy blamed himself for making Elizabeth unhappy. He hated that they were at loggerheads. If her family possessed a larger fortune, possibly Elizabeth would understand his sense of duty. "If only Mr. Bennet had not neglected his duties," Darcy muttered as he stared out the Netherfield library window. "Or if I had less than Pemberley." With a sigh of exasperation, he exited the room to find his sister in Bingley's music room.

The household expected the arrival of Bingley's sister later in the day—something that Darcy dreaded. He had fended off Caroline Bingley's manipulations for the past few years, and knew she would verbally attack Elizabeth. His and Elizabeth's courtship was under enough stress.

"Mesmerizing," he said as his sister finished playing. He had stood in the doorway and listened. It was a brief moment of peace in the past few days' chaos.

Georgiana looked up at him, her eyes dancing. "I did not see you, Fitzwilliam."

He entered slowly. "You, my dear, were too involved in the music's glory to know anyone else existed."

"It is a bad habit of mine." Georgiana stood to greet him.

"I came to inquire whether you were to spend the afternoon with the Bennets. If so, I will happily drive you to Longbourn." He caught Georgiana's hand.

She slid an arm about his waist. "You simply wish an excuse to see Miss Elizabeth," she chided him good-naturedly.

Darcy kissed her forehead. "I may have an ulterior motive."

"You really love her. Miss Elizabeth, I mean," Georgiana blurted out.

Darcy paused, unsure about expressing personal feelings to his younger sister. "I hold the lady in the highest regard."

"Oh, Fitzwilliam. Say what you mean. Maybe not to me, but to Miss Elizabeth."

"Are you offering me advice on love? Since when does an innocent know about love?" he returned a little too sharply.

Georgiana blushed, but she did not turn away, something he deduced that she had learned from Elizabeth. Even though his sister had known Miss Elizabeth for only a few short months, Darcy could observe his intended's influence on Georgiana; and, surprisingly, he considered it for the best. "Tr-True, I have never known love," she stammered. "But I know what a woman wants to hear from *the gentleman she holds in the highest regard*."

"I will not discuss this topic further," he reprimanded her. "Shall you call on the Bennets or not? With the arrival of Bingley's family, I suspect our evening will be taken up with Miss Bingley's conversation."

"I shall call on Miss Elizabeth."

"Then I will have the curricle brought around."

Darcy started to find a servant, but Georgiana's soft voice held him in place. "Thank you, Fitzwilliam, for not bringing Miss Bingley or someone like her to Pemberley as my sister."

Darcy turned slowly to her. "Whatever could you mean, Georgiana? I realize Miss Bingley's behavior can at times be calculating. But she is, in fact, a fine lady, not deficient in good humor. She is handsome and was educated in one of the first private seminaries in London. Miss Bingley is from a highly respectable family in the north of England. You could learn a great deal from the lady, especially as your come out approaches."

Copying one of Elizabeth's habits, Georgiana bit her bottom lip. "I agree with your assessment of Miss Bingley, Brother. It was for a more selfish reason that I spoke."

"Explain, Georgiana."

Her chin rose in defiance, and Darcy wondered if that, too, was a lesson his sister had learned from Elizabeth. "Miss Bingley could teach me how to negotiate the ton; I have no doubt of that fact. However, when I consider the possibility of your marrying...of your placing a woman in my sister's role...I would hope that you would choose a woman who existed in her own right. I am a selfish being; I would prefer that you marry a woman who would allow me to share your attentions. I have no other family; I would be devastated to lose you and Pemberley. I cannot imagine that Miss Bingley would tolerate my presence at Pemberley."

"And you believe that Miss Elizabeth is the superior choice for this reason?" he said.

"You would not have chosen the lady if Miss Elizabeth were not the superior option, and I do not have to tell you that your intended would accept my presence in your life. Whether you realize it or not, Fitzwilliam, you chose Miss Elizabeth as much for *me* as for *yourself*."

Darcy caught her by the arm and pulled Elizabeth behind the door of an empty drawing room. He brought her to him. "Elizabeth," he whispered hoarsely. He cupped her cheek. "I do not want us to be at odds. Can we not start over?"

She turned her head and kissed his palm. "It seems we have spent our entire acquaintance misconstruing each other." Impulsively, she went on tiptoes and kissed Darcy's lips.

"Ah, that was heaven." He maneuvered her closer, so that Elizabeth's cheek rested on his chest. "If we could just stay as such," he murmured.

She snuggled into his body. "Fitzwilliam, we must return to the main parlor." Yet she made no move to leave his embrace.

"Propriety demands that we do, but I would wish to remain as we are now until the vicar pronounces the vows."

Elizabeth chortled. "That is twenty days, sir. Could you tolerate me for so long?"

"Test me," he groaned.

"So Miss Bingley is on her way as we speak?" Elizabeth said sarcastically as she handed Georgiana a cup of tea.

Jane Bennet gave her sister a warning look. "The lady is Mr. Bingley's youngest sister, and therefore my future sister...and, likewise, your relation also, Lizzy."

Elizabeth smiled broadly. "You see. It is as I told you, Miss Darcy. My sister cannot speak ill of anyone."

"And you, Miss Elizabeth?" Georgiana asked shyly.

"Unfortunately, Georgiana, despite how misplaced my opinions might be, I have never held the reputation for swallowing my thoughts. Your poor brother can attest to both the sharpness of my tongue and the firmness of my opinions."

"I cannot imagine that anyone could remain unswayed by my brother's opinions—or his glare," Georgiana blurted out.

Elizabeth squeezed her hand. "We shall both learn to deal with Mr. Darcy in a grown-up manner. Although I suspect your brother still sees you as such, you are no longer a child."

Georgiana looked at both Bennet sisters. "Have I said the wrong thing? I did not mean to insinuate that Fitzwilliam is anything less than the kindest of brothers or the best of men."

"I imagine that Lizzy would agree with you, Miss Darcy."

"Yet we were not speaking of my opinion of Mr. Darcy's kindness or of his glare." She noticed that Georgiana ducked her head in embarrassment. "We were speaking of Miss Bingley's arrival at Netherfield. Which brings to mind Miss Bingley's fine qualities," Elizabeth said with amusement. "I shall enumerate them. No one could object to that." She paused mischievously. "Oh, let me see. I am sure there is at least one item of merit. Yet I am at a loss."

"Elizabeth!" Jane reprimanded her. "You should not speak as such before Miss Darcy."

"Georgiana must learn to deal with my proclivity for the absurd." Elizabeth set her cup down a bit too vigorously. "I shall not pretend, Jane, to forgive Miss Bingley for her part in separating her brother from you. You suffered horribly." Elizabeth refused to mention Darcy's participation in Miss Bingley's plot. "If not for Mr.

Darcy's manipulations, you might still suffer. If the lady had offered you an apology, I might have forgiven her."

"And I have dealt with Miss Bingley," Jane corrected her. "Miss Darcy has no need to hear of Miss Bingley's part in my distress."

"I beg to differ. My dearest Jane, Georgiana will soon be my family. All of us in this room have experienced placing our trust in someone, only to find ourselves smarting." Elizabeth noted Georgiana's fight to keep her composure. Darcy's sister had narrowly escaped George Wickham's perfidy. Unfortunately, Elizabeth's youngest sister had also placed her trust in the man. "I do not wish to turn Miss Darcy against Miss Bingley; yet I would wish to *warn* her to keep her eyes open. For a time, I kept mine tightly shut, and saw only what I wished to see in Mr. Darcy—all his negative traits, magnified and distorted. That is a lesson that I would spare Georgiana. You did not see what others saw of Mr. Bingley's sisters. There are many lessons for a young woman to master: lessons beyond a command of the languages or a steady hand with an embroidery needle."

"And your choice to ignore Miss Bingley had nothing to do with Caroline's setting her sights on Mr. Darcy?" Jane teased.

"It did not." Elizabeth shrugged. "I had not noticed the lady's preference." A burst of laughter followed—all three females imagining Miss Bingley's obvious maneuverings.

<hr />

Darcy and Elizabeth visited the Meryton shops. Elizabeth had thought it important to replace the cloak she had ruined the night of the bonfire. "I can send to London for an appropriate replacement," Darcy had assured her.

"If we choose something too refined, the Lucases will think my family flaunts our match as superior to Charlotte's."

Darcy could not understand such reasoning. "Why would any-one expect me to choose an item of inferior quality? I can afford a fine cloth to replace the scratchy wool of the borrowed item."

Elizabeth rested her hand on his arm. "Maybe that is how people in town think, but not in the country. Although the Lucas women would enjoy the quality of anything you chose, they would not wear the cloak, for fear that someone would remark on their good luck at having had the foresight to make me a loan of the other. The Lucases would be constantly reminded that they could not afford such quality and neither could Mr. Collins. It is best to choose something comparable, with just a hint of finer material. That would express my gratitude without causing Lady Lucas embarrassment."

"I see. Let us follow your plan then." Things between them the past week had improved, and Darcy had decided their problems were a result of premarital nerves on both their parts. He held the door for Elizabeth, but as she preceded him through it, she fell into another man's waiting embrace.

"Matthew Hardesty!" she said and hugged the other man tightly. "I cannot believe you are here."

Darcy felt jealousy clutch his heart. The stranger closed his eyes in appreciation of the woman he held. Darcy knew that moment well; he felt it every time he took Elizabeth in his arms.

She pulled back and cupped the man's face. "I worried...the whole town worried...we have included you daily in our prayers. Your father did not tell us that you were to be at home."

"I did not inform Father of my return. I wanted to be healed be-fore I came home. Father is too weak to tend to a wounded soldier," Hardesty said with a large smile.

"But you are well?" Elizabeth asked.

"As well as a man with one arm might be," the man said.

47

Darcy cleared his throat. "Might you introduce me to your friend, Elizabeth?"

"Oh!" Elizabeth returned quickly to Darcy's side. "Of course. Mr. Darcy, may I present Captain Matthew Hardesty. Mr. Hardesty, this is my intended, Mr. Fitzwilliam Darcy of Pemberley."

Darcy's good manners forced him to offer Hardesty a bow. "You have recently returned to Meryton, Captain Hardesty?" Darcy asked, keeping his tone even as he observed Hardesty's longing look at Elizabeth.

"Two days ago, Mr. Darcy." Hardesty continued to make eye contact with Elizabeth. "My father has several hundred acres five miles south of Meryton. Growing up, your future wife and I shared countless adventures. Miss Elizabeth's cousin and I were close friends. Even signed up together. Unfortunately, as Elizabeth learned many months ago, I left Edgar Linscomb on the fields at Salamanca."

Darcy said automatically, "Yes, I was sorry to hear it."

"Thank God *you* made it back to us, Matthew."

Matthew! Darcy thought it ironic that this man's Christian name came so easily to Elizabeth's lips, but she often called him—her betrothed—Mr. Darcy.

"I am blessed. I had hoped to exit with a major's title before my name, but Bony—Bonaparte—had other plans. I am thankful to have made it out alive. Many others did not."

Elizabeth impulsively touched the man's shoulder and went on tiptoe to kiss Hardesty's cheek. "Well, all of Meryton is pleased you are among us again."

Hardesty bowed to Darcy. "I should go. I wish you well, Mr. Darcy. You have stolen a breath of fresh air: Meryton shall grieve its loss." With that, the man exited the shop.

Darcy bit the inside of his cheek so as not to lash out at Elizabeth for her foolish display. Instead, he directed her to a table containing yard goods and ready-made blouses.

Oblivious to how Darcy's heart raced with anger and sadness, Elizabeth fingered the material of a cloak hanging on a wooden stand. "What do you think of this one?" She stretched out a section of the cloth for his perusal.

Darcy barely looked at her. "I will bow to your taste, Elizabeth. You know better than I in such matters."

Elizabeth gazed up at him. Although he had tried to plaster a smile on his face, he could tell by her reaction that he had failed miserably. "Fitzwilliam," she hissed. "What is it?"

Before he could stop himself, he snarled, "At least, you finally remembered my given name." He placed Elizabeth's hand on his arm. "Tell the proprietor to place the item on Mr. Bingley's bill. I will settle the account with Charles."

Surprisingly, Elizabeth offered no objection. When he returned her to the borrowed gig and turned the carriage toward Longbourn, she finally spoke. "I meant no offense, Fitzwilliam. I forgot myself."

"How often must I explain? When you are my wife, you must have a detachment. You cannot fling yourself into another man's arms." He seethed with anger.

"What can I do, Fitzwilliam? Matthew Hardesty is a dear friend. I will not snub him just to be your wife."

"The man holds a *tendre* for you," Darcy charged as he halted the gig.

Elizabeth's cheeks turned a fiery red. "I will not deign to respond to such a preposterous accusation."

"I saw his face, Elizabeth. Captain Hardesty holds you in his heart."

Elizabeth stiffened. "I believe you should take me home, Mr. Darcy."

He heard the tears hidden in Elizabeth's words, but Darcy ignored her distress. "As you wish, Elizabeth." He gave the horse its freedom.

"Where is Miss Elizabeth?" Georgiana asked as Jane Bennet disembarked at Netherfield.

"I fear my sister is indisposed." Jane shot a glance at Darcy. "A megrim."

Georgiana looked concerned. "We should see to Elizabeth, Fitzwilliam. I cannot bear to think that she is alone at Longbourn."

Darcy took his sister's arm to direct her through the main door. "It is too close to the supper hour to rush off to call on Miss Elizabeth," he whispered. "Besides, I am well aware that when Elizabeth claims a headache, her condition is due to some other cause. I made that mistake before. I will not go rushing to my future wife's side again, only to be turned away."

"Did you argue with Elizabeth?" Georgiana accused him.

"You might better ask when do we not argue," he countered.

"I shall be happy to sponsor your come out," Caroline Bingley assured Georgiana. Charles Bingley had escorted Miss Bennet back to Longbourn.

Only Darcy, Caroline, and Georgiana sat in Netherfield's drawing room. Mr. Bingley's oldest sister, Louisa, and her husband were due to arrive with the morning. Bingley and Miss Bennet would marry in four days. In three, Darcy and Elizabeth's last official calling of the banns would occur. As such, he could not keep his mind on the conversation at hand. He knew, without a doubt, that Elizabeth did not have a headache. She was avoiding him.

"I appreciate your offer, Miss Bingley, but that honor should go to my brother's wife," Georgiana said calmly.

"You jest, Georgiana. Miss Elizabeth may have captured Mr. Darcy's heart, but even he cannot think she is capable of launching you into society. The ton would chew up and spit out the future Mrs. Darcy."

Georgiana shot him an imploring glance, but Darcy was still smarting from Elizabeth's snub. "The ton can be cruel. You might take some instruction from Miss Bingley."

"I mean no offense, Miss Bingley, but I would prefer to make my debut with Miss Elizabeth. She is to be my sister, and I find her opinions on certain individuals very astute." Georgiana raised her chin in defiance.

Darcy glared at his sister. "Georgiana, apologize to Miss Bingley."

Her head down and her hands trembling, Georgiana rose. "I have spoken out of turn. I beg your forgiveness, Miss Bingley. Please excuse me. I will retire if I have your permission, Fitzwilliam." She turned on her heel and exited the room.

"You must take Miss Darcy in hand, sir," Caroline chastised him. "Miss Elizabeth is a poor influence on Georgiana."

Darcy rose in anger. "Miss Bingley, I have tolerated your criticism of my future wife because you are the sister of one of my dearest friends. But I can tolerate your remarks no longer. I think it best if my sister and I remove ourselves from Charles's house. I shall instruct Mr. Jordan to see to the packing." Darcy made a speedy exit.

⋯•⋯

"Miss Elizabeth!" Bingley's butler appeared surprised at her coming unchaperoned to Netherfield.

"Mr. Branson, might you tell Mr. Darcy that I am here?" She tried not to sound as nervous as she felt. She had done Darcy a disservice the previous evening, and Elizabeth had come to apologize.

"I believe Mr. Darcy is in the library, miss. Shall I announce you?"

"That will not be necessary. I shall be only a moment," she assured him and started down the long hallway. If Mr. Branson objected, he did not say so.

Elizabeth hurried along, but the sound of male voices brought her up short. She knew she should not eavesdrop, but they spoke of her.

"Caroline's behavior was beyond the pale when she spoke disparagingly of Miss Elizabeth," Bingley declared.

"I agree," Darcy added. "But what did your sister say that I myself have not thought? I am not angry with Miss Bingley. I am angry with myself for not considering Elizabeth's inability to see Georgiana through a London season. Perhaps I will seek Lady Matlock's sponsorship."

"You cannot mean to ignore Miss Elizabeth? She will be your wife. If you ask the countess to shepherd Georgiana about London, your wife's reputation will suffer."

Elizabeth felt the air being sucked from her lungs.

"What can I do? By ton standards, Elizabeth is incapable of being a proper chaperone for Georgiana."

Elizabeth could bear to hear no more. She tiptoed away. Thankfully, no servants lurked about the halls. Elizabeth turned toward the nearest door. Within a minute, she had escaped the main house and was circling the greenhouse. Away from any prying eyes, the tears began in earnest. "What have I done?" Dejected, she sank down on an abandoned wagon bed.

Thirty minutes later, the tears had lessened, and Elizabeth pulled herself together. "By the time I reach Longbourn, my face will have assumed its usual happy expression." Determined, she set off at a steady clip. The sound of a carriage behind her made Elizabeth want to run away—and to pray it was Darcy.

"Miss Elizabeth," Hardesty said as he pulled up on the reins. "You are out early."

Elizabeth dropped a halfhearted curtsy. "I called at Netherfield...to spend time with Mr. Darcy's sister."

"I see." Hardesty eyed her with some curiosity. "And the gentleman did not steal the opportunity to spend time with his affianced? I cannot imagine a man of Mr. Darcy's reputation allowing you to walk to Longbourn while he leisurely spent hours at Netherfield. Would you like a shoulder on which to cry, Miss Elizabeth?" he said boldly.

"I fear that I have no more tears."

Hardesty climbed down from the carriage to take her hand. "Let me see you home, Miss Elizabeth. Remember, if you wish to speak of this, I am available to listen."

Elizabeth allowed him to help her to the gig's seat. When he climbed up beside her, she graciously said, "Thank you, Matthew."

He smiled at her broadly. "You were always my favorite Bennet sister. Always full of adventure. Of spontaneity. Of a passion for life." He set the gig in motion.

"All the things Mr. Darcy does not wish in a wife," Elizabeth grumbled.

Hardesty did not respond immediately. "I imagine that for a man of Mr. Darcy's stature, spontaneity comes at a high premium. I am sure he plans each detail of his life."

Elizabeth added ruefully, "Probably schedules every minute of every day."

Hardesty leaned closer, as if sharing a secret. "And you are willing to accept such a life?"

Elizabeth sighed deeply. "I am willing to share such a life because I am hopelessly in love with Mr. Darcy. My aunt Gardiner says Mr. Darcy wants for nothing but a little more liveliness. I had thought that as his wife I might teach him to enjoy life more."

"It is a great gamble, Elizabeth. What if your Mr. Darcy does not change? What then? Once you are married, you cannot change your mind. Marriage is forever."

"Even if I wished to terminate the engagement, Mr. Darcy would never cancel our arrangement. He is too much of a gentleman. If I took such a step on my own, I would be ruined socially, as would Kitty and Mary. It is an impossible situation."

Hardesty maneuvered the gig onto a side road. "Now, why do you not tell me everything that has happened of late?"

"What can I do? By ton standards, Elizabeth is incapable of being a proper chaperone for Georgiana. Yet I cannot live without her. Elizabeth is my other half. We have fought a great deal in the past few weeks, but I am of the mind that when we are alone at Pemberley, everything will come together nicely. If Elizabeth cannot adapt to the ton's standards, then Georgiana will find a husband in a less traditional setting."

"My money is on Miss Elizabeth. The ton has been known to appreciate quirkiness. I believe the beau monde will embrace your wife," Bingley declared.

Darcy nodded. "It should be an interesting experience."

"Then you will stay at Netherfield? Four days before my wedding is not a convenient time for you to disappear, old friend," Bingley said.

"Georgiana and I will stay," Darcy said grudgingly.

Bingley rubbed his hands together. "Good! Now, tell me about this Hardesty character."

"How did you know?" Darcy asked. "Never mind. I do not want to know what Miss Bennet has shared with you of my and Miss Elizabeth's private life."

Darcy had called several times at Longbourn, but Elizabeth had refused to see him on either Friday or Saturday. She had accepted Georgiana's calls, but his sister had promised Elizabeth not to discuss their visits with him. At a quiet supper on Saturday evening, Miss Bingley ventured, "I expected to dine with only Georgiana this evening, Mr. Darcy."

Darcy swallowed his frustration. "I am sorry to disappoint you, Miss Bingley." He spoke not another word throughout the rest of the meal.

As he undressed for bed, he said to the empty room, "At least, she cannot ignore me at services in the morning. It is the last day for the calling of the banns. Elizabeth must be present. If she is not, I will ride to Longbourn and *demand* that she see me. This craziness must end. We are meant to share a life. And if we are not, then I must know now."

Darcy waited outside the church for Elizabeth to make her appearance. Finally, the Bennet coach came into view, and he breathed a bit easier. When Elizabeth exited the carriage, she walked directly to where he stood.

"Elizabeth, I am pleased to see you." Darcy caught her hand and brought it to his lips. "I have missed you." She winced but he pretended not to notice.

Elizabeth smiled weakly. "I never meant to give you cause for concern."

Darcy thought that *concern* was too calm a word to describe the emotional seesaw he rode. Yet he refused to voice his reaction. "Will you join me in Mr. Bingley's pew?" he asked as he placed Elizabeth's hand on his arm.

"Papa has asked Jane and me to remain as part of the family today. With Jane's nuptials tomorrow, I believe he is quite melancholy." She bit her bottom lip. "You will forgive me, sir."

"Only if you call me by my name," he teased.

Elizabeth shot a glance at the deacon, who was motioning the congregation to their seats. "We should go in, Fitzwilliam."

Darcy tried to believe that Elizabeth was sincere. However, a shiver shot up his spine. She was too docile. He walked her to the Bennet pew. After saying, "Good morning" to her family, he reluctantly left Elizabeth on the end of the bench.

"Has Miss Elizabeth recovered?" Georgiana asked as Darcy slid in beside her.

He growled softly, "You and I both know my intended was not ill."

Mr. Pinncatch's opening remarks cut short their conversation. The congregation had settled in the pews in preparation for the sermon. The vicar cleared his throat to silence the last of the parishioners who entered. "Tomorrow, it will be my great pleasure to conduct the ceremony that shall unite Miss Jane Bennet and Mr. Charles Bingley in marriage. They are both of this parish and have met all the requirements to marry."

The vicar paused, giving the congregation a moment to react. When silence fell again, he continued. "I publish the banns of marriage between Miss Elizabeth Bennet of this Meryton parish and Mr. Fitzwilliam Darcy of the Lambton parish of Derbyshire. This is the third time of asking. If any of you know cause or just impediment why these two persons should not be joined together in holy matrimony, you are to declare it."

Silence followed, but then Darcy felt the hair on the back of his neck stand on end—a suspicion stung his scalp. A rustling announced the so-called impediment. Darcy turned to see Captain Matthew Hardesty rise to his feet. "I have an objection," he announced to the faces gawking at him. "Miss Elizabeth accepted my suit two years prior. She is betrothed to me."

Part 4

He went cold inside; Darcy was on his feet immediately. "Elizabeth," he demanded, "tell me this is not so." He stared at her intently, his jaw set in fury.

Her mother hysterically called, "Oh, my nerves, Mr. Bennet!"

Sitting with her hands clasped in her lap, Elizabeth refused to look at him. "It is as Captain Hardesty says."

Darcy felt the bitterness swell in his chest. "Why?" His voice rang into the dead silence. "Why, Elizabeth? Why would you perpetrate such a farce?" *She does not wish to share my life.*

Her chin came up in defiance. "It is not a farce. Captain Hardesty and I have a long-held preference for each other." The members of the congregation were quiet. Mrs. Bennet collapsed into Mary's arms.

"I am well aware of the *gentleman's* preference," Darcy growled. He never looked at the former captain; Darcy's eyes rested on Elizabeth.

"It is for the best," she asserted. "By ton standards, I am incapable of being a proper chaperone for Georgiana's debut. You see, Fitzwilliam, I am well aware of how you judge me. Captain Hardesty is not so censorious."

For a moment, Darcy could not speak. Rallying, he said, "Eavesdropping—somehow—my dear? I thought it beneath you!"

Elizabeth's lower lip trembled. "I do not hear you denying the words, Mr. Darcy."

"Why should I deny it?" he retorted. "However, did you stay to hear what followed?" Darcy paused, but when Elizabeth did not respond, he spit out, "I thought not."

"What did you say?" Elizabeth said angrily. "Did you explain to Mr. Bingley how I am too impulsive? Did you tell my sister's intended that my manners will be the joke of the ton? Did you bemoan my poor connections?"

"Miss Elizabeth," Bingley rose to face her. "It was nothing like that. In fact..."

But Darcy cut him off. "No, Bingley. Miss Elizabeth has the answer she desires. The lady deserves no other response."

Mrs. Bennet urged her, "Lizzy, tell Mr. Darcy that you are sorry."

Mr. Bennet rose to defend his daughter. "Mr. Darcy, you will speak to Lizzy in a proper tone. I realize this is a shock for everyone, but I expect you to do the gentlemanly thing. You and Elizabeth will marry. Captain Hardesty never sought my permission. His claim has no merit."

Darcy took a deep breath. "Mr. Bennet, if you will observe your daughter and Captain Hardesty, you will notice no shock on either of their faces. The captain sports a smirk, and your daughter has not shed a tear. This was planned to hurt me enough that I would end the engagement. Miss Elizabeth plans to teach me a lesson in embarrassment. In shame. In mortification. She assumes that I have judged her too harshly in the role she would play as my wife. Elizabeth wishes to emphasize her independence."

Miss Bingley harrumphed.

Darcy took a step to the aisle. "Come, Georgiana." He extended a hand to his sister.

"Fitzwilliam, we cannot!" she protested. "Tell Elizabeth that you love her, and then everything will be as it should be."

"Georgiana, I will not tell you again." Darcy turned abruptly to Mr. Pinncatch. "Thank you, sir, for attending to duty. However, it seems only prudent that I, too, lodge an objection to the ceremony between Miss Elizabeth and myself."

Georgiana drew in a sharp breath. "Fitzwilliam, you do not mean it!"

Darcy turned a cold stare on Elizabeth. "This is what Miss Elizabeth wants." He placed Georgiana on his arm and led her toward the exit, but he could not resist one departing barb. He paused beside Elizabeth. "How far would you have taken your plan to be rid of me, Elizabeth? Would you have claimed that the captain compromised you?" Mrs. Bennet protested and Miss Bennet gasped, but Darcy showed no other emotion. He walked out the door, Georgiana on his arm, never looking back.

"Darcy, you cannot leave," Bingley insisted as servants scrambled to pack Darcy's coach for his departure.

"What do you expect me to do, Bingley? Elizabeth does not wish to be my wife. She made that perfectly clear today. What a fool I have been!"

"But you were to stand up with me tomorrow!"

Darcy stopped his pacing. "Ask your brother Hurst. I cannot face Elizabeth again, and she must be with Miss Bennet for the wedding. Surely you understand that, Charles."

Bingley ran his fingers through his hair. "Of course, I understand. But what will you do? The short season is in full swing in London.

You are not thinking of making an appearance. Your announcement has run in the *Times*."

Darcy's heart sank. "I meant to return to London with Elizabeth at my side. Now, I do not care if I ever see the place again."

"I am amazed. I would never have thought that Miss Elizabeth would go to such extremes. People can speak of nothing else."

Darcy expelled a deep sigh. "Before a hundred witnesses, the lady has agreed to become Captain Hardesty's wife, and although my heart screams with the injustice, I cannot hate Elizabeth. The thought of being *my* wife frightened her." Darcy looked up to see Mr. Jordan at the door. "Be happy, Charles. Be happy enough for the both of us." He shook Bingley's hand before heading for the door.

He fought the desire to turn back—to rush to Longbourn and beg Elizabeth to reconsider. Instead, Darcy helped Georgiana into the coach. Taking the backward-facing seat, he made himself smile at his sister. "What say you to returning to Derbyshire? I have no taste for London."

"Whatever you say, Fitzwilliam."

———◦•◦•◦———

"Lizzy, tell me it is not as Mr. Darcy asserts," Jane Bennet said when she cornered her sister in Elizabeth's room. The family had endured continual whispers throughout Mr. Pinncatch's sermon.

"I did not imagine that Mr. Darcy would recognize my deceit," Elizabeth confessed, feeling the tension draining from her.

Jane towered over her. "Do you understand what you have done, Elizabeth? You have made a commitment to marry Matthew Hardesty. Before our good neighbors and friends, you have driven away the man you love. The man who returned that love. In order to prove a point. To win an argument. You have gambled with your future. Silly, idiotic pride! You have proven yourself to be exactly what Mr. Darcy feared."

Elizabeth did not answer. She simply rolled over and buried her face in her pillow. For long moments, she fought sobs. "I heard Mr. Darcy say that I would be a disappointment." She clung to the last shreds of her pride.

"Mr. Bingley reports that Mr. Darcy also said that, if necessary, he would look for a less traditional way of finding Miss Darcy a husband, and that Mr. Darcy swore his allegiance to you. He thought things would prove less stressful when you were alone at Pemberley. When you had time to get to know each other better."

"Oh, Jane, what have I done?"

⸺

He had spent a week behind a locked door, coming out of his study only long enough to take his meals with Georgiana. He had stared out his window at the changing landscape. "Elizabeth and I were to have married today," he quietly told Georgiana over breakfast. Constant thoughts of what might have been tormented him.

"I know," she whispered. "I am so sorry, Fitzwilliam."

Darcy closed his eyes to shut out the pain. "This is worse than when Elizabeth refused my proposal. At that time, I held the thread of a hope that someday Elizabeth would change her mind. That she would see me differently. That she would learn the truth—"

"About Mr. Wickham," Georgiana finished his sentence. "Yes, I know of Mr. Wickham's failed seduction of Miss Elizabeth," she explained when Darcy looked shocked. "You saved both of us from making a terrible mistake."

"Elizabeth told you of Mr. Wickham?"

"We were to be sisters," she said quietly. Nothing else needed to be said.

Darcy swallowed hard. "I am sorry that I raised your hopes."

"My hopes are nothing compared with yours."

<hr />

"Here you are," Colonel Fitzwilliam said as he strolled into the library. "I have traveled half of England searching for you." He flopped down in the chair across from Darcy.

"I apologize, Cousin, for hiding in my home. Next time, I will seek a more obvious place," Darcy said.

"Very amusing." The colonel looked about the room. "A bit gloomy in here. Why do you keep it dark when the sun shines brightly outside?"

"The darkness fits my mood." Darcy put his brandy glass on a side table. "What brings you to Pemberley, Edward?"

The colonel stretched out his legs. "Well, let me see." He held up one finger. "His Lordship read of your intended marriage in the London papers." He held up a second finger. "He summoned me to Matlock to explain why no one had informed him of such a momentous occasion." The colonel held up a third finger. "Father sent me to Hertfordshire to represent the family and to deliver a sharp reprimand to you for your neglect of him. I arrived, only to find that you and Georgiana had made an early departure, that Bingley had left for his wedding trip, and that the delectable Miss Elizabeth had also left the area."

"Left? To go where?" Darcy asked forlornly.

The colonel smiled. "The lady told no one where she might be found. Miss Bingley, who was delighted with the situation, says Miss Elizabeth left only a brief note. Mr. Bennet has mounted a search."

Staring ahead, Darcy ignored the reference to Caroline Bingley. "But Elizabeth was to marry Captain Hardesty."

"What caused the rift, Darcy? You desired Miss Elizabeth long before we were at Rosings."

Darcy glared at his cousin. "Who speaks of my private life?"

"Do you think Lady Catherine did not inform her brother of your so-called betrayal of our cousin Anne? When Father asked what I knew of Miss Elizabeth, I filled in the blanks that Her Ladyship had omitted from her version of events. Your moodiness made sense in light of Lady Catherine's disclosure."

Darcy ignored his cousin's evaluation of his attempt to cover the fact that he had been heartbroken after Elizabeth rejected his proposal at Rosings. Now, someone had reached into his chest and ripped out the pieces. "I criticized the lady," he said evenly. "Elizabeth has an impulsive nature. She finds herself in embarrassing and even dangerous situations because she does not think before she acts. I tried to caution her that, as my wife, she could not behave foolishly. I wanted to shield Elizabeth from censure. I wanted people to love her the way they did my mother."

"Oh yes." The colonel smiled ruefully. "Miss Elizabeth should model herself after Lady Anne Darcy." An eyebrow raised in amusement. "Tell me, Darcy, where did Miss Elizabeth fail? Was it the fact that the lady could match wits with you? I recall my aunt—your mother—taking your father to task in the same manner. Or maybe it was Lady Anne's artfulness that Miss Elizabeth lacked." Darcy flinched. "Do you not remember snowball battles, with both your parents taking on you, Wickham, and me? Or the time Lady Anne decided that she wanted honey straight from the hive? We left the picnic to the ants as we all dove into the lake, fully clothed, to escape the swarm."

"I have never laughed so hard," Darcy's face softened. "Mama lost her favorite slippers in the water."

"I ruined my new waistcoat." The colonel paused again. "And Georgie reports that Mrs. Reynolds was quite taken with Miss Elizabeth. It would seem to me that winning the praise of Pemberley's paragon of housekeeping would be evidence of Miss Elizabeth's ability to garner the respect of your staff and your tenants."

Darcy groaned. "I have been an idiot."

"What do you plan to do about it?"

<hr />

Darcy knew that Bingley had taken his new wife to Europe for a couple of months. "That is not a source I can use in Meryton," he said as he took foolscap from a drawer to draft a letter. "Where would Elizabeth go?" he mused.

With the colonel's advice, he had already recruited a Bow Street runner to check the Gardiners' household. He thought to call on Elizabeth's aunt and uncle himself, but Darcy knew the Gardiners would protect their niece. "Surely the Collinses would not accept her after Elizabeth's confrontation with Lady Catherine. Collins fears my aunt too much." Darcy tapped the pen's feather against his chin.

Because he was deep in thought, it took a moment for the rap at the door to register. "Come!" he called with some irritation.

"Excuse me, Mr. Darcy." His butler stood by the open door. "You have a visitor, sir."

"I am busy, Mr. Naismith. Who is it?"

"A Captain Matthew Hardesty, sir. The gentleman insists on seeing you."

Darcy growled, "Of all the bloody nerve." Composing himself, he said, "Show the gentleman in, Mr. Naismith."

"Yes, sir."

Darcy fought the urge to find his sword and run the captain through. Then the man was at the door. The captain bowed stiffly. "Thank you for agreeing to see me, Mr. Darcy."

"You should come in, Hardesty. I would prefer that my servants did not witness my tearing you apart limb by limb." Darcy withheld his bow.

Hardesty stepped into the room. He held up his pinned sleeve. "Start with this limb, Mr. Darcy."

"Touché, sir. What are you doing in Derbyshire, Hardesty? I am afraid that I have run out of fiancées for you to claim." Darcy wanted to maintain civility, but the man had cost him his chance at happiness.

The captain looked about the room. "You *are* as rich as Croesus," he remarked. "My selfishness has cost Miss Elizabeth a great estate." He turned defiantly to Darcy. "She has not come to Pemberley?"

"Do you suppose I would tell you if Miss Elizabeth were here?"

"I suppose not, but I promised Mr. Bennet that I would seek his daughter under your roof." The man frowned.

"What makes you believe Miss Elizabeth is not at Pemberley?" Darcy asked.

"The dark circles under your eyes. You are not sleeping, Mr. Darcy." He smiled slightly. "If Elizabeth Bennet were under your roof, you would be gloating. Instead, you are as frantic as I am."

Darcy had had enough of the all-knowing captain. "I am afraid that I have other business, Hardesty. Unless there is something more than your speculations, I must ask you to leave."

"You do not deserve her," the captain charged.

Darcy turned back to his desk, dismissing the man without a word. Angrily, the captain strode from the room. Darcy waited until the sound of Hardesty's footsteps receded before he allowed himself to respond. "I may not *deserve* her, but I *need* Elizabeth Bennet as much as I need my next breath."

———◦•◦•◦———

"Have you found her?" Georgiana asked over supper.

Darcy had finally confided in his sister. Sharing his anguish gave him some peace. "I have people searching in every place of which I can think. When Hardesty was here, he said Mr. Bennet thought Elizabeth might have come to me. That means the Bennets are also in the dark about Elizabeth's whereabouts. So Miss Elizabeth probably left in the middle of the night. I did receive one bit of good news: the paperwork from Mr. Pinncatch. It seems the captain confessed his lie to the vicar. Pinncatch assumed that Miss Elizabeth and I would reconcile."

Georgiana's expression showed her concern. "I have been thinking a great deal on the matter, and I have a theory if you are willing to listen."

Darcy's lips curved into a patient smile. "Why not?"

"If I were Miss Elizabeth, I would realize that you would not give up that easily. She knows she was wrong, and Elizabeth is ashamed of what she has done to you. Yet, like you said about holding onto hope's thread, Elizabeth is hoping you will come for her. She is waiting for you, Fitzwilliam."

Darcy said amusedly, "How do you know all this?"

"Because I am a female. We think differently from men. We want our knight in shining armor. We want men to make the grand gesture."

Darcy's smile increased. "You have been reading too many Minerva Press books."

Georgiana shrugged and said, "Do you want to know where to find Elizabeth or not?"

Darcy frowned. "You really believe that you have figured this out?"

"Of course, I have." Georgiana sipped her tea, prolonging his anguish. "If I were Miss Elizabeth, I would go to the one place you would never consider. I would seek shelter from someone you hated. Someone you would never want to see again."

"Wickham." Darcy saw it plainly. "You are absolutely uncanny, my dear."

"Thank you." Georgiana giggled. "Do you think it possible?"

"So possible that I will be off to Newcastle at first light."

"Would you take a letter to my new sister for me?"

"Georgiana, at this moment, I would give you anything you desired."

"Just a sister. All my own."

Darcy had ridden hard for three days to reach Northumberland. Finally, in the late morning of the third day, he rode into the street where he knew George Wickham had taken rooms. When he first found his old enemy's post, Darcy had made it a point to locate a man who would send him regular reports on Wickham's activities. He tossed a coin to a street urchin who ran out to hold his horse. "Walk him a bit to cool him down."

"Right, Gov'ner."

"Do you know whether Lieutenant Wickham is in?" Darcy looked up at the boarding house windows.

"The fancy one?" the boy asked.

Darcy smiled knowingly. "That is the one."

"Hasn't come down yet."

Darcy handed the boy another coin. "Keep my horse close." Then he made his way into the building. Although it was not in the best area, the house's interior was cleaner than he expected. Within moments, he found the marked door for which he searched. Rapping heavily on the knocker, Darcy waited impatiently for someone to answer. Finally, the door swung wide, and the man he most hated stood on the other side of the threshold.

"Darcy!" Wickham seemed truly surprised to see him. "What brings you to no-man's-land?"

"You know why I am here." Darcy tried to see beyond Wickham to the interior rooms.

Wickham gestured him in, leaving the door ajar. "I am afraid that you have me at a loss. Hopefully, you have found a way to end my marriage, and you have come to take Mrs. Wickham back to Hertfordshire."

"Not likely." Darcy stood in the main room's middle. "Is Mrs. Wickham not at home?"

Wickham picked up his abandoned cup. "I am sure my wife is out spending money we do not have." He gulped the last of the coffee. "I am still awaiting an explanation for your visit."

"I came for Miss Elizabeth." He hated to give away his personal information to someone with Wickham's instinct for manipulation. "Is Miss Elizabeth residing with your wife or not?" he demanded.

Wickham smiled deviously. "I would say that the lady is residing more with *me* than with Lydia. A woman with a broken heart needs comforting."

Wickham had done this to Darcy all their lives—this pulling at Darcy's sense of honor—but the man did not understand that for Darcy reason did not exist when it came to Elizabeth Bennet. The words had no more escaped Wickham's lips before Darcy pounced on the man.

They hit the floor in a mass of arms and legs. Punches landed. Jabs blackened eyes and tore lips, but still the fight continued. Furniture exploded under the force of their combined weight. For nearly two decades, Darcy had concealed his feelings. Now, they poured out in each punch. Each strike. Every taunt. Every manipulation. Every disservice he had suffered at Wickham's hand guided Darcy's assault.

Within minutes, Darcy straddled a semiconscious Wickham and literally pounded the man's head into the wooden floor.

<hr />

"Oh, my God!" Elizabeth gasped as they turned the corner and headed toward her sister's let rooms.

"What is it, Lizzy?" Lydia Wickham reached for Elizabeth's hand.

"Mr. Darcy. He is here." Seeing the waiting horse, Elizabeth caught her skirt tail and ran for the boarding house.

"Lizzy!" Lydia chased after her.

Elizabeth slammed open the outside door and raced up the stairs. The noise from Mr. Wickham's rooms told her trouble waited. She could hear Lydia struggling with the basket that Elizabeth dropped on the first landing, but she did not stop. Completely out of breath, she burst through the partially opened door. "Fitzwilliam!" she called, but he did not hear her. He sat astride her sister's husband, intent on doing the man bodily harm.

"This is for leaving me on Dark Peak for two days when we were twelve!" Darcy caught Wickham's head with his large palms, lifted it, and slammed it into the floor.

"This is for weaseling your way into my father's good graces!" Slam.

"This is for Georgiana." Slam.

"This is for Eliza…"

Elizabeth propelled herself onto Darcy's back; her arms locked around his neck, struggling to pull him backward before he killed George Wickham. "Fitzwilliam! Stop! Please stop!" She managed to knock him sideways, and they tumbled to the floor together. "Fitz-william, I am here," she said to pacify him.

Lydia rushed in and added her hysterics to the commotion. "Wickham!" she screamed and rushed to her husband's side. "My dear Wickham!"

Meanwhile, Elizabeth cooed words of devotion to Darcy, calm-ing him by her presence. She shoved the hair from his face. "You found me," she rasped. "Oh, my sweet William. You came for me."

Darcy twisted to move away from Wickham's body. "I love you, Elizabeth Bennet. You are coming home with me." Darcy held her close to him.

Elizabeth cuddled in his loose embrace before checking on the chaos just over her shoulder. "When you lose control, you create a mess, Mr. Darcy." She smiled broadly at him.

Darcy raised his head to take in the broken furniture and the sobbing Lydia draped over the badly bruised body of George Wick-ham. "Georgiana said that you wanted the grand gesture." His split lip kept the smile from his face. "I need you in my life." Darcy traced a line down her cheek with his fingertip.

A military officer, followed by two enlisted men, rushed through the door. "What goes on here?" the officer demanded.

Darcy pushed himself to a seated position. "Family quarrel," he said, straightening his clothes.

"Whose family? Who are you?"

"Lieutenant Wickham's soon-to-be brother by marriage," Darcy declared. "This is my fiancée, Elizabeth Bennet." He stood and reached out his hand to Elizabeth. "She is Mr. Wickham's sister. In fact, I bought Wickham's commission for him. I am Fitzwilliam Darcy. My cousin is Colonel Edward Fitzwilliam."

The officer frowned. "You did us no favors, Mr. Darcy." He ges-tured to where Wickham lay.

"But you did me one."

The officer nodded his understanding. "It appears Mr. Wickham will have a legitimate excuse for missing his duty today."

Darcy reached in his pocket and took out a fifty-pound note. "Might I entrust that you will see to Mr. Wickham's medical care and the replacing of any damaged goods?"

"Certainly, Mr. Darcy." The officer pocketed the money.

"Might be that Mr. Wickham's nose be broken," one of the enlisted men observed.

"Maybe he will not be so pretty," the officer remarked.

Darcy smiled with satisfaction. "Maybe not." He turned to Elizabeth. "Please pack your bags, my Dear. We need to leave today."

"They are already packed." She moved closer to him. "I bought a ticket to Lambton this morning. I was coming to you. I belong with you, Fitzwilliam."

<hr />

They found a room at the coaching inn. They stayed only long enough for Darcy to wash away the blood and dirt before they set out again. "There is no carriage available to rent," he told her. "So, you will take the public stage, and I will ride beside. Tomorrow we will marry."

"But how may we marry so quickly?"

"Hardesty confessed his part in your staged engagement. Mr. Pinncatch sent me a copy of the banns, and I have the common license. Both are good for three months. It has been three weeks. There is time. Tonight, we sleep in separate rooms, but after the vows, you will sleep with me, Lizzy. I will not tolerate our separation ever again."

"Even after that horrifying sham I put you through?" Darcy heard hope's touch in her voice, and he knew what she wanted to hear.

He raised her fingers to his lips. "You did it because you loved me...because you thought you were not what I needed in a wife."

Elizabeth's eyes met his. "I have treated you so poorly."

Darcy smiled deviously. "Yes, you have, and I expect it will take a lifetime for you to make it up to me. I suggest that we start immediately." He kissed the inside of her wrist, and she rewarded him with a quick intake of air. "Your father is very worried for your safety."

"I should have told him where I was going, but I did not decide until after I was on the public coach," she confessed. "I left him a note of apology for shaming the family."

Darcy swallowed the last of his anger. Elizabeth had suffered on more than one level: her family, the Meryton residents, Captain Hardesty, and him. "We will write Mr. Bennet to tell him that you are safe at Pemberley as my wife."

"You really love me?" she said still in disbelief.

"Elizabeth, I want us to have snowball battles with our children. I want to share honey straight from the hive with you. I want us to go swimming in the lake behind the manor house. I want to dance with you at the tenants' ball. I want to see you heavy with my child. I want our family portrait hanging in Pemberley's gallery. I want our house to be filled with laughter and love." Darcy lowered his voice. "And I want you in my bed. In *our* bed."

"You have thought of us as such? Throwing snowballs, swimming, dancing, and...?" She could not say the words, but Darcy whispered them in her ear. Surprisingly, Elizabeth did not blush this time. "I want those things also, Fitzwilliam."

He saw her into the coach, mounted, and then leaned down to hand her a piece of paper. "A letter from Georgiana," he said. "She wants her sister at Pemberley."

When the coach rolled from the inn yard, Elizabeth sat back into the well-worn cushions and opened the letter.

Dearest Elizabeth,

If you are reading this, Fitzwilliam has found you, and you are on your way to Pemberley. I have executed our plan as you designed it. It was so smart of you to write to me through Mrs. Annesley. You know my brother's pride. He would not have gone looking for you if he thought you were safe. Going to visit Mrs. Wickham was a stroke of genius. Fitzwilliam cannot tolerate the idea that Mr. Wickham might best him. I just hope my brother's recent frustrations do not make him do something drastic. You have certainly had him beyond reason of late. I have suggested to Fitzwilliam that making a "grand gesture" as the way to win a woman's heart. I await you with open arms at our home. Love Fitzwilliam with all your heart, and you will earn my lifetime devotion. He is truly the best of men.

G.

"That he is. The best of men," Elizabeth murmured.

Part 5

"It is a lovely evening, Mr. Darcy," Caroline Bingley said in her most genteel tone.

Darcy's attention remained divided, but he managed to respond, "I am sure I will find it a memorable one, Miss Bingley. It has been more than a decade since Pemberley hosted a formal ball."

To his dismay, the lady lingered, delaying those behind her in the receiving line. Darcy offered Charles Bingley's sister a brief smile as he brought her gloved hand to his lips. Then he shifted his attention to his next guest. Miss Bingley curtsied prettily, revealing more cleavage than was considered proper, but Darcy was already extending his hand to Mr. Hurst. Then he bowed to Mr. Hurst's wife, Louisa Bingley Hurst, who was Miss Bingley's older sister. Miffed, Caroline frostily greeted Darcy's sister, Georgiana, before entering the ballroom.

Georgiana fidgeted with nervousness beside Darcy, and more than once she blushed because of the familiar salutations from their guests. But it did not escape Darcy's notice that a year ago—or even a month ago—he could never have convinced Georgiana to join him in welcoming their guests. It was *her* influence on his sister. In the same way that Elizabeth Bennet had changed him, she had worked her magic on Georgiana. "Welcome to Pemberley, Mrs. Hurst," Georgiana said in her soft voice.

Darcy wondered where *she* was at this moment—wondered what she was doing—wondered if she thought of him as often as he thought of her—wondered exactly how long it would be before he laid eyes on her again. Only God understood how he suffered with their separations. He had once thought of himself as an excellent choice for any young woman of a certain background. He had not realized how arrogant that was. Darcy remembered with heart-clutching pain how he had wrestled with his sense of responsibility to his name and to his estate. The thought of *losing* her had made him feel utterly empty.

At Rosings Park, he had followed her with his eyes, drinking in the pleasure of her presence—the pleasure of her voice—of their war of wits. He had envied his cousin for securing Elizabeth's attentions—actually thought of doing the good colonel bodily harm for daring to look *her* way. Then Darcy had delivered his disastrous proposal. Even now, he fought the urge to clench his fists in anger with himself for his insufferable arrogance and with her for her acerbic response. *You could not have made the offer of your hand in any possible way that would have tempted me to accept it.*

Mr. Steventon, the local magistrate, was next in the receiving line. He thrust his hand out to shake Darcy's. But Darcy's mind was still on Elizabeth's rejection of his first proposal, and he took an extra beat to respond.

Steventon chuckled at Darcy's faraway look. "Don't worry about your guests. Mrs. Reynolds appears to have everything under control. The lady is a marvel."

Darcy's eyebrows rose. "You may not steal away my ace in the hole, Mr. Steventon." he said.

The man laughed obligingly. "The lady has too much loyalty to the Darcy family for anyone to tempt Mrs. Reynolds away."

"I shall convey your compliments to my housekeeper," Darcy said before turning to a another member of the local gentry.

For the next twenty minutes, Darcy responded automatically to each of his guests, his mind never fully engaged. All he could truly consider was a light and pleasing form and a pair of dark eyes.

The tuning of instruments signaled the beginning of the ball. "We should join our guests, my dear." Darcy caught Georgiana's elbow to lead her into the ballroom. His hothouse, he assumed, held no more blooms, for every vase overflowed with floral bouquets. Their scents blended into a nighttime perfume. Every crystal sparkled with reflected light, and Darcy felt excitement, as well as a bit of trepidation, in his gut.

Georgiana's hand tightened on his arm. "This is my first official ball," she whispered.

"So it is," he said close to her ear. "It will be a splendid prelude to your society debut."

Georgiana smiled mischievously and he smiled back. "Meaning that I may trip over my hem or make the wrong turn in the quadrille, and no one will criticize me?"

"You will find, my dear, that gentlemen rarely care to dance, so despite any mistake a beautiful woman makes, they will all be polite." He cupped her hand with his free one and gave hers a squeeze. "So if you trip or make the wrong turn, you have nothing to fear. Your smile, freely given, would stun even the harshest critics into silence."

Georgiana giggled nervously.

"Who shall claim the first set?"

"The colonel." As she said the words, their cousin appeared and took Georgiana's hand to lead her to the floor.

Darcy shot a glance about the room. The people invited for the evening were his friends and family. He had asked Mrs. Reynolds to include his mother's titled relatives, his father's distinguished kin, his close companions from his university days, and the local gentry. These were the people with whom he wished to spend this glorious evening. Dutifully, he claimed his aunt as his partner and assumed the position at the head of the line of dancers.

"You appear to be quite content tonight, Darcy. Your uncle and I are pleased to see it. You have caused His Lordship several moments of concern. My husband takes his responsibilities to your mother's family quite seriously."

Darcy bowed. "I apologize, Aunt, for any uneasiness His Lordship experienced. I promise that Lord Matlock will have no more worry on my account."

The music began, and a lively country-dance opened the evening's entertainment. Despite his longing for Elizabeth, he felt a great deal of satisfaction at that moment. This was Pemberley, and he was its master. He had, at age eight and twenty, finally ascended to his esteemed father's position, no longer railing against the responsibility for which he had been groomed. In the past few weeks, he had come to terms with how much influence—whether for good or for evil—he had.

As the set ended, Darcy returned his aunt to where Lord Matlock stood, discussing business with their cousin, Baron Prestwick. He exchanged a few brief pleasantries before saying, "Excuse me, Your Lordship, Baron, but I must secure my partner for the second set."

"A waltz so early in the evening, Darcy?" Lord Matlock questioned with a bit of amusement. "Are you setting your own standards?"

"Yes, Uncle." Darcy's smile reached the corners of his eyes. He bowed his exit. With a determined step, he crossed the dance floor and headed toward the main entrance. Darcy was a man with a purpose. He paused to whisper to Georgiana, "Wish me well."

"You know that my heart is always with you, Fitzwilliam," she murmured.

As he walked on, he heard Caroline call, "Mr. Darcy!" But Caroline Bingley would not be the woman he held in his arms that evening. He pretended not to hear her and continued on. And then she stepped into the arch of the entranceway, the light of a thousand candles framing her. Wearing a gown of forest green silk, Elizabeth glided a few steps forward to meet him. The gown, trimmed in a delicate lace, clung to her slim figure, and Darcy thought her the most handsome woman of his acquaintance. The emerald-and-diamond teardrop necklace complemented the gown's low décolletage. She glowed. She belonged there. Just as his mother had belonged there.

Darcy extended his arm, and Elizabeth placed her hand in his. She gave him an intimate smile as Darcy brought her hand to his lips. An overly interested, silent group formed behind him, but Darcy had planned this moment's every detail, even the silence. He thought he heard Miss Bingley sob, but his heart could not accept anything besides the extreme happiness coursing through his veins. In a loud and distinct voice he said, "Ah, there you are, Mrs. Darcy. You are just in time for our wedding waltz."

"I hope I have not kept you waiting, my husband." Her voice was joyful.

"It is not a ball at Pemberley without an estate mistress, my dear." He turned and led Elizabeth to the floor's center and then nodded to the musicians. With the violin's first note, he swung Elizabeth into his arms, the place she belonged. They moved as one as they circled the floor.

Darcy edged her closer, pushing the lines of propriety even for a married couple. "Happy, Mrs. Darcy?" he murmured close to her ear.

"Absolutely, Mr. Darcy." She allowed her fingertip to brush the side of his neck before settling her hand more firmly on his shoulder. "I suppose you are quite proud of yourself," she taunted. "You have surprised everyone with this display." They looked deeply into each other's eyes.

Darcy had never enjoyed the waltz until that moment. His countenance softened, while his gaze intensified. "I am content, my wife. I secreted you away for a fortnight, and now I must share you with family and friends." He tightened his hold. "Are you prepared for the onslaught of questions when the music stops?"

"If you believe in me, Mr. Darcy, I am." Darcy observed that her bottom lip trembled.

He spoke only for her hearing: "I will not leave your side."

"I am depending upon that fact, sir." Elizabeth glanced about her as they whirled around the dance floor. "Have we done the right thing, Fitzwilliam, by not telling everyone of our nuptials?"

"Some will disagree," he conceded, "but most will celebrate the fact that I am content, at last." He was silent for a moment as they danced on. "Those in attendance tonight are the ones who—for the most part—will welcome your presence in my life," he confided. She nodded her head, but he saw Elizabeth's confidence waver.

As the music died, Darcy turned to the Matlocks and the colonel, but Elizabeth caught his arm to stay him. "Tell me you love me," she whispered frantically.

Darcy chuckled as he raised their clasped hands to his lips and kissed the back of hers. "This from the woman who dared to thwart Lady Catherine's tactics!" he whispered back, his eyes dancing in amusement. Then, noting her anxiousness, he confessed, "My greatest happiness lies with you. I want nothing more than to spend the rest of my days loving you and raising children with you."

As if his words washed over her, Elizabeth tilted her head, a hint of a grin touching her mouth. She felt the pride of knowing she was his. "You are either crazy or are the bravest man in the world," she retorted.

"Although I admit, sweetheart, that you have driven me nearly insane in this past year, I am neither crazy nor brave—simply a man in love."

She wound her arm gracefully through his and raised her chin in that familiar act of defiance that he had come to cherish. "Then it is time I met my new family."

Darcy's breath caught in his throat, and he felt a simple joy take hold. The couple approached his beaming uncle and Darcy bowed. "Your Lordship," he said, "may I present my wife, Elizabeth Bennet Darcy."

But He Turned Out Very Wild

BY SARAH A. HOYT

Sarah A. Hoyt (sarahahoyt.com) often says no genre is safe from her. She has published fantasy, science fiction, mystery, historic mystery, and romantic biography novels. She has also published over one hundred short stories in various magazines and anthologies. Given all this, of course, she relaxes by writing Austen fan fiction! In that arena, she blushes to admit she has a soft spot for rogues and rakes whose reformation or wholesale rehabilitation she often undertakes in her stories.

As Austen fans well know, George Wickham is a very bad guy. His name, which is close to *wicked*, implies it before you realize. But perhaps he deserves a fair shake, which is what "But He Turned Out Very Wild" proposes to do.

❧

It was dark and wet. Outside the carriage, rain fell in drips and splats from the branches of trees and the gates of the great houses we passed.

Inside the carriage, the air felt cold and damp, and there was the smell of wet wool from my uniform coat and from my collar— soaked through with my tears. The carriage rocked and swayed. The coachman cracked his whip. I had promised him a reward for getting me to Pemberley by early the next morning. Before she... before the woman I loved slipped out of my reach forever. I had—I thought—proof that would render my reputation blameless and me worthy of her.

But why should Darcy believe me now? Now, after all these years. Perhaps I'm going on a fool's errand.

Something like the exhaustion of sadness overcame me. I turned to the window and rested my head on it. And I felt the carriage rock beneath me, rock, rocking me away from the present and into the past.

"No, I don't believe I will give you the living at Kimpton," Fitzwilliam snarled at me. "Good Lord, man, think you I don't know about your scandals at Cambridge?"

I stood, mute and confused, in front of him, in what was once his father's study. From the wall behind Will, his father's portrait looked down at me, his blue eyes softly benevolent and his smile that gentle one that he often gave me. Will's father had been my father's best friend, and had lured my father away from a lucrative practice as a solicitor to manage his great estate of Pemberley.

It wouldn't have been a hard thing to do. My father had been left recently widowed, with no one to look after a baby son, and facing letting that son grow up in cramped quarters in London with no supervision. George Darcy had offered him a chance to live in the country, in one of the most beautiful estates in Derbyshire, and to have his son share the nursery with Darcy's own son. How could my father have refused? Oh sure, it was a diminution of prestige for him, but what did he care for that? George was not someone to hold to the social differences. My father had taken the offer and been contented with it. As had I, till that moment.

Oh, I'd had some inkling before that not all was quite right. When his father paid for me to go to Cambridge with Will, both

Will and I had been overjoyed. We were to have a shared lodging in Cambridge, and we were to take with us, as a joint valet, Curvin Smithen, who had grown up with us—well, as a boot boy—and who had just finished his training as a valet. It seemed to us, then, that we'd achieved our dream of adulthood—that we were finally to enter that marvelous world of privilege and that nothing but happiness awaited us. We were, you see, the best of friends. We were like brothers from the nursery onward. Between us, there was no awkwardness, no feeling of social difference.

But shortly after we got to Cambridge, our friendship cooled. William seemed distracted around me, retiring. He no longer talked to me about his most intimate concerns—his thoughts and his fears.

I recalled Smithen telling me, "Well, what can you expect now, Mr. Wickham? Surely you realize all his other friends here at Cambridge are far above you? Surely you realize that they have made fun of him for his friendship with you?"

Whatever I'd expected, it wasn't this. It wasn't Will, tight-lipped and pale, summoning me into the study right after his father's funeral, and then announcing that he wasn't giving me Kimpton.

"Why? Why ever not?" I finally managed to say. "Why not give me the living your father promised? Why would you dishonor his memory?"

Will's lip curled, the way his lip had always curled since childhood when he was presented with a patent falsehood, an unworthy action, or someone he judged despicable. "Dishonor his memory, indeed. Yes, I would do that and more if I gave that living to you. No, Wickham, give over. I know you too well to entrust you with the souls of Kimpton. I'm not sure I would entrust you with the souls of Hades." He pulled his father's account book from the drawer. "Name your price for what you'd rather have, instead, and I'll write you a note for it here and now."

He looked up. I was speechless.

"Name your price," he said. "Come on, while I feel generous. You must understand that now that both our fathers are dead, there is no occasion for you to come to Pemberley, and you must consider our acquaintance to be quite at an end."

I felt tears burning in my eyes. He would turn me out of the only home I'd ever known? I swallowed hastily, to avoid disgracing myself. "Will?" I asked, not quite sure what this meant. Was it some nightmare in which my childhood friend, my almost-brother became a malevolent stranger? I would presently wake up and be snug in my room in Cambridge, and Will would be sleeping in his room next door. I would wake him up and tell him of my strange dream, and we'd laugh about it.

"Please don't call me that. I will give you a note now, and you will cash it—I'm sure you have gambling debts aplenty, not to mention payments to many tradesmen's daughters—and then you will consider all our acquaintance at an end." He wrote as he spoke, with large, vivid flourishes. "Will ten thousand be enough? Surely, ten thousand will be enough. Good Lord, fortunes have been made on less. You will take ten thousand, and you will leave my home. We shall meet again only as common and indifferent acquaintances."

Numb, not believing any of this could be happening, I received the slip of paper with a hand that felt frozen.

"I...I suppose I could study law," I said. My voice cracked and failed.

Will looked up, looked at me. There was not in his eyes any friendship, any hint of concern, though my pain must have been vividly etched on my face. "I do not care how you live or what you do," he said. "So long as you be gone."

I don't know how I stumbled from that office. I do not remember. I do remember standing in the vast, marbled hall. Darcy had my things packed. Smithen waited with them. He handed me my cane, my hat, and my cape, all curtly and without emotion. "You must know, sir," he said. "You must be gone. He'll have the law on you otherwise."

"The law? For what?" I asked, bewildered.

"Why, sir, that note he gave you. Surely you know he'll change his mind long before you cash it. He'll say you extorted it."

"Why?" It was the question I kept asking and to which I got no answer.

Smithen sighed. "I tried to tell you, sir, in Cambridge, but you would not believe me. Mr. Darcy has fallen in with an unsavory set. All those tradesmen's daughters, the men demanding payment for gambling debts…"

I remembered. There had been women running from our quarters as I approached. There had been men coming to look for me, asking for payment for gambling debts incurred in some drunken game. There had been men demanding I marry their daughters. In that regard, Darcy was right. I owed money everywhere. Save for one thing—I hadn't done any of it. My days were spent studying or walking, my evenings often praying in the Cambridge chapel. I had no carnal knowledge of anyone and I certainly had never gambled.

"*He,*" Smithen said, filling the word with meaning and significance, "gave your name when he went about his exploits."

And that I could see, suddenly. The whole thing became clear in my mind. Oh, Darcy and I look nothing alike. Not in a family type of resemblance. But we are, both of us, fairly tall men and dark haired; both of us have blue eyes. Similar enough to look the same in the darkened gambling dens around Cambridge, and to men too intent on their pleasure to care to fix a face in their memories. Similar enough to sound the same in the description a daughter gives her irate father.

"But why would Darcy do that to me?" I asked Smithen. It was an innocent question, as of a child to an adult.

His blue eyes looked sad, just like the eyes of an adult who has to explain a painful truth to a child. "Don't you know, sir? Have you never suspected? Why, sir, he's always resented the interest and kindness his father showed toward you, of course. Very proud, Mr. Darcy is."

And Smithen had to be right, though Darcy could only have become proud after arriving at Cambridge. But such things happened to people as they grew up. I should not think on it anymore.

My heart broken, all of my worldly possessions in a small bag, I started making my way down the long drive of my childhood home for the last time.

And then I saw her.

At first, I thought that in my pain and grieving I was hallucinating an angel to console me. It was only on looking again that I realized that the angel was none other than Georgiana.

Georgiana was Will's sister and almost ten years younger. Her mother died birthing her, and while she was a small child in the nursery, both Will and I spent hours entertaining her and seeking to make her laugh. In those days, I supposed, I'd thought of her as something between a doll and a sister.

But then at seven she had been sent away to an expensive and reputable school for girls. Mr. George Darcy had judged it prudent that his daughter should have a more feminine surrounding than a home where everyone but a few servants was male. Two years after she'd gone to school, Darcy and I had gone to Cambridge. I hadn't seen Georgiana in eight years.

And what I saw now took the breath from my lungs and the thought from my mind. Even my hurt was gone. All I could think was how beautiful she looked—this blonde lady I could not associate with the awkward child I'd once loved in quite a different manner.

This young lady awakened in me feelings I hadn't been sure of ever entertaining toward anyone. I wanted to fall on my knees and worship her. I wanted to hold her in my arms, protect her, and comfort her. I wanted to put a ring on her finger and call her Mrs. Wickham.

She wore a dark dress—mourning, of course—and held a dark parasol open above her. The darkness only made her seem more beautiful, a statue made of ivory and sunlight. Her eyes were reddened. She would have cried for her father. She hadn't attended the funeral, of course. Women didn't.

"George?" she said. And a small smile appeared on her grief-pale features. "George. You came for the funeral." Then her gaze wandered to the valise in my hand. "But you mustn't leave. You mustn't leave so soon. You must stay and console Will and me. We three have always been quite close, have we not? You're family. Family draw together in times of sadness."

I couldn't tell her what had happened between Will and me. It sounded so insane, even to me. Perhaps Will was insane. Perhaps that was it. It wasn't his fault. Just an illness, a sad event. "I…can't stay," I told her. "I wish I could, but business calls me away to… London." I spoke quite at random.

"London?" She smiled. "Oh, but then you must come see me. Will is setting me up in my own household with my own governess in Ramsgate. You must visit me, George. Promise you will. I will not be denied."

She looked so adorable. As imperious as her insufferable aunt Catherine, but with a whispering undertone of shyness and diffidence. How could I have refused her anything?

I promised.

As the heavens are my witness, I swear I thought I'd visit Georgiana in Ramsgate, and we'd make stilted conversation over tea that had brewed too long—as tea made by governesses is all too prone to doing. Then I'd leave and go about my business, as free of Georgiana as I was of her brother.

I'd never cashed the promissory note—indeed, I dared not, because Smithen was probably right, and any man willing to treat an old friend the way Will had done would be capable of any villainy. I had no intention of being jailed for extortion. With Will's word against mine, they'd surely choose his.

Instead, I'd found menial work in a bookbinder's, reading the final proof before text was printed. I was familiar enough, from Cambridge, with the Bible and all holy texts to catch mistakes efficiently. It paid me enough to keep me in clothes and food and a small room. I lived.

And then I visited Georgiana. And in those moments in her tidy rooms, in the better section of Ramsgate, I was a gentleman. I was sir, and Mr. Wickham again. I was...what I had once been.

I think at first that was the attraction, the reason I allowed Georgiana to invite me back, and then again. Georgiana was beautiful beyond compare, but what chance did I have with that angel? Despite this indisputable fact, something changed. I started going back...for Georgiana.

I think it took me a full six months—as fall turned to winter and winter to shy, blushing spring—to realize I was in love. I was in love with Georgiana Darcy, who was far above my station—a seraphim sent to earth. I was enchanted with the turn of her arm, the movements of her hand, and her little crooked smile. I was besotted with the way her blonde hair curled at the nape of her neck. And not all the perfumeries of the East could create a scent to equal her fresh smell of soap and rose water.

I dreamed of her during the day and then dreamed of her at night. My only hours of golden happiness were those spent in her lodgings, holding her hand.

This is the only explanation I have for proposing to her. Surely, even at the crest of my emotion, I must have known it was foolish. Perilous. Insane. Not to mention self-destructive.

And yet I proposed and she accepted. And then I needed to carry out my purpose—our purpose—without being interrupted. We had to marry before Darcy found us out. Once I was a legal member of the family, I would have some leverage; and if Darcy was truly slipping into insanity, there were excellent doctors of the mind. I could manage it and I would manage it, once we were truly related.

Georgiana agreed to elope. Not happily, I explained to her how people might think, how they might say I wanted her only for her dowry. How certain tongues—those of the Misses Bingley, for example—might attempt to influence her brother's opinion because he was of an impressionable nature. She accepted. She was in love with me. She accepted my explanation because she wanted to marry me as much as I wanted to marry her.

<hr />

I remember that other night of rain and darkness, and waiting inside the carriage for Georgiana and her packages.

It was cold for a summer night, with thunder and rain and a blustery wind that whistled around corners. Georgiana looked giddy, in her pelisse and hat, as she ran down the steps. And stopped.

There were hooves in the night and a horse drew up behind the carriage. Georgiana looked delighted. She ran toward where the horse had stopped.

I believe I knew even then the identity of the rider. I felt no surprise when, after a brief talk with Georgiana, Will appeared at the door to the carriage. He was furious. I'd seen him that furious only a couple of times while growing up—once when his groom had whipped a horse severely, and then again when a gardener had beaten the young gardener boy without mercy. Both times, Darcy—only a stripling —had threatened to have the offender flogged.

Now he was looking at me with a cold rage. He looked so pale that his lips appeared gray. "Eloping?" he asked. "You convinced her to elope?" His lips trembled and his gaze flashed with ire. "She is just sixteen."

"I love her," I croaked. "I want to marry her."

"Oh, I am sure you love her," Darcy said. "Which is why you want to destroy her reputation forever. Out of my sight, Wickham. Take this carriage to whatever miserable hole you huddle in."

"You can't do that. Georgiana. I want to see Georgiana."

"Meaning you want to blackmail me over whatever billets-doux she was indiscreet and innocent enough to write to you. Very well, Wickham. I'll send Smithen with a check, and you will send me every last scrap of paper you have of hers. Do you understand?"

I tried to protest, but he slammed the door of the carriage, and I heard him order the coachman, "Drive on. Drive this villain whence he came."

And the carriage took off, bouncing and jostling through London streets.

I never saw Georgiana after that. Smithen brought me a note, the contents of which I scruple to mention, and a check that I did not wish to—and did not dare to—cash.

He took from me a letter written with an anguished heart and stained with my tears. It detailed, faithfully, all my dealings with Darcy and told Georgiana all that I would have liked to have spared her. It begged her, for the sake of the love we shared, to meet me the next day, at such and such hour, by the coachmen's on Hay Street. I thought we'd rent horses and make our way to Gretna Green in Scotland, where we could marry immediately. I was hoping for a miracle—that Darcy would actually give Georgiana my letter, unread.

Need I say she didn't show up? I sat and waited, in the warm summer evening, by a horses' trough, till the sky turned bright pink in the East. And then I went home with a broken heart.

How I lived, how I survived those few months, I don't know. I seized upon the recommendation of an acquaintance to join the militia. It seemed a good way to leave behind London, the scene of both my happiness and its shattering.

I went to Hertfordshire, to a little place called Merryton. And there found, to my chagrin, that Darcy was a guest at a country house nearby. Neatherfield, it was called. And, as with any man who has ten thousand a year to his name, he was the subject of lively speculation among the mamas and the daughters of Merryton.

Wishing to warn them all—but, for the sake of his father, not wishing to disgrace him publicly—I contented myself with warning one woman, a Miss Bennet, at whom Will was looking with particular intent. I realized my warning was most improper, but Miss Elizabeth Bennet seemed to understand it all.

And then the militia moved to Brighton. I went, happy to get away from Will. Tradesmen in Merryton had been accusing me of seducing their daughters again, and there had been men coming for me for gambling debts I'd never incurred. And Smithen warned me that Will plotted my death. All of Will's other behavior was perfectly normal, so it seemed that I was the only object of his dangerous, mad obsessiveness. I left, hoping it would all improve between us.

But in Brighton, I was pursued once again for payment. Oddly, though Will had left Hertfordshire, I didn't see him in Brighton. Not once. I had to assume he was there, though, because I once glimpsed Smithen from a distance, and Smithen was, after all, Will's valet.

The debts got so awful that the only thing I could do was go to London and cash those old promissory notes. I prepared to do so.

That night, it was raining again. Seemed to be my fate whenever I had to travel by carriage. A note had arrived, informing me that this night I'd be thrown into debtor's prison.

It was not my intention to rot in jail for Darcy's spurious debts in my name. Of course, I might very well end up rotting in jail by cashing a note he said was extorted from him. But it was a risk I had to take.

I had gotten a coach with my last remaining bit of pay, and I was getting into it, when I heard panting and giggling. Puzzled, I looked out the window.

Miss Lydia Bennet, the young and very silly sister of Miss Elizabeth Bennet, was also the particular friend of Mrs. Forster (my commander's wife), and Lydia had been staying with the commander's family. I saw Lydia running toward the carriage, in a flutter of ruffles and laces, an eager grin on her pretty, vacuous face.

As she approached the carriage, the driver opened the door to her—if out of habit or because it was the logical thing to do, I'll never know. She plunged in, in a cloud of perfume and giggles.

Her face was flushed, a not unbecoming pink in a girl still very young and naturally very pretty. She leaned back in the seat, taking deep, racking breaths. "Oh, Lord, I'm fagged," she said. And grinned. "But we're eloping, Whicky." She adjusted her skirts and gave me a sly look. "Imagine your being in love with me all this time. And never to tell me or give a sign of it to me personally, but only to write about it in letters. What a good joke. But I'm glad you did. We shall be married. And I only sixteen." She gave me a sly look, under her quite long eyelashes. "To think I shall have done what none of my sisters has done."

"In love?" I asked, puzzled. Miss Lydia was very pretty, I'll grant anyone that, but really—look at the way she was behaving when she thought she was eloping. Was this proper behavior for such an occasion? And *why* did she think she was eloping? With me?

"Oh, Whicky, there's no need pretending. Your note said it all so well. How much you loved me, how you couldn't live without me. How you'd die lest I eloped with you. And how you'd have the coach here at this time." She grinned at me.

It was the scene with Darcy in the study after his father's funeral all over again. Perhaps I should consider that it was not Darcy who was insane, but I. Perhaps I did those things and...forgot them? But why would I punish myself in such horrible ways? Why would I cut off my access to Pemberley? Why would I marry Miss Lydia Bennet?

The coachman's voice came through the window. "Sir, there's a large group in pursuit. Sir..."

The creditors. And now, if they caught me with this girl.... "Drive, man, drive!"

"To Gretna Green!" Lydia Bennet called out, laughing.

"To London!" I screamed desperately, over her voice.

I confess I sat in my lodgings at Mrs. Young's boardinghouse and drank myself into a stupor day after day for the next several weeks. If I was so insane as to gamble, wench, run up debts, and elope with Lydia Bennet—all without my knowing it—then there was nothing for it but to drink myself to death.

Meanwhile, Lydia—who had been placed in the room next to mine and whom I had not touched, at least that I knew of—whined day and night, "When shall we go out? Are you going to take me to the theater? Are you going to take me to a review? When shall we be married? I'm bored."

How could even the dark side of my soul wish to elope with her?

I had the notes cashed—surprisingly, without any trouble—and forwarded some money to Brighton to pay for the debts there. The rest of it, I invested in good wine. I sat by the window, drank, and dreamed of Georgiana. Georgiana, who didn't love me. Georgiana, who had never loved me. Georgiana, who was now forever out of reach—because of Lydia Bennet.

It shouldn't have come as a surprise that Darcy found me. I had given my address when cashing those notes. What came as a surprise was that he took an interest at all. And that he looked as angry as I'd ever seen him, but controlled himself and didn't punch me into the ground.

He wanted something from me, you see. He wanted me to *marry* Miss Lydia Bennet.

It seemed that, quite unknown to me, his romance with Miss Eliza Bennet had progressed till she was all he could think about. From the tone of his words, and though he'd not said it, he was either at the point of proposing or had proposed to Miss Bennet when the news of my elopement with Lydia had arrived.

To Darcy's eyes, it was all very simple. I must now marry Lydia so that the stain would be removed from the family. Then Darcy could marry Elizabeth.

We were to be brothers. What a good joke. The Almighty, clearly, had Lydia's sense of humor.

I went through with it. What else was left for me to do? Twice, I tried to explain to Darcy that I was out of my mind, that I needed help. But the look in his eyes when he thought I was—as he put it—trying to wiggle out of it, wasn't worth tempting.

He drew up the papers, and he settled the money on me. Darcy in love carried all before him.

I asked about Georgiana once. I think that eventually the scar his signet ring left on my chin might fade. In a few years.

Lydia, of course, thought we were fighting over her. She was the sort of woman whom this kind of thing excited.

And so we were married, on an insipid summer morning, when the milk thin sunlight trickled through the windows of the church on Cheapside.

Her parents—kind, generous people—invited us to their house on our way to a garrison in the far North, where Darcy—for the sake of having me far away from him—had bought me a place in the regulars.

Lydia was still untouched when we headed for the North. And still untouched when news of Darcy's wedding reached us three months later.

◦═◦•◦═◦

Did she know she was missing something—the full state of marriage? I've often wondered. After all, many families don't tell their children anything about their own provenance till the marriage day.

Particularly those children who are female. Perhaps some children are never told at all.

She gave no sign of being disappointed. During our first year of marriage, she went about with a smile on her face and a song on her lips, to all eyes the happiest bride on the Lord's earth. As for me, that was the easiest year in many years, save for Lydia's incessant chatter and save for missing Georgiana night and day. I did not seem to have run up debts. No women claimed to have been seduced by me. Perhaps after saddling me with the erstwhile Miss Bennet and putting Georgiana forever out of my reach, my other, self-destructive self rested at last?

And then, after a year, I got the news that my wife was increasing. Increasing! And I'd never touched her.

But what if the other Wickham had? I didn't ask. I waited in misery to be a proud papa, while enduring the congratulations of well-wishers all around me.

There was no correspondence from Darcy. There was a note from Mrs. Darcy, wishing us happiness on the forthcoming occasion of our child's birth. But such was my state, I thought I saw Smithen around town once or twice. But then I always had that impression, wherever I went.

———

The birth didn't go well. The mother was young. Just seventeen. Too young, it proved.

Though you'd think that someone that buxom and full of interest in such things would give birth with a natural ease, things didn't happen that way.

I called the midwife early in the morning. I called the doctor late in the day. Lydia's screams lost force through the day, becoming mere whimpers by nightfall. And then...nothing.

I sat in a chair just outside the birth chamber, waiting and trying to compose my mind for fatherhood. What would I do? What could I do? The tyke would be my son or daughter, and—please the Lord—sane and healthy and not suffering from my obvious streak of insanity. I would be a father. The best father I could be.

But it wasn't supposed to be like this. My child was supposed to have Georgiana as a mother. He or she was supposed to have Georgiana's eyes and that little crooked smile.

I was crying a little when the midwife came out. I knew from her expression that something had gone very wrong. I stood up, my limbs seemingly tangling on each other, my voice failing me. "My..." I said. And then, "The baby?"

"Oh, the baby is fine, Mr. Wickham," she said, wiping her hands on her already blood-stained apron. "You have a daughter, Mr. Wickham. It is your wife. The poor thing. I—" She looked at my face and seemed to see grief reflected there, because she broke into tears. "I'm sorry, Mr. Wickham. I'm afraid she's dead."

And thus I became a widower.

———— ·•⋈•· ————

It was days before I looked at my daughter, days before I returned to the world of the living. Something about Lydia's awful death confirmed for me that I was cursed, and all those who involved themselves with me would end badly.

I sat in my room and drank myself into a stupor and wished for death. But there were kind friends and concerned officers all around. My officer's wife, she sent a nanny over to look after my daughter, whom I called Lydia. What else would I call her?

And friends sent food and comfort and came and sat with me and tried to console me for the loss I didn't really feel and should have felt.

Guilt and rage swirled in me until one day I woke up, sober and with an aching head.

It was a spring morning. The birds were singing. At breakfast, our housekeeper informed me that my daughter was a fine, lusty child and that my late wife's things still remained in her room, waiting my going through them and packaging them to send to her family or to charity or whatever I intended to do with them.

I went to Lydia's room, a place I'd never—consciously—entered, and started sorting through her effects. She had no less than eighty-five exquisitely trimmed hats, plus ribbons and frippery to trim a hundred more. She'd missed her calling. She should have been a milliner.

There was other stuff, none of any importance. And then, under some lace, in her most hidden drawer, I found a pile of letters tied together with a blue ribbon. I pulled them out, recognizing the handwriting, to my shock. It wasn't mine. Or Darcy's.

The letters—clearly written by the hand of an intelligent man—were from the Brighton time and told Lydia of love, of passion, of undying devotion.

In every letter, he told her to burn the missive. But women never burn such letters.

I stared in horror at the huge, angular handwriting. Once seen, never forgotten. It was Smithen's writing and no mistake.

I stared at it as I realized that he was—also—tall and dark haired and blue eyed. In the darkened, smoky atmosphere of a gambling den, if he dressed like me and said his name was Wickham, who would doubt him? In the darkened bedchambers of tradesmen's daughters, primed by a hundred previous love letters, who would believe he was not me? In my own conjugal bed, in the dark of night, if he threw my jacket over the foot and climbed into bed with

Lydia, how was she to know he wasn't me? It wasn't as though I'd given her anything with which to compare his actions.

The whole monstrous plan unfolded in my mind like a grotesque flower. And I realized I'd been had. I'd been played. My entire disgrace, my horrible marriage, and perhaps even my separation from Georgiana were all a game. Smithen's game.

But why?

I saw the baby and arranged for her care while I was gone. If I had bothered to look at her earlier, I would have known. Her eyes were as close together as Smithen's, and her mouth had a dissatisfied setting, just like his.

But I could not hate her. She'd been conceived because I'd failed in my duty to my wife and because I hadn't examined the events in my life. She was mine in guilt, if not in blood. We would do the best we could. I would try to raise that dissatisfied expression out of her little mouth and to coax her to overcome the duplicity the close-together eyes suggested. I would be a good father.

But first, before I settled down to be a quiet widower with a daughter, I must go see Darcy. If this was not my fault and not his fault, then we must talk to each other and clear up the misunderstanding. I doubted he would welcome me with open arms or let me court Georgiana. And I doubted Georgiana would want to be courted by me after all this time. But still, the truth needed to be out.

With such resolute ideas, I arranged for a coach to carry me south, and I took care of some household affairs. At least no one accused me of gambling debts or seductions. As drunk as I'd been...

But why hadn't Smithen caused trouble for me recently? Something must have happened in the nature of an endgame. But what?

I understood when I got Darcy's letter. Announcing Georgiana's upcoming marriage to the Baron d'If.

It all went blurry. The date of the wedding was a week hence. Enough time to get there, if I rode night and day and rested not.

———————

And that brought me to the carriage, devouring the miles, approaching the place and date of my true love's wedding to someone else. For no good purpose and on a fool's errand. And yet. And yet, Darcy must know and perhaps Georgiana, too, must know that I was not a black-hearted villain. They must, by all that is holy, listen to me.

If Georgiana was marrying this baron, she must love him—and who was I to compete with nobility. Georgiana would marry him still. But she must know before she married that she had never loved a truly unworthy man. Perhaps it would give her peace and make her married life better.

I intended to get there the night before the wedding, to explain all to the Darcys in decent privacy. In retrospect, all it would have earned me was being locked out of the house, perhaps thrown in jail.

Fate had other plans. Due to an unfortunate incident with three cows, a pig, a muddy road, and a much-worn carriage wheel, I ended up getting to Pemberley when the family chapel was full of guests and the grounds gaily decorated with bows for the occasion.

And I ended up bursting into the church—sweaty and reeking of travel, of tears, of wet wool, and of unwashed fur—just as the minister said, "...or forever hold your peace."

"I must speak!" I shouted, bursting into the church.

The august company—and never had Pemberley in its glory hosted such a wondrous crowd of the highest nobility—fell silent. All eyes turned to me. Standing by the altar with his sister—and

some blond youth whose looks I barely remarked on, save for notic-
ing that he was swathed in velvet and golden braid—Darcy turned
to give me a murderous glare.

"Give me leave," I said. "For I must speak."

The minister, astonished, waved me on. Georgiana, lovely as an
angel in her lace and satin, looked as if she might swoon on the spot
and leaned on the former Elizabeth Bennet, her matron of honor,
for support, as if her legs would fail her. She was not, at least, im-
mune to my presence.

I poured my story out. Incoherently and in a confused, tangled
mess, I told it all. The gambling. The tradesmen's daughters. And yet
I, who had been accused of so many seductions, I who had eloped
and been married, had never lain with a woman or, indeed, with
anyone. Not men. Not prostitutes. I saw Georgiana, pale and wan,
lean farther back against her sister-in-law, and my mouth went on,
all uncaring.

"I've never had the slightest interest in whores," I said.

"You're drunk, man," Darcy said.

"Not even a little," I said, and went on to explain my discovery
in Lydia's drawer. As I spoke, I pulled the packet of letters from my
jacket. "And I daresay, if you look, you'll find similar letters with
every tradesman's daughter whom I ever supposedly seduced." I extended the letters. I was aware of some commotion at the back of
the church, but I didn't turn to look.

Darcy extended his hand for the letters, saw the handwriting,
and exclaimed, "Smithen!"

"All right," Smithen said from the back of the church. "So you've
found me out, but you'll do nothing."

I looked back and saw him, unsteadily, point a gun at me. "I will
shoot you dead if you take a step toward me!" he said.

"You forgot you left me nothing to live for!" I yelled.

The gun moved toward Darcy. Darcy took an inflexible step toward Smithen, all the same. "If you shoot," Darcy snarled, "you'd better be very sure of hitting me, for you have only one shot in your weapon. And after that, I'll be on you."

"All right!" Smithen yelled. "Then her." He pointed his pistol at Georgiana. "Take another step toward me, and I will shoot her."

The baron, Georgiana's would-be groom, made a sound like a whimper, removed a lace kerchief from his pocket, and dabbed at his brow, while staring at Smithen.

But Georgiana had the blood of the Darcys in her veins, the very same Darcys who had once opposed a furious Henry VIII. She stood straight all of a sudden, and she took a step forward, away from Elizabeth Darcy.

"You are evil," she told Smithen. "And all evil will be punished."

Smithen laughed. It was a deranged sound. "Not today," he said. And pulled the trigger.

I jumped forward, not quite knowing what I was doing. I jumped in the path of the bullet, knowing only—without thinking—that I must save Georgiana. Georgiana must not die.

The ball smashed into my shoulder. I felt it crush though skin and flesh and bone. I heard screams. I felt something warm down the front of my traveling jacket. Cold spread from my shoulder to my chest. I could not speak. Breathing hurt. My legs felt like running water. I fell.

At the back of the church, there was a scuffle, the sound of fists hitting flesh. But I was all beyond it then. I noted that Georgiana's groom was on the floor also, seemingly unconscious. I wondered if he'd been hit, too.

But Georgiana was by my side, her fingers fluttering softly on my jacket, her voice as commanding and stern as Lady Catherine at her worst, "Bring lights, someone bring lights. And a knife to cut his jacket. And a tourniquet. Quick, man, put pressure on the wound. He's bleeding his heart out. A doctor. Send for the doctor. *Now!*"

Other hands were doing things to me. It didn't matter. Georgiana, concerned and lovely, standing amid a wealth of satin stained with my blood, looked down on me with gentle tenderness. Suddenly, her lips touched mine—a moment of heaven. I tasted salt on them. Why was she crying? It was just me, and I did not matter.

"You must live, my love," she said. "You must live for me. For *us.*"

"My love." I took those words with me into darkness.

I woke up hours later, in my old room at Pemberley. The doctor had patched me up admirably. The valet—obviously not Smithen—who'd been left with me till I woke told me how Miss Georgiana had refused to marry the baron, who'd been so cowardly as to faint at the sight of blood. She'd said, in front of everyone in church, she'd only agreed to marry him because she thought her true love was a villain. Now that she'd been proved wrong, she'd marry for love or not at all.

And Smithen had been on the point of arrest, for fraud and conspiracy and attempted murder, when he turned his pistol on himself, spraying his brains over the walls of the ancient chapel at Pemberley.

Darcy—well, the valet, a good lad of maybe fifteen, wouldn't say anything even ironic about his master. But it was clear from what the valet did say that Darcy was shaken and oddly contrite. Oddly contrite for Darcy, of course.

"He muttered much about his abominable pride that didn't allow him to look behind the seeming facts for the truth," the valet said.

I nodded and started pulling myself up on the bed. "Where are they now?" I asked. "Have they retired?"

"To bed? No. No one has gone to bed. The guests are perhaps in bed in their wing, but in the family wing, no one has gone to bed. Although they're not in the drawing room, and I'm not quite sure..."

I knew then where they were. I knew for a certainty. Sitting on the bed, I looked about for clothes to make myself decent. I spotted a dressing gown thrown over an easy chair by the window. It was blue and silk and I was sure it belonged to Darcy. How kind of him to share. "Give me my dressing gown, man. Quickly."

The valet stared. "Sir, I—" He swallowed.

"Come on," I said. "The dressing gown. Be quick about it."

"Sir, the doctor said as you weren't supposed to get up."

"Boil the doctor," I said. "What does he know?" I had to see Georgiana. I had to talk to Darcy. I had to make sure this wasn't all a fevered dream.

"But sir—" the valet said.

"Now."

He obeyed. Although reluctantly, he obeyed with—it occurred to me—far more alacrity than was owed Wickham, the son of auld Wickham, estate manager for the Darcys.

His hands trembled as he held the robe up for me. "Only, Mr. Darcy said nothing was to happen to you, for you had been his brother. And before the month was out, chances were you'd be his brother again."

My chest expanded as I grinned. The pain in my shoulder meant nothing. "If you want to keep me safe, you'll help me walk downstairs."

"Downstairs, sir?"

"To Mrs. Reynold's sitting room," I said, and grinned at his astonished expression. Clearly, he didn't know that had been our childhood refuge, where the kind lady had fed us milk and chocolate biscuits and listened to all our tales.

But Darcy and Georgiana knew. And I knew where to find them.

"But why would Smithen do it?" Darcy asked.

We sat, all three of us, around Mrs. Reynold's table, as we had when we were small children. Elizabeth Darcy, lovely if disheveled, leaned against the doorsill, in her dressing gown, looking—not left out—but bewildered, as our voices and manners acquired the ease of childhood again.

She was probably having trouble adjusting to the thought that I was no villain. I didn't mind. She would get used to it. Darcy had married a smart woman.

Mrs. Reynold had fed us cookies and was pouring the second glass of milk for Georgiana. She gave Darcy a concerned look, as if hesitating about what to tell him.

"I always treated him well," Darcy said. "Didn't I, Wickham? Did I fail in something I ought to have done?"

Mrs. Reynold turned a concerned look on me. She sighed. She set down the milk jug and sat in her chair, at the corner. "It wasn't either of you," she said. "Or Miss Georgiana either." She sighed. "It was Mr. Wickham's father."

"My...father?" I asked.

"Aye, sir, you must understand, your father didn't want to marry again and subject you to the whims of a stepmother, but he was still a young man with...needs. It is said—and I've heard it from her own mouth—he went down to Bessie Smithen at the tavern. That child of hers, hedge-born, as it were...Well, your father got him a position as a gardener boy, and then Mr. Darcy had him transferred inside. But you must see, Mr. Wickham, he was your brother all along, and he resented that you were treated as a brother of Mr. Darcy's and he was not."

"Envy," Darcy said, and sighed. "Oh, I should have known. And that's why you two look so much alike," he said.

A twinge of pain suddenly stabbed my shoulder, and I winced.

Georgiana put her hand on my forearm. "You should be in bed. But as soon as you can stand up with me in church, I shall be Mrs. Wickham."

"And we'll help with whatever you need for the little girl," Darcy said. "And her education. She is our niece through her mother, after all."

Elizabeth Darcy nodded, by the door.

"And mine through her father," I said. "You know, I believe Lydia thought it was me in her bed."

Elizabeth nodded. "She probably did. She was not the most observant woman around, poor Lydia."

"And the living at Kimpton?" I asked Darcy. "Will you reconsider it, Will? Now that you know the truth?"

"The living at Kimpton?" Darcy asked, with that tilting sneer to his lip. "I wouldn't dream of it."

"But——" I said.

"Not for my brother-in-law. You must keep Georgiana in the style she's used to. There are some lands I'll make over to you both, and Georgiana, of course, brings ten thousand in dowry. We'll fix up the old manor house at the other end of the farm, shall we? That way, you two will be near enough to visit, but not so near it will be like living in the same house."

"When do you think you can stand up in church with me?" Georgiana asked.

I stood. "Why, now, if you wish." The room swam before my eyes, but I would not give way.

Darcy laughed, looking easier than he had since childhood. "My sister and my best friend are not to be married in the middle of the night, like fugitives. Sit down, you fool."

I sat, with relief. Georgiana's arms held me, helped ease me down. Mrs. Reynold gave me another biscuit and poured milk for me.

And a feeling of great ease and happiness suffused me. I had Georgiana's love and Will's friendship.

I had come home.

A Long, Strange Trip
BY ELLEN GELERMAN

Ellen Gelerman was born and raised on Long Island, New York, and spent much of her adult life there. She received her BA in English from Indiana University, leading to a lifelong love of English literature as well as a twenty-five-year career as an advertising copywriter. Though she is largely retired from her formal career, writing is still her passion; she has created many stories based on *Pride and Prejudice*, including several book-length works, and she is working on a manuscript for an original novel. She currently lives in Connecticut with her husband, two college-age children, and two Labrador retrievers, and enjoys volunteering as a teacher of English for speakers of other languages.

"A Long Strange Trip" is indeed a very strange story, and the only story in this collection to violate the events of *Pride and Prejudice*. I read it when it was first published a few years ago, liked it a great deal, and when I was perusing the short stories available for the anthology, I immediately said, "This *has* to go in." There's simply nothing else like it. I hope you will see why.

❧

HISTORICAL NOTE: According to the BBC, the first documented use of psychedelic mushrooms was published in the *Medical and Physical Journal*: In 1799, a man who had been picking mushrooms for breakfast in London's Green Park included them in his harvest, accidentally sending his entire family on a trip. The doctor who treated them later described how the youngest child "was attacked with fits of immoderate laughter, nor could the threats of his father or mother refrain him." From the online encyclopedia Wikipedia .org, under the entry "Psilocybin Mushroom."

"WHAT A LONG, STRANGE TRIP IT'S BEEN."
—THE GRATEFUL DEAD

Jane was by no means better, and Elizabeth was grateful to Miss Bingley for having invited her to remain at Netherfield until such time as her sister was recovered sufficiently to be removed back to Longbourn. Still, her gratitude was tempered by her feeling that she was intruding and unwanted among the family party, and so, at half past six, when she was summoned to dinner, she was reluctant to quit Jane's beloved presence and descend the stairs. Yet propriety demanded that she must. And having eaten very little indeed since arriving at Netherfield that morning, her constitution demanded it as well.

Mr. Bingley asked after Jane's condition with anxiety, and although Elizabeth would rather have given him a more encouraging answer, she was pleased at his concern. Mr. Darcy inquired, too, though it seemed more out of politeness than any actual unease. He then afterward remained silent, although he continued to fix his attention on her in a most vexing manner, causing her to suspect she had done something amiss with her toilette.

Not long thereafter, Elizabeth found herself seated at the end of the table next to Mr. Hurst and knew conclusively that dinner would hold little pleasure for her. Sighing to herself, she stared at the savory concoction of meat, potatoes, vegetables, and mushrooms that was even now being ladled onto her plate by a servant.

Under ordinary circumstances she would eschew such rich fare. But now her stomach growled in a most unladylike fashion—though thankfully none in the party seemed to hear it—and she delicately began to indulge.

"There is nothing I like better than a fine ragout," said Mr. Hurst, digging into his serving with gusto. "Do you not agree, Miss Bennet?"

Suspecting that any meal set before Mr. Hurst would be quickly labeled his favorite, Elizabeth declined to concur.

"In truth, Mr. Hurst," Elizabeth said, "I much prefer a plain dish. A simple roast beef with boiled potatoes is my favorite dinner." Nevertheless, her hunger was such that she ate what was before her in its entirety, and after being served a second time, consumed that as well. The rest of the party seemed in agreement with Mr. Hurst, for they all consumed hearty portions. Only Miss Bingley seemed cross.

"I despise mushrooms," Caroline said, pouting. "Cook has *ruined* the ragout with the horrid, slimy things." She pushed the offending fungi aside. "Dinner is completely spoiled."

"Not at all, Miss Bingley," replied Darcy amiably. "For it has been much enjoyed by the rest of the party, and I see that because they have been added as more of a garnish, and not cooked together with the rest of the ingredients, you have easily separated the mushrooms from the meat and vegetables. There is no reason not to enjoy the remainder of your meal."

Coming as it did from Mr. Darcy, this comment was sufficient to cheer Miss Bingley, and she complied with his suggestion, leaving the mushrooms on the side of her plate.

It was not long after dinner was completed—indeed, the entire party had just retired to the drawing room, the gentlemen declining their usual after-dinner solitude, claiming fatigue—when Elizabeth began to feel rather queer. She found she could no longer attend to her needlework. The room began to swirl around her, the colors of the draperies blended with that of the rug, and the sound of the others' voices took on unnaturally deep tones. She turned her head slowly, for that was all she could manage at the moment, and stared wonderingly at the woman across from her.

"A witch!" she cried, pointing, with great effort, at Miss Bingley. "Fie! Leave us, creature of darkness!" Her own voice sounded slow and wrong in her ears. She tried to stand and run, but found her legs strangely rooted to the spot, her head in a muddle. The walls had started to melt. Trembling, she could only gaze at Miss Bingley in terror.

Miss Bingley was affronted in no small way. "Miss Eliza, what did you call me?" she demanded, aghast.

"There, there, Miss Bennet," said Mr. Darcy comfortingly, making his way on unsteady legs to sit beside Elizabeth on the sofa. He awkwardly began to stroke her arm, as one might stroke a cat. "There is nothing to fear, Miss Bennet. I will protect you. Besides, it is no witch, after all," he added, laughing, "simply a scarecrow!"

"Witch! Scarecrow!" Miss Bingley sputtered. "How dare you!"

Darcy continued to stroke Elizabeth's arm, and she quieted. He was feeling more than a little peculiar himself, and Elizabeth's bare skin fascinated him. It flowed like silk. It *was* silk. Pink silk. How extraordinary! He was using both hands now, drifting his touch delicately over her face, neck, and shoulders. Her usually subtle scent overwhelmed him, and he found himself in a garden of giant pink roses, fondling the tender petals and pressing his whole body into them. He was entranced. His head was spinning—but it was not an unpleasant sensation. Moreover, the satiny feel of the roses was exquisite. Would their taste be as well? He tried one; it melted on his tongue. Delightful! He wanted more.

Elizabeth was now standing under a waterfall of a thousand shining colors. The water flowed down her head, over her shoulders and bosom, and down her legs. The experience was unlike any she had ever known, and was almost unbearably pleasurable. She parted her lips to catch the delicious sparkling waters and found her mouth immediately filled. She had no thirst, yet she was inclined to keep drinking, drinking deep of the sparkling water, while the colors swirled around her.

Miss Bingley gaped in disbelief as she watched Mr. Darcy draw Eliza Bennet into his embrace on the sofa, caressing that unsophisticated chit in a most intimate fashion, his hands flowing over her features, her skin, the material of her gown...gracious Lord, her bosom! Her legs! The brazen hussy was not even resisting his advances. What a harlot! And now he was kissing her in a most outrageous fashion, his open mouth shamelessly prying open her lips. Good heavens, did he actually have his *tongue* in her mouth? Disgusting! Disgraceful!

Her face burning, her chest heaving in jealous distress, Caroline finally tore herself away and turned to remark on this contemptible scene to Mr. and Mrs. Hurst, but found them sitting opposite each other, snorting in barely restrained laughter. The more they tried to control themselves, the louder their mirth became. Finally, they slid to the floor in each other's arms, shrieking uproariously and most unbecomingly. Miss Bingley could not determine what was so frightfully amusing, for they did not acknowledge her presence and seemed quite incapable of rational conversation. Despite her attempts to interrupt their hilarity, their laughter continued unabated.

This was a nightmare; had the world gone mad? Finally, Caroline turned to importune her brother for help. But Mr. Bingley only sat smiling in his chair, staring at nothing, waving his hands in the air, humming loudly. Miss Bingley could not distinguish a melody. "Charles!" she demanded, seizing him by the shoulders and forcing him to look at her. "Charles! What has come over everyone?"

Alas, it did not work. Charles was in heaven, flying through the air amid blue skies and rippling white clouds, attended by an angel. A blue-eyed, blonde-haired angel whose voice was at once all the notes of a heavenly choir. "Charles!" she said. And again: "Charles!" He smiled. Jane. His angel.

Fleeing the room, Miss Bingley nearly collided with a servant. "Do not enter that room. See that no one enters that room," she hissed, slamming the door shut behind her. It would not do to have the servants gossiping about the extraordinary events taking place behind that door. The family's reputation would be ruined. She ran up the stairs and burst into Jane's room. "Jane, my dear," she cried, breathlessly, "what sort of illness besets you? Could it be contagious?"

Awakened from a doze and startled by her friend's sudden entrance, Jane looked up at Miss Bingley with fever-glazed eyes. "I am so sorry, Caroline," she said and coughed slightly. "Of what are you speaking? I fear I am not the best company at the moment."

Caroline could easily see that, despite Jane's illness, she was not afflicted in the same manner as the rest of the household. Aware that it would serve no useful purpose to apprise Jane of the events unfolding downstairs, Miss Bingley apologized for disturbing her, smiled insincerely, and excused herself.

Heading slowly down the stairs, Miss Bingley attempted to make sense of the madness in the drawing room. Were they all possessed? She shook off the idea. Caroline Bingley was not given to superstition. The malady had come upon them very suddenly, not long after dinner. Perhaps they had imbibed too much wine? But no, no one had drunk immoderately, save Mr. Hurst, and that was, after all, his common practice.

What else could have effected such a change in demeanor? Caroline mentally numbered the courses: the hors d'oeuvres, the soup, the fish, the ragout—the ragout! They had all partaken of the ragout, of course, but she was the only one who had not eaten the mushrooms. How could eating mushrooms cause such a reaction? Perhaps they had been tainted. She was suddenly very nervous. What if her relations—and Mr. Darcy and Miss Eliza—were truly ill? Worse yet, what if they all died from contaminated food? Miss Bingley hastened back to the drawing room. She was not yet willing to call a doctor—fear of scandal held her in check—but she did feel it would be best to keep watch over everyone.

When she entered the room, she saw that nothing had changed in the five minutes that she had been gone. No one appeared to be in peril. Charles—the fool!—was still smiling and humming, Louisa Hurst and Mr. Hurst were still upon the floor, laughing boisterously at nothing (one would think they would have run out of breath by now), and Mr. Darcy and Miss Elizabeth were still engaged in mischief on the sofa.

Knowing that she was, in effect, unobserved made Miss Bingley bold. She viewed the two at length with a mixture of mortification, envy, and curiosity. Could this be what transpired between a man and woman during courtship? It seemed highly improper, even for those who were affianced. Perhaps these things were more in the purview of married couples. Another question arose in her mind: Were such attentions really so very pleasing? Miss Elizabeth surely seemed to be pleased, if one could judge by the sighs and moans emanating from her.

Likewise, Mr. Darcy seemed not unaffected. He, too, was making little noises that spoke of great satisfaction. His color was high, and Caroline saw how well the expression of heartfelt delight became him. In fascination, she followed his hands as they traveled over Miss

Elizabeth's person, noting which actions seemed to be responsible for which reactions. The experience certainly was edifying!

It was also most disconcerting. Miss Bingley began to grow warm, and her breathing became more rapid. She wondered if she, too, were becoming ill, but discarded the notion. She left the sofa and paced about the room, fanning herself. How long would this infernal malady last? Attempting to read a fashion publication, she found herself too distracted by the various sounds of laughter, humming, and sighing that surrounded her. Eventually, she sat down at the pianoforte and began to play.

This, finally, had an effect. Although Mr. and Mrs. Hurst continued laughing, Mr. Bingley ceased his humming, and gazed, open-mouthed in wonder, into space. *As if he has not heard this piece a dozen times!* thought Caroline. Better still, Mr. Darcy, finding that the music provided a novel stimulus for the confusion gripping his mind, withdrew somewhat from Elizabeth, and ceased to kiss her, but he did not release her, instead keeping a hold upon a section of her gown and staring intently at it as he stroked it between his fingers. Elizabeth, for her part, began swaying her body in time to the music, her hands clutching Mr. Darcy's sleeve. Meaningless sing-song syllables issued from her mouth, as if she were experimenting with the sound, yet no one else seemed to hear. Miss Bingley felt uneasily like a keeper at Bedlam.

Heartened by the improvement in the behavior of her audience, Caroline played her entire repertoire, and then repeated it two more times. She did not know how long she could perform in this manner, for her hands were cramping and her legs had begun to numb. When she was close to exhaustion and near to tears, she was gratified to realize that the silence in the room meant that the Hursts had at some point left off laughing, and they were now actually sitting up on the rug. Eventually, Mr. Darcy let go of Elizabeth's gown and sat with his hands upon his lap, looking perplexed, while his companion withdrew her own hands and sat back against the sofa with a dazed and dreamy expression on her face.

At length, Mr. Bingley yawned, and yawned again. He stood up, and Miss Bingley held her breath, fearing partly that he would not be able to remain on his feet and partly that this heralded some bizarre new stage in his indisposition. But no. He merely blinked at her, yawned once more, and, enunciating with great difficulty, said, "I believe I will retire now." And slowly, carefully, he made his way across the room and out the door. More yawning followed, from the other occupants of the room, as they seemed, one at a time, to recover from their stupor. Mr. Darcy wavered slightly as he stood, looking about the room in confusion and no little embarrassment. He gazed for several moments at Elizabeth's flushed face and half-closed eyes, a look of some alarm on his countenance. Finally, his eyes rested on Miss Bingley, who had an air of expectancy about her, and said thickly, "You will forgive me. I must have dozed off. Pray excuse me." And with one final glance at Elizabeth, he, too, quit the room, walking stiffly as a result of having sat so long in one attitude.

To Miss Bingley's great relief, Mr. and Mrs. Hurst soon followed suit, rising from the floor in bewilderment and, exhausted from the evening's exertions, heading immediately for their chambers. Mr. Hurst was heard to mutter, "I need a drink," and for once his wife agreed. Elizabeth was the last to regain her feet, her countenance pale and her bearing uncertain. She looked at Miss Bingley quizzically, as if the latter could provide some explanation for the extraordinary recollections she now possessed, which seemed to concern a waterfall and, somehow, Mr. Darcy, but Caroline would not say a word. That fine lady had, during her marathon session upon the pianoforte, determined that her satisfaction at having caught Elizabeth in a flagrant indiscretion was far outweighed by the frightening possibility that Mr. Darcy would feel obligated to marry the country bumpkin, and therefore resolved to reveal nothing with regard to the unusual events she had witnessed. In a calm voice she said, "The hour is late, Miss Eliza. Perhaps you would like to visit your sister and retire for the night?"

"Jane!" exclaimed Elizabeth, her voice hoarse. "Poor Jane, I have been neglecting her. If you will excuse me, Miss Bingley?"

"Certainly."

So Elizabeth fled, her limbs still somewhat uncooperative, but her desire to leave the troublesome memories of the drawing room for the haven of her sister's presence driving her quickly up the stairs.

The following morning, as they all gathered for breakfast, Miss Bingley was prepared. In truth, she had spent the greater part of a sleepless night deciding how to approach the undoubtedly awkward subject that was sure to arise among the party regarding the several hours for which none of them could logically account. She summoned her considerable powers of artifice and waited for the topic to arise. She did not have to wait long.

Mr. Darcy had, from the start of breakfast, been filled with a sense of disquiet, for he felt a nagging familiarity with Miss Bennet that he sensed was very improper. This morning, he had recalled—albeit in no great detail—having been in a lush rose garden that he had found highly pleasurable. He somehow associated the experience with Elizabeth. From out of the corner of his eye, he glanced at her eating her breakfast. She reached out the tip of her tongue to delicately lick a crumb of muffin from the corner of her lips. It was then that he *knew*. As a rational man, he could not explain it. But he knew, without doubt, how her lips and even her tongue felt. And tasted. He ran his tongue over his own lips, and the sensation was unmistakable. As she continued to eat, she smoothed her gown across her lap. Mr. Darcy glanced down at his own hands and stretched out his long fingers. There could be no mistake. These hands surely had touched, nay, had taken liberties with, Miss Bennet's person, for he knew with certainty the smoothness of her skin, the texture of the gown she had wore the preceding evening, and, scandalously, the curve of her breast and the shape of her thigh. This was intolerable! He must find a moment alone with her and beg her forgiveness for having thus compromised her. If necessary, he would offer to marry her.

Miss Bingley, who had been watching the entire party, but especially Mr. Darcy, with concern, knew it was time for her to speak up. Clearly, Mr. Darcy, whose crimson face betrayed a look of anxiety, was on the verge of doing something rash, and she must stop him.

"What a singular evening we had!" she cried, drawing the attention of everyone at the table. "Have you any idea of what transpired?"

Even Mr. Hurst was all attentiveness. Seeing that the party was eager for an explanation, she continued with great animation, "Why, those mushrooms Cook put into the ragout yesterday—they were tainted! They put you all to sleep. And such a sound sleep it was. My word, I had to tend to all of you as if you were children, for I had not eaten of the mushrooms myself, and could do naught but watch you all snore for three hours. It was three hours, I tell you, before you all recovered from your stupor! I would have been inclined to call the doctor, were it not for the embarrassment it would cause you. What a relief when you woke up!" She laughed a bit too heartily. "Is it not amusing?"

Around the table, there was many a relieved sigh. Mr. Bingley began, "And I had the most extraordinary dream, Caroline! I was—"

Miss Bingley, suspecting that they all had been in the grip of some outlandish delusions, did not desire to know her brother's in particular, nor did she wish the others to begin comparing theirs, for that would only confirm to Miss Eliza and Mr. Darcy that the two of them had shared some significant experience. So she hastened to interrupt him: "As you can imagine, Charles, I have severely reprimanded Cook. I would have fired her on the spot, but we cannot do without her, after all, and where would we find another on such short notice? But she has strict instructions from now on: no mushrooms!" Having gained her object, which was to distract Mr. Bingley from revealing too much, Miss Bingley served herself more breakfast, and smiled in satisfaction.

Satisfied, too, were Mr. Bingley, Louisa, and Mr. Hurst. But Elizabeth and Mr. Darcy, in their own ways, remain unconvinced. Their experience had been of a physical nature, and it could not be so easily explained away as a dream. Even if they had been having hallucinations, which to Mr. Darcy now seemed certain, it still did not account for the powerful feelings he retained of intimate contact with Elizabeth. Something had happened—he was sure of it! But the only conscious witness said they had all been sound asleep, a comforting assertion. It would, of course, be better for him—for both of them, actually—to accept Miss Bingley's explanation without question, for that would mean he had *not* compromised Miss Elizabeth, and they would not be forced to marry.

And yet...

Darcy looked at Elizabeth, her head bowed over her plate and her brow furrowed in thought. Suddenly she glanced up, and their gazes locked. She tilted her head, looking at him in confusion. That look alone spoke volumes, for though he could not know of what her hallucination had consisted, he reckoned it might have been similar to his own, and she, too, might have some recollections that she was having difficulty interpreting. Shifting his gaze to Miss Bingley, Darcy stared hard at her until she turned to face him. He peered at her with narrowed eyes, seeking the truth. In return, she gave him as false a smile as he had ever seen, and immediately turned to Elizabeth to ask after her sister. The subject was now closed.

Once breakfast concluded, the party anticipated a visit from Mrs. Bennet, who had been requested by Elizabeth to ascertain Jane's condition. Darcy seized the opportunity, while the others lingered in conversation amongst themselves, to seek out Elizabeth. He found her in the hallway heading toward Jane's room.

"Miss Bennet?"

Elizabeth stopped, her hand on the knob, and raised a brow at him questioningly.

"Before you visit your sister, will you perhaps walk with me a while?"

Reluctantly, Elizabeth released the handle and stepped into place alongside Mr. Darcy.

"You can be at no loss, Miss Bennet," he said in a low voice, "to understand the reason for my requesting a private audience with you."

"Indeed, sir," replied Elizabeth, wishing to come straight to the point, "you seek to know my opinion of yesterday evening's events in the drawing room."

"Precisely. May I be so bold as to presume that you did not believe Miss Bingley when she said we were all asleep?"

"I do not know what to believe," Elizabeth said in a quiet voice. "I know only that whatever happened appeared far more real to me than any dream." With that, she colored, recalling the pleasurable sensations that accompanied her experience.

Mr. Darcy's heart pounded against his chest, for her light blush was most becoming. It was, in fact, the exact color of...

Taking a deep breath, Darcy ventured, "I do not suppose you found yourself...in a rose garden?"

Elizabeth shook her head. "No, it was...a waterfall. I stood beneath a waterfall, and let the water run over me and fill my mouth. It was...most agreeable."

It was immediately clear to Darcy that *he* had been the water-fall—*his* hands, *his* mouth, and *his* tongue—and was strangely proud that he had caused such *agreeable* sensations in Elizabeth. Stifling the burgeoning emotions in his breast, he questioned her further: "Was there..." He cleared his throat. "Was there anyone with you, I mean, at the waterfall?"

"I do not know, I..." Elizabeth could no longer meet his gaze, and directed her eyes to the floor. "I believe that *you* were there, Mr. Darcy, though I do not recall *seeing* you there, exactly. It is more of a *feeling* than anything else, a feeling of your...presence."

Mr. Darcy sighed. It was just as he had supposed. They had indeed been intimately involved with each other the preceding evening, though in not so obvious a fashion as to be clear to either of them. It remained only for him to ascertain whether Elizabeth felt offended by his actions.

"Miss Bennet, it would appear that you and I...that I..." Blast! This was going to be difficult. "That I was concerned in some way... in the creation of...your hallucination, if one may call it that. My own...delusion...was of a rose garden, and I have reason to believe that you were...there, as well."

Elizabeth started, but was silent.

"If, in my altered condition, I did anything to offend you, if you feel I have...compromised you in any way, I pray you will forgive me." He took a deep breath. "Miss Bennet, I am prepared to—"

"Mr. Darcy," Elizabeth interrupted him cheerfully—for despite one pleasurable experience, her opinion of Mr. Darcy's disagreeable manners and arrogance had not changed, and she could tell where the conversation was headed—"I think it is best for all concerned that we acknowledge Miss Bingley's story as truth, and leave it at that. For who among us can say exactly what happened? And now, I must ask you to excuse me, for I must apprise Jane that my mother will soon visit." She gave him a brief curtsy and turned on her heel, heading back toward Jane's room.

As her demeanor did not indicate any residual distress, Darcy decided to let the matter drop, though he suspected that he would always regard the peculiar events of the previous evening with some fondness, even a degree of wistfulness.

Shortly after Mrs. Bennet's visit, Caroline paid an unusual personal call to the kitchens, and met privately with Cook. The servant had made two promises in order to save her job: to ensure that mushrooms would never again be seen in the household, and to turn over to Miss Bingley the small packet containing the remainder of those dried fungi that had caused such trouble the night before. Cook was eager to be relieved of the mushrooms, assuming her employer would make certain that the pigs would not get into them, and sighed in relief as Miss Bingley quit the kitchens.

Walking straight from the kitchens to her room, Miss Bingley placed the packet of dried mushrooms into a drawer and locked it. Certainly, the mushrooms would not be fodder for the pigs; heavens, no! They were far too dangerous. Caroline would keep them safely stashed away. She would put them to use when the opportunity arose for a private dinner with Mr. Darcy.

An Ink-Stained Year
VALERIE T. JACKSON

Valerie T. Jackson was born in rural Texas. She went to school because they made her, and then kept going because it seemed easier than not. She has a BS in psychology, but like most degree holders does not work in her field and is currently in retail. She spends her sadly limited spare time reading, knitting, and hiking. She currently lives in Philadelphia and is time-sharing a dog.

A lot of virtual ink has been spilled over the relatively small character of Colonel Fitzwilliam, who exists more as a plot device in *Pride and Prejudice*, and he is what we would call "a fan favorite." Caroline Bingley, another villain who perhaps deserves more attention than we give her, is the other central character in Jackson's epistolary story, thus killing two birds with one stone when finding time for characters who need a bit of spotlight.

❧

I. COLONEL FITZWILLIAM TO MR. DARCY

June 2

Cousin,

I pick up my pen not three days after I sent my last to you, a testament to my sad plight if ever one could be offered. Did you tell my father of my threat? Yesterday evening, I very nearly made good on it. It was only the awareness that I would discomfort the servants by my presence that kept me from taking myself down to their dining hall and seating myself at the table between the footman and the scullery maid. But, Cousin, surely you are not so desperate as to go dining with the servants, you think to yourself. Oh, but I am! I am not like you, Darcy; I am not satisfied with my own company. I have not your depth. I lack that self-complacency, that strength of character, that makes a man able to withstand the trial of solitude. Yet I have been condemned to spend my summer in London. Such a time! Such a place! It is punishment, rather than pleasure! The streets are bereft, the exhibitions dull, and the parks a dim reminder of the pleasures of the country. I, an innocent man, sentenced to such a fate! A younger son I am, and it is my lot that I must bend to the will of my father and do his bidding. Do not weep for me, my friend! I shall bear up! I shall persevere!

Have I bored you sufficiently with my theatrics? Do you roll your eyes? Very well. I shall leave melodrama behind. In truth, I do rather well, considering the circumstances. Each morning I wake and, after breakfasting, I wander about the house, waiting for the clock to strike a suitable hour for making calls. When it has done so, I do not tarry in carrying out my father's business, and calling upon those gentlemen by whom he is so eager to be remembered. This being done, I go to my club, drink more than I ought, and— after attempting to socialize and finding the society insufferable— return home. Buxton House has never had a very entertaining library, you know, so you will not accuse me of hyperbole when I tell you that I have read every book in the house that can be read, even those by Mrs. Radcliffe that my father keeps hidden in his apartment. I have joined a circulating library in the hope of becoming a man of letters, or at least slightly less ignorant and ill informed. Most nights, I dine alone and go to bed early.

Does this all sound like a plea for sympathy? It is not, and to assure you of that, I will share with you the secret of my endurance: I take very long naps. I am convinced that the ability to nap can get a man through anything. It is rather too bad that one cannot nap entirely at will. I wish to God I'd been able to nap during my time with the surgeon's knife.

Bear up, Cousin, the letter is almost at an end. I pick up my pen one last time, this time to recount to you something that happened early this afternoon. I was returning home from my club via Bond Street, which was remarkably crowded for the time of year. There are other poor souls in town, yet we none of us seem to meet, only to pass, trapped in our own wretchedness and ennui, and never is this more apparent than on the streets, where we shuffle by one another, heads bent, like the condemned marching to an execution that never comes. As I walked, trapped in my own despair, I saw a woman struck by a boy of the lower orders—running, no doubt, from some mischief or crime—and jolted so severely that she was knocked into the streets. Being the heroic sort, I immediately went to her aid and pulled her to safety just as a carriage rumbled past.

I expected that the fair maiden (for it is always a maiden in these sorts of circumstances, you know) would fall into my arms, and I was quite prepared to offer her my assistance through her womanly hysterics. Instead, she cried, "My gown!" And immediately she began decrying, oh, a great many things, from carriages to small children. When she recollected my presence, she blushed, and thanked me prettily for my help. We made ourselves known to each other, and I found her to be none other than the sister of your brother Bingley. I had not time to discover how she had found herself among the condemned before she began chastising her footman severely for allowing her to be jostled into the street. I know Mr. Bingley to be with you at Pemberley. Would you therefore care to satisfy my curiosity as to how his sister found herself in London in June?

I will only add that I found her a pretty sort of woman, but rather too tall and too thin, and with features too strong to be of any real pleasure to my eyes. A shame, because the company of a beautiful woman would not be unappreciated.

And so I bid you adieu, Cousin, until my next.

Yours, &c., R. F.

II. Miss Bingley to Mrs. Hurst

June 2

My dearest Louisa,

You already know that I am wretched. Having detailed at length the evils of London in the summer in my last, I will say only that nothing has changed and I am still as miserable as I was a week ago. London is still hot, the air is still stale, and the company still nonexistent. All the world is enjoying pleasures that are denied me. As if this were not enough, today I was very nearly killed when an urchin knocked me into the street to be run down by a hack chaise. Aunt Lucy's footman did nothing to help, yet still managed to drop my packages in his shock. If not for the assistance of a gentleman, I might not be writing this letter.

Our aunt sends her regards. Those were the last words she spoke to me before she retired to her apartment this morning. "If you should happen to write to anyone I know, do send my regards." She is not fond of me. I do believe that my presence here is as much a punishment to her as it is to me. I have yet to forgive either you or Charles for condemning me to this. I can hear you protesting that it was our uncle who forced my hand, playing upon my guilt until I agreed to stay; but neither of you came to my aid, though you must have known that I have not the temperament to be a companion for an old woman who takes no pleasure in anything.

Oh, but I ought to mention that the gentleman who assisted me this morning was Colonel Fitzwilliam, the cousin of Mr. Darcy. I am sorry to say he is not at all handsome, especially compared with his cousin. I suppose there is a slight resemblance about the eyes, but that is all. He is altogether very plain, and his ears stick out almost comically. He will not do at all. I can see your expression, Louisa! Rest assured, I am not thinking any such thing. I am done with the entire family. I would not let myself have any hopes in his direction, for certainly the moment I even thought such a thing, he would fall madly in love with the daughter of a glove maker.

I hope my brother's ill health has been improved by the waters at Bath and that you are well. As asked, I shall make no congratulations regarding that small line you tucked into your most recent letter, but I trust you will keep me appraised, and give me the honor of being the first to send well wishes when the matter becomes a certainty (as I am sure it will, dearest). Do write to me soon. Your letters are one of the few things I have to look forward to as I carry out my sentence.

Your most devoted sister, Caroline

III. Colonel Fitzwilliam to Mr. Darcy

June 9

Dear Cousin,

I trust my last satisfied your request for "a letter fit to be read in company," with all its idle pleasantries; regards to my father, Mr.

and Mrs. Bingley, and Mrs. Darcy; love for Georgiana; &c. In this letter, I shall indulge myself by writing only to you.

I took the liberty of calling upon Miss Bingley at her aunt's house two days ago. The aunt—who, I am told, is also a Miss Bingley—was not present and had retired to her rooms for the day. It was a pleasant sort of social call. I tried not to lend too much weight to my prior knowledge of her, as my prior knowledge of her came mostly through you, and you can be most severe on women of her sort. For myself, I found her pleasing, polite, and genteel company.

She made it clear that I am welcome to come again, though she, of course, can have no occasion for calling on me. I suppose I see in her a fellow prisoner, trapped in the hot and stale London air, with only the epistles of our friends and relations to remind us that the outside world exists. Commiseration in mutual misery is as steady a foundation for a casual acquaintance as any.

It has been a day since I penned the last. It occurred to me to attend a small exhibition of portraits that I had heard spoken of at the club. I happened to see Miss Bingley there. The gallery was largely empty, as most places are at this time, and we had much time to talk as we walked about, certainly more than is afforded by a social call. I wonder if she has ever held a real opinion in her life; everything that came from her mouth seemed calculated to please, and to conform to the fashion.

But this is an exceptionally dull letter. I suppose I should conclude, lest I spill more ink upon the subject of my two conversations with Miss Bingley, which (and this is a sad commentary) are the most interesting things that have happened in this past week.

Yours, R. F.

IV. Miss Bingley to Mrs. Bingley

June 10

Dear Jane,

I trust this letter finds you and all your family in good health. I shall not hope that you find Pemberley pleasing, for to hope is to suggest something that is uncertain, and there is nothing more certain than that Pemberley will please. I well remember my first visit, and I could write for hours about the pleasing walks and tastefully appointed rooms. It is the work of generations; I do not believe there is a finer estate in all England.

I beg you will forgive me for failing to write earlier, but I have had so very much to do. London is not the ideal place to spend one's summer, 'tis true, but I have so many associates in town that I have had quite a lot of society to choose from. There was a lovely art exhibition yesterday. It was of portraiture, and featured a number of renowned artists, including a few portraits by Mr. Gainsborough, though my particular favorite was a portrait of Mrs. Stanhope by Sir Joshua Reynolds. The conversation was nearly as pleasant as the art itself; it is so fine to exchange reasoned, educated opinions with those of well-formed minds.

Do give my love to Charles, to Georgiana, and to your dear sister, Mrs. Darcy. I beg you will excuse the brevity of this letter. I shall write again as soon as I have the time.

Yours, Caroline Bingley

V. Miss Bingley to Mrs. Hurst

June 10

Dearest,

Can one die of boredom? There is no one here to speak to— this house is bereft of people. My aunt and I have progressed from civil silence to cross words. I am not certain what I have done to offend her, but she scolds me terribly for everything, from the dress of my hair to my playing and drawing. I am at home as rarely as possible, but there is so little to do. There are some small art showings. There will be an exhibition of exotic plants soon, which is the first thing I have looked forward to since I came here.

Colonel Fitzwilliam called three days ago, and I found him pleasing enough. We met again at an exhibition of portraits, and spoke for some time. I did not go with the intent to be pleased. The picturesque is the fashion now, you know, and I am told that portraits are often thought inferior to examinations of nature. Colonel Fitzwilliam says that he prefers portraiture to all other forms of art. He spoke with so much feeling of his pleasure in observing the expressions on the faces of the subjects that I began to like them very much myself. I hope that he calls again. Any company at all would be an improvement over my current isolation.

—June 13—

I left this letter open in the hope that something would happen that would make it worth the cost of the paper. Colonel Fitzwilliam called again, a brief social call, and my aunt held a small card party. Can you imagine anything more insufferable than ten old women playing cards for hours at a time? They talked of nothing but how things were when they were girls—and how stodgy and staid and dull our generation is becoming!

I have tortured myself by reading Jane's most recent letter from Pemberley. She is enraptured with it, of course. Who would not be? She has filled two pages, and half a page crosswise with her ramblings. The walks are lovely. The company is delightful. Miss Darcy plays piano so well. Have you gotten one like it?

Charles added his own illegible scrawl to the end of the letter. I have not the faintest idea of what he has written. No doubt, it is more of the same—mixed, of course, with his own puppyish, slavish compliments for Jane, and Mr. Darcy, and Mrs. Darcy, and the whole lot of them. I care for none of it.

(By the by, when you see my brother next, will you mention how positively shabby my green gown looks? It must be replaced, and the going will be easier if you soften him for me first.)

I have thought a bit more on Mrs. Bingley's letter, and I am decided. It is her revenge. She still hates me for not telling Charles she was in town, and the letter is exactly calculated to drive home to me everything I am missing. Our sister is more devious than either of us knew, Louisa, I am sure of it.

I shall end this letter now. I love you dearly, Sister. You know not how much I wish I were with you.

Yours,
Caroline

VI. Colonel Fitzwilliam to Mr. Darcy

June 15

Darcy,

It is very late, or perhaps I should say very early, but I cannot sleep. Do not concern yourself. There is nothing the matter. I am grown vastly stupid and dull of late. This house is empty and I have so little to do. My father's business is nothing to keep a man truly occupied. It is very hot. I have been in hotter places, places where the sun beats down upon your head with such intensity as to make a man think of the fires of hell. Yet one expects it in such regions. I have every window open, and the noise from the carriages scrapes my nerves raw. I am in such an odd mood. I am cross. My father will return to find that I have driven out all of his servants with my hash words and queer demands.

It is many hours since I wrote the last, and I very nearly took out a new sheet of paper as I read over what I had written (early this morning). But I trust you not to place too much stock in my ramblings. I am much better now, with several hours of sleep and a meal in my belly.

There was an exhibition of exotic plants, which I attended this afternoon. Miss Bingley was there, and greeted me prettily when we met, and we took in nearly the whole of the exhibition together. Did you know she is quite the botanist? I am not one of those men who likes imbecility in females, but she had such an air of superior knowledge about her that I could not resist teasing her.

We were bent over an orchid, a lovely plant, and Miss Bingley was telling me of how they reproduce. I gather that it is a finicky business. I said, "Miss Bingley, do you not find that there is something untoward about a woman knowing quite so much about these matters?"

She looked at me sharply and said, "What ever do you mean, sir?"

"All this talk of male and female and of the way in which the male is joined with the female—it seems almost an affront to modesty."

She blushed and said coldly, "A mind that is always looking to make even things that are innocent seem rife with—with improper meaning—might see it in such a light. But I do not have one of those minds."

She was rather standoffish with me for the rest of the afternoon, and I believe I will call on her tomorrow and set things right between us. She is my only friend in London, you know. It would not do for her to be cross with me.

Yours, &c., R. F.

VII. Miss Bingley to Mrs. Hurst

June 16

My dearest Louisa,

I am so very, very sorry for your loss. Do take care of yourself, and listen to the accoucheur. Would that I could fly out of here and wrap my arms around you. You need only ask and I will leave for Bath at once.

Your most devoted and loving sister, Caroline

VIII. Colonel Fitzwilliam to Mr. Darcy

June 19

Cousin,

I have written another letter fit to be read in company, but this sheet is for you alone. I called upon Miss Bingley on the 16th, but I was told she was "not at home." I have not yet gone back. If she is still cross with me for what I said at the exhibition—which, upon reflection, was perhaps somewhat unkind—I shall not tax her by calling every day. I will try again tomorrow.

We have had rain these past two days, and my hip has ached terribly the entire time. It is eight months since they dug the bullet out, and it is still not right. I begin to fear it will never be right again. Yesterday morning, I nearly wept as I dragged myself from my bed. A very hot towel is the only thing that will do for it, but my valet must replace them every ten minutes, for even in the heat they cool too quickly to be of relief for very long.

No more of this!

I have been reading Mr. Smith's Wealth of Nations upon your recommendation, and recently finished it. I found those pages in which he speaks of treaties of commerce most interesting, that being what I am so much concerned with at present. What would

Mr. Smith think of my so intensely promoting a treaty that would prove advantageous to my father's interests, without regard to its effects upon others? I like to think he would be as disgusted with the whole business as I myself am.

I will return the book to the circulating library tomorrow, if this infernal rain will end.

Yours, R. F.

IX. MISS BINGLEY TO MRS. HURST

June 22

Dear Louisa,

I am glad to hear you are recovered, in body if not in mind. I have every desire to comfort you with words and actions, but you say you prefer that I not make a fuss, and I will respect your wishes.

My aunt and I are getting on rather better of late. We have taken to ignoring each other again, which is a vast improvement over sniping at each other all the day. I am pleased that we have finally seen an end to the rain, and I can once again leave the house at my ease. I left once or twice even with the rain, to escape the confinement of my aunt's company, and returned with all the appearance of a drowned cat. A grand idea this was! Do remind me to thank my uncle for his taking the time and effort to arrange my affairs to suit himself.

Yesterday, I went to the circulating library. My aunt has such a poor collection of books. There is not a novel in the entire house. Not that I read novels, of course, but there are a select few that can be instructive or useful. I hear so many good things about Madam d'Arblay, and I thought to get the first volume of her most recent work. Colonel Fitzwilliam was on his way out when I entered, but he stepped inside with me again when we greeted each other. He did not recommend Camilla, but thought that I might like Evelina. Having read a few pages of it, I find I like it very well.

He apologized for what he said to me at the exotic plants exhibition, which I never did tell you of, and which does not signify in any case. He was very impertinent and I was rather cross with him, but it is forgiven now. He walked me home, but declined to come in. Perhaps he will come again tomorrow. I miss his company. I should say, I miss company, and his is the only I have at present.

I must conclude. I shall take a cool bath tonight, and I will go to bed early. A good night's sleep does wonders for the complexion. Do care for yourself, dearest.

Yours,
Caroline

X. Colonel Fitzwilliam to Mr. Darcy

June 25
Cousin,

Do you cringe when you see my direction on a letter? I have no intention of stopping my frequent epistles, no matter your answer. I am only curious about how they are received.

I thank you for your concern regarding both my physical and mental well-being. Physically, I am much better. I have had only a little pain these past few days, mostly in the morning. I have not touched the laudanum for nearly a week, though I do sometimes require a bracing drink. I fear I may have given up the cane too soon. It helps greatly when I use one, and I have brought mine out to use when I am at home alone. I do not like to use it in company.

I am also much improved in spirits. I cannot account for it, except perhaps it is because I have been about the town more.

I have called upon Miss Bingley several times. I fear I encroach upon her hospitality, for my visits are longer than the usual social call, but she is often the one who begs me to stay a bit longer. Her aunt seems a very unpleasant sort of woman. I am surprised that anyone thought the two of them would be good company for each other. She would be far happier if she were with her brother, at Pemberley. But I suppose I am happier because she is in London, so I will be selfish and say I am glad she is among the condemned.

She is surprisingly pleasing to call upon, you know. She is not what I would call a wit, but her manners are everything polite and engaging, and she is educated in all of those things that a woman is supposed to be educated in, and a few things more. She plays quite well, and she showed me several of her drawings. I was even talked into sitting for her for a spell, and am engaged to sit for her again in a few days. I have seen the beginnings of her sketch, though I had to sneak a glance, for she would not show it to me. My ears do not stick out that much.

I have taken your advice and called upon the Gardiners. It seemed a bit odd, calling upon people I had never before met, but we are family, in a way. Mr. Gardiner was not at home when I called, but Mrs. Gardiner was very hospitable. I was able to meet Mr. Gardiner the following day, and I am engaged to attend a small party at their house next week. I am very much looking forward to it. I mentioned that Miss Bingley was also in town, and after a very long pause, an invitation was extended to her as well. I carried their invitation to her, but she declined it. Is there something I should know regarding the Gardiners and Miss Bingley?

Do give Georgiana my love, and my regards to everyone.

Yours, &c., R. F.

XI. Miss Bingley to Jane Bingley

June 30

Dear Jane,

I thank you for your most recent letter. I am so pleased that you are enjoying yourself at Pemberley. For myself, I find that London in the summer is not nearly so bad as I had feared. There are so many people in town, one begins to forget it is not the height of the social season. Mr. Darcy's cousin, Colonel Fitzwilliam, calls often, and I recently attended a party at the home of your Aunt and Uncle Gardiner. They are delightful company, and they have such wonderful, sweet children.

There have been a great many exhibitions, of exotic plants and of portraits and of all manner of things. My mind is full to bursting with all that is going on here.

I do wish I had time to write you a proper letter. It seems there is so much to say, and yet when I sit down to write to you, I can never say it all. Well, I do hope to hear from you again very soon. All my love to Charles.

Your sister, Caroline

XII. Miss Bingley to Mrs. Hurst

June 30

Dear Sister,

Jane must truly despise me. Her most recent letter is two pages of nothing but what a wonderful time they are all having at Pemberley. I cried when I read it.

No, I must be more complete. It was not only Jane's letter that made me cry. I was already quite out of sorts when I received it this morning. I attended a party at the Gardiners' house. When Colonel Fitzwilliam first brought me the invitation, I declined it, as I thought wise, but a second, written invitation arrived, and against my better judgment, I accepted. I wish I had not. The Gardiners have clearly not forgiven me for the events of more than a year ago. Honestly, Louisa, have they met Mrs. Bennet? The scandal with the youngest only proves what I have said all along: the Bennets are a vulgar, ill-bred family. I was only trying to protect my brother from a most imprudent match! I never thought I would say this, but I am glad, for Charles's sake, that Eliza Bennet managed to catch Mr. Darcy. At least now they will manage Mrs. Bennet, Mr. and Mrs. Wickham, and the two other girls between themselves, and it will not be Charles's lot alone.

I have lost the thread of my thoughts. To return to my point, the Gardiners were cold to me, which truly would not have bothered me, but Colonel Fitzwilliam was cold to me as well. I suppose this means they have told him all about me, and he no longer cares for me. I do not know why this bothers me so, only it was nice to have a friend in London. I tried my very best to make conversation with him, but I found myself rebuffed.

I sat down beside him and said, "You have not called in several days, sir."

"No. I have unfortunately not had the opportunity to do so," he said, not quite unkindly, but not with very great warmth.

"Your sketch is still unfinished. When will I have the opportunity to complete it?"

"I am sure," said he, "that a lady of your talents must have a great many things to draw that are far more interesting than myself."

This was said unkindly, and he moved away before I could say anything in reply, which was a good thing, for I could not trust myself to speak for several moments.

I spoke to few other people the entire evening, and left as early as I possibly could. I very nearly hurled the unfinished sketch into a fire when I returned home. But I could not quite bring myself to do so, especially as a fire would have had to have been made simply for the purpose of burning the sketch, and that seemed rather a big to-do for a spiteful gesture. I know not why I care so much. It was pleasant to have a friend, someone to talk to, and—well, it matters not. Tomorrow, I will attend another botanical exhibit. I had planned to finish Evelina tonight, but as I had only planned it in the hope of discussing it with Colonel Fitzwilliam when he next called, I see no reason to bother.

But do tell me all about how you are faring, dearest. Your spirits seem dull. You write that Mr. Hurst is a great help to you, and that is very good to hear. I am glad also that his health is improving, but then your husband seems the sort of man whose health is most positively affected by Bath: A man who becomes very ill when he wishes to go, and quite well again when he is there.

I send my love to you both.

Your sister, Caroline

XIII. Colonel Fitzwilliam to Mr. Darcy

July 6

Cousin,

I am out of sorts again, I fear. I suppose it is because I have so little to do. One would think that business so vitally important to my father that it must needs keep me in London for more than three months would occupy a greater portion of my time, but it is not so. It is a slow-moving thing, consisting of brief calls to men I hardly know and genial conversation lacking substance, yet always with subtle persuasion underlying every word. Deals and offers made, seeming to have nothing to do with the true aims of either party, but both playing a sort of extended chess match, moving pawns and rooks into place until such time as the final strategy is revealed. I do not speak of myself as a player, you understand, merely a pawn.

I have not called upon Miss Bingley for two weeks. It is a bit cold of me, I suppose, but the sort of duplicity that you described has rather put me off.

The weather has been fine, neither oppressively hot nor miserably rainy, but the air is still thick and choking. The coal dust is dreadful. Why, I wonder, is it worse in the summer than in the winter? One would think that the winter, with the many fires that are burning in the many stoves in the city, would see the worst of it. It is one of the great mysteries of life.

I ought to call again on Miss Bingley. It is unkind of me to cut her so. I was not under any misconception about her, you know. She is much the same as any lady of the ton. (Do you dislike that word as much as I do? There is something very affected about it.) I have dealt with such ladies all my life. I did not expect any more from her. Perhaps I had hoped for more.

Lady Susan O'Brien, the one who ran off with the actor when she was young, and was exiled to the colonies for it, is in town with her husband. He has gotten some appointment or other, no doubt through the charity of her family. I did call. I thought it only proper, because her brother is a friend of my father, but though they are a lovely couple, I was ill at ease in their company. Perhaps my knowledge of their elopement was an unpleasant reminder of things best left unmentioned.

And now I have used up all of my news, and all of the news that I am likely to have for some time. I believe I will call upon Miss

Bingley tomorrow. Politeness demands it. I have no intention of staying for very long, however.

Yours, &c., R. F.

XIV. Miss Bingley to Charles Bingley

July 7

My dear Brother,

Might I impose upon you to write to your uncle and use your not inconsiderable influence with him to convince him to send me an advance on my allowance. I do not think this an unreasonable request, because—and do forgive me if I am failing to grasp some theory of economics that is beyond my ken—the interest from my twenty thousand pounds is, in fact, mine. I know that we poor females are hopeless with money, and I do so appreciate my uncle structuring the annuity so that I am paid only once per quarter, and must put myself to much trouble in order to take any sort of advance on the funds, but if I am willing to take such trouble—for the sake of a lovely necklace, which I am getting at a very good price—I find that I become rather put out upon receiving a letter in which I am talked to like a child.

Further, when you write, do tell him that I am not such a fool as to touch the principal of my fortune, and he need not concern himself about that.

All my love, Caroline

XV. Miss Bingley to Mrs. Hurst

July 7

Dear Louisa,

Colonel Fitzwilliam called today. I was very nearly not at home to him, but I have been very much lacking in company of late, and I could not bring myself to turn him away, though he was so unkind. He stayed a very long time. I hardly noticed how late the hour had become until after he had gone. It is very odd that time seems to fly by when I am in his presence. Our conversation was a bit strained at first. I do not know what he was told about me, and I do not care. We were soon on good terms again, though perhaps not on terms so good as before.

We talked gossip a bit, but there is little good gossip. Everyone is behaving themselves right now, or their misbehavior has not yet come to light in any case. How dull.

As we spoke, I noticed he would occasionally grimace, and shift in his seat, and I finally asked, "Are you quite all right, sir?"

"Well enough," he replied. "I was shot not a year ago. My hip has not yet set itself to rights. I am fine, most days. I think perhaps it will rain again soon."

"I am very sorry," I said. "It must have hurt very much."

His lips twisted into something I suppose you could call a smile. "Yes, very much. It has been many months, and I am still sometimes set off by reminders of—" He broke off abruptly and complimented the wallpaper, for which I thanked him on behalf of my aunt.

"Did you attend the botanical exhibition?" he asked.

"I did."

"It is still open, I believe. I had thought to go tomorrow, but I suppose now I will not have the pleasure of seeing you there."

"Oh, but I may go again," I said. I do not know why I said this, for I had no such plans. It is not as though I want to be in his presence every day.

"I will look for you then," he said, his voice suddenly cool.

I must know what he was told about me! I should not care, but it vexes me to have him think ill of me. The Gardiners, I am sure, made me out to be quite the harpy.

No, I do not care. It matters not.

I had best conclude. I really must pen a letter to Mrs. Darcy. I have been putting it off, but it will not do to neglect her.

Your devoted sister, Caroline

XVI. COLONEL FITZWILLIAM TO MR. DARCY

July 11

Dear Cousin,

On Tuesday, I took in yet another botanical exhibition. It was not quite as grand in scope or perfectly arranged as the former, but I found it more interesting. The plants were those species native to England. I saw Miss Bingley there, though she had been once before. She was far more quiet than the most recent time I had seen her at such a show, and once or twice I said something I knew to be wrong and she did not correct me. I fear she may have taken my previous censure—which was meant in jest, truly!—too much to heart. It was not my intention to quiet her entirely.

We went for a ride in the park, after. I know it is not quite smiled upon to be seen riding in a gig with a woman not one's relation, but Hyde Park was very deserted, and I hardly intend to make a habit of it. In any case, her abigail was with us, which always lends respectability to a situation. She became more talkative then, finding some unkind thing to say about nearly everyone we passed.

"Good heavens, that woman is wearing panniers. Has she been asleep since '74?"

"I do believe I could write my name on that woman's face. Some people ought to have powder rationed out to them in small quantities each day. Was that man's cravat tied by a drunken monkey in the midst of an apoplexy, do you think?"

I am ashamed to admit how much she amused me.

I must say that she is a very pretty woman. Her height is striking. I have always preferred women who were shorter and fatter, but I find I rather like a woman who can look me right in the eye without bending her neck at a painful angle. She looked particularly well this day. I believe it was the light. It is fortunate for her that she does not have her brother's red hair; red hair on women is always a disadvantage. Her hair is a very light brown, and though she was shaded by her bonnet and her parasol, once in a while the sunlight caught the curls at the sides of her face, and it set off her features in a very flattering way. I still think she is too thin, but women nearly always develop a plumpness as they age. I daresay she will be more handsome at one and thirty than she is at one and twenty.

Your news about Georgiana was very pleasing. I am glad that Mrs. Darcy is proving to be the sort of influence you had hoped, and that Georgiana has become rather less shy of late. I am delighted also to hear of her friendship with Mrs. Bingley. I do not claim to know Mrs. Bingley very well, but what I have seen and heard of her I like exceedingly, and I am moreover always happy to see Georgiana making any new friend.

I think that perhaps I am forgetting something. Did you not mention something of importance in your most recent letter? I do not have it here in front of me, and I cannot seem to bring it to mind. It cannot have been so very important if it has slipped my mind. Ah! I recall now! Mrs. Darcy has found herself in the family way, has she? Well, I offer my congratulations, of course. I do hope for your sake that it is a boy. You are outnumbered. You need another male presence, even if he is an infant.

I need not tell you what a fortunate man you are, and unlike other men with wealth, health, beauty, and marital felicity, one cannot even hate you for your good fortune. You are too good. You deserve it all.

Because you have put me in a sentimental mood, I sign myself

Your humble and devoted cousin and friend,

Richard Fitzwilliam

XVII. Miss Bingley to Mrs. Hurst

July 17

Dear Louisa,

How shall I begin this letter? Shall I tell you how I came to my revelation? Shall I tell you every detail, down to the color of my gown and the dress of my hair? No, I will simply say it. I have fallen in love with Colonel Fitzwilliam.

I feel like such a fool for allowing it to happen. I do not know how it happened. He is not at all handsome! He does have very broad shoulders, I must in all fairness credit him with that. There is something in the twist of his mouth when he speaks that is very appealing, and his eyes—I like his eyes very much. They are a light brown, almost hazel, and striking, very striking. But no one could call him handsome.

Yet his manners are so engaging and he is so pleasing to be around that I find I do not notice his less than ideal features, and notice far too much his better ones.

I hate myself for this. I am sure it would not have happened were I not trapped here with nothing to do and no society to interest me. Perhaps I will join you in Bath. My aunt would say good riddance to my leaving her, and I would be away from him.

Louisa, you alone know that I was in love—no, I was never in love with Mr. Darcy, but whatever certain people might think, it was not only his great fortune that attracted me to him. It hurt a great deal to lose him, and to a woman like Eliza Bennet!

And now that I know what I feel for Colonel Fitzwilliam, I find myself very afraid of him. Does that not seem very odd to you? But I am not afraid of him, I am afraid of losing him, which will inevitably happen. He leaves town on the 4th of August, which seems at once too soon and not soon enough. Perhaps if he had not heard such a bad report of me from the Gardiners, I might entertain some hope. Perhaps if he were not such good friends with Mr. Darcy, and Mrs. Darcy, whom he thinks excessively well of, and talks about far too often in far too complimentary terms, perhaps then I might...But he is such, and I cannot and will not allow myself to entertain any hope that he feels anything for me. Even if he did, Mr. Darcy would surely dissuade him. I know from my reception at the Darcys' house in town this season just past that I am welcome there as Charles's sister, nothing more.

I have not yet told you how I came to this knowledge, this accursed knowledge about myself that I wish I did not have. He called again, yesterday, and stayed for quite a while. My aunt deigned to grace us with her presence, and we played at cards for a time. We played at piquet after she left us, and I won two guineas. We talked a while more, after the cards were set down, and I picked up the sketch I had begun several weeks earlier. He agreed to sit for me, and I made good progress, but it became late in the day, and he took his leave of me. It was all so unexceptional. Having him with me seemed the most natural thing in the world, and I could not remove him from my mind for the rest of the evening. I read books, and thought of passages he would like. I worked at my embroidery, and caught myself daydreaming of embroidering his handkerchiefs and making small items for his rooms.

I had always thought falling in love a dramatic sort of thing, with swoons and declarations, but it happened so quietly, and now what am I to do about it? Oh, Louisa! If I avoid him, I will take from myself the only interesting companion I have. If I allow myself to be in his presence, I will surely give myself away. Your advice will be very welcome.

Yours, Caroline

XVIII. COLONEL FITZWILLIAM TO MR. DARCY

July 18
Cousin,

I am not quite certain what your design was in sharing with me the information that Mrs. Darcy received from her aunt regarding Miss Bingley. I suspect it was to amuse me, but I fear that it has failed. Indeed, the effect may be quite the opposite from the one you intended, for I feel terribly guilty now. Miss Bingley did indeed keep much to herself at the Gardiners' party, and I suppose one could say that her air was conceited, though I do not think she thought herself above the company so much as she did not know the company. It should have fallen to those who knew her to make her feel welcome. I do not censure the Gardiners in any way, for they were everything hospitable to everyone. But for myself, my behavior to her was so cold that I am not surprised she left as soon as she could.

I think I will call on her this afternoon. It would not do to bring the subject up, of course, but I will feel a great deal better after seeing her in good spirits.

—July 19—

I have called upon Miss Bingley, yesterday and today, but she is not at home, at least to me. I saw a young lady admitted entrance as I was leaving, so it seems that it is only my presence that is not desired. I can think of nothing that I have done of late that might have occasioned such a response, but I cannot concern myself with it overmuch. I will try again tomorrow. Very likely, we will meet in general company. I will go to an exhibition of paintings of landscapes on Monday, which is the 21st. Nearly the end of July! My time here is almost at an end.

Perhaps Miss Bingley will be at the exhibition. I will have to see if I can discover what I have done to remove myself from her good graces, and coax myself back into them if I can.

Yours, &c.,

R. F.

XIX. Miss Bingley to Mrs. Hurst

July 19

Dear Louisa,

I am quite relieved! I have not yet received your response to my last, but I had to write and tell you that Mrs. Weston has come to town. She was a schoolgirl friend of mine, you may recall. She is here because her husband must have an operation, and it is serious enough—perhaps I should say interesting enough—that he has gotten the attention of several prominent London doctors. He has some sort of tumor, which they will try to remove from his leg without taking the whole leg. Dreadful business! I quite feel for her, poor woman. But—and here I am being selfish for a moment (which, as you know, I always give myself permission to be)—if the operation goes well, she will almost certainly be a frequent caller here as her husband recuperates. So I may avoid Colonel Fitzwilliam without depriving myself of the only tolerable company in London. I will call on them both tomorrow, and I will be sure not to mention to poor Mr. Weston that his misfortune has aided me considerably, for I really do feel terribly for the man.

I am not so selfish as to be happy he is suffering, for all that Mrs. Weston's presence has heartened me considerably.

Your sister, Caroline

XX. COLONEL FITZWILLIAM TO MR. DARCY

July 22

Dear Darcy,

You have taken leave of your senses! I must thank you for the most diversion I have had since my exile began. Your letter provided me with great amusement, and even now I chuckle to think of it. I assure you I am in no danger from Miss Bingley. She is nothing more than a friend, and hardly even that. Because you cite as your evidence the fact that I have mentioned her in my every letter since the beginning of June, I will write you a very long letter without mentioning her once, which should not be difficult at all, as I have not seen her in several days.

How is everyone? Good news of Georgiana always cheers me, and I am very happy to hear that she has mastered the concerto to her satisfaction. Tell her I will expect a private performance when I see her next, so she must make certain to keep practicing the piece.

I trust Mrs. Darcy does not suffer too much from her condition. Dare I hope that when you reference her waking you early each morning, you refer to more pleasurable pursuits than listening to her vomit? Ah, but I can see your face even as I write the sentence, the way your brows have drawn together in annoyance and the very slight blush that has appeared on your cheeks. Do remember that your cousin is a military man. If you knew the sort of talk that goes on among the bloody backs, that even we officers engage in at times, you would see that what you think of as my cruder speech is actually very restrained.

I am glad to hear that Mr. Bingley approves of the estate you have chosen for him, and I am sure the steward that you have picked out will suit him very well. Tell me, will you let him choose the furniture for his study, or do you intend to direct him in that as well?

So my brother arrived at Pemberley last week! What does Mrs. Darcy think of him? Andrew is very eccentric, and I daresay she finds him amusing. I hope she does, and that she is not annoyed with him. Keep an eye on him, I beg you. You know what he is like around my father, and what my father is like around him.

I have finished reading Paradise Lost and Paradise Regained, and I have nothing which with to follow them. I am in the mood for something heavy and theological. I am sure you have suggestions. Nothing in Latin. My Latin is very poor and worse for being out of practice. I prefer to read in English.

Give my regards to everyone, and my love to Georgiana.

Yours, R. F.

XXI. MISS BINGLEY TO MRS. HURST

July 25

My dearest Louisa,

I thank you so very much for your letter. Do stop apologizing for not being able to invite me to Bath. I am not sure I would wish to go on any account, and you are entirely right in your actions. If the dowager Mrs. Hurst is in Bath, you must pay your respects. Meddlesome woman that she is, she will no doubt be very much in your business—and you recall correctly that we do not get on at all. I am sorry to hear that John has had occasion to mention your loss to his mother. A handsome man your husband may be, but he is not always very clever. No doubt the odious woman will find some way to make it your fault. Do not pay the least attention to anything she says.

I have heard that Mrs. Darcy is in the family way, yes. I did not mention it to you only for fear of upsetting you. You have my sympathy, Louisa. It is not fair that you have been without a child for three years while she finds herself in such a happy situation not a year after her marriage. Perhaps it is the country breeding, and you should take to running about the countryside with no concern for decorum or propriety. No, you had better not. Mrs. Hurst would only criticize you for it, as she criticizes you for everything. I worry for you, dear. I know how that woman upsets you, and you do not need to face anything more when you are still recovering.

As to your advice about Colonel Fitzwilliam, I have taken it to heart. My hopes that Mrs. Weston would provide me with company have been dashed. I understand that the operation did not go as well as we all had wished and prayed for, and that they had to take the leg. She is with her husband, and I doubt very much that she will make any calls in the foreseeable future. He seemed a very nice sort of man when I called on him, and I am very sorry for him.

I do think you are being very optimistic about my chances. I am not a capital match for him, I fear. I do not mean I would be a poor match, only that he could easily do as well, or better, being that he is the son of an earl, and well connected in the military, though he has said that he may retire from the army soon, if his hip does not improve. I would be glad of it. I do not like the idea of people shooting at him.

Still, I will not avoid him. I will do my best to succeed in making him love me. I will not talk about botany. I will let him direct all of the flow of the conversation. He mentioned reading Paradise Lost. I will read it as well, or enough of it that he will think I read it. I despair of it working, but you are right. I must try, or I will regret it.

Your loving sister, Caroline

XXII. Colonel Fitzwilliam to Mr. Darcy

July 30

Darcy,

May I speak of Miss Bingley without raising your suspicions if I speak only to criticize her? I was readmitted to her presence yesterday, but she has grown very dull. We did not have a conversation so much as she agreed with everything I said. I wonder if she was out of spirits, and not up to conversation, but then I wonder why she admitted me at all, if that was her condition. I did not stay long.

As to the concern that you raise—that my behavior will raise expectations regardless of my intentions—I have thought seriously on it. There is some validity in what you say, and it is possible I have been imprudent. My calls have been very frequent. However, she lives at present with her aunt, a respectable woman. We have done nothing with even the appearance of impropriety, except perhaps my calls have been longer than society dictates acceptable. As to Miss Bingley's feelings, I would be concerned indeed if I thought myself raising her expectations, but I believe we understand each other perfectly. I have seen nothing of pursuit in her, and certainly she shows no symptoms of love.

I will furthermore be leaving town altogether very soon. I go on the 4th, if all is well, and I hope to see you at Pemberley by the 10th of August at the latest. I look forward to seeing you, and Georgiana, and Mrs. Darcy. I believe Mr. and Mrs. Bingley will be gone by the time I arrive, to spend a few final months at Netherfield while their new estate is prepared. I am glad to hear my father is gone. Ashbourne is surely more at ease. I am vastly pleased that he and Bingley have struck up a friendship. My brother is so odd, and one never can know if he will take to a person or not, but from what you have told me of the man, I think Bingley is just the thing for him. You and Ashbourne are too much alike in certain things to be good friends. (Do not make outraged faces at me. You know it is true.)

I may go to the theater tonight.

Yours, R. F.

XXIII. MISS BINGLEY TO CHARLES BINGLEY

August 3

Dear Brother,

I would be happy to join you and Jane at Netherfield on the 1st of September. I do not know the exact plans of Louisa and Mr. Hurst, but I imagine they will accept your hospitality as well, when they leave Bath. I look forward to seeing you in town on Tuesday sennight. I am, however, perfectly happy with my aunt, and I see no reason to change accommodations for so short a time as you will be spending in town.

All my love to Jane.

Your sister, Caroline

XXIV. COLONEL FITZWILLIAM TO MR. DARCY

August 5

Dear Cousin,

All has not gone well. I am trapped in London a fortnight at least. I will not bore you with the details, but it will be quite impossible for me to join you at Pemberley before the 25th—at the earliest. I need not convey to you how much I would rather be with you and Georgiana and Mrs. Darcy and even my brother, for I am sure you already know.

I called upon Miss Bingley again, but her behavior has not changed from what it was the most recent time I saw her. She has designs upon me. Once the idea occurred to me, it became quite obvious. I wonder why she has chosen to pursue me now, when all summer we have had a pleasant friendship. Do you think perhaps if I propose, she will go back to being as she was before? I am not serious, of course, though the idea did tempt me for a moment, if only because it might have gotten me my friend back. Not that I wish to marry her. She is very pretty, and I enjoy her friendship and her company. She is not unintelligent, though I would not call her bright or witty. She is actually rather amusing, in her own way. She is very critical of everything, but she has genuine feeling in her. When I called upon her most recently, she was making a sweet-smelling sachet for the sickroom of her friend's husband, which I thought very kind of her to do. Sickrooms always have a dreadful odor, do they not?

Matrimony, however, is quite out. She will not do for me, though I'll not ramble on with all of the reasons why we are unsuited.

I only wish that she were not so determined to pursue me in such a clumsy fashion. It vexes me to see it, not least because I want better from her. I want better for her than a man who would take her while she acts in such a way, a man who cannot have either sense or respect for her.

I have spent too much time thinking about this. I will end now, and sign myself.

Your servant, R. Fitzwilliam

XXV. MISS BINGLEY TO MRS. HURST

August 7

Dearest Louisa,

Oh, how I wish you were here!

Colonel Fitzwilliam came yesterday. Of late, he does not stay long. I blush to reveal how much his visits mean to me, though I am careful. That is, I try not to seem overeager. Charles will arrive in town on the 11th, and I am to go to dinner at his house on the 12th. He asked me to dine with him and stay at the house he has recently let, but I would rather not have him know how miserable I have been with my aunt while he has been at Pemberley. So I declined, saying that I was so very happy with my aunt that I saw no reason to leave her. (Foolish, yes, but I have my pride.)

—August 9—

He has not come at all. I am going out of my mind. I do not like being in love.

—August 13—

I dined on Grosvenor Street yesterday. It was a small family party. Miss Kitty Bennet was there, which was just the thing to lift my mood, as you can well imagine. She has been staying with the Gardiners since the beginning of July, and is returning home with Charles and Jane. She is not quite so stupid as she used to be; that is the best that can be said of her.

I had to force myself to eat, and be myself. I have not seen him since the 6th, which is a full week! I truly have lost my mind. I shall be far, far happier when he is gone, and I can begin to put myself to rights, and forget him.

I will send this letter now, for it is meant as a letter, and not a journal.

Yours, Caroline

XXVI. Colonel Fitzwilliam to Mr. Darcy

August 20

Darcy,

I beg your pardon for not replying to your last in a more timely fashion, but I have had a trying few weeks. In an ill-judged move, I agreed to a fencing match with a friend from my club and while I enjoyed it a great deal, my hip was less pleased by the exercise. I woke the next morning in terrible pain, but was not at leisure that day to stay in bed, so I swallowed my pride and took up my cane and made my way to St. James. All would have been well, but as I was making my way down a flight of stairs, a skitterbrained fool tried to rush past me, my crippled hobbling being too slow for him. I lost my grip on the handrail and took a fall. He was everything apologetic and helped me to my chair, and what was I to do but pardon the whole thing? I suppose I could have knocked him about the head with my cane, but they do frown upon things like that these days.

I spent the next two days at home, often abed, or hobbling about the house, snapping at the servants. I was, moreover, forced to decline an invitation to dine with the Bingleys during their short stay in town.

Mr. Bingley called on me the next day, but I am vastly prideful at times, and I did not want to reveal my weakness, so I said nothing of my hip. I only pled exhaustion as my reason for declining his invitation. We talked of my brother for a time, and I—quite casually, I promise you—asked after Miss Bingley.

She will return with them to Netherfield. I should say, she has returned with them to Netherfield, for they left on the 19th. I believe that she was not supposed to travel to Netherfield until the 1st of September, but I suppose the allure of leaving her aunt's company could not be denied.

It is likely for the best. Her decision to pursue me put me in a very awkward spot, as I have no intentions in that direction. I have been imprudent, I confess it. I hope I have not done very much mischief by spending so much time with her. A separation is best for both of us.

On to my good news. My father's business is complete, and I leave tomorrow to join you at Pemberley. I hope to see you by the 23rd, or the 24th at the latest. This letter is, therefore, somewhat excessive, but I have done so much for Post Office revenue this summer, I could not resist stuffing their coffers just this much more.

Yours, &c., R. F.

XXVII. MISS BINGLEY TO MRS. HURST

September 4

Dearest Sister,

I am glad to hear you will be leaving Bath, and joining us here at Netherfield soon. I eagerly await your company. The Bennets grow no more tolerable by long association than they were at first blush. Oh, Jane is pleasant enough, and though I am severe on Charles at times, I do love him dearly, but the rest of the company here is unbearably stupid when they are not insufferably dull.

I have decided to put Colonel Fitzwilliam out of my mind. He was to come to dine with my brother before we all left town, and I put myself to such pains with my toilette, and even finished reading that dull book so that I might have something about which to speak, when he sent his apologies! My preparations were wasted, for there was no one to appreciate them but Kitty Bennet and my own brother and sister!

He seemed so reserved with me the last few times I saw him. I am entirely discouraged from the whole scheme. I hope I never see him again! As that does not seem likely, I hope that I do not see him again for several months. I am sure that several weeks out of his company will leave me wondering why I cared for him at all.

This will likely be the last letter I send before I see you next, and can embrace you properly.

All my love, Caroline

XXVIII. Colonel Fitzwilliam to Mr. Darcy

January 5

Dear Darcy,

Arrived in Bath two days ago, after as comfortable a journey as one could expect in January. I have taken lodgings, and settled in. I doubt very much that the waters, or anything else offered in Bath, will be of much use to my hip, but I will not complain. My father is paying for me to spend six weeks here, and I only have to allow myself to be examined by some physician who will no doubt agree with me entirely in my assessment of the situation: to wit, my hip aches because a French soldier shot it.

Did I tell you the best part of our discussion? I believe I was still too upset when I saw you to speak of it. My father accuses me of dissembling. He says the pain, if there is pain, is caused by a desire to free myself from my responsibilities. My responsibilities are to be at his beck and call, you understand.

Forgive me. I am perhaps still somewhat out of sorts with the whole thing. I will not think any more of it. I will focus instead on the six weeks I have ahead of me in Bath, all of them paid for out of my father's purse.

I suspect I will again begin contributing a great deal to the revenue of the Post Office, as I have few associates here. My friends are all in London—what irony. I hope Mrs. Darcy is well, and that she continues well, and that neither you nor Georgiana suffer the start of nervous disorder as Georgiana's coming out draws near.

Yours, &c., R. F.

XXIX. MISS BINGLEY TO MRS. HURST

January 9

Dear Louisa,

Now I am in Bath and you are not! And he is here. I need not specify who "he" is, for you know too well how my hopes have persisted despite my best efforts to conquer them. I am determined that I shall make a conquest while I am here in Bath. Not of him, but of someone. I will marry this year. There is a Mrs. Bingley now, and I am a guest in my brother's home, no matter what pains he may put himself to in order to pretend that I am not.

I suspect Jane is in the family way. They have not said anything, but she has been twice visited by a medical man, and she and Charles smile at each other even more than is usual for them. The Bennet women do breed prodigiously, do they not? First Mrs. Darcy and now Mrs. Bingley. And Mrs. Wickham gave birth to a surprisingly large, healthy lad, for all that he was born only seven months after the wedding. I hope Mrs. Darcy has nothing but girls.

I shall marry. I want away from it all. I am not without my charms, and I have received at least one offer every year that I have been out. Fool that I am, I declined them all. I shall not make such a mistake again. The next unobjectionable offer I receive will be the last.

Your sister, Caroline

XXX. COLONEL FITZWILLIAM TO MR. DARCY

January 13

Darcy,

I have visited the physician and endured much pain as his assistant manipulated my hip this way and that. Mr. Schofield himself even condescended to palpate the affected area. His guess is that a fragment of the bullet remains, and is irritating the nerves and the joint. There is nothing for it, unless I will consent to go under the surgeon's knife. He says that such a course carries serious risks, as there is no guarantee that a bullet fragment is even there, or that an operation will not do more harm than good. (This, of course, assumes that an operation does not kill me outright.) In his discussion of the arguments against an operation, he neglected to mention that such a plan would require me to suffer to allow myself to be sliced open, and poked at in the hope of finding something. If I am so fortunate as to indeed have a fragment in my hip, it will, no doubt, be ossified and have to be wrenched out. I am sick to my stomach just thinking of it. I will not do it, and Mr. Schofield quite agrees with me that it is better for me to manage the pain as best I can than undergo such agonies with no sure expectation of a good outcome. He therefore suggests that I set aside my pride and take up the cane at all times, and prepare myself to go through a great many hot linens throughout the remainder of my life.

Physicians and talk of operations aside, my time in Bath passes pleasantly. The Bingleys are here, I imagine you know, and my brother has recently joined them. I have seen Miss Bingley several times. Her behavior toward me is somewhat cold. I confess to being rather conflicted in her presence. I want her as a friend, but I am afraid to put myself forward, for fear she will misinterpret me. My behavior this summer past was imprudent, and things are awkward.

I am vastly amused by Ashbourne's friendship with Mr. Bingley. They are so different, Mr. Bingley at ease in every society, Ashbourne at ease in none, and yet they seem to get on famously. I do not understand it at all, but I think it a very fine thing for my brother. I have not previously been much in company with Mr. Bingley. I confess I never knew quite what to make of your friendship with him, but I find that he is agreeable and not altogether unintelligent. I give you leave to continue arranging his life. You have condescended to direct the lives of far less worthy individuals.

Yours, R. F.

XXXI. Miss Bingley to Mrs. Hurst

January 14

Dear Louisa,

I have this comfort, at least. I waste my time pining for only one Fitzwilliam. Colonel Fitzwilliam's brother, rich and titled though he may be, holds not the least interest for me. I have never met a queerer, more disagreeable man in my life. I do not know what Charles was thinking in bringing him into the house, to stare morosely at walls and blunder through conversations. Charles claims he is "agreeable, once you become acquainted with him." I ask you, how does one become acquainted with a man who barely opens his lips except to say something impolitic.

He is more to be despised because he brings Colonel Fitzwilliam himself round quite often. Louisa, how can a man's mere presence be agony and joy at once? And why can I not be rid of these abominable feelings?

Enough! I will be rational now.

Do you recall Sir Frank Watson? We had a minor flirtation during my first season, but nothing ever came of it. He is in Bath, and we have seen a good deal of each other. His wife died about a year ago, and he is out of the blacks now. He pays me the kindest attentions of late, and I encourage them all. We flirt quite shamelessly. You would blush to see it. He is an idiot, of course, but he is handsome and rich and I would be able to manage him without the least trouble.

Have you had the news? Jane is indeed in the family way. I said everything right and congratulatory when they told me. They expect the confinement in June. I can only hope to be married by June.

Your sister, Caroline

XXXII. Colonel Fitzwilliam to Mr. Darcy

January 20

Darcy,

Were Bingley any other sort of man, I would fear for your friendship with him. After the spectacle my family has made of itself in his very house, I would not blame him for casting the entire family off.

My father came unexpectedly to Bath on the 15th. He disagrees with my assessment of my situation, and has found a physician to parrot him. I must submit to the operation; anything less would be unworthy of me. Unworthy of him, he means. The man is senseless! Am I to risk my life and put myself to agonies for an operation that offers no sure hope of success or relief? Our discussion became quite uncomfortable and heated. It is not the first time my father and I have traded harsh words, and yet I am not able to dismiss some of his more cruel statements from my memory easily. This, fortunately, happened within the walls of my own lodgings.

Unfortunately, my father then decided to call upon Andrew, at Bingley's house. Andrew, in a rare showing of fraternal loyalty, declared himself to agree with me. Moreover, I understand, he said that even if he did not, he should not pressure me to change my mind, I being the one who must live (or not) with the consequences of any decisions that are made. This uncommon filial defiance did nothing to calm my father, and he upbraided him most severely.

Perhaps this, too, might have passed without much consequence, but I happened to call upon Andrew while my father was still there. I found Andrew, seated in a chair, being scolded like a child and not saying the least in his own defense. You know that I am not given to protecting my brother. We are not always on good terms, partly because I find his unwillingness to act as a man before my father unseemly. But I could not stand by and watch this display without saying something.

The end of it is that my father and I shouted at each other for a time before my father stormed from the house, and Andrew locked himself in his room and did not come out of it for two days.

Mr. and Mrs. Bingley are of such yielding tempers and easy characters that I daresay they were excessively shocked by our display. I apologized as best as I could, and forgiveness was both freely granted and declared utterly unnecessary.

There is something else, which I hesitate to tell you. I went back yesterday to see Andrew again. I found him in surprisingly good spirits. I saw Miss Bingley also, and she reminded me so much of herself, her true self, the woman she is when she is not preening and pursuing, that I engaged her in a very long, very agreeable conversation. I think perhaps some of my speech was imprudent, for I revealed to her things that I am now embarrassed to have told her. Nothing improper, I assure you. But I have been more troubled about this sorry business of my hip than I have let on, even to you. I should not have spoken so candidly to her about the subject.

She is much occupied with Sir Frank Watson at present. He is a fool and she deserves better.

I am exhausted from the events of the past few days and beg your forgiveness for my lack of civilities. I trust everyone is well. Tell Georgiana I will be in London for her presentation at court.

Yours,

R. F.

XXXIII. Miss Bingley to Mrs. Hurst

January 27

Dear Sister,

Forgive me for not writing sooner. I have had headaches of late, and when I am not laid up with them, I am occupied with Sir Frank. He makes his intentions very plain, and I am in daily expectation of an offer. I will accept him. A fool he may be, but he is a rich and handsome fool. I only wish I did not see the colonel so very often. Is it not odd, Louisa? Colonel Fitzwilliam has not more than a few thousand a year, and even I am not so smitten as to think him Sir Frank's equal in looks, and yet I would—

Well, there is no use thinking about it. I shall tell you more of Sir Frank. He is very handsome. There is something very delicate in his features, but they are not effeminate. The curl of his hair and the curve of his jaw puts one in mind of a classical statue. He is tall, but not overly tall. And his eyes are a shocking blue. He is entirely perfect for me. He never teases me, and treats me as though I were a princess. Sir Frank defers to me in everything. I am sure I would be very content to be married to him.

Did I mention to you the conversation that I had with Colonel Fitzwilliam some time ago? He was so candid with me, and our speech flowed so easily. No, never mind, I will not speak of it. It has not been repeated, and it will not be repeated. There is no use thinking on it.

I do wish Lord Ashbourne would leave. He had made some noise about going, but Charles begged him to stay so earnestly. You have the intelligence of the affair between him and his father from Jane, I know. No doubt, she put the whole thing in an absurd light, which made it all an unfortunate misunderstanding. Well, the truth of it is, Lord Buxton is a very disagreeable man. Colonel Fi I am sorry for his sons, but glad that I am not part of such a family.

My head begins to ache again, and I expect Sir Frank shortly. Perhaps he will make his offer today. I will be glad to have this matter settled.

Your sister, Caroline

XXXIV. Colonel Fitzwilliam to Lord Buxton

January 31
Dear sir,

I regret to inform you that I will not accede to your wishes. As you have expressed your intention of withdrawing all financial support of my stay in Bath in such a case, I have taken the preemptive step of repairing to plainer lodgings and have enclosed my new direction, should you care to write to me here. I cannot give any intelligence regarding my brother's failure to answer your letters, but as he spends money on nothing but dead insects and religious books, I suspect your threats to cut his allowance will not have the effect you desire.

Your respectful son, Richard Fitzwilliam

XXXV. Colonel Fitzwilliam to Mr. Darcy

January 31

Cousin,

My brother has discovered himself. Just today he wrote to my father, refusing his lordship's demand that he return to London. I was privileged to see the letter before it was sent, and I must say that it almost borders on the insolent. We will make a man of him yet. The moment the post left, Ashbourne seemed to realize what he had done. I left him to Bingley's care, that gentleman having far more patience for my brother's anxieties than I do.

I saw Miss Bingley at the Upper Rooms two days ago. She was in company with Sir Frank Watson for much of the night. I blush for her when she is with the man. She acts like such a simpering idiot, agrees with every word he says, and pretends to care about his cravats and coats as much as he does. I am too clear-sighted with respect to my own sex to fail to realize that many men are pleased with such behavior, but it would never do for me. She can be rational, you know, and I infinitely prefer her when she is.

I asked her to dance. I should not have, but something in her eyes told me that she had had enough of Sir Frank's inane conversation, and I felt duty bound to come to her rescue. She seemed at first pleased, but she was ultimately very dull with me, and seemed eager to be out of my company. I had hoped we could be something like friends again, now that she has turned her attentions to Sir Frank, but I suppose that we shall not ever be as we were last summer. Is it not odd how I now look on the summer months wistfully? At the time, I longed for them to end. And yet yesterday I found myself thinking on nothing so much as the ride Miss Bingley and I took through Hyde Park.

My letters are dreadfully self-centered of late. I do apologize. I am glad to hear that Mrs. Darcy is in good health. Anxiety about an impending confinement is only natural. As to your suspicions that the ladies of the neighborhood are adding to her fears by telling her horrid tales, I daresay you are correct. It is the same in the army. No green soldier goes into battle without having been first terrified out of his wits by stories of fearsome injuries, gruesome deaths, and suchlike things. It is far from kind, but that seems to be the way of the world. (This reminds me, I have it that Ensign Wickham is being sent to the West Indies and may see battle. I really must write to him before he goes.)

My love to Georgiana.

Your servant, R. Fitzwilliam

XXXVI. Miss Bingley to Mrs. Hurst

February 2

Louisa,

Forgive my poor penmanship, but I write to you in agitation. I saw Colonel Fitzwilliam at the Upper Rooms some few days ago, and he asked me to dance. I was so pleased, but he was so agreeable that it was soon all I could do to keep myself from bursting into tears. I do not want to marry Sir Frank Watson! I despise being in love. It makes me such a fool. Sir Frank is rich and handsome and his connections are good. He is a baronet. I would be presented at court as his wife. And he is perfectly—

He is perfectly dull and stupid, and his company is a trial. But what am I to do? Yesterday evening, he gave me to understand that he will call today, and he was so particular about finding me alone. I have not slept a wink this night, and I write to you now by candlelight, my hand shaking and my head throbbing. I cannot stay in this house. I will not be nothing but my brother's sister any longer. Once the child comes—I must marry. I must have an establishment of my own. To be Lady Watson would be an answer to my hopes and dreams. Why can I not see my way to letting go of foolish, childish, romantic thoughts?

It is later now, just after dawn. I have spent some time crying, and it has done me good. Things seem clearer now. When Sir Frank comes, I will make the only prudent choice.

Sir Frank has come and gone, but my headache was so bad that I could not possibly go down to see him. The matter is thus delayed. I feared he would think I was avoiding him, so I sent a message through my brother that I very much hoped he would call again tomorrow. Perhaps Colonel Fitzwilliam will come to the house today, declare his love for me, and save me from this wretched decision.

Perhaps also I will learn to fly tomorrow.

All my love,
Caroline

XXXVII. Colonel Fitzwilliam to Mr. Darcy

February 2

Dear Cousin,

I saw Andrew today and found him in surprisingly high spirits. No reply has yet come from my father, but Andrew is determined to hold fast and not return to London until the beginning of March. I never thought I would pen these words, but I am proud of him.

Miss Bingley was upstairs with a headache when I called. She has had several recently. I made a joke about her wishing to avoid me, but Bingley assured me that was not the case. He seemed worried about her. She is prone to migraines, I recall that from our conversations this past summer, but she told me they were infrequent. It seems that of late she has been troubled with frequent headaches. I hope it is nothing serious.

I saw Sir Frank Watson today also, and I felt I had to greet him, for all that he is such dull company. He acted very strange with me, and more so when I mentioned I had just come from Bingley's. He said something about hoping Miss Bingley would not be cross with him and that he would "much rather have been with her this afternoon" and being so sorry that her headache delayed him and some other things that I could not quite make sense of. He seemed somewhat agitated. I do not know what to make of it, but I am once again convinced that Miss Bingley could do far better. Why is she prepared to waste herself upon a man like Sir Frank Watson? Bingley is good to her and she is still young. She need not rush headlong into an imprudent match. If it were not so terribly improper, I would speak to her and try to dissuade her from the scheme, but I cannot imagine how I would broach the topic.

Forgive me for spilling so much ink upon a topic that cannot interest you. I am oddly troubled by this.

I send my regards and love to everyone.

Yours, R. F.

XXXVIII. Miss Bingley to Mrs. Hurst

February 4

Louisa,

I have never been so wretchedly miserable or so embarrassed in my life. I will never leave my room again. Nay! I will leave my room and flee to the Continent. Perhaps I will flee to another continent. Even Australia could not be a greater evil than Bath is at present.

Caroline

XXXIX. Colonel Fitzwilliam to Mr. Darcy

February 9

Darcy,

I received your most recent letter this morning. You were brief and to the point, but then you always are. Do I acquit myself if I tell you that I had already come to the same conclusion? Yes, I am in love with Miss Bingley. I particularly liked your decision to send me a few of the letters that I have written since June, with certain passages marked for my review. I have perused some of them, and it is so apparent, I take exception to my own foolishness.

I have said that I had already come to the realization before your letter arrived. That happened yesterday, when I went to Bingley's house. Have you heard that Sir Frank Watson proposed to his cousin? It is a great upset, Sir Frank having been so blatant in his attentions to Miss Bingley. For myself, I can only think of it as a bit of good fortune, but I do feel for Miss Bingley. Not for the loss of Sir Frank—she is well rid of him—but his cousin, Miss Watson, has been unkind to her. It seems the family expected him to propose to Miss Watson as soon as he was out of the blacks, and his attentions to Miss Bingley were not looked upon kindly, least of all by Miss Watson herself. The matter has been set to rights, as far as the family is concerned, but Miss Watson is still put out, and as she cannot vent her ire on her future husband, she has made Miss Bingley her target.

I do not fear for Miss Bingley's reputation or comfort in the long term, but she and Miss Watson have several mutual acquaintances, and the whole thing must be very uncomfortable for her at present. I further have it from Bingley that Miss Bingley is quite determined to marry this year, and Sir Frank's defection has upset her greatly.

To return to my story. I went to Bingley's house to see Andrew, but I had also hoped to see Miss Bingley, to determine her state for myself. When I asked after her, I was told she was not taking guests, but Andrew happened to mention she was in the downstairs sitting room, and I confess I purposely lost myself in the house in order to find her.

The door was slightly open, and opened fully with a slight push. She was lying on the sofa, a pillow clutched to her chest. My heart quite broke for her. I realized then what you have known for months. I could have gone to her, and I desired nothing more than to gather her in my arms and comfort her, but I only backed quietly out of the room. I needed time to think.

My mind is a whirl. Tonight, I am glad of the ache in my hip. It provides an occasional distraction from my thoughts.

R. F.

XL. COLONEL FITZWILLIAM TO MR. DARCY

February 15

Darcy,

Miss Bingley has agreed to marry me. In a month, you may make me the subject of as much raillery as you like, but I beg you to defer your teasing for a time. I have been made to understand the depth of her feelings for me, and I am perfectly disgusted with myself—I had thought her attempted pursuit of me dispassionate.

Rationally, I realize that I had no way to know her heart, but what has rationality to do with a man in love?

Yours,

R. Fitzwilliam

XLI. Miss Bingley to Mrs. Hurst

February 15

Dearest Sister,

Colonel Fitzwilliam has asked me to marry him. Upon writing that sentence, I stared at it for some minutes. I still cannot credit it.

He came today to see his brother, and I was determined to meet him. I will not have the world thinking that a Miss Watson who is so ugly and stupid that she must have her father bully her cousin into marrying her can have any effect on me. I am so glad to be rid of Sir Frank. We would have been wretched together.

I looked quite well today, I think, though I did not take particular care with my toilette. My hair has been cooperative of late. That always puts me in a good mood.

We met in the drawing room, myself, Colonel Fitzwilliam— Oh! But I am allowed to call him Richard now, and he particularly asked me to. Lord Ashbourne and Charles were there as well, though Jane had gone to lie down. It was strange and awkward at first, for he kept staring at me, and I had not seen him in several weeks. Charles and Lord Ashbourne went away for a time to I do not know what they went off to do, only Colo Richard watched them leave with an odd expression on his face. I was suddenly overcome with distraction, and I could not think of a thing to say. I started to talk of something—I cannot remember what—and then he came across the room and sat beside me and said—

No, I will not tell you what he said. Those words are for me alone. Only, he gave me to understand that he cares for me, and I—

Do you remember when we were girls, and we used to practice just how we would respond to our marriage proposals? "Your Grace, you have made me the happiest of women, and I would be honored to accept your proposal." I was always so poised and composed and graceful in my acceptance. Well, there was nothing of composure or poise in this. Were I in a different frame of mind, I might be able to see my way to being embarrassed, but I am only—

Ah, but I am getting ahead of myself. The moment he had made plain to me that he was asking me to be his wife, I burst into tears. Oh, Louisa, it was awful. They were not even ladylike tears of happiness, they were sobbing tears of relief. I suppose I somehow communicated to him that there was nothing in the world I wanted more than to be his wife, for when Charles returned and saw us, me sobbing into his handkerchief and Richard with his hand on my back, I heard Charles say, "What on earth is the matter?" And Richard said, "I think your sister has just agreed to marry me."

Despite my joy, I am seeing my way to be embarrassed about all of this, but it was all settled in a few minutes more. I managed to restrain myself and speak with tolerable composure. Charles gave his blessing to the match. I suppose I will have to write my uncle, but I care not a fig what he thinks. I am sure he will be glad to be rid of me entirely.

What a fright I must have looked! Richard did not seem to mind, and stayed for several hours.

I can hardly think. He comes again tomorrow. You must come to Bath, and then my every happiness will be complete.

Yours, Caroline

XLII. Colonel Fitzwilliam to Mr. Darcy

March 5

Dear Darcy,

Ah, Cousin, would that you were in Bath and had witnessed it for yourself!

I wrote twice to my father following my engagement. My first letter went unanswered, and my second was returned unopened. I was prepared to leave the matter at that, but Caroline begged my leave to pen a letter of her own to my father, and I gave it. I know not what she said in her letter, but my father came to Bath.

We have met him four times. The first visit saw him at his most unkind. The treatment Mr. and Mrs. Bingley and, especially, Caroline received was not to be borne. I could have tossed him from the house—and would have, had it been my house and not Bingley's but Caroline cajoled me into being civil. After he had gone, she told me she feared her fortune and connections were not smart enough for him, but I assured her that I could have been marrying a German princess and my father still would have found it exceptional that I had chosen a bride for myself without first consulting him.

My father returned the next day and the day after, and Caroline was in fine form each time. It was a masterful display of obsequiousness and toad-eating that would have made Lady Catherine's parson green with envy. I would have choked on my own vomit had I attempted such blandishments. The end of it all is this: I am once again on good terms with my father, solely on the basis of my having chosen for myself "a woman of sense and good breeding" as my bride. I moreover have it from Ashbourne, who has it from my sister, that my father may make a wedding present of one of his houses in London—not a mere lease on good terms, but an actual transfer of property. This is not to reach Caroline's ears until it is certain, however.

Well, I am not entirely pleased with her methods, amusing though they were, but I will not argue with good results. She is not under the least misapprehension about what sort of man my father is, and even at the height of her fulsomeness I heard her tell him that she would not agree with him that it was better for me to suffer the surgeon's knife than "give myself up to my weakness" (his words). Because I have mentioned it and you specifically asked in your most recent letter, I will tell you that my hip is better. I use the cane nearly every day now, despite my hatred of displaying my infirmities for all to see, and it does help. Caroline scolds me when I leave it at home.

Do not worry overmuch about Mrs. Darcy. It was only the accoucheur's educated guess that she would be confined in February. These things can never be known exactly. Children come when they are ready to and not a moment before.

Tell Georgiana that if she trips and falls at her presentation, I will provide her with a set of men's clothing and procure her passage on a ship to the Indies (East or West, whichever she prefers). Never mind that, I will write to her myself and try to reason her out of her fears.

I had best conclude before I am forced to reach for yet another sheet of paper. I send my love and regards to you and all your household.

Yours, R. Fitzwilliam

XLIII. Miss Bingley to Lord Buxton

March 10

My lord,

I could not wait another moment to take pen to paper and tell you how grateful I am for the kindness you have seen fit to bestow upon your most unworthy servant. How can I ever give proper thanks for such kindness? I shrink from the thought of taking on such a task. Dear Richard has been forced to tell me every detail of the house—all that he can recall, for he has only seen it once. This does not surprise me, your holdings being so vast that one cannot expect your children to know every detail of every house, but I do wish he could tell me more. I am sure it is a delightful home. Richard said that it is grand and stately, and only a little old-fashioned. I am sure that we will be able to bring it up to the standard that is worthy of a son of yours with only a small outlay, though perhaps we will have to wait some time before going forward with the expense. Weddings are such costly things, you know. No, upon reflection, it will not do to wait. I would never have anyone seeing your son and, if I may take the liberty of calling myself so, daughter living in a house that is anything but a proper reflection of your rank and position. I am sure we will find the money somehow.

I was furthermore delighted to receive your kind invitation to stay with you at Kentridge when we return from Weymouth. I am so eager to see Lady Mary once again. You have a very fine daughter, sir. I have never met a more accomplished young lady. You have done very well by her.

Richard wishes to make his greetings in his own hand, so I will end here.

With most heartfelt respect and deepest gratitude, I am, sir, your lordship's most obliged, humble, dutiful, and obedient servant, Caroline Bingley

Sir—I am sure I cannot exceed Caroline in expressing my gratitude for your gift, so I will not try. I will say only that I thank you for your kindness. Caroline and I will marry in the church at Kentridge, as you have asked us to do. The Bingleys leave for Pemberley along with my brother in a few days. I will be about three weeks behind them, as I have some business to attend to in London before going on to join them.

—R. Fitzwilliam

XLIV. Colonel Fitzwilliam to Miss Bingley

March 17

My dear Caro,

No, I will not stop calling you by that name. I like it. What is more, no one else uses it, so it is mine alone.

I hope this letter finds you well. I know that traveling with my brother can be a trying experience. I recommend a glass of wine and a nap to help you recover. Have I ever told you my philosophy of napping? Remind me when I arrive, and I will enlighten you.

My father has given me two thousand pounds, to be used in the renovation and repair of our house. Your abilities frighten me, woman.

Shall I ask you to give my love and best wishes for her recovery to Mrs. Darcy, or would that be testing your forbearance? I think I shall send it through Darcy instead. I look forward to seeing the little one. I must begin instructing Master Richard Darcy on how to be as charming as his namesake.

God willing, I will arrive at Pemberley no later than the 1st. It occurs to me that this is the first letter I have ever written to you. Am I making a mess of it? I have no talent for letters of love. There should be more verse and less sarcastic prose, but I would laugh too hard to hold my pen if I attempted to write you a sonnet, and I see no occasion for transcribing the words of another.

Caro, this is the man you have accepted: not always properly serious, given to much complaint, and with a bad hip besides. In scant weeks, you will be joined to me forever. If you wish to cry off, you had best do it soon.

I will be earnest for a moment. I miss you terribly. I have a picture of you in my mind. Do you recall when we went riding in Hyde Park? I think I fell in love with you that day, but I was too foolish to know it. You looked so well with the sunlight in your hair. You critiqued the dress of each person we passed, and some of your comments amused me greatly. It is a memory that I will use to carry me through the next week.

Your most devoted, Richard Fitzwilliam

XLV. Miss Bingley to Colonel Fitzwilliam

March 20

Sir,

I am ill equipped to speak on your talent with love letters. The letter I have just received seems to me the most perfect specimen of its kind. I have no wish to cry off. Your complaints will always have a willing ear if you will endure mine.

I give you leave to call me by That Name, if you must—but not in public. It took me years to dissuade my brother from using it, and I will not have you return him to the habit.

I have seen Master Darcy. He has that odd, unfinished look that newborns always do, but he is a healthy, well-looking child and I am happy for them. Do not make a face; I am in earnest. I will let Mr. Darcy transmit your love and wishes. I doubt very much Mrs. Darcy would be able to keep her countenance if they came from me.

I recall very well the afternoon in Hyde Park. It is one of my happiest memories. I did look very handsome that day, did I not? Ah! I have found a flaw in your letter. You have praised my hair, but not my smile, or my eyes. In fact, now that I read it again, I think your letter quite lacking in admiration of my good looks. I trust you will remedy this when you arrive. We must go riding in Hyde Park when we take possession of our house in London. And only think, we will be able to ride out as husband and wife, with no need for maids or footmen to lend us propriety, and we may go out every day if we wish.

I miss you very much. Charles teases me for being lovesick. He is as troublesome as he was when he was a child. I confess I am easily distracted, now that you are not here. I spend too much time staring at my sketch of you, and now that I have a letter to read, I will read it until I know every stroke of the pen by heart. I am so eager to see you.

I left this letter open while I walked out with Jane and Miss Darcy. I am bad company at present, too given to staring into the middle distance and not attending to anything that is said, but as this is to be expected in a woman whose lover has chosen the company of bankers over her company, I am excused. Miss Darcy thinks nearly as highly of you as I do, and Jane's patience is never exhausted, so at least I do not fear censure when I speak of you at length, and I frequently do.

I will be genuine with you for a moment (this, sir, is a rare event, I think you know). You have honored me with your proposal. I want you to know that I will do my best to be worthy of that honor. If you will only tell me what you want in a wife, I will do my best to fulfill your wishes.

I sign myself as your devoted, Caroline

XLVI. COLONEL FITZWILLIAM TO MISS BINGLEY

March 24

Dear Caroline,

I was not intending to write any more letters from London. I leave in but two days. After reading your last, however, I have decided to send this letter ahead of me. I had better not arrive at Pemberley and find you bent over The Improvement of Human Reason, or some other book that I have mentioned in passing. Such reading would well be a torment for you.

You have been genuine with me, and I will return the favor. I have seen enough simpering, idiotic females, and enough women who play the part with varying degrees of success to know that I do not want one of them. What do I want in a wife? I am not a man who has either the inclination or the patience to take a Child Bride in hand and mold her into my ideal. Your brain, Caroline, does more than hold the sides of your skull apart, and that is not a trait that is as common (in women or men) as one would hope. I expect you will take advantage of this.

I do not expect you to change to suit me. Moreover, I am well aware that any such changes would be superficial and halfhearted, at best. I know you better than you might think, thanks to long, hot London afternoons, when there is nothing to do but converse. Those afternoons have largely passed into the dreamy haze of idealized memory, not because I particularly enjoyed sitting in your aunt's parlor sweating through my shirt, but because of you.

I love you, Caroline, and I trust we are capable of making each other happy. I can only hope that you are entering this marriage with open eyes and a clear head, as I am. I'll not have you put me on a pedestal, Caro. It will not do.

I hope that I have set that bit of foolishness to rest for good. Here I am writing to you again, so I will address the failure of my earlier letter and say that I look forward to seeing my beautiful Caroline once again. Her smile, as bright as summer sunshine, is the light of my world, and her eyes are the clear blue of Caribbean waters.

I do hope the pimple on her chin has healed.

Yours, Richard

XLVII. Mrs. Fitzwilliam to Mrs. Darcy

June 2

Dear Mrs. Darcy,

I thank you for your kind invitation to Pemberley, but Colonel Fitzwilliam and I have no plans to leave London at present. The summer in London is so delightful, and we would not go away from it for the world. We will be at Tetley Hall in August, and I look forward to seeing you there.

I send my regards to Mr. Darcy, Miss Darcy, and young Master Darcy.

Yours, &c., Caroline Fitzwilliam

The Potential of Kitty Bennet
BY JESSICA KELLER

Jessica Keller is a lifelong devotee to all things Austen. She is a graduate of Trinity International University where she majored in communications; while there, she was the editor for the campus literary magazine, as well as the editor of the weekly college newspaper. She works full-time at a local police department but spends her free time reading period drama, baking, watching *Masterpiece Theatre* adaptations of the classics, running, and writing freelance. She lives in the Chicago suburbs with her husband and two cats, Bruce Wayne and Clark Kent.

Kitty Bennet was never a particularly interesting character to me, possibly the least interesting of all five Bennet sisters and without many distinguishing characteristics. When I was collecting stories for this anthology, I said that if someone could write a decent Kitty story, I would put it in. Jessica Keller did.

❦

As unbecoming as eavesdropping is, that was just the predicament Kitty Bennet found herself in on that late spring morning.

She had not meant to listen to the hushed conversation between a man and his wife; she had only wanted to ascertain whether Lizzy had planned any errands for them, in which case Kitty needed to change from her blue sprigged morning dress into a walking out dress. But upon hearing the Darcys' conversation, Kitty shrank against a tapestry in the hallway, grasping the thick emerald green fabric in her fists behind her back like a lifeline.

"She is so very changeable, which could be a threat, but I believe it to be an asset for us. She will do well here under Georgiana's guidance." Even though she was speaking low, Elizabeth Darcy's voice carried into the hallway.

"Ah, but remember, my love, Georgiana is even now in her room, packing. A carriage will be prepared within the hour. Her visit to Anne is long overdue, and I've a mind to get her out of the house as quickly as possible."

"Of course, Darcy. Georgiana must not be influenced for ill. In truth, she should have been gone yesterday. But even without her here, I know it will all be of no trouble to us."

"It would not have been my choice, but there is not much that could have been done otherwise. I will not have her, or any young girl, near Wickham for any reason, and with them lately imposing upon the Bingleys, Pemberley is the only safe place." Elizabeth's husband, though still wary of the arrangement, could only agree.

There was a pause and Kitty held her breath. She had to strain to hear Darcy continue because he then spoke softly: "You know, you must know that I am thinking only of you. With all that has happened...after...I cannot have you distressed."

Lizzy answered, "Take heart, Darcy. Kitty will be no harm to anyone here. Granted, she is silly, but..."

There.

They had been speaking of *her.* She had known all along, but her own name on her sister's lips put away any doubt. Blinking back tears, Kitty tried to decide what to do.

It was one thing to *feel* herself an unwanted guest; it was altogether another thing to *know* herself unwanted.

The choice to come hadn't even been Kitty's to make. She had been staying at Netherfield when Jane received a missive from Lydia, announcing that she and Wickham would descend upon them in a day's time. At that point, Jane called for a carriage and sent Kitty promptly on her way to Pemberley, with only a letter in her hand to announce her reason for showing up at the Darcys' front door.

Turning, Kitty ran the length of the hallway and down the large front staircase, startling Lark, Pemberley's butler, as she tore open the front door and rushed outside.

"Miss Bennet!" Lark called after her. "I implore you! The morning air is still chilled and you have not your bonnet or pelisse!"

Quickening her pace even more, Kitty called over her shoulder, "I care not, Lark! Please let me be."

The ground was still wet from the heavy evening rains, and her slippers would quickly be ruined. But she pressed onward, walking in long strides around the side of the house toward the back of the property, where the wooded hills could hide her progress.

Ladylike or not, half of her had wanted to burst into that morning room and reveal what she had overheard. She wanted to shout at Lizzy and Darcy that she was not so changeable as they believed her to be. Kitty knew to what they were referring. Yes, she had made many bad choices and impressions when she spent her time gallivanting with Lydia.

But could not the folly of youth be forgiven already? It had been a year since she had even seen Lydia. Kitty well remembered it, because it had been when Lydia and Wickham came to Longbourn to announce their marriage. Since then, Lydia had written, begging Kitty to join her, but Mr. Bennet had strictly forbidden her from answering any of Lydia's missives, and Jane had quickly invited Kitty to Netherfield. For a year, Kitty had subsequently been passed back and forth between Netherfield and Pemberley, and had returned home to Longbourn only once, to attend the wedding of her sister Mary.

"This is not to be borne. I have become the unwanted spinster sister. They will cart me from house to house as they need help with their children. I will be the pitied aunt," Kitty huffed as she skirted past a felled tree.

And that was the rub of it. Kitty found herself utterly alone in the world. The outcast. The last of five sisters to be married. Her younger sister, Lydia, had married quickly, and even plain and dreary Mary was lately wed. How could Mary have found a husband before she, Kitty, had?

"I am not so changeable," she muttered. "I just don't know myself." It was cold, but she wasn't ready to return to the house yet, so she pressed onward despite her numb toes.

Kitty's dark mood continued as she cleared the woods and walked into a large overgrown pasture. Tall grasses and wild heather swayed in an enchanting dance with the wind. Unassuming homes stood guard on either side of the field, and the distant horizon was dotted with the smaller dwellings of the workers of Lambton and those who made their living at Pemberley. One stone home stood out from the others on a well-kept piece of land to the north of the field. It drew Kitty's notice because it had a more genteel look than the others, much like her papa's home.

Turning to walk the path toward Lambton, Kitty's foot caught, as if someone had seized it between their hands. Her whole body lurched forward, and she tumbled with a great sloshing sound onto the ground.

"Ow! Ow! Ow!" Kitty was only momentarily stunned before sitting back up. Her foot was wedged tightly where it had become stuck, so much so that she had to use her hands to jerk her left foot out of the offending foxhole. She was wet through and through, and speckled with mud. Biting her bottom lip, Kitty pressed her palms to the ground and rose on shaky legs. She tested putting weight on her left foot, and promptly crumbled to the ground again.

Smacking a puddle with her fist, she let out an agitated, "Well done, Kitty! You've made a real fool of yourself!"

She couldn't rightly sit there all day, nor was crawling an option, so she rose again, albeit more slowly and then gingerly hobbled forward. Wincing, Kitty turned back in the direction of Pemberley and walked on—as much as a walk as it could be called. She would take a step with her right foot and do a quick little hop with her left, plant the right and dangle the left for a moment and then repeat. At that rate, it would be nightfall before she even got into the woods.

"Miss! Miss, you are unwell."

Kitty was in the left-foot-dangle-stage, and the man calling to her in close proximity caused her to lose her balance again.

He ran forward and Kitty glanced up. The man wore a simple single-breasted black frock coat, and as he leaned over her, his hat tipped off, revealing butterscotch-colored hair tinged with red.

"Miss, I was watching you walk just now, and I fear you are either foxed or injured."

"Sir, I assure you I am not, nor have I ever been foxed in my life. I do not take strong drink. I did, however, succeed at lodging my foot in a foxhole."

The man's lips twitched with a suppressed smile. "Ah, so it would seem you were foxed in quite another way, then."

Kitty crossed her arms and peered up at the stranger, and in her normal fashion—which always greatly shamed her two eldest sisters—she answered with the first thought that came to her head: "Sir, I must know if your purpose will be to continue to jest or to assist me in some way."

The man broke into a full smile, and it had the effect of making Kitty feel a little less chilled to the bone. Leaning over, he offered his hand. "Mr. Denton at your service, Miss."

Kitty grasped his hand, her cheeks flaming when she realized that hers were gloveless. What must Mr. Denton think of her? Breaking contact the moment she was on her feet, Kitty smiled bravely, though her ankle hurt like the blazes.

"Thank you, Mr. Denton. You have been most helpful. And now I must return home." Kitty turned, trying to hide the grimace on her face as she put weight on her foot, but Mr. Denton, seeming to finally completely take in her circumstances, stopped her.

"I would be remiss in my duties as a clergyman...my duties as a gentleman...if I did not ascertain how you came to be in this situation. Has someone...you can tell me, Miss...has someone used you ill and left you here?" His voice was reassuring.

"Mr. Denton. I feel I have been used ill, but not as you imagine. If I have been hurt by someone, it has not been bodily. My only physical aliment is a pained ankle, which I caused myself, and now I must get back to Pemberley."

"Pemberley? Then you are—"

"Mrs. Darcy's sister. Miss Bennet."

"Miss Bennet, you will have to forgive the impropriety, but I feel I must carry you back to Pemberley. I could hardly leave the sister of Mrs. Darcy in such a state—or any person, really. And in truth, I have business with Mr. Darcy and was on my way to the estate when I came upon you."

Kitty had colored before; now the flush grew infinitely deeper. She peeked up into his eyes—impossibly blue eyes. They were a remarkable mixture of many different shades and depths of blue, as if the sea and sky met at the horizon in them.

"I couldn't possibly allow you," Kitty answered.

"Miss Bennet. My gig has a broken wheel at the moment, or else I would have been in it. You will be perfectly safe with me, I promise."

He took a step toward her and muttered. "Poor dear, you're wet through." Before she realized what he was doing, Mr. Denton removed his coat and placed it about her shoulders. Then he reached and picked her up in his arms without ceremony.

Denton moved swiftly, her weight not seeming to burden him in the least. Kitty felt a small semblance of shame because she found herself enjoying being carried a man. Throughout her whole life, she had hugged her sisters and mother, and they had been very soft—their bodies melding with an embrace. Being held by Mr. Denton was a much different feeling. She had rarely hugged her father, and had never been this close to any man before. Her body was being carried so snugly against him she couldn't help but realize how firm his chest and arms were, and it struck her that it was nice to cling to someone so solid.

Kitty suddenly envied her married sisters in a way she never had before. How inexpressibly nice it would be to lean against the strength of a man in times when life seemed too much to bear. How wonderful it felt to be surrounded by someone else and depend that they would take care of her.

Kitty sighed.

Mr. Denton's deep rumble of laughter snapped her back to reality. "Comfortable?" Catching her gaze, he quirked an eyebrow.

The thud of approaching hooves saved Kitty from having to supply an answer. A giant black horse bearing a similarly tall and dark rider reared fifteen paces in front of them. The rider reined in his steed and dropped to the ground, exploding toward them.

"Mr. Darcy!" Kitty yelped.

"Catherine? That cannot be you!" Darcy's eyebrows dove into a deep V as his eyes surveyed the scene before him. "What happened here?" His gaze flicked to Denton and he growled, "Do not make me regret giving you the benefice."

"Do not cast such a grave look my way, Darcy. Miss Bennet tripped. I believe her ankle is compromised."

The line between Darcy's eyes became more pronounced as he stared at Denton. "Indeed. I will unburden you of her." Before Kitty could protest, she was passed from Denton to Darcy.

"I was on my way to speak with you on a church matter, but I will come back tomorrow. Miss Bennet, I pray you will be mending by then." Denton bowed and turned to leave, but Darcy called him back.

"It seems I didn't think this through. I mean to ride back with her. You'll have to hand her up to me." Darcy passed Kitty back to Denton, and then clucked to his horse.

"Mr. Darcy, I cannot possibly ride with you. That horse is enormous and my riding is nothing to boast about," Kitty protested as Darcy swung up onto the great black beast.

"Nonsense. Tabor is fine under my command." Darcy reached out as Denton lifted Kitty up to him, placing her in front of himself. Darcy wrapped an arm around her and took up the reins in the other. He tipped his head to Mr. Denton and nudged Tabor to movement.

"Whatever were you doing outside, Catherine?" Darcy's tone was clipped.

"What were *you* doing out?" Kitty shot back.

"Looking for you."

"Are you in earnest?" Kitty asked. Only an hour earlier, he had been calling her an unwanted guest, so why would he come out in the damp to find her? *Send a servant to search.*

"Of course. The moment Lark informed me you had fled the house, I came immediately."

"Why didn't you send a servant after me?"

Darcy's groom, Barlow, stepped out of the stables and collected Tabor as Darcy helped Kitty down. The master of the estate strode with her in his arms toward the house. He began to speak again, his words more gentle than before. "You are my sister. I could do nothing but come after you myself."

<hr />

"Lizzy, there is something I want to ask you. Promise you will hear me out?" Kitty spoke from her place on the settee. She was glad to be alone with her sister. Being in the same room as Mr. Darcy on the same day that he had carried her mud-caked self into the house would have only made her feel more embarrassed. Kitty knew the events of the morning had only confirmed in their minds how foolish she was.

"Speak at your leisure." Elizabeth sat with a book open on her lap.

"I know you and Mr. Darcy seldom use your townhouse because you are so rarely in London."

"That is true."

"I was wondering, hoping, if there was any chance you could be persuaded to spend the season in London this year. And if you do, I'd be eternally thankful to you if I could go along. I long to see a true season." There. She had said it.

Lizzy's eyebrows shot up. "Kitty, you cannot be serious. My husband and I greatly dislike London, especially during the season, and I assume you're asking us to sponsor you for it?"

"I would like to find a husband—not immediately, to be sure. But soon."

"And we would wish the same for you, but you hardly need to go to London to find a suitable man." Lizzy smiled and set her book down on the side table.

Kitty let her words quickly tumble from her mouth like marbles off a table. "But I do if I am going to find the sort of man I want to marry!"

Elizabeth regarded her sister. "And what sort of man would that be?"

Kitty could do little to help the long sigh that escaped. "Rich. Gloriously rich, like your husband. I want to shop on Bond Street and keep a townhouse and have as many servants as you and Jane have."

Lizzy's smile faded. "Kitty, it is hardly likely a man that wealthy would be tempted to marry you."

"That is unjust, Lizzy! Do you believe that only you and Jane are good enough for such men?"

"You mistake me. Remember, Jane and I did not marry for fortune, we married for love. I would love Mr. Darcy and live with him had he not a bank note in the world."

Kitty hadn't thought of that, and it gave her a moment's pause, but suddenly she remembered her other sisters. "But I do not want to struggle like Mary and Mr. Overton either! He is only Uncle Philip's clerk and their home is *so* small."

"Honestly, Kitty! All my letters from Mary say she wants for nothing and has never been happier in her life. This one here." Having marched across the room, Lizzy took up the correspondence from her desk. "She writes, 'Each night after dinner, Mr. Overton listens to me play and sing for him, after which he praises me, saying, "Indeed, I believe I have robbed the stage of its finest talent."' We spend so many peaceful days together that I cannot imagine there used to be a time I said I would never marry.'" Lizzy thrust the letter at Kitty.

Kitty scanned the page. "Mary does not sing or play well. Mr. Overton lies."

"No, Mr. Overton loves Mary, so to him her performance is enjoyable."

"But I'd rather have fine carriages than someone so enamored with me that he praises me falsely." Pursing her lips, Kitty crossed her arms. "You will not take me to London, will you?"

Mrs. Darcy shook her head. "No. And you would do well not to let Mr. Darcy hear you talk of marrying rich, because it would vex him greatly. I don't know why you even entertained the thought of London. All four of your sisters found husbands without having a season. You will, too."

Kitty smiled to herself as she reread the letter that had been delivered that morning to Pemberley with her name on it. Receiving her own mail on a meticulously polished salver from a white-gloved servant made her feel royal.

Miss Bennet,

I pray that you are well and have not suffered any ill effects after your run-in with that malicious foxhole. I gave a moment's consideration to eradicating all of them from the field, but then I recanted and decided to love the little red scoundrels all the more,

*because without them, I should not have met you, and I greatly
enjoyed meeting you. I look forward to our next encounter and hope
it will be equally memorable, just not one that brings you pain.*

Sincerely,

Mr. C. Denton

She had seen Mr. Denton on one other occasion—the day after her fall, when he kept his appointment with Mr. Darcy. The master of the house had allowed Denton to see her briefly before the two men sequestered themselves in Darcy's study for three hours.

Kitty had wondered what could keep the men talking so, but then, Kitty hadn't realized that Darcy held the advowson to the Lambton parish, nor had she known that he had only recently appointed Denton to the position.

What a great amount of responsibility Darcy held—appointing clergymen, acting as magistrate, caring for tenants, and making sure the land was producing enough so all in the area had jobs and food to eat. Her respect for the brother-in-law who had once terrified her grew.

"Are you sure you're well?" Kitty jumped at her sister's voice, so engrossed in her letter and thoughts of powerful men that she had not heard Lizzy walk into the room.

It had been three days since Kitty's foxhole incident, and she was more than fine—she was feeling downright caged. She wanted to walk and knew her ankle could withstand it, but Dr. Wendington had recommended three *full* days without walking, and Darcy insisted the instructions be followed to the T.

"You know I'm mended, Lizzy." Kitty looked at Elizabeth, who was standing behind her, her hands gripping the settee where Kitty reclined. Lizzy was the one who didn't look well. Her skin was pale and she had lost weight. "But arc *you* well, Sister?"

Mrs. Darcy clasped her hands together and looked up at the ceiling. Looking back down at Kitty, Lizzy said, "I have been meaning to speak with you about it."

The drawing room door swung open, and Darcy strode toward his wife. "Lord and Lady Chalmer have just arrived. Lark is showing them to their rooms, and they should be down presently." Darcy took his wife's hand, pressing a kiss to her fingers, and then held it between both of his. "You are up to this? They need not stay overly long."

"How long, sir?" Lizzy smoothed his cravat.

"He tells me no more than a fortnight. His mother does not travel well, and they mean to continue on to London thereafter."

Husband and wife turned toward the door as it clicked open.

"Darcy, you old dog! It is a pleasure to see you looking so well, and Pemberley is the jewel I remember." A thin, dark-haired man, wearing a pomona green dress coat and gleaming Hessian boots, declared in a lazy manner as he walked into the room. The man, whom Kitty assumed was Lord Chalmer, had the most delicate wrists she had ever beheld on a man.

"Lord Chalmer, we are at your service." Darcy bowed.

"Nonsense, Fitz, none of this 'Lord' stuff for you. You have pulled too many devious pranks on me and we share too many secrets, so I believe 'Lord' will not do at all."

Lizzy smiled. "Was my husband truly a menace?"

"I am afraid to shock you, but yes." Lord Chalmer straightened his jacket and ran two fingers over his mustache.

Elizabeth smirked as she regarded her husband with a sideways glance. "I am rather pleased to hear it."

Darcy coughed, but Lord Chalmer continued: "On one occasion, he told me he would have my gig prepared. It would seem Darcy's idea of preparing a gig is very different from mine. The scoundrel gathered a few of our classmates and they took the wheels off my carriage. Imagine, coming out ready to go to the club and finding just the box sitting there on the ground. He put the wheels back on later, but it ruined one good evening for me, to be sure."

Kitty pictured the whole scene in her head, and thinking of this stylish man striding out to his carriage only to find it unusable— and it being Darcy's doing—brought on a fit of laughter.

"Ah, I see you've lost your good manners, Darcy. You have been remiss, letting me speak of Pemberley as a jewel and not introducing me to this very pretty jewel in the room." Lord Chalmer gestured toward Kitty, his words causing a flame to spread up the back of her neck.

Darcy rolled his eyes at his guest. "Lord Chalmer, may I have the pleasure of introducing you to my sister, Miss Bennet."

Lord Chalmer bowed deeply and then proclaimed, "I should have known by your beauty that you were a relation of Mrs. Darcy."

"Lord Chalmer, it is an honor to meet a friend of Mr. Darcy's. He tells me you are to be here a fortnight? What business are you on?"

"Kitty!" Elizabeth chided her.

"I see you are direct." Lord Chalmer regarded her with a smile one bestows upon a clumsy puppy.

Lark announced that dinner was served, and Darcy took Lizzy's arm.

Lord Chalmer rounded the settee and addressed Kitty. "Miss Bennet, may I offer you my arm?" She giggled, accepting it.

At dinner, they were joined by Lady Henrietta Chalmer, Lord Chalmer's mother. She sat regally, her back ramrod straight as she surveyed the room.

"You have a large home, Mr. Darcy." Henrietta announced.

"We find it accommodates our needs," he answered.

Lady Chalmer stabbed at her asparagus. "Where is your young sister? Why have you hidden her from my son? And from me as well?"

Everyone stopped eating. Lizzy stole a look at Darcy before she spoke. "Georgiana has been lately called to visit our aunt and cousin. She was sorry to miss your visit."

The older lady harrumphed and addressed Kitty. "And you, you are the unwed sister of Mrs. Darcy. What is your name, child?"

"It is Kitty, ma'am."

Henrietta's eyebrow twitched. "Kitty? Your parents named you after a ratting animal? It is a shame I wasn't there at your birth. I would have convinced them to name you something acceptable. I believe the name Florence would have suited your countenance."

Lizzy kicked Kitty's shin under the table in warning. "It is short for Catherine, ma'am," she said.

At this, Darcy let out a deep, rarely heard laugh. "Forgive me. I just imagined calling my aunt—Lady Catherine de Bourgh—Kitty. I believe she would send me to my room without dinner."

———◆◦◆◦◆———

"Of all the flowers in Pemberley's impressive gardens, you—dear Miss Bennet—are the most beautiful." Lord Chalmer patted Kitty's hand as it rested in the crook of his arm. Lizzy was abed that day and Darcy would be holed up in meetings with his steward for much of the morning, so Lord Chalmer had suggested a walk to distract Miss Bennet and himself from the dullness of having no entertainment afforded them. Kitty had begun to disagree with him because there was much to amuse guests at Pemberley, but he would brook no refusal.

"I thank you, my lord, although many would call you a toad eater for such fine words."

Chalmer flinched, and then gave a small nod. "My, you speak as no young woman of my acquaintance."

Kitty stopped in her tracks, forcing him to do so as well. "Forgive me, did you take offense? It was meant as a joke."

He pursed his lips, and placed both of his hands upon her shoulders. "Pretty Kitty. If you want to tease me…there are, well, many other ways I would like to be teased." He slowly traced his fingers up and down her arms—feather light—as he spoke. The sensation made her tremble, noting which, Chalmer gave a Cheshire grin and then leaned down, his lips brushing her ear as he whispered. "And, my dear, I picture you *teasing* me in such a manner all the time; in fact, I can think of scarcely anything but that when I am near you, you are so intoxicating."

———◦◦◦◦———

Darcy crossed the room to where Elizabeth lay in their bed. He sat beside her, tracing his fingertips down her cheek.

"Have I told you yet today, dear Wife, how much I love you?"

Mrs. Darcy placed her hand over his, drawing his palm to her lips. "Only a hundred whispered times or so, but I do not tire of hearing it."

Lacing his fingers through hers, he voiced the thought that had been nagging him the entirety of the past month. "I cannot be silent any longer, Elizabeth. I must know, I must know how you are feeling. I am afraid—"

His voice caught and Lizzy seized the opportunity to sit up and lay a finger over his lips. "I have caused you so much grief," she whispered.

That bit of nonsense needed to be dispelled from her mind. Darcy pulled her into his arms, cradling her head against his shoulder. "Oh, my sweet wife, you could never, ever grieve me." He took her shoulders in his hands and set her at arm's length, so he could look into the brown eyes he adored. "I was grieved by the loss of our child, but that was not your fault. However, I am worried. You have grown ill."

Elizabeth blinked back tears. "I cannot argue with you. I don't know what the matter is. In the past fortnight, I have come to tire rapidly, my head often aches, and anything I put into my stomach turns sour."

Darcy nodded. "You are dwindling before me and it is torture to watch. You are so pale." He brushed a stray tear from her cheek.

Elizabeth smiled. "Don't men like pale women? Isn't that quite fashionable?"

Darcy shook his head. "Not my wife. I fell in love with a browned beauty who refuses to wear her bonnet while out on her walks. She lets the sun kiss her cheeks and her nose freckle, and I love her for it."

"I love you so much, Darcy." Lizzy leaned against him and his arms immediately came up around her.

Between planting soft kisses in her hair, he said, "You feel warm. I will call for Dr. Wendington tomorrow, and I will send away the Chalmer."

"I cannot have you dismiss an old friend."

Darcy flopped onto the bed, a sardonic laugh on his lips as he put his hands behind his head like a pillow. "Friend. Friend indeed!"

"Are you serious, Darcy? You so rarely speak poorly about someone. What on earth is your relationship with the man?"

"We were roommates at school, but never friends. Albert Chalmer had all the same haunts and downfalls as Wickham. Gaming. Drinking. Women. He spent his years in that fashion."

"No wonder you sent Georgiana away!"

"Indeed. If only we could have shielded Kitty, too, but I did not believe her ready to deal with my aunt for a long duration. But as to

197

the Chalmer, I received a note from a friend in town informing me that they are just short of losing everything. Both of their homes, their horses, and most of their staff—virtually gone. And they owe to creditors. I do not know the amount, but I must believe that they are in a great deal of debt. I am sure he was hoping to entice Georgiana to marry him and live off her fortune, the monster. Even if his worth were great, I wouldn't let her near him. It is beyond that man to love a woman."

"But I cannot comprehend why you allow him to stay here."

"Honor—or my old imprudent pride." Darcy turned to his side and propped his head up on his fist. "I made a mistake in school. I tried my hand at gaming once, the races to be exact, and I lost a great deal. I did not have the courage to tell my father, whereas the late Lord Chalmer kept a steady stream of money flowing to Albert. I begged him to pay my debt and he did, but he made me promise that I'd be accessible to him had he ever a need. I have paid him back a hundred times since then, but he will not let me forget the promise. I made a deal with the devil that day."

"We will endeavor to make sure he is not comfortable here, then." Lizzy smiled at Darcy.

"Come." He moved over on the bed and opened his arms. "I want to hold you."

Kitty was attempting to read a book the following morning, but Lord Chalmer would not allow it. He sat within inches of her, reading aloud over her shoulder until she snapped the book shut.

"Lord Chalmer, a woman cannot think around you!"

He gave a seductive smirk and spoke just above a whisper. "I should hope you feel that way about me, pretty Kitty."

She gasped. "My lord!"

"I cannot stay silent, Miss Bennet." Lord Chalmer picked up her hand and squeezed it. Kitty cast a quick look toward the other occupant of the room, Lady Chalmer, but she seemed to pretend they didn't exist.

"I know it has been only three days, but I find myself quite besotted with you and—" His words halted upon Darcy's entrance. Darcy's eyes went straight to their clasped hands. And Kitty dropped Chalmer's hand as though it were a hot iron.

"Miss Bennet, I require your assistance. It would seem Mrs. Darcy is unable to accompany Mr. Denton into the village to deliver church baskets, as was originally planned for today. Might you fill in for her?"

Kitty rose to her feet. "Of course, Mr. Darcy." She looked to Chalmer, hoping he would offer to join them, but he turned and looked out the window.

The day with Mr. Denton progressed much to Kitty's liking. Although wary of going into the homes of the poor, Kitty decided not to voice her fears and simply followed Denton's lead.

She found herself amazed because Denton knew every person in every cottage by name. He asked specifics about their families and ailments, and prayed with those who welcomed it. Kitty handed out peppermints and butterscotch treats to the children, and cheese and bread from the baskets for each home. If felt good to do something tangible for needy people, and Kitty found herself wondering why she had never considered the poor before.

"We made a good team today." Denton relieved Kitty of the baskets, and they walked side by side.

"Thank you for taking me with you. I have never done such before, and would like to go again with you the next time. Until today I have not given much thought to those who have less than I do. I did not think there were such people on Mr. Darcy's property."

"Don't mistake me, Miss Bennett. Darcy is an exceptional master and does all he can for the people who live near Lambton, but surely it is the church's duty to see to these people as well. I believe I am called to care for them, and as you've seen, it was Darcy's money that bought the provisions. These people are proud and don't seek handouts, so between Darcy and myself, we try to give them all we can without causing offence."

"But, do these people work at Pemberley? I cannot say I recognized any of them."

"No. Darcy's staff lives well—he would allow nothing less. But, even in a small bustling town like Lambton, there are never enough jobs to go around and people make due with very little."

They walked in silence for only a minute before Denton spoke again. "Miss Bennet, forgive me, but something you said more than a week ago now has caused me some restless nights."

Kitty started at that and squeezed his arm. "I did not mean to cause you distress. What did I say?"

"You said someone had harmed you, but not bodily. It kept making me think about my sister Phoebe, you see, we had an unhappy childhood and she was so often downcast with no one to speak to. I couldn't bear thinking that you were grieved without a chance to speak about it. It may not be my place, but it has made me worry for you."

"Mr. Denton, you are kind to remember. And I will reward you with the truth, because it means a great deal that you actually cared about my rambling that day."

"Actually cared? Of course I cared, and still do."

Kitty sighed. "Mr. Denton, on the day in question, you found me brought very low, and not just by the fall I took. You see, I am the only one of five daughters to remain unmarried, and I found myself, in that moment, quite downcast about my situation. I came upon a realization that I did not know who I was at all."

"That is a startling realization. How did you come to such a thought?"

"Well, it has been a lifelong idea that I have finally put words to. Please understand that I am not asking for your pity, Mr. Denton."

Denton nodded.

"In my family, my papa loved my sister Lizzy best, and that fact was one well known because he often voiced it himself. He and Lizzy would sequester themselves together to laugh at the rest of us. All the while, my mama adored my charming youngest sister, Lydia, and praised our eldest sister, Jane, for her beauty—which left Mary and me without any mooring in our home. Mary tried to win praise by studying books and practicing music. She seemed not as affected by my family's lack of interest in her. I was not so strong."

Kitty paused to see if Denton would just pat her hand and tell her that he was sure she was mistaken, but he didn't do anything of the sort. He turned toward her and lifted his eyebrows.

Kitty pressed on. "My eldest sisters treated me as though I were a bug in their ear. Understand, Mr. Denton, I just wanted someone to notice me...someone to tell me that my existence mattered and I was valued. The only person who gave me any thought was my sister Lydia, and now I see she wanted my company only to indulge her fancies. Thinking upon it, I feel ill used by them, because not even one of them wanted to know me, and they are my own family."

"I can see how you would feel as though you had lost yourself among them. You were a sketch, not a painting, or an afterthought, not the main subject," Denton said. Kitty nodded. "That is exactly how I felt. And so I spent my time trying to be the person I thought Lydia wanted me to be, and then she was gone and I found that I had never even been there. I didn't know who Kitty Bennet was."

Denton pointed at a felled log, and they sat down together. He turned toward her and asked, "Have you found her now?"

Kitty looked out over the homes of Lambton. "I don't know. I believe so, but I also believe no one likes who I really am. You see, the day you found me, I had just overheard my sister and her husband speaking about me in an unflattering way."

"What did they say?" Denton tilted his head and furrowed his brow.

"They were accusing me of being changeable, which I was in the past. But they also sent Miss Darcy away because they thought I would be a bad influence on her."

"I can scarcely believe that. Enlighten me. How could you be a bad influence on anyone, Miss Bennet?"

Kitty twisted her fingers together and bit her lip.

Then she looked up into his eyes and the calming sea of blue drew the words right out of her. "They believe me silly. You see, when I was younger, I was a flirt and I fell in love often. And if that isn't a grave enough offense, I also often speak what I am thinking— whether it is socially acceptable or not."

Denton's lips twitched with a hidden smile, and he took hold of her hand, securing it safely between both of his. "I do not think you are the cause of the Darcys sending their sister away. It cannot be for these reasons."

Kitty began to speak, but Denton shook his head and went on. "What I mean to say is, are not the abilities to love and speak truth admirable qualities?"

"Mr. Denton, you have just made all my youthful folly somehow seem virtuous!" Kitty laughed. "If you only knew, Mr. Denton, there is so much in life, and in my own mind, that I do not comprehend."

He stood, offering his hand to her, and then tucked it into the crook of his elbow. "Which is precisely how it should be. What fun would there be to existing if we understood and knew all? Half the joy in life is figuring it out and making mistakes along the way."

"And you are a clergyman...encouraging mistakes? Because, sir, you will find that I muddle many things in life."

Denton winked at her. "I am pleased to hear it. That means you actually live life. Miss Bennet, too many people merely exist without taking any risks at all."

⸺⬥⸺

Lord Chalmer leaned against the mantel in his assigned bedchamber and allowed the flames of the roaring fire to mesmerize him. Soon, he told himself, soon warm fires and richly appointed rooms would be his lot in life again. He licked his lips with the thought of expensive wines and roasted quail dinners instead of the tavern drinks and stews that had lately made up his meals.

He turned when the door opened.

"Ah, Mother, how nice of you to join me," Chalmer purred.

Henrietta jabbed a finger at her son. "What is going on, Albert? Despite our circumstances, you are well bred. But the attentions you are paying that *Kitty* belie that."

"Tsk. Tsk. Kitty? That is quite vulgar of you. Do sit. And I will tell you my plan." Albert gestured to a high backed chair, and his mother swept forward.

"Please do, because it is beyond me why we have stayed on at Pemberley after we learned of Miss Darcy's absence."

"Miss Darcy, yes. Fitz saw me coming, so to speak, and sent her away. The blackguard!" Albert scratched his chin in thought.

"Darcy must have heard that I had pockets to let and knew I'd try to wed Miss Darcy. Such a pity, too. Her dowry would have secured us, Mother, and I have heard she is not painful to look at either. I had thought I could talk sense to the man; what brother would deny his sister the opportunity to marry a lord? Wealthy women are leg-shackled to poor men of title all the time, and it's considered a fair trade. But the man is too proud for it, and believes dear Georgiana deserves far better than the likes of me, which is rich, seeing as Darcy chose a common mousy wren without a ha'penny to her name for his own wife," Chalmer said as he sneered.

"How bad is it, Albert? How far below the hatches are we truly?"

"The entail is killing me; the expense of maintaining it is simply too much to bear. Mama, we have rented out the London townhouse, and now the papers for Eddenwall are complete. Kicked out of our own home. Only Bates and McDonnagal have been kept on from our staff, and I do not know how long we can depend on their grace, with only the promise of back pay to entice them."

"I would say your gaming habits have done little to help us as well," the lady added.

Albert squared his shoulders and faced her. "Would you deny me the one thing that brings me any pleasure, any pleasure at all, in the world?"

Lady Chalmer sighed and patted her son's hand. "Of course not. You are right. Men must have their escapes."

"Of course, I am right on that account. The real matter at hand is, what is to be done? I received four letters from creditors the day before we left. It cannot be long until all of London knows of our situation—renting out both our properties without letting a new one. I need to make an advantageous match as quickly as possible. And that...that is where Miss Bennet fits in."

"But she is a farmer's daughter! A gentleman farmer—but a farmer!"

"Yes, but she is also sister to Mrs. Darcy, and therefore her future is tied closely to Mr. Darcy. Darcy would never let a relation of his be in want; it is not in his character. If I marry the child and my debts are made known, I have no doubt that Darcy will pay them all. The rumor is, he has done so already for a brother-in-law. Just think! When we have not the bank notes sufficient to let a house, Darcy will give it to us—or we will live here at Pemberley."

Albert began to pace as he walked, his hands clenched together. "But time is of the essence. The marriage must take place before Darcy hears the totality of our loss. It is our only hope, outside of traveling to America and trying to find a rich man's daughter there."

His mother shuddered. "America! I would be loath to be related to an American. Yes. I see. *That* would be much worse than a farmer's daughter."

Kitty gaped at the bundle on the bed she knew to be her sister. When had Lizzy taken so ill? She had never seen her sibling thus.

Kitty stole to the edge of the bed and grasped Elizabeth's hand. She was shocked by how sweaty it was. She looked from Lizzy, covered in many blankets, to the blazing flames in the fireplace. No one would be comfortable in such a hot room. Surely, Elizabeth would feel better if the windows were cracked and the fire doused.

At the touch, her ailing sister's eyes fluttered open.

"I did not know you were this bad," Kitty whispered.

"How long have I been abed?" Elizabeth's voice held nothing of her normal liveliness.

"Two days. Mr. Darcy is worried. He paces your hallway like a lion, and will not come down to eat with us, because he says he must stay near you. He is just outside the door now, giving Dr. Wendington a comb over about your care."

Kitty was ashamed to admit that her sister's illness had afforded her many happy hours in Lord Chalmer's company. The man had such a way with words! He was always whispering "pretty Kitty" to her, and often sitting closer than proper. He was so attentive and everything she had dreamed of in a man.

They had been on three walks in the garden and played a round of cards both nights together. When no one was listening, he would lean over and say that he couldn't leave Pemberley without an understanding.

An understanding!

This very morning after breakfast, he had asked how soon he could call her Lady Chalmer.

Ever since her eldest sisters' weddings, Kitty had promised herself she would marry well, but she had never imagined she would marry a man of title. Her sisters would finally have cause to be jealous of her! She might have had to wait the longest for a match, but hers would be the best of all.

Her thoughts returned to Elizabeth, lying in the bed before her, a wisp of a breath passing through her mouth. "Mr. Darcy will not tell me what the matter is, Lizzy; will you?" Kitty knelt beside her sister, still holding her hand.

Lizzy licked her cracked lips. "The doctor says it is infection, but the fever is too much, Kitty. Please put a cold rag on my forehead. I cannot bear this."

Kitty did as Mrs. Darcy asked, bathing her sister's face and arms in cool water until she fell back to sleep.

Conrad Denton prided himself on the fact that he had done much in his life alone. His late father had often been violent and inebriated, and Conrad's pretty young mother had died so young. His elder brother, Henry, cared not for the rest of the family. Conrad had spent much of his youth keeping his only sister, Phoebe, safe and comforted. Upon their father's death, Henry had inherited the family fortune and forsaken his responsibility to care for his younger siblings. Conrad had taken Phoebe under his protection until her marriage three years ago. He dearly missed her companionship, but it gave him pleasure to see his sister finally cherished and cared for by a man other than himself—something his elder brother and father had never done.

All of that had been training for Conrad's adult life as a clergyman, or so he figured. He could spend his years caring for the downtrodden in his community, and all with the help of his benefactor, Mr. Darcy. He could come home to his residence and glebe, Graceacre, and recharge...alone. Denton was simply happy to have a roof over his head and food on the table, with no fear of a brother belittling him, a father hitting him, or a sister sobbing to haunt him.

Alone was the only safe way to exist.

But suddenly the thought of living life alone didn't seem so appealing to him anymore.

He knew it was downright bacon-brained of him, but he couldn't deny that he was in love with Kitty Bennet. But admitting that to himself would have to be enough.

What right did a clergyman have to cherish the relation of his employer? No, Miss Bennet was too far out of Conrad's reach to even consider—but surely, he could enjoy her company.

As she walked beside him, her stride matching his, he watched—out of the corner of his eye—the woman who was consuming his thoughts. He memorized her face, from the slight upturn of her nose to the velvety flush of her plump cheeks to the bounce of her delicious chocolate curls. She was a diamond of the first water, of that there was no doubt, but more than that, the woman was a perfect mixture of fire, laughter, and frankness.

"Miss Bennet, I see you were unable to persuade Lord Chalmer to join us." He spoke not because he cared a fig for Lord Chalmer's company, but simply to talk.

"Yes. I tried, but he said that he could not stand to go anywhere near those people who live in rat's nests. His words, not mine. I attempted to explain to him that helping them, doing something, is good for one's soul, but he would not hear of it."

"I am pained to hear it." Really, Denton was not; he was glad to have Kitty's company without prissy Chalmer along.

As the pair traveled round the trees, Conrad held his breath. He had offered to show Miss Bennet his home, Graceacre, and she had enthusiastically accepted the invitation. Denton found himself jittery about Kitty taking in her first view of it. What if she was disappointed and did not like it? He would feel less than a man.

When his two-story stone home became visible, Kitty gasped.

"This is your home? This is Graceacre, the parish of Pemberley?" Her eyes were like saucers, and they grew wider and wider as she gazed over the land that made up the glebe and the house.

Her overt pleasure elicited a comfortable laugh from his lips. "Well, most would call it the Lambton Parish, but you would be right in saying we have very close ties to Pemberley."

"Mr. Denton, I have loved this home from the first moment I saw it, which was the day you rescued me!"

"Are you in earnest?" He beamed, delighted.

"Certainly! I saw this home and it stood out from the rest and looked so genteel, so like my papa's Longbourn, although I believe you have taken better care of your land than Papa ever has."

"Allow me to show you the inside and see if you are just as enchanted with it." He offered her his arm.

Kitty bit her lip and seemed to hesitate.

"We will not be unchaperoned. I keep two servants, and my housekeeper, Mrs. Sawford, is at this hour within."

◆◆◆◆◆

"My lord," Lark said and bowed to Albert. "There is a man waiting in the parlor. He will not give his reason for being here, and refuses to leave until he has spoken to you."

Albert ran a finger around his collar, which suddenly felt constricting. His heart began to beat a death march within his chest and his hands felt clammy.

The creditors could not have found him so quickly, he assured himself. He had not sent any correspondence from Pemberley, on the off chance that his mail was being monitored by a postmaster, either in London or near Eddenwall. And besides his mother, only the two servants left at Eddenwall knew where he was. Albert gulped. What if he had been foolish to trust them?

Lark addressed him again: "I fear you will have to see the man, my lord."

Chalmer straightened his cravat. "Of course. Lead me to him, Lark."

But what would he do if it was a creditor—jump out a window and run away? Or, worse yet, what if it was a constable, there to take him to debtors prison?

Lark opened the door, and at the sight of Eddenwall's long-time steward, Bates, Albert experienced a tide of relief so overwhelming that it almost brought him to his knees. The servant had served his father faithfully for almost his entire life; the man knew nothing but Eddenwall and Chalmer.

After Lark left the room, Albert smiled at the humble man before him. "It is good to see you, Bates. What news from Eddenwall?"

Bates, a small, balding man, bowed before his master. "Edden-wall is as beautiful as ever, but the joy is gone without you and the lady there. We are preparing it for the renters, who mean to move in at the start of next week."

"Good, good. But why in the blazes did you come all this way, Bates? Do you know how dangerous it is? For all we know, you've been followed, and now my creditors know where to find me."

"I had to take the risk, Lord Chalmer." Bates twisted his dusty hat in his hands. "It is regarding the creditors."

"Speak on," Albert commanded.

"There are more than six of them camped out near your property. They come to the house every day, and more letters come daily, too. Sir, they are saying that if the debts aren't paid in full, then the deed to Eddenwall will have to be forfeited—and you will be taken to debtors jail for the interest and for the funds that the sale of Eddenwall might not cover. Moreover, my lord, they are saying that payments need to be made, in full, within the fortnight, or else all of this will happen."

Albert began to pace the room, his hand raking through his hair. "Are you certain, Bates? This is worse than I thought. The renters will be thrown out of Eddenwall, and my story will be made known to all. A fortnight to pay all—are you sure?"

"Quite sure, my lord. They brought signed documents and showed them to me."

"This is a blasted business! They will take my very life away from me. I curse the day my father died and left me that infernal entail! Oh, don't look so shocked, Bates. You've done well, man. Return to Eddenwall, and I will do what I can to make certain that none of these things come about."

After Bates left, Albert spent an hour in a chair, with his head in his hands, thinking. Only one solution came to him. He had run out of eggs in his basket. Truly, his only hope now was marrying Kitty Bennet as quickly as possible. In fact, it would have to be by the end of the week if he was to have time to convince Darcy to pay off all his debts and save Eddenwall. There wasn't time to start afresh with a new girl. It was Kitty Bennet or jail for him.

It shouldn't be too difficult. The girl was in obvious awe of him and his title, and his mother had promised to make herself scarce to afford them hours alone together.

Albert rose from the chair and picked up the decanter that rested on the sideboard. He needed a distraction, something to bolster his mood. He shook the bottle, watching the amber liquid swirl. He uncorked the container, poured a glass, and swallowed the liquor in one gulp, his lips curling as it burned his throat. Wiping his mouth with the back of his hand, he decided that one was enough.

A pity there weren't any gaming tables or race tracks near Pemberley to take his mind off his troubles, if only for a few hours. But there were other ways for a man to divert himself. Surely, there was a pretty little maid within the estate who wouldn't mind entertaining a lord's fancies.

Yes, he had seen a petite, well-endowed blonde girl among the upper servants. She would do nicely. He'd entice her and then turn his attentions squarely to securing Kitty Bennet.

Kitty made her way up the stairs and headed directly to Elizabeth's bedchamber. She wanted to see if Lizzy was any better, and if she was, Kitty sorely needed her advice.

The past few days had been so confusing. After seeing the parish house from top to bottom, Kitty couldn't help but be, as Denton called it, enchanted. She suddenly felt that a house similar to Longbourn would suit her perfectly. An estate such as Pemberley was nice to visit, but she had a feeling she would never truly feel comfortable in such a grand home.

Seeing how much pressure Darcy was constantly under also gave her pause. Did she truly wish to have a husband with so many demands on his time? She would not mind if she could be involved and work side-by-side with her husband one day, but Darcy's duties were carried out solely by him. These thoughts, however, went against her longstanding dream to marry a rich man…a man like Lord Chalmer.

But she knew nothing significant about Chalmer, save for information about his ancestral home, Eddenwall, which he spoke of often. Eddenwall and fashionable dress seemed to fill the man's head, so much so that Kitty suddenly realized he had never asked about her thoughts or her life. He knew naught of her, her background, or her family, yet professed to love her ardently.

Then there were these startling feelings in her stomach whenever she was near Mr. Denton. The man was so easy to speak to, and she knew his entire background and he knew hers. He was such a well-cut man in every way—other than his purse.

And that was that.

Kitty's dream required a wealthy man, and so, she told herself, she would just have to get over all her worries about the size of the home and the duties of such a husband.

In her slippers, she padded down the hallway and found Elizabeth's chamber door open, but what she saw stopped her in her tracks.

Mr. Darcy had his back to Kitty as he ran his hands over his wife's face. A deep, low, heart-wrenching sob broke from his lips, and he dropped onto the bed. Gathering his unresponsive wife in his arms tightly, he rocked back and forth, with her against him.

"Fight, Elizabeth," He left a trail of kisses down the right side of her face. "Fight this for me. I cannot…I will never…"

His voice broke and he seemed to pull his wife even tighter against him. Kitty knew she should turn and walk away, knew that it was improper to view her brother's tortured moment of despair. But something held her there.

She gawked at his unkempt appearance. She had never seen a man so undone. His hair fell limp over his eyes, his neck was bare, and his shirttail only half tucked in. Darcy's shoulders heaved as he wept.

"I cannot live without you, Lizzy, you are my very life. Speak to me, dearest, and tell me how I can make you better. I will sacrifice anything to make you well. You are the very core of me. I love you. I love you. I love you."

Finally able to break her trance, Kitty backed away from the doorway without a sound. What would it be like to be loved as Elizabeth was loved by Darcy? Kitty doubted she would ever know such devotion.

Shaken by what she had just witnessed—her sister unconscious and Darcy broken—and by her own thoughts about her life, Kitty padded down the hallway like a ghost. She was a breath away from the grand staircase when a flash of puce caught her eye. It disappeared quickly around a corner, near where the servants' stairs must be. Had not Lord Chalmer been wearing a puce waistcoat that morning?

There was no reason for Albert to be in that section of the home. But, although Darcy kept his servants in excellent dress, their uniforms were black. None of them would have been so fashionably dressed.

Curiosity pushed her onward. She rounded the corner and pushed aside the curtain that hid the servants' staircase from view, only to fall back against the wall, her hands coming up to cover the gasp escaping her lips.

There before her was Lord Chalmer, his body pressing Alice—Kitty's lady's maid at Pemberley—against the wall. His lips drank of Alice's mouth as if she were living water, and his hands inched up her skirt. Alice's hands intermittently caressed his back and raked through his hair as she moaned.

Regaining her composure, Kitty balled her fists at her sides. "Lord Chalmer, how dare you!" she cried.

Chalmer staggered back, as if physically hit, and Alice froze to the spot, her face white. Spinning, Chalmer glared at Kitty, and it made her insides roil. "How dare *I*? How dare *you!*" His voice was a growl. "You little vixen! You've no right to be sneaking about this area, and I find it entirely unrespectable of you to creep up on a gentleman."

Kitty knew she was shaking, but didn't know if it was with rage or fright. "A gentleman? I seriously find little proof of that in your current pursuit." She spat out the words and turned to retreat, but Albert grabbed her arm and pinned her against the wall.

His voice changed to a purr as he grabbed her chin between his fingers. "Listen here, my trifling hoyden, it's about time you grew up and realized what the world is like. Did you truly think you alone could satisfy a man? Ha! Did you think that after our wedding, I would keep to just you? Ridiculous child!"

Albert released Kitty and straightened his waistcoat. He glanced over his shoulder at Alice, who stood, seemingly rooted to the spot, wringing her hands. "Be off with you, chit. Have you nothing to employ yourself with?" he barked at the little maid, and she rushed down the stairs.

Turning his attention back to Kitty, he spoke as if he were a solicitor laying out a transaction. "I will secure a special license, and we shall wed by week's end. You will grow used to these…happenings…but I promise to pursue my dalliances in a way that will not bring undue embarrassment to you as my wife. In fact, I could be persuaded to take but one main mistress, whom I would keep in a separate apartment, which would alleviate gossip." He bowed his head, as if making a great concession.

"But sir, I cannot desire marriage with a man who, even before the establishment of it, wishes another woman."

"You speak such feminine drivel. My dear Kitty, there is not a man alive who does not have a mistress. It does not negate a marriage—a wife is first in a husband's heart, and a mistress is first in his bed. It ends up being a comfortable arrangement for all. Besides the point, you are growing older, no man has sought you out. What options besides me are afforded you? We are comfortable together and you will gain a title. I know we could have a successful marriage."

Kitty shook her head. "No. I cannot believe it as common as you say. Mr. Darcy, for one, does not keep a mistress; he loves my sister and her alone. My papa—"

Albert's guffaw cut her off. "Are you completely blind? This is the way things are. You are right to say Mr. Darcy does not keep a mistress. No, he probably keeps ten. And you must have looked the other way when your dear papa went off for company."

He could not be right. Darcy—ten mistresses? Surely not. Lizzy could not love him so dearly if that were the case. And Kitty knew well that her papa's only other company was that of his books and a comfortable chair in his library.

Lord Chalmer must have mistaken her silence for consent, because he pressed his body close, his fingers tracing her neck. "Is it that you are jealous, Miss Bennet? Because you need not be. We can away to my chamber this minute and fully explore each other."

Her senses tingling with alarm, she shoved against him and tore down the servants' stairs, all the way down through the kitchen, and then erupted out the back doors. She took in two huge gulps of air before taking off at a run toward the wooded hills. Head down, she charged forward, stumbling as she went.

She needed to think, to breathe, and, most of all, to be away.

Suddenly, she terribly regretted her words to Lizzy more than a month past now—when she had told her sister smugly that she would rather have fine carriages than someone who truly adored her. After seeing Mr. Darcy with Lizzy, Kitty didn't think she could ever be satisfied with anything less than the same dedication. But was there such a man in all the world who could love *her* like that?

Lord Chalmer didn't care for her in that way, but he was right about his offer, no matter how distasteful, was still her best...her only...offer. She didn't want to end up a spinster, a burden to her relations. Certainly, a marriage without love would be preferable to no protection or home of her own. Wouldn't it?

"Miss Bennet!" a familiar voice called out to her. Kitty spun and spotted Mr. Denton picking his way over the field toward her. She took in his wide shoulders and sighed. He was such a well-cut man, although not quite as tall as Mr. Darcy.

Conrad's gut clenched while he watched sweet Miss Bennet palm her tear-streaked face and endeavor to smile in his direction. He would find out what had caused her unhappiness.

"Mr. Denton! How good it is to see you. I am out for a walk just now, but I promise you I will be on the alert for foxholes."

He laughed. "Take my arm, Miss Bennet, and I will walk with you and protect your feet from any evil that might be lurking in this very field." Kitty took Denton's arm as he winked at her.

He tucked his other hand over hers as she rested it in the crook of his arm. In a subdued tone, he said, "Unless my eyes deceive me,

Miss Bennet, you have been crying. Please unburden yourself and tell me as a friend what troubles you."

Kitty heaved a sigh. "You have been a good friend to me, Mr. Denton, but I fear that you will grow weary of hearing all my dark thoughts."

"Have no fear on that account; I could listen to you talk all day without tiring. Your voice has quickly become one of my favorite sounds."

It was brazen of him to say such a thing, but he was rewarded by a brilliant light in her eyes and a small upturn of her rosebud lips.

"Oh! Mr. Denton, I believe I have made a right muddle of my life."

"You know how I feel about muddles—speak on," he encouraged her.

"I do not believe I will ever find a man who will cherish me as I am. You see, Lord Chalmer wishes to marry me speedily, but I have lately learned that he has no intention of remaining faithful to me as his wife. I do not believe another option is open to me, however. I forfeited all that in the folly of youth," she said, drooping her head.

His fingers tightened around her hand as she spoke. Lord Chalmer was a right blackguard! What man could want the company of another woman when he had sworn before man and God to love just one with heart, body, and soul? Especially when that woman was Kitty Bennet? A man would have to be daft not to see what a treasure this woman was. Even burdened by terrible circumstances, she had chosen to smile at him and pretend she hadn't been crying. Miss Bennet had more strength than he had ever seen in a woman. His own sister, Phoebe, had needed constant encouragement when she was down, and getting her sister to open up with her thoughts had required hours of work. But Kitty, she didn't dance around the truth. Conrad asked a question and she answered him honestly. He loved that about her.

Denton wanted to tell her of his own love, yell from the top of Pemberley for all to hear that she had another option in this world—him. Conrad wished he were a firstborn son. Were he, he would have the fortune and then be able to recommend himself to a woman of Miss Bennet's quality.

Denton bit back the words of his heart. Instead, he said, "Why, Miss Bennet? Why do you believe you forfeited your happiness such that you are now punished with the prospect of a loveless marriage?"

"When I should have been spending my time becoming a woman worthy of a good man, I did not take the opportunity to do so. Instead, I indulged in flirtations with officers and whiled away my days dreaming of men in regimentals. I was most likely passed up by men of quality because they saw me for who I was then, a girl with nothing of value in my head. Now those decent men are all taken."

"I wouldn't worry on that account. I believe a man in uniform makes many a girl lightheaded. My own sister wed an army man, and they have been happily married for years now. I sometimes wish I had chosen the military route; then I would have had sweet angels like you batting their eyes at me. But, in truth, such a life would not have worked. Fighting requires a great deal too much fearlessness for me. I prefer the church—taking care of the people here and standing up for a sermon once a week."

"I grant you that standing up in front of a church full of people takes a different sort of courage than facing an opposing army—but it is courage, nonetheless. I, for one, would never be able to mount the nerve to do what you do every Sunday."

"I cannot believe that! Miss Speaks-Her-Mind Bennet couldn't get up and talk in front of people. Utter hogwash."

"I am in earnest, sir. I could never do it."

"Then you do not know yourself."

"And you presume to know me better?"

Denton nodded.

"Then speak on, man."

"You, Miss Bennet, are beautiful without knowing it. Those you love, you love deeply. Those you do not know, you think well of. You approach everything—whether it is delivering food to the poor, or going for a walk—as a grand adventure, which, in turn, makes those around you savor life all the more. You are quick to laugh, and quicker to forgive offenses. You speak what you think, which few women do. It is an utterly refreshing and truthful way to be. All in all, Miss Bennet, I find you are a young woman full of potential."

"Ha, potential! That means that I might never become who I am supposed to be."

"True. But take heart, Miss Bennet. You possess your own brand of courage, one that will not let you rest until you become that woman."

"Have you such faith in me?"

"You inspire it without knowing."

<hr />

Elizabeth thrashed about in her bed, her hands trying to push away the layers of blankets piled on her. "So hot. Too hot," she mumbled in her delirium.

Darcy hovered over her, his brow knitted with worry as Dr. Wendington forced the bedding back over Lizzy. "It is imperative that all these covers stay on her."

Standing a few feet back, Kitty looked from her sister to the roaring fire. Kitty's own back was damp from the heat, so it was no wonder that poor, feverish Lizzy was suffering.

Their mama had never prescribed such measures whenever the girls had come down with fevers. No, Mama had always cracked the window to let fresh air fill the room and had sent them to bed with a wet cloth draped over their eyes to help induce sleep.

"She is not getting better. Nothing you are doing is working!" Darcy boomed at Wendington.

The doctor stammered, "Mr. Dar-Darcy, all that can be done for Mrs. Darcy is being done. A fever is the body's attempt to stay alive. The only way to balance her humors is to sweat the fever out with fire, hot liquids, and blankets."

"But we are losing her!" Darcy's agonized voice rang painfully in Kitty's ears.

"Then Mr. Darcy, please relent and allow me to bleed her."

Darcy shoved Wendington away from Elizabeth's bedside. "You *will not* bleed her!" He ground out each word with force.

Kitty stepped forward and touched her fingertips to Lizzy's cheek. "She is so hot. Much too hot. We need to cool her down. She is so uncomfortable. Mr. Darcy, have mercy and let her be at ease."

Darcy turned his head slowly and regarded Kitty, his eyes vacant. "How?" he whispered.

"My mama says that when a fever comes, a body just wants to rest, so give it whatever it wants. Lizzy wants to be cooled down. Douse the fire for one, her body is hot enough without it. Throw open the windows. We will pour cool liquids down her throat. Order cold water up and let us bathe her skin."

"Absolutely not!" The doctor's eyes blazed. "You foolish girl! Do you presume to know more than a man of medicine? Your treatment would cause Mrs. Darcy certain and quick death." The man turned his back on Kitty and addressed the master of the house. "Mr. Darcy, I understand that you are greatly grieved and that you want what is best for Mrs. Darcy. I must bleed her immediately."

Anger flickered in Darcy's eyes and he exploded. "Do you really believe you understand? My entire reason for existing hangs in the balance, and you say you understand. You would have to kill me before I let you bleed her. Butcher! You are dismissed. Leave us; there is nothing left for you to accomplish here. If my wife is to die, she will do so in comfort."

Aghast, the doctor gathered his things and left the room.

Darcy turned and caught up both of Kitty's hands. "Instruct me, Sister; tell me what we should do for Elizabeth."

———

Her back aching from kneeling on the ground all night, Kitty was holding Elizabeth's hand when her sister's eyes fluttered open. Kitty put her hand to Lizzy's forehead—cool and dry. The fever had broken.

"Good morning, Sister." Kitty whispered.

"I do not ache anymore." Lizzy's voice was raspy.

Kitty smiled. "You are out of danger. Let me wake your husband." She nodded her head toward the chair Darcy was sleeping in. His lips, even in slumber, formed a grim line, and deep, dark circles were evident under his eyes. She knew exhaustion must show in her own face as well.

Kitty and Darcy had spent the entire night awake, removing cloths from Elizabeth's brow the moment they became warm and replacing them with cold ones, bathing her skin to bring down the temperature, and spooning cold water down her throat. Near four in the morning, Kitty had told Darcy he was no help to her because growing weariness made him clumsy. He had fought her, but in the end had collapsed into the chair beside the bed, where he still remained.

Crawling toward the chair, Kitty laid her hand on his forearm and whispered, "Mr. Darcy, wake up. Your wife wishes to see you."

His eyes snapped open and he almost tripped over Kitty in an effort to get to the bed, where Lizzy regarded him with bright eyes.

Darcy laughed and gathered his wife in his arms. "You are well, aren't you?"

Elizabeth nodded.

"I can tell just by looking at you! I thought I had lost you and didn't know how I could live, but you are well and I love you more than ever. I will let you rest, my Wife, so you can regain your strength."

Smiling, Darcy clapped Kitty on the back, as if she were a schoolfellow. "Well done, Kitty! It looks as though your mama has some sense in her head, after all."

"Indeed, sir, it is there, just deeply buried behind all the shiny things that so easily distract her," Kitty said and grinned at him.

Taking a seat by Lizzy, Darcy took his wife's hand, and then his face became somber. "Forgive me. I should not have said that about Mrs. Bennet. Please do me the favor of never repeating it."

Kitty pretended to lock a bolt over her mouth and nodded. "Your words will die with me, Mr. Darcy."

"Then, Sister, I pray that you will have to hold my secret a very many years."

⁂

Lord Chalmer crossed the room when Kitty entered. It was a good thing Mrs. Darcy had recovered, because if she had not, then marrying Miss Bennet would be pointless. Darcy would have had no reason to care about Catherine Bennet's welfare if they were no longer related. He would have no temptation to pay all of Albert's debts—and now, more than ever, Albert sorely needed those debts paid.

"My dear Miss Bennet, may I say how much joy it gives me to wish you well now that your sister is mending." Albert took up Kitty's hands in his own. He thought back to the day she had caught him with Alice, and he knew he had made a right brumblebroth of his courtship with her. But he would right it now, assure her of his love and remind her how much pin money he could afford her once they were wed. And if that didn't work, he could always carry her off to Scotland by force and marry her there, where the laws were loose.

She seemed to hesitate as she bit her lower lip. That was all right with Chalmer; better a quiet wife than one who would challenge him at every turn.

He pulled himself up to his full height and began: "Miss Bennet, I need only your consent and I will ride today to acquire a special license for us to marry. Now that your sister is in good health, I believe our wedding should not be delayed another day longer."

He felt her try to remove her hands from his grasp, but he didn't allow it. A woman needed to learn to be obedient to her husband, and the child might as well get her first lesson now.

"Please, Lord Chalmer, let go. I cannot believe a word you say. You do not wish to wed me, not truly. I do not understand why you press your suit." She inched toward the door, but he moved and slammed it shut.

Enough of these niceties! There are ways...things I could do to her to make her wed me and ensure that Darcy forces a marriage as well. The thought spurred him to act.

"Kitty, I have tried to reason with you, but enough is enough. I am through with reasoning, because you are beyond it." He grabbed her wrist and dragged her across the room, tossing her bodily onto the couch. As he came down upon her, she screamed.

"Shut up." He yanked the edge of her dress down off her shoulder. She was a pretty little thing, so the act wouldn't be odious. "Because you will not relent, I will simply have to take you." He kissed her collarbone, at the same time securing her flailing arms.

"You see, Darcy has all the money in the world, and I need it, and I need you to secure it for me."

"Help!" Kitty shouted at such a decibel that he released her for a moment to cover his ears. She pushed against him and made to run, but he was quicker, and grabbed her hair, yanking her backward.

The ruckus distracted him, so he did not hear the door erupt open, nor did he know that Darcy was charging across the room until the man jerked him back with impressive force and threw Albert down to the ground. Darcy moved and stood between Albert and Kitty, becoming a formidable shield.

"You are to leave my house and never return. You are to never write to me or speak to me again. Leave now, before I summon a constable." Darcy's normally soft voice held a very hard edge.

Albert rose from the ground, making sure his hands were up in mock surrender. "Now, now, old chap, the girl was begging me. We are to be married, Kitty and I. I am to be tied to you forever, Darcy."

"Not while I live," Darcy growled.

"But Darcy, you cannot throw me out; you made a promise," Chalmer said, reminding him of the stupid oath Darcy's pride had forced him to keep all these years.

"Hang the promise! I have paid you back a hundred times, and I am sick of your face. Out of my house this instant! Or I will have you thrown in jail. I am the magistrate and I promise I will not be an impartial judge."

"Miss Bennet, are you sure you're all right? We could call a doctor." Mr. Denton sat in the chair across from Kitty as she tried to regain her composure.

She had not known he was in the house, meeting with Darcy, until he rushed into the room while Mr. Darcy was yelling at Lord

Chalmer. The ever-considerate Denton had come to her side and held her hand. He had spoken to her in his calm, reassuring manner, telling her she was safe now.

And that was it.

As he held her hand while her brother-in-law yanked Albert out of the room, it came to Kitty that Mr. Denton was the only man she wanted to spend the rest of her days with. If she couldn't be with this kind man, then she'd be a spinster.

For the longest time, she had thought she needed a wealthy man in order to live comfortably. She had dreamed of a man who could provide her with fine horses, fashionable bonnets, and vacations abroad. But suddenly it came upon her that she cared not if she ever saw Vauxhall or shopped the stores on Bond Street. Once, those things had seemed so important, but she had been sorely wrong.

What she had wanted, and what she dearly needed, were two very different things.

She needed a man who was patient with her, one who drew out her secrets and wanted to know every inch of her mind. Kitty needed a man who would want her beside him in his labors, who enjoyed her company, and who looked forward to all their shared moments. She needed a man who loved her as she was.

"I need not a doctor, Mr. Denton, but I finally know what I do need."

He raised his eyebrows questioningly.

She swallowed hard.

"You."

"You need me? I am at your bidding. I will do anything for you, Miss Bennet," he answered, oblivious to her meaning.

"All this time, I have been blind and foolish, looking for my future in all the wrong places. And now I see that it is right before me, with you."

His expression changed to shock and his jaw dropped. "Are you sure? Could you care for me?"

"I do care for you very much, Mr. Denton. I believe I'm in love with you, though I realized it only just now."

Denton dropped to one knee. Taking Kitty's hand, he pressed a kiss to the back of her fingers that set her heart to pounding in her chest like a runaway carriage.

"I have loved you since the moment I saw you in that mud puddle. I wanted to scoop you up in that instant and take you home. I haven't much to my name, but I promise to adore you for the rest of our days. I love you, Kitty Bennet. Say you'll marry me."

A flood of warmth washed over her as she looked into the blue horizon of his eyes. "Yes. Of course." Her voice was only a whisper.

Denton let out a joyful laugh as he swept Kitty up in his arms. But then, a breath away from kissing her, the color drained from his cheeks. "But what of Darcy? Your brother will have my head. I should have spoken to him first."

"Mr. Darcy won't reject you. He cannot! He is your friend." Kitty gave Conrad's hand a reassuring squeeze.

"It is his right as your protector. I love you, but your brother knows I'm just a clergyman, Miss Bennett. You deserve a man of Darcy's circumstances. He can't possibly accept my suit."

"Hush. We'll make him see that you are the only man I could ever love."

A laugh at the door drew both Kitty and Conrad's attention. Darcy smiled broadly and strode forward. "Look at the two of you, presuming all manner of things about me."

Kitty spoke up. "Mr. Darcy, before you speak, I must tell you that Mr. Denton is the best man I have ever known, I *love* him."

Darcy nodded. "And Mr. Denton is exactly who I would pick for you Kitty. The union has my full consent."

Denton clasped Darcy's outstretched hand. "Thank you Mr. Darcy, I don't know what to say. I promise to treasure your sister forever. I don't deserve her or your blessing, but I will endeavor to live a life worthy of both."

"We'll run the banns this week and you shall be married by the end of the month." Darcy placed a hand on each of their shoulders as he spoke.

<hr>

Neither Darcy nor Kitty heard from Lord Chalmer or his mother again. There was a rumor that mother and son lived out the remainder of their days in America, but who could give credence to such an outlandish report?

Mr. Darcy was true to his word. Kitty became Mrs. Denton by the end of the month, and she filled every inch of Graceacre with her love and laughter.

On a warm summer's eve, Kitty and Conrad would sit in the gardens and watch their four children, playing in the woods with their three Darcy cousins. Occasionally, the six Bingley children could be found running among the same trees, sharing secrets and finding frogs with their relations.

At such times, Kitty would sigh and think of her wedding day. At precisely the moment that the couple were being pronounced man and wife, she knew that—for the first time in her life—she was number one in someone's heart.

And so she was, and remained.

A Good Vintage Whine

BY TESS QUINN

Tess Quinn is a right-brained individual working in a left-brained profession who writes fiction to feed her soul. A fan of Jane Austen since her first introduction at age thirteen, she indulges in what-if scenarios and exercises in character, and at present is working on her third novel-length piece. When not writing for fun, she gets equal pleasure from traveling wherever funds will take her, photography (though she's running out of wall space), or relaxing in a comfy chair with a good book, her cat, Fergie, in her lap, and a nice cup of Yorkshire Gold tea. She is a U.S. native currently living in New York, yet her heart often can be found in other places and times, mostly Regency England.

This short, humorous engagement story is based around a simple conceit (being locked somewhere) and what it does to people (makes them say things they normally would not).

❦

"Bingley, how on earth did you manage this?"

"I am sure I do not know, Darcy—it just…happened!"

"Well, stand aside, man, and let me try once more."

Bingley moved to the other side of the enclosure, well behind Darcy, and watched as that gentleman put all his concentration—not to mention his shoulder and considerable weight—into forcing the door to open.

"It is of no use!" He finally gave it up, rubbing his shoulder. "It will not budge; indeed, our attempts to force it, I believe, have only wedged the obstruction more tightly."

He glanced at his friend, laughing in spite of his own irritation at the panicked countenance Bingley wore, and said, "It appears we shall rest here yet a while then, until we may be discovered."

Despite Darcy's outward calm, Bingley was quite clearly agitated. "But...what if we are *not* discovered?" He looked around him frantically. "What if we are not missed and are confined here for days? How long can we survive? The air will become putrid—we have no food or water. What if there are rats—?"

He looked to go on indefinitely, his words coming faster and louder as he spoke. Darcy walked back to his friend and put his hands on Bingley's shoulders, holding them there with some steadying pressure until Bingley looked at him. "Get hold of yourself, Charles!"

"I beg your pardon, Darcy." He tried to settle his mind, to focus it upon his friend. "I am afraid I do not do well in confined spaces. I have not the temperament for it. I cannot think...cannot breathe." His eyes darted about the room. "We are lost—we shall expire here! What a singular turn of fate—just as I have secured my happiness, it is cut short!"

"Bingley!"

Having both silenced Bingley and drawn his attention yet again, Darcy set about to ease the man's nerves.

"Consider, man. We are hardly lost. We are in your own wine cellar, for pity's sake." He picked up a lamp from the nearby table and moved it slowly around. "We have a lamp—and spare," he added as he pointed the light toward candles resting on a low shelf. "It is only two hours or so until the Bennets arrive for dinner. Do not you think if we fail to appear by then, we should be searched out?"

"Do you truly believe it, Darcy? We will be found? Two hours?"

"Very likely sooner. The housekeeper will send a footman for wine for this evening; we could meet our rescuer at any moment." He added, "And you will have forgotten it all by the time you face your lady across the table."

"Oh! Yes, of course. My gratitude, Darcy, you have indeed put my mind at rest." Bingley calmed somewhat at that, though he could not fully relax.

Darcy guided Bingley over to the table and into a chair to await their rescue. He had not been completely truthful. Keeping the man calm, for both their sakes, had forced him to give in to a little falsehood. He rather thought any wines or spirits for this evening's dining would already have been collected for the decanting of those which required it. It could well take the failure of their appearance when guests arrived to initiate a search for Darcy and Bingley. The best hope was that, on discovering them missing, some servant or other might recall having seen them descend to the wine cellar. Darcy was certain they would be detected, but not so assured of its imminence. They could be here for some while. And the last thing either of them needed in their close quarters was an outbreak of hysterics.

Now that he had somewhat assuaged Bingley's fears, he wanted a diversion to maintain the calm.

"Shall we?" he asked, pointing to the row upon row of libations around them.

"What?" Looking up from the table, Bingley caught Darcy's meaning. "Oh! Yes, I suppose we may as well. Pick what you like; it is all the same to me at the moment."

Darcy had only just arrived back at Netherfield, having been in town the past several days, when Bingley returned from an afternoon of shooting. Darcy had not been expected for another two days, but Bingley's welcome was warm. Bingley wasted little time in confirming that an engagement had been formed between himself and Miss Bennet; whereupon he added that he expected the Bennet family to dine that evening and was delighted that Darcy would now join their party. Darcy's own delight, had Bingley but known it, was tempered by anxiety about how his presence might be received by that family—and one member of it particularly—given the regrettable events of the day before.

They were disheveled from their activities—Bingley from the hunt and Darcy from the dust of the road—and determined that, as each must bathe and change his attire, they might as well dress early for dinner. Upon doing so, they then met in the billiard room, where, over a game, Bingley asked Darcy for his assistance. He wished to select a particularly fine port for Mr. Bennet's enjoyment after dinner. And so, armed with glasses and a wine screw—for which Darcy now silently thanked Providence—the two men had ventured down into Netherfield's cellars. They had only begun to peruse the casks and shelves when the heavy door had in some manner broken free of its holding latch and slammed shut. The loud clatter which immediately followed suggested that something additional had dislodged and fallen across the door as well, resulting in their present predicament.

Darcy passed by the port now—their situation called for something slightly less heavy—and settled at last upon a pinot noir of good vintage. Bingley watched him as he took up a nearby rag to wipe the bottle of its fine coating of dust. He inspected the cork down in the neck before applying the screw to it; it came free a moment later with a satisfying *puh*.

He filled the two glasses and placed one in front of Bingley on the table. Placing the other glass across the table, he took a seat in one of the remaining two chairs. Another chair lay in pieces on the floor at the entry. Bingley had employed it unsuccessfully to ram the door. *Blasted English oak!* thought Darcy. *It could withstand any barrage.*

Bingley had continued to follow Darcy's every action with concentration, as if only the sight of his friend could keep his own alarm at bay. Now, as they sat together, they raised their glasses.

"To your happiness, sir!" said Darcy.

"To an early release!" replied his friend. "That will ensure my happiness!" Both laughed, though Bingley's held an element of nervous disposition.

Oh, blast, thought Darcy. *I must take his mind from this imprisonment.* Reaching into the interior pocket of his coat, Darcy brought out a small book. He offered it to Bingley.

"Poetry, Darcy? You surprise me, I confess."

"I comprehend no reason for your astonishment. I read a great variety of material—treatises, essays, and, yes, poetry—even, if you will credit it, the occasional novel."

"I do credit it, all of it," replied his friend. "I know you to be a great reader. Nonetheless, I find it a revelation that you carry verse in your pocket."

"It is Cowper—lyrical without being too maudlin or sentimental, for the most part." He added, "The nature of verse allows one to peruse it in brief moments of idleness." He stopped, considered again, and said, "Must I justify my choice of reading to you, Bingley? Do you desire the book or no?"

Bingley took it then. He opened it at random, somewhere in its middle, and began to read, moving his lips as he went through the words. After only a moment, however, he broke off and handed the diversion back. "It is no good, Darcy. You know I am not much for reading at the best of times."

Darcy began to return the book to his pocket when Bingley added, "Perhaps if *you* were to read it, Darcy—*to* me. I might find more comfort in hearing the verse spoken aloud."

Darcy regarded Bingley incredulously, prepared to offer a caustic remark; but he was met with an earnest appeal in the man's eyes. At length, he sighed, flipped through the small book to a random work, and, stopping first to refill their glasses, he began to read:

"Ask what is human life—the sage replies, / With disappointment lowering in his eyes, / A painful passage o'er a restless flood, / A vain pursuit of fugitive false good, / A scene of fancied bliss and heartfelt care, / Closing at last in darkness and despair..."

Darcy glanced up at Bingley and saw that perhaps this was not the selection to soothe his breast. He moved forward through several pages and settled upon an offering a bit lighter in tone, first slaking the thirst his exercise had induced before beginning again.

"Though nature weigh our talents, and dispense / To every man his modicum of sense, / And Conversation in its better part / May be esteem'd a gift, and not an art, / Yet much depends, as in the tiller's toil, / On culture, and the sowing of the soil."

This was better—Cowper's observations of a less dire nature:

"Words learn'd by rote a parrot may rehearse, / But talking is not always to converse; / Not more distinct from harmony divine, / The constant creaking of a country sign. / As alphabets in ivory employ, / Hour after hour, the yet unletter'd boy, / Sorting and

puzzling with a deal of glee / Those seeds of science call'd his A B C; / So language in the mouths of the adult, / Witness its insignificant result, / Too often proves an implement of play, / A toy to sport with, and pass time away."

Darcy's deep, well-modulated voice and the cadence of his recitation did appear to assuage Bingley somewhat, and so he continued, breaking off now and again only to taste of his wine.

When Darcy had finished *Conversation*, for which he received the compliments of his audience for his measured recitation, he filled their glasses yet again and moved on to *The Task*; but soon he noted that Bingley's interest—and, indeed, his own—had waned considerably. "Shall I go on reading?"

"No. I thank you, Darcy; I feel I have had enough poetry for one afternoon." He gave it thought a moment before adding, "Do you know, I do not understand the penchant for this poem. The first you read, I found superior; it had a pattern to it, at the least. But this latter one—what purpose can there be in calling it poetry if the composer can stop and start wherever he pleases? I believe even I could write such lines without the onus of forming rhymes. But then what would be the *point*?"

Read aloud he might, but Darcy was not inclined to lecture on the merits of free verse, nor the delight that Lady Austen took from it, at whose request *The Task* had been written. He did not offer reply of any sort, nor was one expected. Bingley had left the matter as soon as he had raised it. Darcy surreptitiously drew his watch from his pocket and glanced at it. An hour had elapsed since they were shut in the cellar. How many more must they endure before they would be found?

Rising, he took a lamp and returned to the shelves, selecting a second bottle identical to the first. He opened it and set it on the table to settle in the air a few moments. Its bouquet was delightful, redolent of its black cherry undertones. Though full-bodied, it had a smooth texture that slid easily—and gratifyingly—down the throat.

"How long have we been here?" asked Bingley during the wine preparation. "Do you know, Darcy?"

"Mmm. Upward of an hour, I should think." He raised the first bottle, now empty. "Long enough to enjoy this," he said and laughed.

Bingley laughed as well, but with trepidation. Darcy sat down again and, to divert his friend, said, "Tell me. You have secured the hand of Miss Bennet. How did you go about it? When I departed for London, you were yet hesitant in your address of her."

In truth, Darcy cared little for the details of Bingley's courtship with Jane Bennet beyond that it had been put to rights, as had their own friendship once Bingley had forgiven Darcy's part in the couple's separation of several months. But it was a topic sure to draw Bingley's full attention and thus draw the same away from their continued incarceration.

"I can tell you that I am glad to have the thing decided!" said Bingley with a laugh. "I believe I resolved on at least three occasions—no, four—to offer to Miss Bennet. If I had endured one more supper with *Mrs.* Bennet without its being settled, I am certain I should have gone mad." He smiled as he recalled his lady. "She is most beautiful, Darcy, is not she?"

"Mrs. Bennet?" The name had been pronounced with wry amusement as Darcy poured servings from the second pinot noir, but Bingley took his friend's question seriously.

"*Good God, no*, man! It is of *Miss* Bennet that I speak!" He looked at Darcy in some astonishment until he realized the man was making sport. The smile returned, along with a dreamy mooning: "My Jane…"

"Indeed, she is very fair. You deserve no less." Raising his wine glass, he added, "To Miss Bennet, soon to become Mrs. Bingley!"

"To Miss Bennet!" Bingley could hardly drink without dribbling, so wide was the smile upon his countenance.

"It was torturous, Darcy. To be so near and yet feel so far removed from my beauty, simply for want of words."

Darcy nodded sagely. "I gather a constant audience did little to free your tongue."

"Indeed. Although…in truth I cannot lay blame at any feet but my own. Mrs. Bennet hinted for me to get on with it at every turn, and then contrived pointedly with each of my visits to arrange for my privacy with Miss Bennet. On each occasion, the echo of her hints —*Mrs.* Bennet's hints, that is—lodged the words in my chest. Blasted awkward, it was."

Bingley went on, sighing at the memory of it. "And when the words would come to me, there was always some sister about. I tell you, Darcy, but for the love of my Jane…well, it would have been akin to living in a…a ribbon emporium!"

Darcy laughed. "And Mr. Bennet? Surely, there could be little doubt of your design with such studious attendance upon them. Did he nothing by way of advancing your suit?"

"I scarcely saw him, in truth. He closets himself in his study during the day, and escapes to it again directly when dinner concludes."

If he could not condone his actions, he could at least understand Mr. Bennet's motives in such a household. But did not the gentleman see that to further an understanding between his daughter and Bingley would be greatly to his own advantage?

"I might still have failed to speak, were it not for Miss Elizabeth!" added Bingley.

"Miss Elizabeth Bennet?" Darcy, who had been listening idly to his friend's recounting, now gave him his full attention. Indeed, up to that point, as Bingley had related his tale, his friend had given half his thoughts to that young lady. She was never far from his consciousness these months past; and events of the preceding day had only escalated the frequency and intensity of his imaginings. It was she, in fact, who had precipitated his early return to Netherfield. He struggled now to put aside those thoughts and listen to Bingley, who had already begun his explanation.

"...nothing she said, but I am certain she saw the situation with clarity. Soon after tea, she excused herself to go into another room to write a letter. A ruse, I suspect."

"A letter? And this loosed your tongue and your resolve?" Darcy asked, jealously wondering to whom the lady wrote.

The two men had been draining and refilling their glasses whilst the one had been reliving his proposal. By now, a third bottle had found its way to the table and stood awaiting their attentions. Bingley applied the screw to it as he continued.

"No, no. But as she passed, she gazed upon me directly and smiled, Darcy. The simple gesture carried such an understanding—such earnest friendship—that it provided me the encouragement, indeed, all the fortitude I had been lacking. Imagine that, Darcy. Nothing more than a smile!"

Darcy could imagine it with ease, particularly the smile of that lady. It had been etched in his mind since the day they had met by accident at Pemberley two months earlier, when he himself had been a shocked and grateful recipient of Elizabeth Bennet's smile. He smiled now, recalling it. Bingley took no notice, however, of any alteration in Darcy's mien, being intent on the task of pouring their libations as he continued.

"We had been establishing a table for cards at the time, but immediately upon Elizabeth's departure, Mrs. Bennet herself recalled some errand or other and begged that we postpone our play for a few moments only; and shortly thereafter, she required the assistance of Miss Catherine and Miss Mary."

At Darcy's sideways glance, Bingley said, "Oh, I comprehend that it was yet another of her attempts to push me along. I am not a perfect fool. But it was done with less preamble—less nonsense, if you will—such that on this occasion, it did not put me from my purpose."

Darcy poured another glass for each of them as he asked, "And the lady herself? How did Miss Bennet compose herself through these myriad moments of privacy?"

"Oh, Darcy! She was the very example of decorum. At first when left to ourselves, she was a bit quiet, shy of her relations' presumptions. I am quite sure it did not help when I flustered about as well. But once we moved past believing any understanding would be ventured, she was sweetness itself and I found my own manner yet again."

Darcy could wonder if the lady had indeed been as serene as his friend suggested, but it would serve no purpose to question, as the issue had been resolved successfully.

"Hic!—Oh, Darcy, forgive me," said Bingley, as he placed his empty glass on the table. He sighed.

"Do you know, Darcy, ladies are the strangest of creatures. As delightful as they are, I wonder if I will ever understand them."

"Why is that, Bingley?"

"Do you know, when at last I screwed up my courage and professed my love to Jane, what she did?"

Now that he had at last come to describing the proposal, Darcy tried to give him his full attention. "What did she do?"

"She cried, Darcy! She cried!"

"She cried?" repeated Darcy. "How extraordinary. Did she offer you no immediate answer?"

"No! And that is the wonder of it!" Bingley's countenance took on a moment's beleaguered sadness before brightening yet again. "She could not speak for the tears, and I began to wonder if I had misread her affections after all and placed her in the awful circumstance of having to reject me kindly." His eyes softened as he thought of Jane. "I could not have borne it, Darcy. I adore her with complete abandon."

Darcy smiled with understanding from having borne such disappointment himself. "But how did you finally arrive at a settlement, then?"

"She noted my alarm growing and managed to stammer out a yes, hesitated, and then said yes again with more force. I tell you, Darcy, I was beside myself with joy to hear that one small word."

That one small word thought Darcy. *I wonder if...* Suddenly, he felt very tired, as if he were an old man. His friend, on the other hand, was wound tight as a clock spring with his joy. Darcy once more pulled his watch out and squinted to see the face clearly: another circuit of the hands and more. They had now been in the wretched cellar well over two hours. The Bennets would arrive at any moment, expecting dinner with their new son. Miss Elizabeth could be there even now, at Netherfield, little knowing and perhaps little caring that Darcy sat, consumed by thoughts of her, so near.

"I gave Miss Bennet my handkerchief, and once the tears sub-, er, subseed, er, subsided—do you know, that is a dashed hard word to say—when once that was got past, she told me she loved me, Darcy, has done all along."

"I am truly happy for you, sir. Very happy, indeed." Darcy forced a smile for his friend's good fortune and raised his glass yet again. "To Miss Bennet."

"Does it grow cold in here, Darcy?" asked Bingley some while later. "I wonder, could you ring for the fire to be lit? I am not secure in my legs, I think, to do so."

Darcy frowned and looked about him. "There does not appear to *be* a fire here, Bingley." He looked around once more. "For that matter, there is no servant bell."

"Ah! A pity, is not it? I believe I could find this room quite homely if only it held the addition of a fire."

His friend only grunted by way of reply, his attention now claimed by the precarious task of replacing a spent taper in their lamp with a fresh one without losing the flame. For the moment, it required all his concentration, as his fingers for some reason fumbled about, having swelled to twice their customary thickness.

That task finally accomplished, Darcy accepted another glass of wine from his friend. "To what shall we drink now?"

"Hmm..." Bingley's face screwed up to consider this important decision. Then suddenly, his countenance cleared as inspiration was found, and with great satisfaction he proclaimed, "To a fire!" and lapsed into a fit of giggles at his own cleverness.

Darcy scowled but he raised his glass and drank nonetheless.

"Bingley, I believe you are in your cups...well, inebriated, at the least. Perhaps we should make this our last," he said as he raised the bottle and noted with surprise that it, too, was empty.

"Nonsense!" cried Bingley. "I am as sober as you!"

They considered the statement a moment, pronouncing it acceptable finally before Bingley offered, "But we should exercise care, I daresay; we shall be called to dine soon."

Darcy nodded by way of reply, and then picked up his glass and drained it. "Right, then. It is enough."

Bingley followed his example. The two sat then, staring alternately at their glasses and the empty bottles, fingers tapping the tabletop, until Bingley offered, "One more, do you think? If we change to a lighter grape, perhaps..."

"Yes, of course! A lighter grape..." Darcy stood and then placed his hands upon the table for support a moment before carefully approaching the shelves. His gaze moved down them slowly. He squinted and peered at labels before selecting a bottle and returning to his seat. When he had some difficulty in aligning the wine screw, Bingley moved to assist him. He held the bottle firmly on the table whilst Darcy, with two hands gripping the screw, guided it to the cork; after several attempts, the bottle was opened.

"This looks remarkably like the wine we had earlier, Darcy, does it not?" Bingley was studying his glass near the lamplight.

"No," chided Darcy, swirling the garnet liquid in his own glass. "They are nothing near alike. Our former were pinot noir, and this..." He read closely the bottle's label. "*This* is a pinot noir. There, you see?" He gestured at Bingley's wine.

"Ah yes, of course. My mistake. I beg your pardon."

———◦◦◦◦———

"To Miss Elizabeth Bennet!" offered Darcy as they raised full glasses yet again.

"Miss Elizabeth Benhic..." Bingley met the toast and drank, but then frowned as he considered what he had heard. "No, no, Darcy, surely you mean Miss Jane Bennnn…" He studied his friend and, smiling then, repeated, "My Jane."

"No, no." Darcy waved his finger from side to side. "I must object, Bingley. Miss Jane Bennet is indeed your sweet lady, but we have drunk to her enough, I think. I wish now to drink to *my* lady! My lively, lovely Elizabeth and her fine eyes!"

Bingley's elbows rested on the table, and he leaned forward on them now. He stared at his friend across the short distance, attempting to make sense of what he had just heard. Darcy took no notice, his own eyes gazing into his glass as though he could see *her* countenance within the deep, rich spirits. His lips were turned up in a distracted manner that Bingley took for a smile.

When Darcy raised his glass to drink yet again, he noticed his cell mate. "Bingley, your jaw hangs down nearly to the table. Are you ill, man?"

Bingley promptly closed his mouth, which act allowed him speech again. "*Your* lady?"

"*My* lady? My lady who?" He chuckled on his repetition, finding it enormously humorous as the sound filled the room.

"Darcy! Did not you claim just now my Jane's sister Elizabeth Bennet for your own? Could I have mistaken my ears?"

"No one could mistake your ears," his friend said, laughing as he pointed at the organs under review. "They turn as red as your hair when you imbibe too much."

Bingley's hands flew to his ears immediately to seek truth in Darcy's claim. "*Do* they?" He pulled on his lobes, holding them extended between thumb and finger whilst trying unsuccessfully to inspect them from his side vision, as he added, "They do not feel warm. Indeed, they do not *feel,* Darcy. I have lost all sensation in them."

Darcy snorted at this pronouncement. But immediately after, his expression sobered; his mien became doleful as he said, "Would that *I* could lose all sensation, my friend. For I am in a miserable state."

"You are ill?"

"Yes!" Darcy curled his frame over and rested his brow atop the table. "I am sick with love, Bingley."

"Sick with *what?* I cannot hear if you speak into the table, man."

"Love, Bingley." He sat up again. "*Love!*" He winced at the volume of his proclamation. "There is no hope for me. I am doomed. '*A painful passage o'er a restless flood,...Closing at last in darkness and despair.*' Such is my allotment."

"Do you mean...Miss Bennet?" Bingley screwed up his face as he said this, testing the possibility. "Miss *Elizabeth* Ben——?"

"The very same. My Elizabeth Bennet. Elizabeth. Lizshy." He tried out the diminutive name, but it felt awkward.

"But...that is wonderful news, man. I had no idea of it——it is...a wonder!"

"But for the complication that she despises me, I might agree."

"No! *Despise* you? I hardly can credit such a thing."

"It is so, Bingley. And I have only myself to blame for it. I do not deserve her estimation."

"Nonsense! You are the best of men——"

"No——I have behaved dreadfully toward her."

When Bingley once more began to demur, Darcy launched into his tale of woe. He acknowledged first his haughty disdain on his and Bingley's initial foray into Hertfordshire a year past, a recital Bingley could not but concede to have a measure of truth in it by his own recollection. Then began a slow rendering of Darcy's growing admiration of Miss Elizabeth Bennet even as Bingley was making

love to her sister; his reacquaintance with her in Kent the preceding Easter and the realization that he must act to secure her hand.
Bingley sat rapt throughout the singular recounting, hardly able to
take in his friend's words.

"Darcy. I have had no inkling of your sentiments these past
months. My poor friend!"

"No, do not pity me, Bingley, for I am undeserving of such goodwill after my actions to separate you from your own lady. I was
wrong to do so."

"Darcy, you know, surely you must know, that is all resolved; I
have long dropped the matter."

"Ah! But you do not know all, you see. I did not admit of it
before; my...confession...to you was not complete." He paused,
grimaced, and then said, "My actions damned me all the more for
having attempted to gain for myself what I withheld from you."

Bingley regarded Darcy quizzically whilst his friend's gaze
moved to a knothole in the table's surface, his countenance reflect-
ing pain at the memory until finally he roused himself to regard
Bingley again.

He sighed softly. "I proposed to her, Bingley...there in Kent this
past April."

"Did you?" Bingley asked with benign interest until his faculties gave meaning to the utterance, and then: "Darcy! You *proposed
marriage?*"

"Indeed I did, sir. Most abominably, but nonetheless I sought a
match similar to that which I denied you. Do you see now what a
wretched friend I have been?"

"But..." Bingley was at a loss. Finally, he stammered, "How...
what did she—"

"She upbraided me most efficash...violently." As Bingley
had made no more of his own injury at his friend's hands, Darcy

continued, telling Bingley of the horror of his realization that the woman he esteemed so highly—loved most ardently looked upon him in the worst possible manner. Bingley listened with all the attention at his disposal.

"Darcy, I do not understand. What you describe is grave, indeed—"

"Indeed. She forced me to look at myself; I could not admire what I found."

"But…" Bingley struggled with his memory a moment to frame his question. "But did not you entertain Miss Elizabeth at Pemberley not two months past? I did not guess—could not have done—of any bad blood between you! Do you jest with me?"

Darcy took a long drink from his just-replenished wine and then admitted of more—of his letter to Miss Elizabeth Bennet (though not all its contents) and the effects it must have had in softening that lady's regard for him; of his anxious joy at their accidental meeting in Derbyshire; and of his renewed hope of a change of her heart before the crisis of Lydia Bennet's elopement had once more separated them, it seemed forever and without hope.

"No, Darcy, this will not do! If you love her, truly love her, can you now hold against her the sister's shame? The circumstance, as I have it, was sufficiently resolved, was not it? You *cannot* despise Miss Bennet, yet—"

"By God, *no*! Indeed, I—" Darcy stopped suddenly and could not go on. He had nearly betrayed information he had determined never to make public, not even to Bingley.

"Ah. P'raps I understand."

"*Do* you, Bingley?"

"It is Mr. Wickham."

Darcy's head snapped up at the name as his eyes fixed sharply upon Bingley.

"I know well your dislike—your abhorrence—of the man, Darcy, but—"

"Charsh, you know *nothing* of it."

His friend quieted at that, and Darcy put his head into his hands, with his eyes closed and his face drawn tight in anguish. Finally:

"I love her, Bingley. I love her. And nothing...not her odious mother nor her silly sisters nor her lack of fortune, no, not even... *Wickham*...would keep me from renewing my suit—but the lady herself does not wish it."

"Do you know this? How is it you know this?"

"Do you forget, Charles, our calls upon the Bennets these weeks past?"

"Of course not—you attended me to make determination of my Jane's affections, as well as my own—"

Darcy wagged his finger again at his friend. "No, Bingley, no. Or rather, it is true after a fashion. But I had other motive as well. I wished to judge if there was any hope to be had with Miss Elizabeth."

With a longing look at his empty glass, Darcy slumped in his seat. Bingley waited expectantly, but no further communication was forthcoming.

"Darcy?"

"Yes, Bingley?"

"What did you conclude?"

"When?"

"When we called upon Longbourn!" Bingley threw up his hands in exasperation, nearly toppling his chair with the gesture. Both men winced at the scraping sound of its restitution.

"It is no use, Bingley. She cannot care for me." He held his head up then and looked at his friend, his eyes miserable in the light of the lamp.

"Was she not civil to you? How do you draw such a conclusion? I confess I was too enamored of my Jane to take particular note, but I recall no unpleasantness."

"No, no unpleasantness; her manners are too well schooled for such." His face fell.

"But I found no encouragement, Bingley, no renewal of the amiability we enjoyed in Derbyshire, in her words or in her looks. Indeed, we hardly spoke but for the 'civilities' of our comings and goings. I could take no encouragement from our few discourses. I am certain she accorded me her attentions only on the basis of my being *your* friend. You must have noted the differences in the welcomes afforded us generally."

"But Darcy! Could you let the matter drop on such small judgment? Can you be so certain of her opinion?"

"There is yet more to my miserable tale of unrequited regard, Bingley."

"More?"

Darcy sighed with resignation. "Only yesternight, my aunt— Lady Catherine de Bourgh —accosted me at home in town, in a high dudgeon."

"Lady...? But—she was *here!* Or rather, at Longbourn."

"Indeed, it was her call upon Miss Bennet yesterday that she wished to report to me."

"But we—none of us—could make sense of it, Darcy. She simply appeared in all her state, held converse with Miss Elizabeth in private, and departed again—and Miss Elizabeth would not divulge their discourse."

"Shall I reveal it to you, Bingley?" He proceeded to detail Lady Catherine's attack on Miss Bennet, as his aunt had recounted it.

"Oh, my. How perfectly horrid that must have been for Miss Elizabeth—and she never said a word."

"No, I imagine she would not. But do not you see now, Bingley, the hopelessness of my situation? Miss Bennet can only despise me after this treatment at the hands of my relation. The tenuous goodwill we established this summer could not survive such an onslaught." He stared at his hands on the table, confusion on his face, and whispered nearly to himself: "And yet she refused her, Bingley..."

"Refused her?"

"Mmm. Refused to make a promise to my aunt never to enter into an engagement with me. But does this mean that there is yet some hope, no matter how small? Or was she simply being obstinate in the face of an odious challenge? You must admit Miss Bennet to be capable of such obstinacy."

Bingley grimly nodded his head.

Darcy laughed hoarsely, and his voice nearly broke as he added: "I cannot continue without some resolve. I had to come immediately. I must know, for good or ill. Had I set aside my pride, my reserve—had I spoken sooner, in Derbyshire some weeks ago perhaps...but I fear it is too late. I am half hope, half agony. My feelings have not changed; I admire and love her and would have her for my wife. I had hoped with Lydia settled and your understanding with Jane concluded, that proximity to Miss Bennet might allow me to make further amends to her. But this...this *outrage* of my aunt's! I believe it to be more than can be overcome."

Darcy had come to the end of his tale. In the ensuing silence, Bingley concentrated for some time before adding, "But just this morning, she asked after you."

"Did she?"

"Yes, or...well...I believe it was she, was not it?"

"Bingley! Think, man! This is critical to me. Was it Miss Elizabeth? What was her manner?"

"Yes, yes, all right. I am certain it was she." He closed his eyes tightly to help him remember. "Yes, yes, it was, and she was all civility. She asked me if you still intended to return to Netherfield soon..."

The sun shone brightly as Bingley and Darcy approached the lane to the Bennet house—a little too brightly, perhaps, for their preference that morning. They squinted as they walked to relieve the sun's assault on strained eyes. Bingley's carriage had, by his direction, set down the gentlemen at the top of the turn to Longbourn, both men admitting that a bit of air and exercise would well serve to prepare them for the coming meeting. Their rescue from Bingley's cellar had come eleven hours after their incarceration—and, if it may be revealed, seven bottles of wine had been consumed in the interval without the benefit of food to offset its effects.

When Mr. Bennet and his family had arrived for their dinner engagement and Bingley did not appear to greet them, Mrs. Nicholls undertook to discover his whereabouts. No one could recall having seen him for some time, and his man, Hodge, who had been given the evening for his leisure after Bingley had dressed, was visiting away from Netherfield and could not be applied to for intelligence. At last, a servant was found who suggested Mr. Bingley might have gone off with the man with whom he had been seen approaching the billiard room; but when questioned further by Mrs. Nicholls, the servant—who had been taken on only within the past fortnight—could not identify Bingley's companion, beyond that he was certainly dressed in the mode of a gentleman. He could offer no further description, as his own concentration had been directed toward disappearing from the hallway at the master's approach, so that he himself would not be seen.

As no guests beyond the Bennet family had been expected for the evening, this new information carried with it as great a mystery as that of the master's whereabouts. Mrs. Nicholls took charge then, establishing the Bennets in the parlor with a footman to serve them drinks while the remaining staff began a search for Mr. Bingley and the unknown visitor. After an hour, the flustered housekeeper had the onerous task of returning to the parlor to report their lack of result, grieving at the understandable distress this caused the eldest Bennet daughter.

After much discussion, Mrs. Nicholls convinced her master's guests to adjourn to the dining room for dinner, providing assurances that she herself could not wholly trust that Mr. Bingley would arrive midcourse with some reasonable explanation for his tardy appearance. Such event did not transpire. Indeed, two courses came and went, and Mr. Bingley's absence was still felt.

Mr. Bennet seemed to quite enjoy his repast, acting for all the world as though nothing were amiss. His wife made amends for his indifference, spending the entire evening caterwauling about the effects of Mr. Bingley's neglect on her nerves and appetite, while said appetite became fully sated from the selection of meats, savouries, and vegetables appearing at each course. Miss Bennet, it need not be said, ate nothing, but sat staring in silence at her dishes in obvious distress. Miss Elizabeth Bennet ate but little and concerned her discourse with attempts to console her sister. Their sister Mary Bennet held forth on Mr. Bingley's breach of manners, while the youngest sister in attendance, Miss Catherine Bennet, offered that perhaps Mr. Bingley had changed his mind concerning his betrothal, and then, following a swift kick under the table from Miss Elizabeth Bennet, spoke no more but glowered at the table in front of her as she ate.

The family did not remain for dessert or coffee when, ninety minutes later, Mr. Bingley had still not appeared; rather, they called for their carriage and departed in various states of curiosity or anxiety, the entire departure narrated by Mrs. Bennet's high-pitched squawk.

Although Mrs. Nicholls was relieved at their departure, still the mystery of her master's whereabouts was yet to be resolved. A servant had been dispatched to Meryton at once on the discovery of Mr. Bingley's absence—a footman who could be trusted to approach inquiries with discretion, so as not to excite gossip   and he had returned, having discovered nothing. No one he had engaged in converse admitted to seeing his master that day. The house at Netherfield had been searched from ground floor to top, as well as the stables and gardens: what if Mr. Bingley had met with an accident and was incapable of calling out for assistance? As the evening wore into night, such thoughts came more frequently and with greater intensity.

In the wee hours of the morning, Mr. Bingley's man returned from his leave to a house in an uproar. One mystery he could solve. The gentleman with Mr. Bingley could be confirmed, in fact, as Mr. Darcy, who had returned before schedule from London. But this information did not offer intelligence as to where, indeed, these gentlemen might now be found. If anything, it compounded the confusion, being that he was not a visitor Mr. Bingley was likely to have left the estate with for any reason, nor had Mr. Bingley indicated any intention of going out until morning. It also occurred to Mrs. Nicholls that the heretofore imagined accident scene might be less likely, for which she was grateful, but for the fact that she now had *two* missing gentlemen to account for.

Subsequent to this intelligence, however, Mr. Darcy's customary suite of rooms—which had been prepared the day before in anticipation of his return in two days—was visited. His man, Grayson, was found in the dressing room, where he had rested in perfect ignorance, absorbed in reading a novel, since he had seen to his master some hours previous. A glance from the housekeeper was all it took for a maid to admit to neglecting to search these rooms initially, assuming that they were unoccupied. This spurred yet another full house search, leaving no room or closet untried. Immediately, Grayson joined in the search with the others.

Finally, when the house had been searched a third time, it occurred to a timid upstairs maid to ask if anyone had surveyed the cellars. The staff in attendance for this profound utterance looked at one another, shrugging and shaking their heads. At once, Mrs. Nicholls herself led two footmen and the valets to the cellars.

On first glance, nothing appeared amiss. They entered the main cellar in silence and heard no cries for help. Then, waving their lamps here and there as they approached, a footman noted a long iron bar lying across the entry to the wine room, and wedged into a corner in such a way as to have the effect of blocking the closet door. The lock itself had the kitchen key protruding from it. The footman tugged to remove the bar and—being unsuccessful on the first attempt, as it was stuck fast—he passed his lamp to Grayson and used two hands to finally yank the bar free.

Thus were Mr. Bingley and Mr. Darcy finally emancipated from their incarceration. Mrs. Nicholls opened the wine closet door and peered cautiously inside to find two gentlemen seated at the table in the center. They looked a fright—hair tumbled about, their ascots long discarded, and their coats lying on the floor next to them— and the gentlemen themselves languished across the table, resting on their elbows. At the entry of the valets, Bingley and Darcy both raised their heads and smiled in a slow, languorous manner, which suggested they were only marginally alert. Grayson and Hodge stepped in straightaway then to assist in escorting the gentlemen to their chambers. During their slow progress up the stairs, the housekeeper managed, between the two men, to hear an account of how they had come to be found there.

Despite their having been found after three in the morning, and their consumption of a significant amount of Bingley's pinot noir inventory, neither Bingley nor Darcy found himself able to sleep long once he was restored to his rooms. Both rose early after only a few hours; and, following extended attentions from their valets—including a celebrated concoction of Grayson's, which served to restore each to himself somewhat—the gentlemen determined to travel to Longbourn at the earliest moment in person. They had been grateful to find that Mrs. Nicholls had at once dispatched a messenger in the middle of the night to the Bennet family with word of the circumstances of Mr. Bingley's disappearance and subsequent restoration in good health. She admitted, however, that so flustered had she been at the entire episode that she had quite forgotten to mention Mr. Darcy in the missive.

And so the gentlemen found themselves now on the path to the Bennet residence, prepared to offer apologies and assurances of continued goodwill. Bingley could not wait to be reunited with his Jane, while Darcy held his hands together to keep them still as he pondered his likely reception by another Bennet daughter.

"Bingley," said Darcy as they approached the arched entry to the manor yard—having determined that he would speak with Miss Elizabeth Bennet this day, no matter the risk to his pride, and now wanting to take his mind from the less sanguine possible consequences of such discourse—"have you any recollection of how we passed the night?" His friend looked at him, and he clarified, "Surely, we must have done something—held some converse—during our detention; yet I confess myself unable to recall a single detail." He looked to Bingley with a quizzical brow.

"Do you know, Darcy," replied his friend after some concentration, "I have no idea!"

Georgiana's Voice
BY J. H. THOMPSON

J. H. Thompson grew up in St. Paul, Minnesota, as the second youngest of seven children. She began writing short stories at the age of twelve as a means to escape a torturous, spoiled little brother. In 1995, she married her high school sweetheart, and they lived briefly in Wisconsin before moving closer to their families. She has since made up with her little brother and now lives with her husband and two sons in Plymouth, Minnesota.

Many authors have tried to give voice to Georgiana Darcy, a character who is referenced far more than she appears in *Pride and Prejudice* but obviously had quite a bit of influence behind the scenes, particularly in the latter half of the book. Thompson's story, "Georgiana's Voice" is, in my opinion, one of the best attempts.

❧

Mr. Julius Pritchard is not the most well-known music master in the city of London, but every Tuesday, in a large and stylish townhouse in Portnam Square in London, he is hailed as the best. A servant of the Darcy family for twelve years, he knows the styles and preferences of his pupil well, and when he brings new pieces to be learned, it is always with the confidence that she will accept the challenge and, eventually, play the piece as it was meant to be played.

The girl is tall—quite too tall for her age—thin, and with sadly arranged brown hair. The room holds her one friend in the form of a well-used pianoforte, which she hammers at relentlessly. Poorly, too, for she is not paying attention to the music sheets. That girl is me—I am Georgiana Catherine Abigail Darcy.

I am waiting for Mr. Pritchard to arrive to deliver my lesson. This has always been the best part of my week, and I am especially eager to see him, as I have not had a proper lesson in more than three months. He believes that I no longer truly need his instruction, that my talent is natural and that as long as it is always nurtured in me, it will always exist. For my part, I at least believe that my love of music, if not my talent, is natural.

Mr. Pritchard has been my master since I first sat down at the keys. My only sibling, my brother Fitzwilliam, had chosen him for me after having had many complaints from my nurse that I would not stay out of the music room or away from the pianoforte. I was only four years old then; my mother had already passed away. With clarity I can recall the first time ever I played a piece right—some nursery song or other—and Fitzwilliam was there. My dear brother clapped and praised me and told me how well I had played. I really adore him; when I was a child I wanted to marry him.

When Mr. Pritchard comes in from the dreary London day I greet him fondly; he gives me one of those smiles that make me wish he were my grandfather. "Miss Darcy," he says, fluttering papers about, "I am quite gratified that you are returned from Ramsgate. I trust your stay there was all you hoped?"

I smile sadly and take his hand. "It was not, in fact; but let us not talk of it. What have you brought me?"

"If you are in a somber mood, Miss Darcy, perhaps the selection I have brought today is more appropriate than I knew." He smiles and flutters some music sheets in front of me. "Now, come and play.

You will enjoy the piece, I hope. But first, warm your fingers and play me something merry."

I sit next to him, and play a Mozart piece which I have known for many years, which he likes. When it is over he claps and praises, and I smile, for his sentiments are truly felt. How much easier things would be, if only everyone were as open and honest as Mr. Pritchard!

He bids me to play my new piece. I read the notes, one by one, and then I play the whole piece through, hearing the tick of the pendulum, the deep timbre of the notes, the slow progression of the piece, but not the music. Mr. Pritchard tells me to play it again. He has moved to the chaise to sit back and listen. "Truly, you are paid for nothing," I tease him.

"Play your lesson, Miss Darcy," he says, and tries to sound stern. I smirk and turn back to the instrument. "And listen when you play—oh, you will like this piece."

I play. The music is haunting—it is low and deliberate and each note rumbles in my stomach. I am carried away by the melody, melancholy rushing over and through me. Suddenly I am no longer in the music room, but away again—back in Ramsgate, where the ocean pounds the rocks and the air smells warm and salty; I am with him again—with the man who has, since I departed that place, haunted me with every step. I can feel his gentle hand upon my chin and his firm lips on mine; I can hear the tender words whispered in my ear. Silent tears roll down my cheeks.

I ought to be paying attention to the music sheets, but I cannot think and stumble several times. I cannot control the bent of my thoughts; they always turn toward him. I know he does not love me. In my head, I know. In my heart, though, I hope even still, for though I now understand that he never loved me as he professed to so passionately, I love him still. Oh...my heart aches for him.

The piece is over. Without looking up I ask who has written it, not hearing the answer. Mr. Pritchard touches my hand gently and leaves the house in Portnam Square.

———•◦•———

I clearly remember the day my father died. I was not yet twelve years old, and on that morning I had risen with the determination to go outside and walk, as I had not been allowed to for several days. Fitzwilliam came to my chamber before I was quite ready, and I recall being angry with him for that. I could never forget the words he said—"Georgiana, Papa died in the night..."—words delivered in such a low, soft voice as I had never before heard from him. My heart broke.

I simply cried for an hour straight. My brother, you see, does not lie and does not exaggerate, so any information he delivers, no matter how shocking, must be taken at face value. There was no need to question, reason, or see for myself. My Papa was gone, and the only two Darcys left in the world were young, devastated, and quite alone.

It was then that Fitzwilliam developed that controlled facade that I hate so much. I know the very moment it first appeared—right before he delivered the news to me. For a while, I really believed him as indifferent on the inside as he appeared on the outside. Then I learned to read his eyes—windows to the soul, Mrs. Reynolds (our housekeeper at Pemberley and a very dear woman) once told me. It could not be more true in the case of my brother. His face could be absolutely blank and yet if one were intuitive enough, one could read Fitzwilliam's eyes.

He almost always wears that infernal mask, but I have learned how to tell when he is teasing me, when he is frustrated, when he is tired, and when he is pleased. Very occasionally, when it is only the two of us together, I can get him to take it off—I can get him to open up and talk with me. These times are the only moments I truly spend with my brother. They are always very brief, but I cherish them with all my heart.

Tonight is one of those nights. The mask is definitely off, likely because he wishes to cheer me. He is just returned from Pemberley, and tomorrow he promises a visit from someone whom he says that I should like very much.

"Mrs. Priscilla Annesley is the widow, if you recall, of the late rector of Hunsford Parsonage. Our aunt disliked her greatly, so I am certain we shall find her a sensible woman. I have applied to her to visit, and if you like her, dear girl, you shall have a new companion."

I long to observe that I do not want a companion, but a sister; or, better still, to have my brother always with me. But I know that neither is very likely. "She is a young woman, if memory serves," I reply, looking into my tea. Then I look up, and with the expression on his face that begs for liveliness from me, I cannot help but oblige him a little. "Shall she try to charm you?"

He smirks. "As you well know, my dear sister, I am not easily charmed. And I do not think the widow of a clergyman would be quite suitable," he says. My face falls, but my brother does not know why, and he asks.

"Who would be suitable?" I ask him. "Who is good enough for you?"

He looks away, uncomfortable.

"There is no one good enough for you, Fitzwilliam," I say in absence of any reply from him, shaking my head and looking away. "What woman exists, among those who would be suitable, who does not fawn over you without having been acquainted with the fact of your fortune? And what man exists who will not hunt me for mine?"

He takes my chin in his hand. "These are questions too heavy for a girl your age," he says, sadness descending into his eyes. And then, carefully, he adds, "There are those whom I trust—honorable young men, with integrity, who are artless."

Knowing exactly of whom he speaks, I look away, not wanting to talk about Mr. Charles Bingley. At some point, I ought to marry and ease my brother of the burden of caring for me, and in the absence of a gentleman I might really esteem, Mr. Bingley is not an altogether bad option. Fitzwilliam *wants* Mr. Bingley to marry me; and though he is amiable enough, it is unlikely that Mr. Bingley would have me, despite the wishes of his awful sisters.

I wish that I could tell my brother this. I wish he would not hint at a marriage between his sister and his dearest friend. It is not because I do not like Mr. Bingley—he is kind and a good friend to my brother. It is, rather, that due to my knowing him most of my life, I do not think I could look upon him as anything but a brotherly figure. I am fortunate in that I am still young for marriage, despite what I may have thought some months ago. It will be another year at least before I am even out.

I dodge Fitzwilliam's comment. "And what about for you?" I ask.

"Do not worry for me," he replies. "A gentleman may stay unmarried far longer than a lady and still be considered eligible. I shall find someone, I am sure."

I take a sip of my tea and decide a change of subject is in order. "Has Lady Catherine found a suitable replacement for Mr. Annesley?" I ask, referring to the late rector of the parsonage connected with our aunt's estate.

"I believe Hunsford parsonage is again occupied, at last," he replies, smiling—a sure sign that he is grateful for the new topic. "Though I must admit I am not looking forward to meeting the man. His noble patroness *herself* has described him to me as a bit of a sycophant."

"That cannot be a good sign," I agree as my head fills with the image of a tall, rail-thin, elderly gentleman scraping his elbows whilst he follows after my aunt, which is just the sort of person Lady Catherine likes to have about.

"I shall meet him soon," continues my brother, reminding me of his unfortunate, but annual, invitation from Lady Catherine to spend Easter time visiting Rosings Park.

"Yes," I say, grateful that my presence is not required. "Please be sure to send me a full report."

"I am sure he cannot be so bad," says my brother. "You might ask Mrs. Annesley about him; she must have shown him the parsonage and introduced him to the servants."

"I beg you would forgive me if I should happen to forget," I say in reply. "But when you meet him, you must be sure to tell him how curious I am about him, and invite him to write me." My brother grins—a handsome sight. "I wish you would smile more often, Fitzwilliam."

For a moment, he looks as if he wants to say something further. He does not. The mask goes up and he returns to his tea.

———◦•◦———

When Mrs. Annesley arrives the next day, I am summoned to the sitting room. From the hallway a light, young voice can be heard mingling with my brother's; I pause before going in.

"She tends to be very shy," he is saying. This is not untrue, however much I wish it weren't pointed out. "She had a very troublesome summer at Ramsgate, which has caused her to withdraw even more, but I hope you will be able to help cure her of that."

I do not want her to hear the complete tale of my disgraceful summer, so quickly I pop my head round the corner to announce my presence.

I am a little astonished by what I see—Fitzwilliam is sitting rather closer to Mrs. Annesley than I would have imagined, and more surprising than anything, there is no mask. I smile at this, forgetting about Ramsgate or Mrs. Annesley's worth—for, I reason, if my brother can converse so openly with her, surely she can have nothing lacking. She smiles at me with lovely dark blonde curls framing her face.

My brother makes the introduction and we take tea. During the course of the conversation I say very little, but my brother and Mrs. Annesley talk openly about a number of subjects, mostly relating to my studies and my family. Familiar with my aunt, she inquires after the most senior member of the Fitzwilliam family, my uncle the earl, mostly curious about whether I am required to visit.

"It is likely that they will not issue Georgiana any invitations until she is of age," my brother informs her.

"Have you lately visited them, Miss Darcy?" asks Mrs. Annesley.

She directs the question at me particularly, with a quizzical look upon her kindly face. Fitzwilliam is looking at me the same way.

"I—I...have not, no," I stutter, looking earnestly at the forget-me-nots on my teacup. I glance upward, fully expecting them to fall into conversation between them again. They do not. They are looking at me—kindly, but *looking*. "Um...But...but my brother shall be visiting my aunt. He goes to Rosings each year...at about the same time of year."

"And will you take your sister, Mr. Darcy?" asks Mrs. Annesley, tilting her head toward him.

"I will visit my aunt with my cousin Colonel Fitzwilliam. We are always invited the week of Easter, for about three weeks."

There is again a pause in the conversation that makes me uncomfortable. "I understand you have met the new rector at Hunsford," I venture, looking up, but only a little.

Mrs. Annesley smiles. "Yes, I have. He is a peculiar creature, to be sure, but he suits Lady Catherine quite well. He is not yet married, but I am sure that will be rectified quickly, with your aunt's assistance."

My brother smiles. "She does love to be useful." He takes a final sip of his tea and then sets the cup back down, addressing Mrs. Annesley again. "I am afraid I have some time scheduled with my solicitor, to discuss some business that I have been putting off longer than he would like. Georgiana, would you be so kind as to give Mrs. Annesley a tour of the house?"

"I would be delighted," I reply with a smile, and stand to do it. Mrs. Annesley and Fitzwilliam exchange their parting pleasantries and we begin the tour with what is, in my opinion, the most important room in the house—the music room. By the time we are through, nearly an hour has passed and I am feeling quite comfortable with her. She leaves soon after.

Fitzwilliam and I dine together quietly, as we always do. He asks me a few questions about Mrs. Annesley, and between us it is determined that she is quite a suitable companion for me. He is left only to investigate her references. I wonder if this is necessary, as Lady Catherine has particularly recommended her and that lady would rather perish than be wrong, but I hold my tongue. My brother does not like to be questioned, and it will give him peace.

Within a few weeks, Mrs. Annesley and I have fallen into a nice routine. I practice every morning, and on Tuesdays Mr. Pritchard comes to instruct me; after he has gone, Mrs. Annesley tutors me. She has introduced some new subjects, so there is something to learn each day. She thinks my French is good, but it is not; she unrelentingly spends the first full hour of our lessons speaking nothing but French, no matter if we are studying history or geography. For five or six hours we study, and in between we part for dinner. She is serious about the lessons, which although sometimes vexing, is a grand departure from my former companion's style. *Her* French was worse than *mine*.

One morning, about a month into Mrs. Annesley's employment, I wake to find that my regular maid, Clara, is nowhere to be seen. Instead, Greta, one of the upper maids, is waiting for me. I have seen her a handful of times but have never spoken with her. Dressed in my nightgown and a robe, I greet her.

"Good morning, Greta."

She smiles nervously and inclines her head, but says nothing.

"Can you tell me where Clara is this morning?"

She smiles and nods again, but still says nothing.

"Did Mrs. Edstrom send you?" I ask, referring to the housekeeper.

Once more, the smile and nod, but no words. She holds out some towels and a cake of soap.

She does *not* speak, apparently. I tilt my head and crease my brow and gesture to the dressing room where I bathe.

"Is my bath ready?"

She lifts the towels and soap in the air slightly, she must understand the word "bath."

I smile, a little amused by the game. I pass her gently and walk into my dressing chamber. My bath is indeed ready, but it does not explain the mystery of my missing maid.

The quietest bath I have ever had commences, and afterward, Greta fights with my hair. It is incredible, unruly stuff—stick straight, thin, and mousy brown. No one has ever been able to arrange it well, except one of my cousin Anne's maids, but she was as prickly as Anne herself. This morning, it is only pulled into a tight but simple bun, and there is little left to frame my face. When she is finished, I go down to join my brother at breakfast.

He seems a little agitated this morning, and begins speaking almost immediately. "I cannot stay long with you, as I have to meet with my solicitor and Mr. Albertson, who has come to town this morning," he says. "However, you will be quite busy with Mrs. Annesley, selecting a new maid. Clara has left us this morning."

"I noticed that," I say under my breath. Louder, I ask, "Did she tell no one why she left?"

"Her mother fell ill a day or so ago," he explains. "She left to tend her and does not expect to return."

"I see." The news is disappointing, for I liked Clara and would have liked to hear her reasons for leaving from her own mouth. "I hope all is well at Pemberley," I offer to my brother. Mr. Albertson—a sticklike fellow without sons, or even a wife—is his steward, and almost never comes into London, which he hates. On the whole I have found him to be a disagreeable, fussy sort of man, but his character is of little significance to me, as I hardly ever see him, and when I do, he barely dips his head in acknowledgement.

"All is well," he assures me. "I must settle some things with him before I go into Hertfordshire with Bingley in a few weeks."

My face falls, even as I fight against it. My brother does not know that his presence in the house is what keeps my mind calm enough at night to sleep, somewhat unencumbered by dreams of Ramsgate. I did not know that he was going away, but I must learn to accept that we cannot always be in the same place.

"Bingley has taken a house there, which he may like to purchase. I promised that I would visit him, to help him assess it properly."

I want to scream at this and observe that Mr. Bingley is fully capable of making his own decisions, if he would just stop consulting Fitzwilliam. This, you see, is another reason I do not want to marry Mr. Bingley—what woman would want her brother to monopolize her husband's time?

My brother observes my somewhat crestfallen look and takes my hand. "I did not tell you," he says. "I am sorry, Georgiana. I have already promised Bingley...I did not mean to neglect you."

I turn my palm up and squeeze. "It is all right," I say. "How long will you be gone?"

"About a month," he replies. He looks worried.

"Do not fret," I say, patting his hand. "My time will be adequately occupied with Mrs. Annesley's lessons, and with Mr. Pritchard."

"And how fares Mr. Pritchard?" asks Fitzwilliam, taking a bite of his bread. "He is well, I hope."

"Yes," I reply, pausing to think on it. I have not taken any great notice of anyone since returning to London, but Mr. Pritchard has always been very special to me. "Though I confess I worry for him. His step is not quite as light as it used to be."

"It is only age," he says, and tries to make it sound comforting. "I am sure Mr. Pritchard has many more lessons to teach."

I hope silently that he is right. "Where is Mr. Albertson?"

"He is waiting for me in my study," says my brother, in no particular hurry to finish his breakfast.

"Has he eaten breakfast?" I ask, setting down my teacup. "Should we not invite him to join us?"

"He is not a guest, Georgiana, he is my steward. He will wait for me."

"Of course," I mutter into my eggs. Not much more is said during the meal, and soon enough he leaves to confer with Mr. Albertson while I go in search of Mrs. Annesley.

The next afternoon, I am occupied with her in the yellow drawing room, speaking with girls who might fill the position left vacant by Clara. Most are French girls, who speak lovely English, though there are a few English girls, who are all quite serious and never smile. These applicants were sent to us by Mrs. Annesley's sister, who is the proprietor of an agency.

There are ten of them. After I listen to Mrs. Annesley speak to nine of them briefly, the tenth comes into the drawing room. I instantly like her. I do not know why, but I like her.

"My name is Michelle," she says in a thick French accent. She is a lovely girl, about a year older than me, I think. Her hair is curly blonde and arranged neatly, and a genuine smile is upon her face.

"I am Mrs. Annesley, and this is Miss Darcy," says my companion. I smile and curtsy to Michelle.

"How do you do, Michelle?" I say, hopeful that she will be different from the nine other boring and identical girls.

"I am well, *merci*," she replies. She sits down and then asks, "Your maid…she is gone?"

"Yes," I volunteer, which is unusual for me, as I ordinarily let others who would talk do so. "She left us a day ago."

My good companion continues by asking the same questions of Michelle that she asked of the other nine girls. Michelle likes to talk, apparently, and mixes her French and English, but they are all words that I can understand. She talks of her cousins, who are farmers and soldiers, and of her uncle, who is a baker. She came to London when she was fifteen.

When she leaves, Mrs. Annesley asks me whom I liked best of the ten, and I smile a little. "Oh, I liked Michelle the best," I reply, uncertain of her own opinion. "She seemed the most straightforward."

"That is just what I thought, too," she replies, sitting down with her needlework.

"You did?" I ask, a little surprised. "You think Michelle is the best choice?"

"Oh, I think she is the most straightforward," she clarifies. "Strictly speaking, I think perhaps Mary is the most prudent choice. She is the most skilled of all the girls."

"Oh."

She smiles up at me for a moment. "This is a choice you must make on your own, Miss Darcy. All of the girls are qualified; my sister would not have sent them to interview for a position with the Darcy family if it were not so. It is *you* the girl must work for; *you* who must manage her. If you liked Michelle best, then why not choose her? Have a little faith in your own ability to judge character, my dear."

My heart plummets into my stomach, and my expression falls with it. "That is not something that I can do," I say, shaking my head.

Mrs. Annesley puts her work in her lap and gives me a curious look. "Is there something you wish to talk about, Miss Darcy?"

"No," I reply loudly, rising. "No, not at all." I rush to the door and turn to look at her. "I am going to retire now. Good night."

She stops me at the door with a hand on my upper arm. "Miss Darcy, please turn around."

I do as she asks, to find her looking at me with kindness in her eyes. "Yes?"

"It is three o'clock in the afternoon, Miss Darcy."

I look away and want to cry. "Yes," I say. "Of course. I meant...I just want to rest a while."

Mrs. Annesley takes my chin in her hand and turns my head so that she can look at me. "If you ever *do* want to talk," she offers gently, "I hope you feel you can talk to me." She pauses to let the offer settle between us for a moment.

I look back at her, incredibly uncomfortable. "Thank you," I say quietly. She smiles at me and I turn toward my rooms.

The next morning, I am forced to make a choice—I cannot continue to try to instruct Silent Greta, as she clearly wishes neither to learn English, nor to be a lady's maid. Reminding myself that if Michelle ultimately does not succeed, she can be quickly replaced with no harm done, I write to Mrs. Annesley's sister to request that Michelle come to work for me.

She joins us three days later, and shopping ensues. I confess I do *love* to shop and have a bit of an obsession with bonnets. I must have *something* pretty to cover my awful hair, after all. I almost cannot wait to be married, so that I can wear a cap to cover it all the time.

Michelle is fitted for a wardrobe suitable for a lady's maid, which she almost does not accept. It takes quite a bit from both Mrs. Annesley and I to convince her that it is all quite proper and perfectly all right, and then her thanks are profuse. When we return from Mildred Townsend's shop one afternoon, in the hall we meet my brother, who greets me and kisses my cheek. "Shall we have tea together?" he asks me. "I will leave in the morning for Hertfordshire."

I smile. "Of course," I reply, and hand him Mrs. Townsend's bill. "For Michelle," I explain. "Oh, and one for me."

He takes the paper and glances at Michelle, who turns crimson. After looking at it, he looks up at her again. "Do not fret about this," he says to Michelle. "Georgiana, you are to be congratulated. I did not think it could be done."

"Of what do you speak?" I ask, confused.

"You now own bonnets enough to cover every head in England." He kisses my cheek again and heads to the library.

I smile after him and look at Michelle. She smiles back at me, a little more at ease, and follows me up the stairs to my rooms. A few moments later, the footman knocks on the door to deliver the bandbox containing the newest addition to my collection. I thank him and hand it to Michelle to be put away.

"I do not yet know where to put it," she says, a little embarrassed.

"Oh—in my dressing room. I will be right in to show you where."

I follow her after a moment and find her staring into an open closet. My bonnets are all inside—some forty-five of them—all arranged neatly in order of season, and then type, and then color, from the darkest blue to the brightest yellow. Looking over her shoulder, I spot my favorite one—it is light pink with little roses made of ribbons and the loveliest ivory lace trimming it.

"You can put it next to this one," I say, tapping the shelf.

Michelle turns to me with an awestricken face. She shakes her head. "*Mon dieu!*" she exclaims. It is all she can muster...there are *quite* a few bonnets, I suppose.

My dear Georgiana,

There is not much to tell about the past week. I hope the same is true of your week, excepting perhaps a new piece of music from the formidable Mr. Pritchard.

Mr. Bingley and his sisters all send their best to you. One, in fact, is watching over me at present, eager to ensure that I have someone to mend my pen if it should break. I am sure you can guess who the solicitous young lady is.

After my arrival last week, there was an assembly held in the little town of Meryton. You can imagine that I attended with some reluctance, but as Mr. Bingley is my host and he was eager to go, I obliged him. There was not much to be seen there, except the overly eager new acquaintances of Mr. Bingley's. I did meet one young lady, however, whose company I think you might enjoy.

Miss Elizabeth Bennet is the second in a family of five daughters. Her father has a small estate near Netherfield, entailed away from the female line. Her older sister, Miss Jane Bennet, is the only other that merits mentioning. Miss Bingley and Mrs. Hurst have taken a liking to the eldest Miss Bennet. She is, however, quite reserved. The younger three Bennet sisters are, in my opinion, too young and too silly to be out. Miss Elizabeth, however, is possessed of a sharp mind and quick wit. You and she would get along well.

Yesterday, Miss Bingley invited Miss Jane Bennet to dine with her and Mrs. Hurst while we were dining with the officers. It seems Mrs. Bennet sent her eldest daughter on horseback. She rode in the rain and was wet through by the time she reached Netherfield. She has taken ill and so must stay with the Bingleys and recuperate. Miss Bingley also invited Miss Elizabeth to stay when she came to nurse her sister.

That was an odd enough circumstance in itself. It seemed that Miss Elizabeth's father had needed the carriage—again—on the day following Miss Bennet's falling ill; however, her sister was not to be deterred. Rather, she chose to walk the three miles from Longbourn to Netherfield, in ankle-deep mud. Miss Bingley observed, after Miss Elizabeth had been shown to her sister's sick room, that Miss Elizabeth was not fit to be seen. Miss Bingley was all astonishment at what she perceived as a spectacle made upon Miss Jane Bennet's behalf. She immediately demanded my assurances that I should not like to see you do the same. Of course, I acquiesced, but I could not help teasing her a little by commenting that Miss Elizabeth's eyes had been brightened by her exertion.

My brother goes on for another quarter page, in his smooth handwriting, about Miss Elizabeth Bennet. He has never mentioned any of his new female acquaintances to me in his writing. I had assumed this was because he had *made* no new acquaintances—he is not an easy person to speak with. And when he is with Mr. Bingley, his sister Caroline—who has quite made up her mind to marry Fitzwilliam—tends to circle round my brother like a vulture when there are other young unmarried females in the room. I used to think her kind, before I realized the motive behind her attention. Now I do not know what to think, and try to avoid her as much as possible. Most of the time it is easy, because she is dressed all in beads, feathers, and swooshing silk, and can be seen and heard a mile away. Mrs. Reynolds calls her a peacock when she thinks no one is listening.

I ponder this Miss Bennet and wonder what she looks like. I assume she is at least tolerable, because there is no mention of her looks anywhere in the letter.

I have gotten another letter today, from my cousin Anne de Bourgh—the daughter of my mother's sister, Lady Catherine de Bourgh. Anne is only about five feet tall and wears saffron shades of yellow (but does not look good in them). She has hair so dark it is almost black, skin the color of spoiled milk, and eyes that are small and gray. I was afraid of her as a child and have always thought her looks putrid. However, she is as warm-hearted as a person who has been raised to think chiefly of herself can be. She writes brief but constant letters to me, and when I visit Rosings she does her utmost to sit with me, which can be difficult at times, as she is always being shown to her rooms to rest.

This letter is no different than most that I receive from her. The lovely thing about them is that she never bothers with opening pleasantries, and she writes just the same as she speaks—bluntly.

Dear Georgiana,

It has been at least three weeks since your most recent letter; I had expected one from you sooner. You know you are the only person with whom I ever correspond. I am not allowed out, and my other cousins do not have time for me.

Mother is well and sends her best wishes. She will assist me in selecting a new maid this week. Nicole has gotten too old. I did like her, inasmuch as I have ever liked any servant, so I wonder what she will do after she is finished here.

Anne's kindness is not perfect—she has had almost as many abigails in two years as I have bonnets, dismissing all of them either because of age or attitude. I do think her more sincere than curious about Nicole's future employment, however. She may be just as demanding and blunt, but she is more gentle and generous than her mother. I do not mean to say that Lady Catherine is not charitable, rather, that her charity is limited.

I believe Anne when she says that I am the only person to whom she writes. I try to make my replies cheerful and interesting, but I am sure I fail miserably most times.

Sighing, I put down her letter. Each time she writes she speaks of the same things—first her mother, and then herself, and then, if she is permitted to write so long, of other goings-on in the world with which she is acquainted. It is a very rare occasion indeed when I receive a letter from her that does *not* bore me to tears. However, it is a nice challenge for me to come up with things to write about. I have the same difficulty thinking of things to speak of in company.

I leave the letters on my writing table and wander to the music room. My fingers dance across the keys involuntarily as I sit down. I wonder on the young lady mentioned in my brother's letter—Miss

Elizabeth Bennet of Hertfordshire. Given that my brother clearly likes her, I am predisposed to approving of her. Second of five daughters, living in an estate entailed away from such children... she would not be so very self-important or imposing, as Miss Bingley is. I wonder if she has any fortune to speak of, or whether she has any noble family. I should like nothing more than to have a sister to love—a friend of my own gender and near my age.

Ensuing letters from Netherfield are quite full of Miss Bennet. Fitzwilliam talks about the day on which the Misses Bennet leave Netherfield and how quiet the evenings become. He talks of meeting her at other homes in the neighborhood, and says that he watches her interact with young Lucases and older Philipses, and how much he enjoys talking with her when he does speak. And in one letter, I am struck by his saying, quite bluntly, "She is so expressive, and so full of life, with such striking eyes." He gives no indication, however, that his sentiments are returned. When he speaks of their conversations, it occurs to me that they debate more than they discuss, so I wonder whether there is any tenderness of feeling for him on her side.

He does, apparently, pay her more attention than he has ever paid any woman, excepting perhaps Miss Bingley, but that can only be because she asks for such attention. In his most recent letter, he mentions that Mr. Bingley is not as satisfied with Netherfield as he had hoped to be, and that they will return to London as soon as matters there are settled.

He arrives sooner than expected. Within a few days of his return, we fall into that same, comfortable routine that we have both come to rely upon. I adore my brother and cherish every moment that can be spent with him. It does not really matter that neither of us is terribly inclined to speak.

My dreams of Ramsgate are becoming less frequent, but they still trouble me. I do not sleep well and am afraid that Mrs. Annesley notices my fatigue. The dreams are generally the same—my mind flashing back to moments when I was alone with him—with the beautiful, charming, and deceitful man who followed me there. The dreams feel so real that I wake up confused, and then feel my anger at him renewed.

One morning, after I have slept very, very little, I try to plead illness with Mrs. Annesley.

"You are not ill," she says gently. "Miss Darcy, I know that you are not sleeping well. Is there not something that I can do to help you? Will you not tell me what is troubling you?"

I remember the day that she told me she hoped that I would talk with her if I ever felt like talking. There is not anything to tell her that my brother does not already know, so I take in a breath.

"If I were to tell you something in utter confidence," I begin in a low voice, "would you keep it to yourself?"

"I will keep any secret you tell me, as long as it is not to your detriment."

I sigh. Taking Mrs. Annesley's hand, I lead her to the settee and sit myself upon it. She sits next to me. "Let me first assure you that there is nothing that I am about to disclose to you about which my brother does not know every particular," I say. Tears begin to well in my eyes; Mrs. Annesley squeezes my hand and readies her handkerchief. With a deep breath, I continue. "When my brother was a younger man—a boy, really—he had a good friend named George Wickham. He was the son of our father's steward, and our father was very fond of him. He supported him at school after his father's death—the elder Mr. Wickham died so very young, you see. My father had intended him for the church, and had left provisions in his will for the living at Kympton to fall to him." I pause and let a smile come over my face.

"Your father must have been a generous man," says Mrs. Annesley in my silence. "I had wondered where your brother got his example."

I nod. "My father was an excellent man. I wish I could have known him better. He had such faith in Mr. Wickham. My father, you see, lost both of his parents at an early age, just as Mr. Wickham did. I suppose that was why he was so fond of him." My smile falters and I heave another sigh. "But his faith was misplaced. Mr. Wickham learned to enjoy gambling and whiskey, and other things a young lady is not supposed to know of, more than his studies. His relationship with my brother crumbled. Mr. Wickham asked him for money, and he asked him to lie.

"Fitzwilliam, of course, would have none of it and tried to encourage Mr. Wickham to be an honorable man. He did not succeed. Of all of this, of course, I was perfectly unaware." I pause here, letting out a breath and looking around the room a little.

After a moment I breathe deeply again to steel myself for Mrs. Annesley's reaction, and then continue, determined not to stop until I am finished. "My companion, Mrs. Younge, whom my brother and I liked very much, suggested that we holiday in Ramsgate this summer. She did this knowing that my brother would not be able to accompany me—there is simply too much to be done at Pemberley during summer. But with his blessing, we set out.

"When I first met Mr. George Wickham at Ramsgate I was surprised—I recalled a young man who paid almost no attention to me as a child. I had always thought him handsome, and if I am at all honest with myself, I still do. I was quite surprised that he even approached me—but unbeknownst to me, he was there by design. I did not recall at that time, as he smiled charmingly at me, that he had left Pemberley the same morning my father was discovered to have passed away. I did not know at that time, that upon leaving Derbyshire he left debts, knowing full well that my brother would discharge them. I did not recall that he did not write my brother at all, and though his relationship with my brother was quite thinly worn, Fitzwilliam was distressed by this. All I could see was that he was paying attention to me. It was not many days later that he told me that I was beautiful, and that I played the pianoforte more brilliantly than ever he had heard. A few days more and he was falling in love with me, until a fortnight after he first encountered me—quite unexpectedly, mind you—he declared himself and made the suggestion that, because he and Fitzwilliam were estranged, we should marry first and then seek consent. That way, Fitzwilliam could not help but give it. He would see that his sister was happy, and he and Mr. Wickham could renew their friendship.

"All the time he knew what he was doing—he knew what he wanted and it was not me. I trusted Mrs. Younge, and she deceived me. I was completely taken in by him, by her design and by his. But I ought to have known that none of it was true—nobody falls in love in two weeks' time, except in romance novels."

I pause for a long time and examine my fingers. "I was thoughtless, and I hurt my brother," I finish finally.

Mrs. Annesley squeezes my hand again. "What happened to stop you?" she asks.

"He came to Ramsgate. Fitzwilliam came to Ramsgate."

"And did he confront Mr. Wickham?" she asks, her brow contracting.

"I told him what Mr. Wickham said to me," I say, my eyes flooding with tears at the memory of my brother's expression. "I asked him for his blessing. He asked me if I loved Mr. Wickham."

"And what did you say?"

"I said that I had very strong feelings for him, which I believed constituted love. He simply shook his head, kissed me, and sent me to my room. He wrote to Mr. Wickham; I do not know what he said. I expected some kind of response—a letter, a visit, anything. There was none. I have not seen him again."

"And do you still have those feelings for Mr. Wickham?"

I look away. "They are waning." I sigh and shake my head, thinking on it. "My brother, generously, never told me that I was not in love, nor did he ever attempt to direct my feelings in any other manner. He simply explained some things to me...the things that I mentioned earlier, and reminded me of the attractiveness of my fortune." I sniffle a little and take the handkerchief from my sleeve to pat at my eyes. "I wish the whole thing had never happened. I dream of it every night—and sometimes, during the day, if someone mentions the sea...or falling in love. Or even fishing nets, sometimes—I do not know why."

When I look up at Mrs. Annesley, there is only kindness in her eyes. "Miss Darcy, I think it is probably true that your brother has suffered because of this, but it may not be so much because of your actions. You are young; Mr. Wickham is not. His actions were calculating; yours were not. Consider that your brother and Mr. Wickham were friends as children. Do you not think that perhaps part of what your brother is experiencing is the pain of being betrayed by a friend?"

I smile sadly, truly never having considered this part of the matter. "I had not thought that, no."

"Your brother adores you, my dear. He almost lost you, and I think he may be blaming himself for what he allowed to happen. He may feel that he left you unprotected. Do not take too much of the blame upon yourself."

I smile and thank her, and though I do not know whether I believe them or not, I try to remember her words.

———————

My dear Georgiana,

I hope that you are well. I have arrived safely this morning in Kent at Rosings Park. Our aunt sends you her best wishes; Anne snarled at me. I assumed she meant it as a welcome.

The next handful of weeks, I expect, shall be rather dull. There is not much to do at Rosings Park, as you recall—there is no one to play or sing, as you do, and only Fitzwilliam and I visiting. At least, however, I shall not be forced into society, as I was in Hertfordshire.

My brother is not a social man; he is shy, like his sister. He does not look forward to social invitations in general, especially when he is acquainted with only one or two guests, but he also tends to dread them when he is acquainted with everyone in the room. He seems, to most, to be rather taciturn. He is seen as uninterested in any manner of conversation and considering himself quite above all of them—which, in my opinion, he is. Truly, all that my brother lacks to be considered as good as a prince is a title, which he most definitely does not want.

I remember a time when my brother told me what he did want— before Papa died and before my governess was discharged. He used to be quite open with me, and there was one particular conversation I recall with some clarity. We were sitting in the servants' dining room on a cold and wet day in early March, eating cake. I do not remember where the cake came from or why it was baked, but I recall that it was a secret and I was not to tell my governess under any circumstances. It is likely that Fitzwilliam was behind the scheme.

As we sat quietly eating and whispering, he asked me, "Georgiana, what do you dream about?"

"At night?" I think is what I asked, probably giggling the whole time.

"At night, and during the day. What do you wish for?"

I started running through the list of things I wanted—mostly hair ribbons and dolls—and when I was through, I stuffed another bite of cake into my mouth and asked Fitzwilliam what he dreamed about.

He paused before he answered. "Sometimes I dream about Mama."

It was the first time he had ever mentioned her to me, and I got very quiet and wide-eyed, and whispered, "What did she look like?"

He swallowed and put down his cake. "She had very dark hair," he quietly said, looking away. "And she was tall."

"Was she very pretty?"

"She was beautiful," he whispered, smiling at me. "When I was a very little boy, Mama and Papa gave a ball at Pemberley. I was not allowed to go downstairs, but she came up just before it was time for me to go to sleep. When she walked into my bedroom, I thought an angel had descended from heaven."

"Sometimes I wish I could see her," I said, putting down my own cake. "Did she not sit for a portrait?"

He looked away suddenly, with what was, even to the eyes of an eight-year-old, obviously pain. "No," he replied. "She did not."

I took his curt reply to mean that he was not to be questioned about it further. My stomach then began to protest the richness of the cake and its delightful icing; I sat back and put my hand across my midriff with a sigh. After a brief moment, Fitzwilliam looked back at me and smiled a little.

"How about a bit of milk?"

I am thinking back on that day now, after so much has changed, while sitting on my chaise in my rooms in London after preparing for bed. I like the city a great deal, but I prefer Derbyshire and Pemberley, and I know that when my brother marries, we shall spend almost all of our time there. Unless, of course, the lady prefers the city.

I rise and go to the window to look out into the starless night. My thoughts turn again toward my brother, who has been in Rosings these two weeks. He does not discuss his personal matters with me, but I think on them every once in a while, even though I ought not to. Given his conservative nature and his dedication to his duty, I know he will marry. And I know, unless he is particularly struck as I thought he might have been with Miss Elizabeth Bennet, he will marry the type of young lady whom he is *supposed* to marry, rather than the particular lady whom he *wishes* to marry.

Putrid Anne and Caroline the Peacock are out of the question— he has assured me of that on more than one occasion. But I do wonder whom he will marry. I wish to be able to so much as tolerate my future sister-in-law, whomever that might be, but dearly hope that I could come to like her, or even love her, as my own sister. And perhaps there is a way that I can encourage him in his choice.

I turn to the writing desk and ink my pen.

My dear Brother,

I hope you are well and enjoying yourself at Rosings. Please convey my love to my dearest cousin the colonel, if you would, and please tell him that I would very much like to see him if he is able to visit us.

Now I must come to the purpose of my letter. I have a concern, my dearest Brother, that I sincerely hope you will take to heart.

It concerns you, Fitzwilliam. You have said that I should not be thinking about marriage at such an age, but I know you must be, and I confess I have been thinking on yours. I know you will not marry our cousin Anne—I know she has never liked you, and you have never liked her. You have also said repeatedly that you have no interest in Caroline Bingley—for which I could never thank you enough. I do not know what other ladies have caught your fancy— with the exception of the apparently formidable Miss Elizabeth Bennet of Hertfordshire, whom you will likely never see again—but I do not want you to be unhappy in your marriage.

I have been witness to a few marriages, but those handful have been marriages of prudence—marriages in which families benefit, financially or socially, but where the principal parties are not matched well. I give you the earl and his wife, for example, who, I am sure, have never said a kind word to each other in the unnaturally long span of their lives together. I would not be entirely surprised to know that our aunt does not spend a moment in her husband's company except, at meals and social gatherings.

I know that it is not for me to worry about your life, that you are quite capable of handling your own private affairs. But Fitzwilliam, I have always loved and admired you and that kind of life is not the kind of life that I would want for you. And so I beg you, for your own sake, to marry a woman whom you truly do admire, and one who admires you in return. I want you to be happy with yourself and with your wife, and I know that you are capable of looking beyond the surface to the person behind the silk and feathers. Our family does not want for anything except another loving member, and so I hope that you will not look for what you do not need in your wife.

Now, I am tired, and I am sure I have quite overstepped my boundaries, so I shall go to bed. I will expect to see you in about five days at the house in Portnam Square. Please travel safely.

Your loving sister,

Georgiana

⁕

The following Friday, when Fitzwilliam arrives, he is very distant. He takes his tea alone in his study, and stays there for several hours.

At supper, he will not speak with me beyond a few curt sentences. Afterward, we sit in the music room, and he is still as silent as stone. When I ask him what is wrong, he gives me a peculiar look.

"I received your letter, before I left Rosings."

I do not like the sharp tone of his voice at all, and my heart immediately plummets to my stomach. "You did?"

"Yes," he says, looking away. Then he looks back and says quickly, "Georgiana, I know you are still very young, but I do wonder what gets into your head sometimes."

This comment catches me a little off-guard. The letter that I wrote to him, I felt, was perhaps not thought out very well, but it was sincerely meant, and Fitzwilliam has always encouraged me to speak with him about what does, in fact, get into my head. I am saved from having to reply, however, as Fitzwilliam begins a rant.

"As it happens," he says as he stands, looking out the window and folding his hands behind him, "Miss Elizabeth Bennet is a particular friend of Mr. Collins's new wife—you do know who Mr. Collins is, Georgiana?"

I lift an eyebrow at his back and wonder where this line of questioning is headed. "Yes—the rector at Hunsford," I say, tentatively, wondering what the only woman who, to my knowledge, has ever caught my brother's fancy has to do with his irritability.

"Miss Bennet is visiting Mrs. Collins, and on a few occasions, the Collinses, and their guests, came to dinner, while Fitzwilliam and I were at Rosings. I spoke with her several times."

Still without a hint as to what the problem is, and what I have to do with it, I reply, "And how is Miss Bennet?"

He stuns me into silence by replying, "I have made an offer of marriage to Miss Bennet, and have been turned down quite soundly."

It was clear to me that, from the first time he ever saw her, he liked her, but this is quite unexpected. Now I am wondering what has gotten into *his* head. And what got into *her* head to make her refuse him?

"*Your* encouragement in this whole affair was really quite unnecessary, you know," he continues, turning around. "Your letter to me was received the day before this cursed event took place. I cannot say that if I had not received it, I would not have made the offer, but it certainly did play a role, Georgiana."

It takes me a moment to figure it out, but I think I am offended by this comment. "I played a part in your proposal?" I ask, bringing my hand to my chest. "What part?"

"Your *letter*," he snaps at me. "The one you wrote to me, which I received not three days ago. Surely you remember writing it? You encouraged me to propose to Miss Bennet."

"Fitzwilliam, I did not know that Miss Bennet was even in the same county as you. I assumed that after you left Netherfield, you would never see her again. I do recall writing the letter, but I did not specifically request that you marry her."

"But you knew that I admired Miss Bennet, and you encouraged me to, and I quote, 'marry a woman whom I truly do admire.' You went on for a page about how you did not want to see me unhappy in my marriage."

"But you never gave me any indication that she liked you in return," I say, my dander up. "You said that she consistently sparred with you. Why would I assume that she liked you if she always quarreled with you?"

My brother looks at me sideways. It is true I never argue with him, but for Heaven's sake. I had *nothing* to do with this.

"Did you assume that she liked you?" I ask him. "Did you assume that she would accept your proposal because of your consequence in the world?" He says nothing, so I assume that he did, which angers me. I rise and stomp my foot. "Why would you do such a thing?"

It is clear that he is embarrassed, and he turns his face away. "Georgiana—" he begins, but I stop him.

"Do you truly not realize how taciturn you seem to strangers? Do you not realize that no one you know ever offers a contrary opinion to yours because you intimidate them? Fitzwilliam, you told me that Miss Bennet refused your offer to *dance* with her—why on earth would she accept an offer of marriage?"

"Georgiana—"

His face has softened a little, but I have not. "What I asked of you," I say, in an even tone, "was that you marry where affection was mutual. Meaning, of course, Fitzwilliam, that she liked you as well. And in any case, no woman of good sense would ever accept a man whose main form of communication was silent stares."

When his eyes widen, I know that I have gone too far. Rather than apologize, however, I only look at him while my heart slows to its normal rate.

"Georgiana..."

I wait for him to continue in that dark voice, but he does not. I blink, finally. It pains me to know that I have hurt my brother, but there is nothing that I have said that is untrue, and I can have nothing more now to say. "Good night, Fitzwilliam."

I manage to make it to the sanctity of my rooms before I collapse on the bed and burst into tears. Michelle is upon me in less than a minute, asking what is wrong, and ignores me when I dismiss her.

"*S'il vous plait*, Miss Darcy, allow me to help you. You cannot get yourself out of your clothing."

She is trying to be helpful, but all I want is to be alone. "I will do very well *myself*, thank you!"

Michelle snorts and mumbles some French words that I am fairly certain translate to "silly English girl." Then, from under the pillow in which I have buried my head, I hear her sigh. "Please. Miss Darcy. I do not mean to be rude, madam, but I do not intend to leave you as you are."

Tossing the pillow off, I rise to stand in front of her, scowling and tearful with my arms crossed. "Michelle, I am giving you an order!"

"I would happily comply if I thought you could reach all of your buttons and untie the knot I have put in your corset laces."

She is not defensive as I would be in her place, but infuriatingly confident, her hands folded respectfully and her brow arched. I let out a huff. "If it will get rid of you faster!"

The ghost of a smirk touches her lips as I turn around to let her do her job. Later, when she has left me tucked safely into my bed, I am grateful for her dedication, because she is right—I would not have known where to begin undressing myself.

Mr. Wickham makes no appearance during what little sleep I have—my angry brother takes his place. I do not emerge from my room the next day and Fitzwilliam does not come to inquire after my health. For many days, we avoid each other entirely. I throw myself into my lessons instead.

Mrs. Annesley has, in the past, encouraged me to venture into the library when I am looking for something to do. Saturday afternoon is quiet and rainy; I take her advice and head there, hopeful that I will not encounter my brother.

The library is an imposing thing; all high walls and dark oak. The first thing that one notices upon entering the library is the smell of leather which permeates the air. There must be a thousand books here, arranged perfectly and dusted neatly. The room is handsome, but authoritative and stern—a bit like its chief occupant. I peek inside to make sure no one is there before I enter into it. Quietly I run my hand down the volumes upon the shelf closest to me and pick out the one on which my fingers stop. It falls open and there is a loose page inside.

The paper is folded and yellowed and the ink is thick; it has bled through. Curious, I replace the book it was resting in and open the note.

Dear Father,

Today is my birthday and you spent the whole day with me.

I enjoyed the picnic with you and Mama, and I enjoyed riding with you in the park.

I know you are very busy, so today was special.

I shall always remember it.

Yours,

Fitzwilliam

Tears blur my vision. I have intruded on something very private and personal and while I am not sorry to have come upon it, I am sorry for the offense of reading it. When I reach up for the book it was hidden in, my hand rests on my brother's.

"Oh!" I exclaim, startled. "I did not see you."

"May I have that note, please?" he asks, turning up his palm. His voice is emotionless and his face is stone. I cannot look into his eyes; he must be angry with me.

"I am sorry," I say, my voice choked. My face turns red as I refold the note, place it in his hand, and turn to leave the library. I hear my name as I reach the door and stop.

My brother approaches me. "Where did you find this?"

I still cannot bear to look at him. I bite my lip to try to stop my tears and look at the books instead. It is a moment before I can answer him; my throat is constricted and I want to run and hide. "In a book on the shelf."

He pauses, and then, to my surprise, gently asks, "Can you show me which book, Georgiana?"

I still cannot look at him, so I move to the shelf upon which I found the book and remove it. I hand it to him, still looking down.

The binding of the book cracks as it falls open. Fitzwilliam draws a sharp breath. "Shakespeare," he whispers, his voice reverent. "Father read this to me countless times before he sent me to bed." He leafs through the worn pages; I finally look up. Softness has descended into his features and there is awe in his eyes. He turns back to the note in his hand. "I wrote this in the evening on my ninth birthday. I did not know he kept it."

"I am sorry for intruding on your privacy," I say quickly. "I did not mean—"

But he silences me when his maskless, gentle eyes meet mine. "Georgiana, please do not apologize. There is very little that Father left behind; I'm quite pleased to have this." He kisses my cheek and departs the library, leaving me quite confused indeed.

The next weeks are wet and quiet in London. My brother and I speak little to each other, and the air between us is strained. At long last, one evening he startles me by entering the music room and laying a hand upon my shoulder while I am in the middle of a

Beethoven piece. I stop and look up, curious. He meets my eyes; his are tired.

"You were right," he says quietly. "I did presume that she would accept me. I assumed, because of our different circumstances, that she would want—that she would be obliged, even, to accept me. I went to the parsonage that evening certain of my success."

"Will you tell me what happened?" I ask, my voice small.

"It is quite a story, my dear girl," he replies. "I have been mulling it over these many weeks. I feel...drained." He lets out a breath.

"If you would rather not—"

"No, no," he assures me, sitting down upon the bench. After a pause, he offers, "I would, perhaps, prefer to abridge the story for you. I am afraid that I have violated your privacy, and you ought to know of the circumstances."

"Did you tell her of my letter?" I ask, rather wishing I had burnt the cursed thing after writing it.

"No," he says, shaking his head. "I was obliged to tell her about Ramsgate."

I am quiet for a long moment. "Do you trust her with this secret?" I ask, not certain whether I am angry.

Fitzwilliam settles me by taking my hand. "I know you have no way to know it," he says, "but Miss Elizabeth Bennet is most scrupulous; she will not make it public."

"Why did you tell her?"

My brother then tells me of Mr. Wickham's enrollment in the militia, and his stay in Hertfordshire. He tells me of his chance meeting with him, in the streets of Meryton. He tells the not astonishing tale of a young and charming gentleman with exquisite manners who captivated the whole of the county.

"Making his true character known to Hertfordshire would have only succeeded in my being even more disliked," he says with a wry kind of smile. "But he took a particular liking to Miss Elizabeth Bennet, and when I tried—albeit halfheartedly—to put her on her guard, she would not hear it. He had told her that our father had willed the living at Kympton to Wickham and that I had denied him it upon Father's passing."

"But it was willed conditionally only," I protest.

He smiles again. "I know that, Georgiana, and Wickham knows that, but all of Hertfordshire would have made the issue my word against his. You of all people know how I hate to be questioned."

"Fitzwilliam, were you really so terrible? Did no one see you truly?"

"They all saw me truly, Georgiana, and that was the trouble. I did not force the issue of Wickham's character because I thought it beneath me to lay my private actions open to them. I paid almost none of them attention, excepting Miss Bennet, and I did not encourage Bingley in his acquaintances either."

I have never heard my brother utter an admission of guilt so readily before, and am a little stunned, but not displeased. It is comforting to know that sometimes the great Fitzwilliam Darcy makes mistakes. "How did this come to light?" I ask gently.

He draws breath slowly, staring at the keys instead of looking at me, and a sadness creeps into his features. He speaks deliberately. "I went to the parsonage that evening knowing that Miss Bennet was quite alone. I thought of a number of approaches, and then, deciding that a direct one was best—"

"You always do," I say, laying my hand on his knee.

He smiles a little and takes it. "Yes—I do. I declared my feelings for Miss Bennet—she was surprised, as I had expected. And then, after foolishly letting her know the difficulties of such a connection, I asked if she would not become my wife." He then looks at me with a heartbroken expression. "She would not. I have been over it so many times in my head, Georgiana, that I could quote her reasons for refusing me—my arrogance, my conceit, my selfish disdain for the feelings of others...and then she accused me of having ruined Mr. Wickham...among other things."

"What other things?" I ask, curious. I would not wish him to hide anything from me.

"Nothing that signifies, dear girl." He pats my hand. "I wrote her a letter...a very long letter. In it I detailed my dealings with Wickham. I delivered it to her in the grove at Rosings the next morning. I do not expect to ever see her again."

Smiling, I squeeze his fingers. "I am sorry that your heart was broken."

He is quiet for a moment, and then turns to face me more squarely. "I...I know I am not perfect, but I truly never knew..." He looks away.

I take his dimpled chin between my thumb and forefinger, as he has wont to do to me at times. "Your heart will mend, Fitzwilliam," I say quietly, "and you can improve your behavior. Our closer acquaintances know the truth of your character; they know of your charity...that you are simply shy, like me. You can show it to others beyond your own circle."

He smiles. "Georgiana," he says, and then kisses my cheek. He pulls away and sighs. "I am exhausted. Take your brother to bed."

I walk with him up to his rooms, and then decide to retire myself. An odd feeling grips me as Michelle, yawning all the while, brushes out my hair. I feel almost giddy; as if something unexpected and wonderful is about to happen. For not only have I this moment reconciled the one and only disagreement which I have ever had with Fitzwilliam, I have realized that I have not thought or dreamt of Mr. Wickham since my brother's return from Rosings some three weeks earlier. He has not crossed my mind in a lazy, melancholy moment; he has not crept into my dreams to unsettle me; and he has not walked off the pages of a book I ought to be concentrating on. He is slowly melting from my memory, as ice off the meadow in spring. The lessons left behind are a nutrient to help me grow and blossom in the splendor of the season.

———————

"Being at Pemberley, with guests," says Mrs. Annesley in the carriage, "will be excellent practice as hostess for you. Your age will excuse you from any faux pas that you might make, and with the Bingleys—one in particular, mind you—you cannot make a mistake that is not charming."

It is early August. We are on the last leg of our journey from London to Pemberley. We are in the first carriage, and Miss Bingley and the Hursts are behind us in a second, with our servants in a third. Mr. Bingley rides beside us on his horse, and my brother rode ahead of us after receiving a message from Mr. Albertson.

"I do hope you are not referring to Mr. Bingley," I say, looking sideways at her. Mrs. Annesley likes to tease; I do not always appreciate it.

"Oh, yes," she replies, a most serious look upon her face. "He is quite smitten."

"He is not smitten with me," I assert. "If he is he shall be sorely disappointed." I lift an eyebrow and turn to look out the window again. We drive but a few feet more and then stop. As we alight from the carriage, my brother is there to hand me down. He greets me in a reserved way, as he usually does, but he smiles and I tell him how pleased I am to be at Pemberley. Mrs. Reynolds is there, as well, and I introduce her to Mrs. Annesley, whom I think she will like very much. A maid offers to guide Mrs. Annesley through the house and she and Michelle make themselves busy directing footmen with our trunks. As the Bingleys and Hursts descend from their carriage, taking their time, my brother says nothing out of the ordinary, but in his eyes I can see a certain pleasure. I think he has got a secret—perhaps a surprise for me.

He takes my arm and we walk inside. The Bingleys and Hursts disperse to rest and direct their servants; Fitzwilliam steers me toward the main rooms of the house.

"I am sure you know that I have a surprise for you," he says, his eyes twinkling.

"Yes," I say impatiently. "What is it?"

We turn into the music room—my favorite in this house, as well—and he gestures into one corner. I am confused for a moment, until I realize that the pianoforte that used to stand there is gone, and a new one—ornately carved, painted, and polished—stands in its place. "Oh!" I gasp, covering my mouth and smiling. "Fitzwilliam, it is beautiful!" I run my fingers across it and sit down upon the bench, declaring that I cannot wait to play it. I begin the first few notes of a scale but discover that it is not tuned and wrinkle my nose.

He smiles fully and his cheeks flush. "I am glad that you like it. There will be someone here to tune it this afternoon, and you may play me something after supper this evening."

"It is too much!" I declare, but would not have him send it away for anything. "Thank you. For what reason, may I ask, did you go to such trouble?"

"Nothing is trouble for my dearest sister," he replies playfully, which causes me to suspect that there is something more to surprise me with. "It was purchased to thank you for your honesty and generosity. Despite all that we Darcys have, Georgiana, those are two things we receive rarely."

I smile sheepishly and pull my hands away from the keys. "If I am either honest or generous, it is because of you, sir."

Dipping his head solemnly in acknowledgement, he folds his hands and sets them on the top of the instrument. He smiles slowly, and then lets his eyes dance at me again. Now I am certain that there is something more. "I have another surprise for you, which you might like better than your new instrument."

"I cannot imagine what it is," I say. "As it is, I shall drive you mad and play this all day long." I gaze over it, and up at him again. "Thank you, again."

He bends down and kisses my cheek. "It was nothing, if it gives you pleasure," he says. "Now, you must go and change out of your traveling clothes. There is someone I would like you to meet at last."

I look at him, fiercely curious. "Who is it?"

"Miss Elizabeth Bennet and her aunt and uncle are touring Derbyshire. They are all staying at the inn at Lambton. I asked if I might introduce you to her while she is there."

My stomach begins to flutter in nervousness, but I take hold of his arm. "Oh, yes!" I declare, all nerves. "Oh—whatever shall I wear?"

Fitzwilliam laughs. "Anything will be fine. I have got the curricle coming around. Mr. Bingley will follow us on horseback once his sisters are settled. I shall meet you downstairs." He kisses my head and I turn toward my room, calling for Michelle.

———◆———

Miss Elizabeth Bennet is only a little shorter than I am. She is raven-haired with round cheeks and a pleasing figure. She is dressed modestly, which suits her open and sincere face. She smiles at me, and the fine eyes about which my brother has raved brighten the sitting room. Oh, I quite like her. She is lovely.

My brother lets Miss Bennet know that Mr. Bingley is also coming to call upon her. She smiles, and for the briefest of moments, my dear brother's face is graced with such an expression of tenderness that I smile. It is clear, to me at least, how much he really likes her. For this reason, I cannot think what to say, and am sure I seem quite silly when she tries to engage me in conversation and I make only brief replies to her comments.

Her uncle and aunt, Mr. and Mrs. Gardiner, are kindly-looking people and I like that same openness and sincerity in their features which I observe in Miss Bennet's. Mr. Bingley makes his appearance in quick succession to our own, and comes into the room all smiles and eager to talk and please. I find it amusing that Mr. Bingley, a man who misplaces his pens upon the surfaces of writing tables, recalls the precise date of the ball he gave at Netherfield. I wonder if something particular occurred then, as it is evident that there is something more he wants to say about it. He keeps his inquiries general, however, and though Miss Bennet is kind and clearly pleased to see him, there is no special attention paid to him, and neither has anything truly noteworthy to say.

My brother is perfectly composed and relaxed in her presence—on the surface, at least. We stay with them for about a half an hour and then, just before we leave, my brother persuades me to invite them to Pemberley for dinner, which I do quite nervously. Mrs. Gardiner accepts for the party, and smiles encouragingly at me. We settle on the day after next, and then must take our leave. Fitzwilliam and I are both close to silent, but smile stupidly on the return to the house.

To my vexation and delight, Mrs. Gardiner and Miss Bennet call upon us the following morning. Her uncle had accepted an invitation to go trout fishing at Pemberley, issued the previous day by my brother, and they had set out earlier in the morning with a party that included Mr. Bingley. Miss Bingley and Mrs. Hurst greet our visitors coldly. I wonder if something happened between them in Hertfordshire and rather suspect the sisters of being less than gracious neighbors.

Mrs. Gardiner is as open and friendly as she was yesterday. She talks easily with Mrs. Annesley, and Miss Bennet listens respectfully to their conversation, joining in occasionally. I, of course, say next to nothing, as I am afraid of saying something silly.

I am afraid Miss Bennet is not very comfortable in the presence of the Bingley sisters, for she seems quite anxious. After remaining silent since her arrival, Miss Bingley screws up courtesy enough to inquire after the health of the Bennet family, and receives a reply formulated with as much consideration as Miss Bingley showed in waiting more than a quarter of an hour to ask.

After this exchange, finally I notice Mrs. Annesley looking at me as though something is expected of me, and I am reminded that I am the hostess and must ring for some refreshment. Some lovely fruits are brought, and we all gather round the table, and not long afterward, Fitzwilliam comes to join us.

He issues a general greeting to the room, and I smile a little as I see Miss Bennet's cheeks flush. He explains that he had heard from Mr. Gardiner that the ladies intended to call at the house, and that all of the gentlemen were still enjoying themselves at the river.

I observe Miss Bennet as he speaks. After some moments she seems more relaxed and at ease, which pleases me, and I think her smiles must please my brother. It does not escape my notice that he seems particularly anxious for she and I to speak, and I do exert myself more to do so.

Miss Bingley, unfortunately, also notices that my brother is attempting to forward conversation between Miss Bennet and myself, and from the expression upon her face, she is not pleased by it. She proves it then, by asking Miss Bennet whether the regiment of militia, which I knew Mr. Wickham had joined, had not removed from Meryton.

"They must be a great loss to *your* family."

Knowing the nature of Miss Bennet's acquaintance with one in particular of those officers, I would feel more for my new friend if I did not more clearly recall what connection I had with the same officer. Miss Bingley has never heard a word of the incident, and would not have posed the question if she knew of it, but the comment was made out of anger and jealousy, and with the intention of injuring my brother's opinion of our visitor. It has the unintended side effect of silencing me for the remainder of the visit.

Miss Bennet answers quietly and disinterestedly, and they do not stay much longer. When they have gone, Miss Bingley begins abusing her abominably. I can see she wants me to join her, but I cannot. My first introduction to Miss Bennet through my brother's glowing descriptions in his letters was enough to ensure my good opinion. Now that I have met her for myself I have no objection whatever, and so I ignore Miss Bingley, and go quietly and smilingly with Mrs. Annesley to my French lesson.

Fitzwilliam does not join us for tea that afternoon, but Mr. Bingley does. He and I have pleasant conversation, while his sisters are uncharacteristically quiet. Soon Mrs. Reynolds pops in and tells me that my brother would like to see me. I cannot think what for, so curiously I go in the direction of her pointed finger. My brother is waiting in the hallway.

"I should like a turn in the garden with you," he says, his hand extended. I smile and take it.

We reach the garden. It is so beautiful at this time of year. Fitzwilliam tucks my hand into the crook of his arm and smiles at me.

"You and I did not have the chance to talk yesterday evening," he says. "What were your impressions of Miss Bennet?"

Honestly, Brother. Don't beat around the bush. A direct approach is always best, after all. "She is lovely," I say, to quickly assure him of my regard. "I very much like her."

"I am glad to hear it," he says. Then he stops and turns to me, squeezing my hand. "I think that it is time we had a talk."

"What about?" I ask, my stomach aflutter.

"You know that I must marry," he says, his voice low. "I know that you do not know her well...but...do you suppose that you might like to have her for your sister?"

Though I am rather inclined to call his valet and send him back to the inn with our mother's wedding ring, I consider the question. I do like Miss Bennet, very much. My first impressions of her are everything good and amiable, and adding to that my brother's own good opinion of the lady, the fact that the dogs do not growl at her as they do at Miss Bingley, and Mrs. Reynolds' rapture over her the night before, I do not think I have greatly erred. As to her fortune and connections, I am perfectly indifferent and always have been to anyone's. But if she is my sister, then she is my brother's wife. This means many things and I sit on a bench to ponder them. Fitzwilliam looks nervous and a little surprised.

"I should very much like to give over housekeeping to your wife, Fitzwilliam," I say, which is not the answer he was expecting at all. He stares uncomprehendingly at me for a moment but then realizes where my thoughts have gone, and sits next to me. "I should have to share you," I say quietly. "Rather a lot, I conjecture."

"But with a woman worthy as I believe Miss Bennet is," he whispers to me, "would you share willingly?"

I look up at him. "Do you remember the Weldons?"

He quirks an eyebrow. "Of course—Philip and his sister Agatha. What makes you think of...oh."

My cheeks are crimson, but I meet his eyes. Agatha was several years older than me, but the only other young lady who lived in Portnam Square, so I knew her reasonably well. Like Fitzwilliam and I, there were more than ten years between her and Philip, and their parents had passed on.

"She adored Philip," I remind my own, dear brother, "but when he married, she was left in London without a visit from him for an entire year."

"I would never do such a thing," he replies. "Georgiana, you know I would not."

I feel silly for even thinking such a thing, and smile sheepishly at him. "I do."

He tilts my chin up with his crooked finger. "And—assuming everything turns out the way that I hope it shall—Miss Bennet would not hear of leaving you behind."

"I should dearly love to have a sister," I tell him, smiling. "And I do like Miss Bennet very much."

"And so," he continues, uneasily, "if I were to court Miss Bennet—properly—and if I could show her that I am not the vicious beast she must have thought me at times, perhaps she would consent to marry me. You would approve?"

I smile at him. It is rather endearing to hear him speak in terms so uncertain. "Yes!" I declare. "Unless of course, you think Miss Bingley would like to fill the office."

He raises his eyebrow at me. "If a lifetime of torture was what I wanted, I would choose Anne first. At least it would be quiet torture," he retorts, and we continue our walk. He is smiling all the way, and I know his head is full of Miss Bennet. "We will have a new family at Pemberley," he declares just before we reach the house again. He kisses my forehead and leads me inside.

The next day I rise and practice early in anticipation of spending the remainder of the day getting ready for, and enjoying, Miss Bennet and the Gardiners' visit. My brother leaves the house before I am finished and when he returns he has distressing news: Miss Bennet has been called home unexpectedly and will not be joining us today. I am disappointed, but my brother—who had the day before been talking of marriage and new families—is, quite clearly, both angry and brokenhearted. This combination of emotions I have seen before, regarding the same woman, and I do not know what to do. He is close to silent for the remainder of the day, and in the evening I want to suggest that perhaps he should join Mr. Bingley when he returns to Hertfordshire, but am too afraid to speak to him.

I try to outlast Mr. Bingley's sisters, but as I do not wait until ten o'clock to rise, I cannot. Fitzwilliam approaches me and recommends that I retire with a kiss on my head, which I know is not a suggestion, but a command. I sigh and bid him good night, walking slowly to my room. The day has turned out quite differently than I had expected and hoped and I wish that I knew why.

When the house is finally dark and quiet I hear his footsteps. They are distinctive—strong, sharp, and quick. He is pacing. He walks up and down the hallway at least four times before his steps slow down, and before long he is shuffling his feet. When I hear his footsteps stop at the end of the hallway opposite his chamber door, I rise and put on my robe. I step out to the hall.

He is sitting slumped on the cold marble floor, his arms resting on his legs, bent at the knee. There is—not surprisingly—a bottle of wine resting between his feet. I sit next to him.

"Go to bed, Georgiana."

"Tell me what is troubling you."

"No."

"I am not a child, you know, Fitzwilliam. You can confide in me. I may not be able to do anything for you, but at least I can listen and help bear your burden."

He looks at me with eyes swollen from sorrow and narrow from anger. "Go to bed, Georgiana."

"No," I say emphatically, quite perturbed with him. "I beg you, Fitzwilliam, just talk to me. It will do more good than drowning your troubles in that bottle of wine."

His head thumps against the wall; I wince for him but he does not seem to feel it. "Oh...my dear sister." He shakes his head now, back and forth, in a rather exaggerated manner. "You would be too distressed by what is going through my head."

"And what is going through your head?"

"The fact that I am in love with a woman who will never have me."

In any other circumstance, I would rejoice at his confession of love. "You are speaking of Miss Bennet?"

"I am."

"And why will she never have you?"

"Because her youngest sister has run away with damned Wickham, and she knows that I could have prevented it."

Stunned, I stare for a moment. "What has Wickham done?"

Fitzwilliam flops his head in my direction. "He ran away with Miss Lydia Bennet." He reaches for his wine. "She has nothing— no money, no connections, few friends. Nothing that will tempt Wickham to marry her. She is lost to her family and I could have prevented it." He lifts the bottle by its neck to his lips and takes an untidy swig.

"He has ruined that poor girl," I whisper, covering my mouth with my hand. "Miss Lydia Bennet could so easily have been me."

"No," drawls Fitzwilliam, "for Wickham would have married you. He will not marry Miss Lydia Bennet. She has nothing to offer him."

"Truly, they have nothing?" I ask, beginning to worry for my new friend. How distressed must she now be! "There is no way he would marry her?"

"If she had what you have, perhaps," he replies with another swig of his wine, "but she has not, and so he won't."

We fall quiet for a moment. I know not what my brother is thinking, but my head is swimming with the words that he used to describe Miss Lydia Bennet's situation.

She is lost to her family.

He will not marry Miss Lydia Bennet.

I could have been lost to mine—despite what my brother might say, had I married Wickham I would eventually have figured out that he did not love me, and only wanted my fortune. I am enough ashamed of what I almost did; had I actually eloped, I would never have been able to face my brother again.

I eye the bottle and am tempted to drink of it myself. Instead I shake my head. "She will now never see her parents and four sisters again. Oh…poor Miss Bennet." My words are but a whisper, but my brother hears them.

Fitzwilliam, astonishingly, belches and then sighs. "I do hope, dear sister, that the poor Miss Bennet to whom you are referring is Miss *Elizabeth* Bennet, because while Wickham is a complete rake and I would like to throttle him for what he has done, Miss *Lydia* is not exactly…bright."

This declaration disquiets me and I sit back against the wall. Is this what my brother thinks of me—that because I fell for Wickham's charms and deceitful ways, that I am similarly obtuse?

"Which makes it all the more shameful!" he declares, starting his rant again. "He *knows* she does not realize he will not marry her." He sighs and drinks again, letting the wine dribble down his chin before wiping his mouth with the sleeve of his shirt. "The man could charm the scales off a bloody snake."

It is an interesting thing, hearing my brother talk in clichés. And curses. Belching, with wine dribbling down his chin. I look him over, and for perhaps the first time in my life, I see him not as my older brother, deserving of respect and deference; a young man born not just to wealth but to tremendous responsibility, forced upon him before he was ready. Before me instead I see a sulking little boy who has not gotten his way, and I want to giggle before I recall what the cursing and wine is all about.

"Fitzwilliam, all is not lost. You do not know that Miss Bennet would never have you."

"No," he dismisses me, "she will not. I have had a hand in ruining her family; what woman would not hate such a man?"

"You do not deserve hate," I say sharply. "Wickham does. And how on Earth could you have prevented this? You did not know he would do this."

"But if I had not felt it beneath me to explain the rift between Mr. Wickham and myself, none of this would have happened. None of it, Georgiana, none at all. For God's sake, I might even be married already."

I laugh a little. "Oh...my, brother, what a dramatic streak you have got," I tease. He ignores me. "What would you have done— would you have exposed your entire past, and mine, to all of Meryton? No one should have to do such a thing. This is not your fault.

And let me be the first to assure you, being a young lady myself, and knowing what it is to be deceived by the man, that Miss Elizabeth Bennet is at this moment likely blaming *herself* for what has happened. She also knew what he was, Fitzwilliam...." I sigh and look earnestly into my brother's tortured eyes. "And neither of you are to blame. It is Mr. Wickham and Lydia Bennet's doing."

"She *did* blame herself," he says quietly, and shakes his head. "But she is not to blame. I am." I start again to protest, but sobriety has suddenly overtaken Fitzwilliam and he stands. "And so I will have to do something about it." He picks up his wine bottle and begins down the hall, striding confidently as though nary a drop of alcohol had touched his lips.

I rise to follow after him. I have to walk quickly to keep up with his long, purposeful stride. "What are you going to do?"

He slows to a stop. "I must find him. I have no doubt that Mr. Bennet and Mr. Gardiner are intelligent and resourceful, but they will not know where to look. I am the only one who can find him, and find him I must." He puts his free hand on my shoulder. "Georgiana, I will have to go to London early tomorrow. Mr. Bingley will not want to stay long and will encourage his sisters to return to Grosvenor Street in a few days. I will write to you every day and will return as soon as I possibly can."

I kiss his cheek before I turn back to my chamber. "You must do one more thing."

"And what may I do for you, dear sister?"

"You must hope."

He pauses a moment, looking me in the eyes. Purpose has returned to his, but that is not what I want to see.

"I will if I find reason to."

It is all I can ask for. I smile and enjoy an embrace from my brother before turning in.

In the morning I am left with the unenviable task of making my brother's excuses and playing hostess to the Bingleys and Hursts. Mrs. Annesley tells me not to fret over it. "It is good practice," she says. "You will one day find yourself hostess to less gracious visitors." Mr. Bingley and Mr. Hurst are well able to entertain themselves; one out of courtesy for me, the other out of habit. It is the Bingley sisters that have me flustered, since I am certain that at some point I shall be questioned about my brother's reasons for returning to London so hastily. When the time comes, however, I find happily that a general explanation of business satisfies and bores them into changing the subject.

The next day, the Bingleys and Hursts depart Pemberley, no doubt at Miss Bingley's urging. My brother's first letter arrives the day after. He says only that he has arrived, that he has been rather occupied with his task and that he is hopeful that Wickham can be located. I wish that I could write to Miss Bennet and ask how she is faring; to reassure her that my brother's regard is steadfast, but I did not have the opportunity to ask her before she left Derbyshire.

The weeks pass slowly, and I receive a letter at least every Wednesday from Fitzwilliam. He does not mention his quest at all and in his words there is a tone of distance. I can almost see him as he writes them to me, with the mask in full force.

Mrs. Annesley's lessons provide much-needed routine and purpose for these long days. She seems to think my French is improving and she wants to teach me German. I hope she allows me to concentrate on one language at a time. I have barely mastered English, after all.

Five weeks after my brother suddenly departed Pemberley, I receive a letter to lift my heart.

Dear Georgiana,

It will be but a few days before I am home again. I am sure I am as anxious to be there as you are to have me return.

I have not mentioned the purpose of my coming to London to you since I arrived. This has been largely due to the general unpleasantness of the situation and the fact that I did not wish to trouble you. However, I think that you should know that Mr. George Wickham and Miss Lydia Bennet were married this morning. The bride at least was pleased with this event, although I believe Mr. and Mrs. Gardiner mourn somewhat for their niece. I do not know whether they will travel into Hertfordshire before he is obliged to join to his regiment in Newcastle, but it does not signify. However ungrateful they both are, my task has been accomplished and perhaps my mind can now be at ease.

That would, indeed, be welcome. Fitzwilliam continues the letter by telling me all about Mr. and Mrs. Gardiner's children, and how kind that couple was to him during his search. When I am finished with the letter I tuck it away and prepare the house to receive him in the next day or so.

When he arrives, he is somber and quiet. He does not talk much and he spends several days almost exclusively with Mr. Albertson. We spend every morning at least together and many afternoons walking in the park; I play and sing for him every evening, but weeks pass before we have meaningful conversation.

"Georgiana," he says, hesitantly, as we have our breakfast some three weeks after his return from London, "may I ask...does it trouble you?" His shoulders are tense and there is gravity in his look; he fidgets with his butter knife.

"Does what trouble me?"

"Wickham's marriage. You...you at one time had some very strong feelings for him."

I look into my teacup. "I do think on it sometimes," I confess, "but beyond wondering how Miss Elizabeth Bennet is faring, it does not trouble me."

"It does not?" he asks. My assurances seem to have lifted some weight from his shoulders.

"No," I say quietly. I take a breath to steel myself and then continue. "If I still believed Mr. Wickham loved me, or that I loved Mr. Wickham, I am sure it would bother me. I...I am still angry at him." I look my brother in the eyes and can see what Mrs. Annesley sees... the pain of a betrayed friend. "For what he did to you as well as for what he did to me. But I shall ever be grateful to you, Fitzwilliam, for making me see what he truly is."

I want, desperately, for my brother to embrace me, but I know he will not.

Instead he draws a mighty breath and informs me, "I have taken every precaution to ensure that Mr. Wickham will not importune our family any longer. I may not say it very often, Georgiana, but I do adore you and I would be heartbroken if I ever lost you."

Tears fill my eyes as I exhale. "I love you, my dear brother." Proud of both of us, and knowing he will want to collect himself, I rise, kiss his head, and leave the breakfast room.

The following afternoon when we gather for tea, Fitzwilliam is quiet and I amuse myself by watching a pair of rabbits play just beyond the window. Mrs. Reynolds enters the room and quietly addresses my brother. She leaves quickly, and then he approaches me.

"Georgiana," he says, while taking my hand gently in his, "I have a confession to make.."

I set down my teacup. This statement was not lightly made. I prepare myself for some shocking news. "What is it?" I ask.

"When you were a little girl, you asked if our mother had not sat for a portrait. I said that she had not. It was not true."

This, I am shocked at. Not so much that there should be a portrait of my mother, but that my brother should have lied about it, and that he should remember my asking so long ago. "It was not?"

"No," he says solemnly, shaking his head. "Though I did not know it at the time, I have known it for a number of years. I am sorry, Georgiana."

"Then there is a portrait of my mother? May I not see it?"

Fitzwilliam smirks a little. "Yes," he says, and tucks my hand into his arm. We leave the sitting room, bound for the gallery. He explains himself as we walk. "There are two. She sat for one when she was sixteen, and another shortly after her marriage to our father. When she died, he requested that the first, which hung in Matlock, be sent to him. He was very, very angry...he was bent on destroying them both." In the gallery we stop before two portraits draped in black. "No one knows who put them away, but Mrs. Reynolds found them after his death and asked if I would not like them to be hung. I did not even look at them—I was too upset. I told her to put them away...but I remembered them a few days ago."

"Why were you both so very angry with her?" I ask. This does not seem rational at all.

"I was not angry with her," he tells me, but his voice is sharp with the emotion. "Our father was. His anger I cannot vouch for, nor can I say when it ebbed. He sent me to school but a day after she was laid to rest and I did not see him for two full years."

"You were angry at him." I am starting to understand some things—dare I think one of these could be my brother?

He is quiet, staring at the shrouded portraits. Oh, and there it is—that strong, controlled facade. I hate it when this happens.

I clutch his arm. "Please," I beg him. "Please tell me what you are thinking." He turns his head, and for a moment, he will not look at me. "Fitzwilliam, please."

He turns back to me, and the mask is gone. Sorrow fills his eyes. "Yes, I was very angry with him. It was not her fault that she died... it is not my fault..."

He turns away again. After a moment, he turns back, and without looking at me, removes the black covering from our mother's portraits.

I am stunned. Absolutely stunned—I cannot think for several moments. I understand now. I understand why my father always spoke highly of Fitzwilliam, only to decline to visit him at school. I understand why he wrote such long letters, with every intention of assisting Fitzwilliam in whatever he asked for, but relegated himself to London during the summers. Oh, I understand—for here before me, immortalized on canvas, is my mother, and there is not one feature of hers that she did not give to my brother in birth. Fitzwilliam's beauty is merely a copy of hers. My father could not bear to look at Fitzwilliam—at his own son.

"And it was not only this," he says, gesturing severely at the portraits, trying desperately to control his voice. "Every mannerism... every tilt of my head or gesture of my hand reminded him of her. Now I ask you, Georgiana, what young boy would not be angry at a father who refused to look upon him, as though he were hideous?"

His voice becomes choked at the last; I silently stroke his arm and wish I knew what to say. Faster than I realize, connections are being made in my head. My father could not stand to look at his own son, but his steward's was a fine replacement for the affection that he missed, for he could look at a Wickham and not see his wife—a wife whose death he blamed on himself, for she died in childbirth, which was a circumstance he brought upon her.

"Why did he not hate *me*?" I ask. "If she died giving me life, then why did he not despise me?"

He takes a breath and turns, smiling a little at me. "Nobody can hate such a tiny little thing as a baby," he says softly. "Especially a little baby girl with golden curls, such as you had. He fell in love with you from the moment he laid eyes on you."

My eyes fill with tears as I look again upon my mother. "How can you bear all of this, Fitzwilliam?" I ask him. "He fell in love with me, as you put it, at the same time he resolved on never looking at you, his son and heir. It is not just." My voice breaks and I look away for a moment. "It is not reasonable."

He is quiet for a moment before he answers me. "Many things in life are unfair, my dear," he replies. "I was angry with Father my whole life for this reason, and I never truly got to know him. Now he is gone and I have not the chance."

"You may regret the anger, but it is not unfounded. I never understood, until now."

"There is more that I regret," he continues softly. "I regret ever having hidden these away. Not for my own sake, for I recall Mother's face with clarity in my mind, but for yours, Georgiana. You might have known your mother all this time, and because of me, you have not." There is that heaviness in his voice which is a clear indication of the self-reproach he is unfortunately good at.

"You take too much upon yourself," I say quickly. "Truly, my dear brother. You are not to be blamed for every little thing that goes ever slightly amiss in my life. I know you think you could have protected me from Wickham, but you were misled about Mrs. Younge's character, and I should have known better than to arrange to run away with him. And these portraits…" I pause, turning to them. "I am just grateful to have them now."

Fitzwilliam embraces me. "My dear sister," he whispers into my hair. "Whatever would I do without you?"

"You would be thirty thousand pounds richer with a less heavy heart," I reply in all seriousness.

My brother pulls away and solemnly takes my chin between his thumb and forefinger. "Georgiana, that is not true. You mean so much to me…I do not know how to tell you how much."

There is a rather unexpected rap on the wall at the far end of the gallery. We both look up, but my brother is not surprised at it.

"Yes?" he addresses the footman, patiently.

"The carriage is ready, sir, and your horse is 'round front."

"Thank you, Davis." He nods and walks away.

"Carriage?" I demand impatiently. "Where are you going?"

He hesitates before he answers. "I am going to join Bingley at Netherfield. I have some rather important personal business with him." He pauses again and swallows. "It concerns a young lady he is exceedingly fond of."

My heart plummets into my stomach and my face turns white. Before I think what is about to come out of my mouth, my lips move. "Oh, for Heaven's sake—not *me*, I hope?"

He smiles and lays his hand against my cheek. "Georgiana, I am sorry. Mr. Bingley is fond of you, but he is in love with the lady of whom I speak. There are some things about her that I said to him, which I ought not to have, and some things I did not say, which I ought to have. I must set things right. It is quite likely that he will be engaged within the month—within a *week*, if I know Bingley."

I let out a breath. "Oh…I am pleased for Mr. Bingley," I say, but really more relieved for myself.

He shakes his head and takes my hands in his. "I presumed too much when I matched Bingley with you," he says. "It was only in my own head, I know, but my desire to see you settled safely within my reach interfered with my good judgment. For that I must apologize, and do what I am able to do for my friend."

My face shines with a smile; I am so very proud of him. "How long must you be gone?"

"I do not know," he replies. "I should think not longer than a week, but that should depend upon Bingley. Then I will be on to London."

"Perhaps Mrs. Annesley and I could come to London in a few days, in case you decide you rather enjoy London too much to come home?" I ask, hoping he will agree. I hate to be away from him now.

He smiles. "Yes, I think that shall do nicely. You can make the arrangements to travel with your companion, and write to let Mrs. Edstrom know to expect the pair of you."

I smile and kiss his cheek gleefully, until a thought occurs to me. "Fitzwilliam," I say slowly, "do you expect to see Miss Elizabeth Bennet while you are in Hertfordshire?"

His face turns somber. "Yes, I do," he replies quietly. "The lady that I spoke of, who Bingley is in love with, is Miss Elizabeth's elder sister, Miss Jane Bennet."

"Will you send her my best wishes, and invite her to write to me, if she will?"

My brother lays his hand in mine and smiles a little. "If Miss Elizabeth and I get the chance to speak, yes, I will." He swallows and continues, in that pessimistic way he has, by saying, "Keep in mind, however, that I do not expect that Miss Elizabeth and I will have the opportunity to speak privately, or that she will speak to me at all." I just shake my head and kiss his cheek. He promised, so he will do it.

After a whirlwind of preparation with Mrs. Annesley and Michelle, we arrive in London on Wednesday and expect my brother on the following morning. He arrives in relatively good spirits and though he has some business to conduct with his solicitor and a handful of calls to return, he and I are able to spend much of the day together.

That afternoon, on a search for a boring letter from Putrid Anne which I have misplaced, I take myself into the front drawing room. I am not paying much attention to anything but surfaces and the placement of the items upon them, so I am startled to find a young man standing next to the fireplace. I jump and cover my mouth, and then begin to apologize profusely.

The young gentleman holds up a hand to reassure me. "I beg your pardon, Madam," he says. "I am sorry to startle you. I am waiting for Mr. Darcy."

"I am here," comes my brother's voice from the entrance to the room, and with a happy look on his face he strides swiftly over to the young man and holds out his hand.

The man takes it, smiling as well. "It is good to see you, Darcy."

"And you, Henry," replies my brother, shaking his hand firmly. "You look well."

"I am well; thank you."

My brother looks to me with a smile. "Miss Georgiana Darcy, this is Mr. Henry Beresford. Henry, this is my sister, Miss Darcy."

I used to think that my brother was the most beautiful man that I had ever seen, but oh…how wrong I was. Mr. Henry Beresford has the most clear green eyes I have ever seen, and as they focus on me, he smiles and they turn joyful. I am so stunned that I have quite forgot on what purpose I came into the sitting room. As I go through the motions of my curtsey, I almost cannot bear to take my eyes off of his.

"I am pleased to meet you, Miss Darcy," he says. "I have heard much about you over the years."

My brother goes on to explain that Mr. Beresford is an old friend of his, and while he and my brother have written very faithfully they have not had a chance to meet in several years.

Fitzwilliam then invites Mr. Beresford into the library and we part. He is gone by the time my lessons with Mrs. Annesley are all complete. I am disappointed, but take the opportunity to question my brother about his friend with the bright green eyes as we take our tea.

"Tell me more about Mr. Beresford. Where is he from?" I demand.

Fitzwilliam smirks and sips tea. "He is from Northhamptonshire, where his family has lived for several generations."

"And have they an estate?" I ask. "Has he any brothers or sisters?"

"They have a vast estate," he replies, "possibly as large as Pemberley. And he has two brothers."

"And how long have you been acquainted with him, my dear brother?"

Fitzwilliam chuckles a little. "I met him several years ago in London, where his father introduced us. His father and ours were great friends."

"They were?"

"Yes. Is it such a shocking thing to know that our father had friends?"

I smile at his remark. "No. It is only that I do not remember any of them." I fall quiet for a while, wanting to ask more but too embarrassed to do so. Fitzwilliam watches me as I look idly around the room.

"The elder Mr. Beresford is still living. It is very likely that you shall meet him one day...perhaps he will have a tale or two to tell about our father."

I look at him shyly. "I would like that." Then I sniffle, for no reason, and look around the room some more. I catch my brother shaking his head.

"What is the matter, Fitzwilliam?" I ask in all sincerity.

"Georgiana..." He pauses and looks thoughtful for a moment. "Please understand, dear girl...your upbringing has been something I would not have let another do for anything, and I am not going to let you go so easily. I will not give *any* man my consent—I would not even have given it to *Bingley*—until you are eighteen."

I want to laugh at him but dare not. "What has effected such a statement from you, sir?"

He smirks. "Let me say only that in the library, Mr. Beresford was quite as curious about my sister as she now is about him."

My cheeks turn bright red. "He is not married, then?"

Fitzwilliam sighs. "No, he is not." He then adds quickly, "But I beg you to be careful, Georgiana...I do not want to see you hurt again."

My heart fills and I smile at him as my eyes glisten. "With your guidance, Fitzwilliam, I shall be well. I promise." He smiles at me, and out of the corner of my eye, I finally see the item for which I have been searching. I jump up, kiss Fitzwilliam's cheek, and twirl out of the room, waving Putrid Anne's boring letter.

⸻

In the late afternoon on that Saturday, we receive a most unexpected caller—my esteemed aunt, Lady Catherine de Bourgh.

"Georgiana," she says, before the poor butler has the chance to announce her, "you will leave your brother and me to speak privately."

I gaze at her. Her entire face is red and puffy and there is a sharp gleam in her eye which I do not like—she is *furious*. I am too stunned to move and would prefer to stay and hear what she has to accuse my brother of.

"Georgiana, you are not hard of hearing. Go find something useful to do; we have important business to discuss."

Finally my brother rises and manages to stammer, "Lady Catherine, it is a pleasure to see you here."

"Mr. Darcy, I have had quite enough cheek for one day," warns my aunt, and then she turns back to me. "Georgiana, I will not repeat myself."

After a confused pause, Fitzwilliam tilts his head to me. "Georgiana, perhaps you should go."

I purse my lips and glare at him and plan to quiz him later. With a significant look of displeasure at both of them, I rise to leave the room.

To my surprise, Mrs. Edstrom is standing there with a drinking glass. She hands it to me, and I take it.

"Whatever is this for?" I ask, wondering if the world has gone suddenly mad.

She says nothing, but takes the glass from my hand. She steps left of the drawing room door and places the rim of the glass against the wall and presses her ear to the bottom of it. Then she hands it back to me. Curious, I copy her and hear my aunt say, "...speak with your sister about her growing impertinence. I have read her letters to Anne..."

I smile at Mrs. Edstrom in thanks and turn back to the wall as she walks away, intently listening.

"What is the purpose of your visit, Madam?" He sounds impatient.

"What is the nature of your relationship to Miss Elizabeth Bennet? I demand a straightforward answer."

"I am acquainted with Miss Elizabeth Bennet, and have been for about a year. Why do you ask?"

"And have you made Miss Bennet an offer of marriage?"

My brother says nothing for a moment; I am nervous for him. "What has you asking these peculiar questions, Lady Catherine?"

"I will tell you," she snaps, and I can hear her cane tapping on the floor as she paces. I imagine her circling my brother as a vulture does his prey. "On Thursday evening Mr. Collins paid me a visit. He was very alarmed and knew that I would be, and when you know the reason for it, I hope you too shall be alarmed. Mr. Collins informed me that your friend—that Bingley fellow—is lately engaged to Miss Elizabeth Bennet's sister. He lamented, as he should, for your friend; I hope you know that his choice is not a wise one."

She pauses here, and I assume she is waiting for my brother to agree. He does not; she continues. "He then informed me of a particular report currently circulating in Hertfordshire which concerns you."

"And of what does the report consist, Madam?"

"It is said that you will soon be, if you are not already, engaged to Miss Elizabeth Bennet. Although I know this to be impossible, we must now formalize your engagement to my daughter. I will not have these rumors flying about and upsetting my Anne every time you smile at a young lady."

"I do not smile at young ladies, Madam." Fitzwilliam's tone is dark; he is clearly upset.

"Nevertheless, these things cannot be allowed to get out of control, Darcy. I have already secured the young lady's assurances that the report is false, and there is no more reason to delay the engagement."

I wonder where the rumor came from as I wait for my brother's reply. He is quiet for an uncommonly long time. He coughs. "You have…*her* assurances that she is not engaged to me?"

"That is what I said."

"And how came you by this information?"

"From the lady herself, of course," she replies, nettled.

"You visited Miss Bennet?"

"I did. She was impertinent and willful and I was too long in her company."

"What did she say?" Here my brother's voice is slightly raised in pitch; he is nervous.

My *brother* is *nervous*.

"If you must have the narrative, I will give it to you," she snaps, and the cane begins tapping again. "I arrived at Longbourn this morning and was greeted only by silence and open-mouthed stares." This, of course, is a clear indication that she was exceedingly rude. I am not surprised. "I applied to Miss Bennet to walk out with me, which she did reluctantly. I came directly to my point, as I always do, by demanding that she contradict the report which I received from Mr. Collins two days ago. She pretended not to know of it and then informed me that she may choose not to answer some of my questions, if she did not like it. She had to be consistently reminded of my superior consequence. She paid no mind to my position. It was outrageous! That girl is headstrong, conniving, and foolish, and Darcy, if you do not take care, she will ruin you!"

Fitzwilliam coughs. "Did you happen to mention your desire for Anne to marry me?" asks my brother, with that nervous pitch in his voice.

"I did. For my part I explained too much—she ought to have accepted my wishes and made the promise which I asked of her."

A pause. "Promise, Madam? What did you ask of her?"

My aunt snorts. "Of course I asked for her word that she would never enter into an engagement with you," she replies. "She would not give it, though if she did I doubt that I could trust it. She is perfectly obstinate. I do not want Georgiana in her company, Darcy, if you should choose to visit Mr. Bingley and his unfortunate new family after he is married."

"She would not promise?"

"No, she would not. You see how serious this situation is. Therefore, I must demand—"

"I thank you, Lady Catherine," says my brother hurriedly, "for bringing this to my attention. As it happens, I shall be in Hertfordshire this Tuesday morning. I shall do whatever is in my power to settle these matters while I am there."

There are footsteps heading toward the door, so I am forced to dash for the kitchen while Fitzwilliam shows Lady Catherine out. When I am certain she has gone, I search for him again. He is pacing in the drawing room.

"Fitzwilliam?"

He turns at my entrance and rushes toward me, taking my upper arms. His eyes are wild with nervousness and excitement. "She did not promise she would not marry me."

I try to feign ignorance. "Who did not promise?"

"Georgiana, I know you were listening," he admonishes with a silly kind of smirk. "I am speaking of Miss Bennet, of course!"

I blush and bite my lip. "You are not upset that I was listening?"

"No," he replies, "I am too anxious to be concerned about what you are doing."

I laugh at him. "Fitzwilliam, I told you!" I declare, laying my hand against his cheek. "I told you that you must hope, and now you see that there is *reason* to hope."

He looks earnestly into my eyes, and his soften. "I thought I *did* hope, Georgiana," he says quietly. "She would not give her promise to Lady Catherine never to marry me; if she had decided totally against me, she would have issued what Lady Catherine asked for."

"What are you going to do?" I ask, smiling.

"I will join Bingley again at Netherfield, as I had planned. I will leave on Monday and be in Longbourn by Tuesday morning. From there, I cannot say what I will do. It depends upon Miss Elizabeth."

I smile and happily kiss his cheek, leaving him to prepare for his journey and extracting a promise for a letter with any news as soon as it occurs.

———◆———

On Friday, after much patient waiting on my part, I receive a letter from my dear brother, dated the previous Wednesday.

My dear Georgiana:

At last, today I am able to write to you. I have every hope that this missive finds you quite well, studying, and entertaining Mr. Pritchard.

I have visited Longbourn, and as I know you are anxious to read all I will write about the ladies living therein—and one in particular—I shall delay no longer in relating their conditions to you.

Miss Mary Bennet, who looks much like her father, is a quiet young lady to be sure, though I think you might like her. I have observed that she shares your love of music—or at least your determination to play it. She is very studious, and reads a great deal, though I think she might benefit from some variation of topic.

Miss Catherine Bennet is a pretty young girl, closer in age to yourself than Miss Mary. I think you would like her, as well. Her sisters call her Kitty. She is petite, blonde, and with a very interested mind, much improved, I think, by the marriage of her sister.

And now, dear sister, you shall hear of the one Bennet about whom you must be the most curious—

My heart races at the anticipation that I might hear good news relating to Miss Elizabeth; I jump up and smile.

Miss Jane Bennet ——

Oh! That teasing man! He will be punished.

—— is, according to her mother, quite the prettiest of all her daughters—no mean feat, I assure you, for she has five of them. Bingley must agree with her; I must not. But I am sure you shall like Jane very much, and I have fixed it so that you and Mrs. Annesley may travel to Netherfield to meet her, some two weeks before the wedding, and stay through a month, and perhaps you might like it better to stay at Longbourn after the wedding. It is not a very large house, but I am assured that there would be room for you—Mrs. Bennet has a few guest rooms, which might be used by the Gardiners; however, if that be the case, Miss Bennet's room will no longer be in use, and Mrs. Annesley could stay there. You, of course, would stay in Miss Elizabeth's room. She will be traveling to London, and as I am going with her, there will be no need for the Bennets to accommodate me.

I pause. I go over my brother's cryptic lines to be sure of what I have read. There is only one reason—one reason which supposes proper behavior—that my brother would travel with Miss Bennet to London, quite by themselves, and that would be that they were married.

Oh! Married!

I jump up again, smiling, and I read on:

I am sorry, my dear girl, that you are not with me at such a time as this. I should very much like to share my joy with you. I could not help teasing you—Miss Elizabeth's tendencies to do so must be contagious. As you are likely the sole member of my family very much pleased by my choice, your support will be missed when I receive replies from my uncle and aunt.

"Miss Darcy," interrupts Mrs. Annesley, "what has your brother to say that has gotten you so excited?"

I spin around. "Oh! It is such wonderful news. My brother is getting married!"

She declares her joy at this information. "To whom shall he be wed? I hope not to his cousin," she teases, knowing the answer full well. "She must be a great lady to have secured his affection."

"Miss Elizabeth Bennet," I reply, impatiently reading through the rest of my letter. When I am done, I put it in my lap. "She is from Hertfordshire. She visited us in Derbyshire this August, when we were there with Mr. Bingley and his sisters."

"I remember Miss Bennet and her aunt and uncle," replies my good companion. "More particularly I recall the way Miss Bingley glared at her."

"Miss Bingley will not take this news well," I say, wondering whether I should laugh or be concerned. Her hopes were all in vain from the very start, after all...but nonetheless, I think she might be hurt.

"Everything happens for a reason, Miss Darcy," says Mrs. Annesley. "This might be an eye-opening experience for Miss Bingley. Perhaps she might learn that the charms she possesses, which she assumed would attract your brother, have no real merit."

I think it more likely that she will learn to be bitter, but keep my opinion to myself. "But my brother is a particular kind of man," I say cautiously. "Don't you agree? He is not like other men. I am sure I have not met any quite so generous or kind, or genuine and artless."

Mrs. Annesley laughs at me. "Georgiana, dear, he is your *brother*. Of course you think so well of him. And I might remind you that you are not yet out, and the list of young men with whom you are acquainted can be counted out on one hand and half are your own relations."

I smile and turn pink—she is right, of course. "But you must at least agree that a full quarter of them are rakes," I counter.

She laughs again. "Yes, a full quarter." She shakes her head and gazes at me, and I can see a little affection in her eyes. "One man, Georgiana. *One man.* Do not give him another thought; he is not worth it."

I smile at her. "No, he is not." I look back at my happy letter. "Married!" I shake it in the air. "Not to Putrid Anne. Not to Caroline the Peacock. To someone he loves." I sit and read it again, and sigh when I am done. Mrs. Annesley is laughing at me still.

It is Friday. The morning is bright and cold and I rise to put on my new blue silk gown. My expectations for another letter from Fitzwilliam are high; it has been nearly two weeks since his last arrived.

There will be no letter today, however, for the gentleman himself is standing there as I walk into the breakfast room. And with such a smile! He holds out his hands; I take them.

"Fitzwilliam?" I smile. He kisses my forehead, but does not speak for a moment. To encourage his affection, I rest my head on his shoulder.

I feel his firm stance soften; he holds me close. "I am so happy," he whispers. "Dear sister, I have not been this happy."

This admission brings tears to my eyes. He rubs my back and I pull away to look at him. His eyes are wet, but he is not embarrassed. "Everything is settled?" I ask, smiling as I squeeze his hands.

"Yes," he replies. "We are to be married alongside Bingley and Miss Bennet at the end of November. If you like it, you will come to Netherfield in a few weeks' time—"

"Fitzwilliam, I do not care about your plans for me," I reply. "I will do and be whatever or where ever you wish; you have only need to say. But I do want to hear all about it." I pull him toward the table and sit him down at his place. Then I fire off questions—What did you say? How did you ask? Where were you? How did you come so quickly to an understanding?

He laughs—something which my brother has not done in quite some time. "Dear girl, these are questions best asked of Miss Bennet herself. Why do you not write her?"

"Would she wish it of me?" I ask, a little astonished.

"Silly question," he replies. "When I left her she asked me to bring you this." He pulls a piece of paper from his breast pocket and hands it to me. I read what she has written in flowing hand:

My dear Miss Darcy,

Today I send your brother home to you quite unwillingly. Though I know he goes to a lady he very much adores I cannot help but be a little jealous and hope for his safe and speedy return. Mr. Darcy assures me that you will come to Netherfield to stay for a fortnight before the wedding. I hope you will allow me to introduce you to my sisters Mary and Kitty, who are about your age, and I should like to spend much time with you myself.

Miss Darcy, I hope with all my heart that you approve of your brother's choice and that I shall meet every expectation you have in a sister. Please write to me, if you like, and I look forward to seeing you very soon at Longbourn.

Very truly yours,
Elizabeth Bennet

About a month later, after I have written to Miss Bennet and she back to me, and my brother and I have called upon her and her aunt and uncle in Gracechurch Street while she was in London, and she repaid the visit, we are on our way to Longbourn. We traveled this morning first to Netherfield and stayed there only long enough to change horses and clothes. As we pull into the drive, I see Miss Bennet's home, and note the way that Fitzwilliam smiles and relaxes, as though what lies inside the stone walls is the key to all his happiness.

Longbourn House, I judge, is little more than half the size of Netherfield Park; however, there is a kind-looking older gentleman standing out front, ready to greet us, who I assume is Mr. Bennet.

My brother hands me down and introduces me to Elizabeth's father. "I am very pleased to meet you, Miss Darcy," he says to me. "Your brother speaks very highly, and very often, of you."

"Your daughter speaks the same way of you, sir," I reply with cheeks ablaze.

Mr. Bennet smirks and tosses a glance in the direction of the house. "You are very welcome, Miss Darcy." I nod quietly and smile as he turns to my brother to welcome him. We then go into the house, as it is rather cold outside. There, Miss Elizabeth Bennet greets me warmly and I am able to sit between my brother and his fiancée in the Bennets' drawing room.

"I hope your journey into Hertfordshire went well," she begins.

"It did," I confirm, without much else to say. "Thank you."

"When did you arrive at Netherfield?"

A little embarrassed by my eagerness to see Miss Bennet again, I hesitate to answer. Fitzwilliam encourages my response with a kind look. "Little more than an hour ago," I say.

Elizabeth smiles. "I hope your brother did not rush you, for I should have to punish him if he did. Really, Mr. Darcy, you ought to know by now never to rush a young lady."

I am a little struck dumb by her playful teasing, even though it is good-natured. As I look to my brother, however, I see no offense, just a look on his face that I have not seen before. I do not know what it is, but I am certain he is not displeased. Still I feel I must defend him.

"It was rather the reverse, Miss Bennet. Please do not scold him. It is I who did the rushing."

"It is true, Miss Bennet," replies my brother, who embarrasses me by continuing, "I rather suspect she had some encouragement from a visitor to her chamber at Netherfield."

Elizabeth smiles gleefully. "And how is Miss Bingley today?"

I cannot help but return her smile. "I thought she said she had a headache," I reply.

"I dare say she does," says Elizabeth quickly. "Mrs. Bennet is visiting Netherfield with Jane and Kitty."

I want to laugh but am not entirely certain whether it should be appropriate in the presence of Mrs. Bennet's husband. I sneak a glance at him. He is smirking, and from this, there is only one thing that I can conclude.

The Bennets are going to take some getting used to.

The next four weeks are a whirlwind. I cry at my brother's wedding and vastly enjoy my time with Kitty Bennet. The time spent with her is like none I have ever spent. I have never had the benefit of a friend my own age. When my brother and new sister arrive at Long-bourn to collect me on their way to Pemberley from London, they are both glowing, refuse to stay long, and promise to invite Kitty to Pemberley in a few months. We promise to write faithfully when we part and Mr. Bennet kisses my hand affectionately.

When we reach Derbyshire, my brother announces that the Beresfords will be coming to visit us the next week, to meet the new Mrs. Darcy. It is quiet at Pemberley until that day, and then a mass of activity takes place to welcome the Beresfords.

Mr. James Beresford and his wife Camille have brought their three sons. Henry, of course, is the eldest; David, the middle son, is lately engaged; and George is the youngest, no more than fifteen.

I am more than pleased to see Mr. Henry Beresford again, and during the evening on which they arrive, he does not leave my side. There is not much to know about me, but Mr. Beresford talks about his family, which by my measure, is large. Beyond those he has brought with him, he has a grandfather still living, and aunts, uncles, and cousins too numerous to recall. Since David will be married in little more than a month, he muses that soon enough he will be able to add sister to the list.

"Elizabeth, of course, is my only sister," I say, "though she herself has four of them."

"Mrs. Darcy, you mean?" he asks, looking in her direction. "She is a lovely woman, and it is clear your brother is happy. You must be pleased with his choice."

"Very much," I say. "Though I am the only one of my family who has always been so."

Mr. Beresford laughs—a delightful sound, low and gentle and melodic. I smile and look down and know I am blushing like an idiot. "It is unfortunate that we cannot always choose our relatives," he says.

"Yes," I agree. "But Fitzwilliam has done very well, I think, in choosing my sister. I only hope I can do so well for him."

Mr. Beresford smiles at me but says nothing. Later in the evening we converse with his two brothers, who are very cheerful young men. Elizabeth smiles at me several times—an affectionate, proud smile that she has, no doubt, adopted from my brother. Fitzwilliam also glances my way on a few occasions during the course of the evening, and also has his protective eye trained on his friend Mr. Beresford, who occasionally looks his way with an amused expression on his face.

I finally retire to my rooms to prepare for bed, but am too excited to sleep. I knock on Elizabeth's chamber door. She is not in bed yet, and invites me in.

"Did you enjoy yourself this evening, Georgiana?" she asks me while brushing her hair.

I giggle a little. "I think it is obvious that I did."

"Yes," she laughs. "And I think Mr. Henry Beresford did, as well. Tell me, did you like his brothers?"

"Oh, they were very kind," I say, but I am not thinking about David or George. Only the eldest son of that family is in my thoughts. I sigh, flopping down on Elizabeth's chaise. "I will not be able to sleep tonight."

"The Beresfords will be here all week," she replies. "You will see Mr. Beresford tomorrow. Do not be too anxious."

"I could have talked with him all night long," I reply, not really listening to Elizabeth.

"I think the feeling is mutual, Georgiana." Elizabeth looks at me, her expression serious. "But do take care, my dear sister. I know what you are thinking—when I was your age I had the same thought about a young man or two."

"You must not say that, Elizabeth," I tell her, feeling chirpy. "You have only ever had eyes for my brother; admit it."

"I will not!" she declares with a laugh. "I hate to break your heart, but my feelings for your brother when I first met him were much different than they are now."

"Oh, do be serious, Lizzy," I say, admonishing her a little. "I know you have not always got on as well as you ought to have, but you must have liked him from the very beginning."

Elizabeth laughs again, to my astonishment. "Absolutely not! And why should we have got on from the start? There is no reason to always be agreeing with your brother, you know. What would vex him, then?"

Elizabeth's chin is turned up and she is grinning, and I suspect she has had more wine than she ought to have had. I smile back at her. "Do you mean to tell me you did not like him?"

"No, no, no," she says, waving her hand. "I disliked him. A lot. I even promised my father that I would never dance with him."

"But why?" I ask, folding my legs up into my chest and wrapping my arms around them.

"He slighted me, you know," my sister states, raising her eyebrow and shaking her hairbrush at me. "I am quite surprised you did not have this story from my mother when you stayed at Longbourn after our wedding." And she then begins to detail my brother's first foray into Hertfordshire society.

"But he is not like that," I tell her, as if she needs to know it. "It is only he is uncomfortable around strangers. And," I admit, almost holding my breath, "at that time he did tend to be a *little* proud."

"A *little*, Georgiana?" laughs Elizabeth, getting up to finish brushing her hair. I blush and bite my lip. I am so happy that he met her, and though I would wish to at this moment, I cannot even begin to express myself, so I remain silent. She sighs as she sits down at her dressing table, and continues her tale. "And then, you know, Mr.

Wickham came into the neighborhood and filled my head with lies that I found all too easy to believe, for more reasons than one."

I become somber for a moment. "Lies roll easily off Mr. Wickham's tongue," I say slowly. And then I realize exactly what Elizabeth has just told me. "You believed his lies?"

"Yes." Then she turns around and looks me in the eye, her face so serious that I would think her suddenly sober if she were not flailing the hairbrush again. "He came into town dressed handsomely in a red coat and a charming smile and had all of Meryton swooning at his very presence. And when the subject of Mr. Darcy came up between us, he wasted no time in informing me—and later, everyone else—that he had been very ill-used by your brother; that he was denied a living willed him by your father." She turns around and pulls the brush slowly through her hair again. "And I believed every word he said—so much so that I laid the accusations at Fitzwilliam's door when we met in Kent."

I am a little shocked. If someone as intelligent and sensible as Elizabeth could be fooled by Wickham, then perhaps I am not quite so silly as I had thought. As if she can sense my thoughts, Elizabeth sets down her brush and moves to sit next to me. "He did the same thing to you that he did to me, with the same objective—revenge upon your brother. He saw in you a young girl in need of attention and affection and that is what he gave to you, with the intention of taking your fortune in return. Had you not been shy or modest he would have found something else in you to exploit." She focuses on braiding her hair for a moment, and when she has tied the ribbon around the end of her braid she turns back to me. "I was mortified to know the truth, but at least, dear Georgiana, I did not lose my heart to him."

"My heart is not lost," I assure her, and then smile as my thoughts turn toward Mr. Beresford again. "Not yet."

She smiles. "Do you know what the worst part was about his running away with Lydia?"

"You were unable to attend your sister's wedding?"

She laughs outright. "That was a blessing!" she says. "But no. The worst part was that my holiday was cut short and I was just starting to fall in love with your brother." She rises and kisses my forehead as I laugh back at her. "Now, go to bed. It is late and I am sure you will have pleasant dreams tonight."

I rise and kiss her cheek. "Thank you, Lizzy." She hugs me and wishes me good night, and I do the same. I shut her chamber door and pause in the hallway to sigh and smile to myself a little, and hear Fitzwilliam entering her chamber though the door to his own.

"Did Georgiana come to discuss Mr. Beresford with you?" I hear him ask his wife.

"Oh, yes," she says. "Her head is quite full of him right now."

"I heard you talking about me, my love," comes my brother's strong voice, "and about my old friend."

"Yes?" says Elizabeth. "And do you always eavesdrop on ladies' conversations?"

"Absolutely. How else would I know what was going on in my own house?"

"You are being silly."

There is a pause. "Madam," I hear from my amused brother, "you are tipsy."

"Yes," she replies, "and I mean to exploit it to the fullest."

I wait, but that is the last I hear from them. I slip away to dream about Mr. Beresford.

Secrets in the Shade
BY BILL FRIESEMA

Bill Friesema lives just outside Chicago in Oak Park, Illinois, a few blocks from Ernest Hemingway's birth home, where he has been a volunteer docent for over a decade. His interest in Jane Austen's writings began after viewing the 1995 BBC production of *Pride and Prejudice*. Over the years, he has written a variety of short stories for his friends at Austen.com. When he is not engaged in his principal task of software development, Bill enjoys baking bread, playing chess, reading, watching classic movies, and running.

"Secrets in the Shade" gives us a look into Darcy and Elizabeth's marriage years down the line, reintroduces Wickham as a possible convert to the side of good, and gives the Darcys a mystery to unravel concerning family scandals from the past.

❦

Chapter 1—Intimation

"William!" Elizabeth called out as she walked briskly down Pemberley's great hall with James in tow. "William, it is useless to hide—we are determined to find you!"

James giggled, ever so appreciative of his mother's playfulness.

"I am here in the study, my dear. Is anything the matter?"

"No, nothing at all. I merely wished to inquire whether we should have the good fortune of your company as we take a turn about the grounds."

James broke away from his mother's grip and ran toward the sound of his father's voice. The loud patter of leather shoes on oak flooring gave Darcy ample warning to set aside pen and paper, and catch the young lad flying onto his lap.

"Papa, you promised that we should all promenade when the weather turned fair, and it is ever so agreeable now."

"That I did, James, and so we shall; but I must first complete some correspondence that I have postponed as long as I could. Have no worry; I am nearly finished, and I shall overtake you and your beautiful mother within the half hour." Darcy smiled as he brushed his son's hair to the side and kissed his forehead. "Run along now; your mother is waiting by the door."

James was more surprised than disappointed, so accustomed had he become to his father's ready attention. Indeed, to the surprise of the Darcy intimates, it was the father who had evolved into the more indulgent parent, always eager to amuse, praise, and forgive. The lad's chief source of disciplined instruction was his mother's cajoling voice, augmented only rarely by application of a firm hand.

Lizzy collected the six-year-old, and they waved in unison before closing the door to the study. A bright afternoon sun had finally dispelled weeks of cold temperatures and dreary wet skies; it was the first truly pleasant day of spring. Elizabeth could by no means decline such an invitation to delight, but first she had to check on the well-being of her other child. She popped into the nursery and found Jenny, her lovely, dark-haired two-year-old, napping. Marion was in watchful attendance. Elizabeth smiled and quietly backed into the hall. Mrs. Reynolds helped outfit mother and son with light coats, and they set off in high spirits toward the shed in search of food for waterfowl.

As they leisurely approached the pond, James looked thoughtfully into his mother's face. She smiled at his innocent intensity.

"What is it that you wish to ask me, James? I can practically read the question on your brow."

"I'm sure you cannot guess what I am thinking."

"Can I not? Oh, I am certain that you are marveling how in the world I could have been so fortunate as to have been blessed with a son so delightful as you!" Elizabeth teased.

"No, Mama, you have it all wrong," James scoffed. "I was just wondering, who is older—you or Papa? That is all."

Elizabeth grinned. "Why, James, do I suddenly look so old to you that you cannot tell? Ha! Your father must be wearing his years very happily, indeed, for he is eight full years older than I am. That is hardly the sort of question to ask of a woman when you wish to make a favorable impression! But what prompts your question, my dear?"

The boy's face brightened with relief. "Oh, I was just worried that you were older than Papa and so you would be the first to die. I am so happy that you will be with Jenny and me for many more years."

"Die, James? What makes you think of such a thing? Was it because Caesar died last winter?" She brushed his cheek with her hand and added softly, "Yes, I miss him very much, too—he was such a good dog and such a good friend."

"Yes, Mama, I have been thinking a lot about Caesar and how he couldn't walk after he broke his leg and couldn't get better."

Elizabeth smiled and hugged James. "No, I'm afraid Caesar was far too old, but he was our ever-faithful companion, and we will always have fond memories of our playtimes with him, won't we?"

After walking a little farther, she added. "Life is such a sweet mystery, James. Perhaps someday, when you grow to be much older, you will understand why beautiful creatures such as Caesar die, and you must promise that when you do, you will explain it all to me. But until then, you must not worry about your father and me, for we shall stay with you and your sister for a very, very long time." She stroked his cheek as he hugged her waist.

As they approached the bench by the water's edge, they were welcomed by cacophonous quacks and honks as ducks and geese swam furiously toward them from the far side of the pond. James began flinging chunks of stale bread toward the ducks to prevent the geese from devouring more than their share. Soon, he knelt down and let the ducks eat directly out of his hand; their furious nibbles tickling his palm so much that he giggled uncontrollably. James was careful, though, to hold his head away, having learned his lesson well the previous autumn when a drake mistook his lower lip for a worm and nipped it hard enough to draw tears.

Elizabeth leaned back on the bench, enjoying the tranquil scene. After half an hour, James had exhausted the supply of bread, and tried to hold the attention of the ducks and geese by throwing twigs and stones into the water. They quickly caught onto the deception, however, and swam away. Soon, James found a supply of flat skipping stones and a new preoccupation.

Elizabeth relaxed in the warm sunshine and closed her eyes for a few moments. The past seven years had been nearly ideal. Life at Pemberley was grand, and although she did enjoy its advantages— including the balls, the music, the solitude of the library, and the walks in the magnificent garden—such pleasures had no lasting hold on Elizabeth's heart. Darcy had claimed that for himself long ago. Yes, Darcy was a good man, a faithful and loving husband and father; but Elizabeth was relieved to have proven that he was not without fault. She would have found it nearly as impossible to live with an unblemished man as to live with dull Mr. Collins! On certain occasions, Darcy had proven himself human enough to suffer poor temper and insensitivity, so he was certainly human enough to complement her own failings. Their life together, although not always smooth, was at least rich with laughter about their own absurdity and with the pleasures of increased intimacy that accompanies reconciliation.

Lizzy was lost in recollection when a sudden shadow broke her reverie. She opened her eyes, expecting to see that a cloud had intercepted the sunlight, only to be startled by a man's shadow slowly approaching from behind.

"Darcy, how naughty of you to give me such a fright! Whatever possessed you to sneak up on me?" But as Elizabeth rose and turned, the shock of recognition made her smile quickly vanish.

Chapter 2—Intrusion

The intruder was all meekness. "Mrs. Darcy, please forgive my sudden appearance. It was not my intention to cause surprise or unease—"

However much the sudden appearance of the interloper perturbed Elizabeth, she quickly regained her composure.

"Mr. Wickham!" she sharply interjected. "You are perhaps the last person I should have expected to encounter here! Whatever could have prompted you to appear, unannounced?"

Wickham was taken aback more by her pointed delivery than by the justice of her sentiment. His hesitation suggested to Elizabeth the possibility that some tragic event had prompted his visit. Her tone softened.

"Is all well with Lydia and the little ones? Is it on their account that you have come?"

Wickham felt relieved that the conversation had taken a more conciliatory turn. "No, that is not the case; Lydia and the children are very well, I thank you. Mildred, Agnes, and Humphrey are growing up in quite a lively way, inventing fresh challenges daily for their mother's patience, it seems. Lydia is unaware of my stopping at Pemberley, or else she would have sent her love; but I shall be delighted to pass along your kind greeting."

Wickham, wanting more time for Elizabeth's temper to abate, bent down to address his nephew, who had walked over to investigate the disturbance. "And this must be James. You have changed much since you visited us three years ago. That was too long ago for you to remember me, I'll wager. But you are quite the young man now, are you not, James, so fancily attired in your handsome coat and boots!"

James retreated behind his mother's dress. "Is that the man that Papa dislikes so fiercely, Mama?"

Elizabeth could only smile at the child's forthrightness. "James, perhaps it would be best if you were to go to the house now, as I need to talk to your uncle for a bit. I shall return to collect you soon; then we shall continue with our walk."

Resenting the interruption of his pleasure, James scowled as he picked up his cap, slapped it against his leg to shake off the dirt, and trudged back toward the house. After he had walked out of earshot, Elizabeth's attention returned to the visitor.

"Mr. Wickham, I am having great difficulty in accounting for your coming to see me without my sister's knowledge. What is the urgency of the matter that prompted such a spontaneous action? What is so important that you could not give notice of your desire to call at Pemberley? And why did you seek me here by the pond, rather than call for me at the entrance of my home?"

"I must ask your forgiveness once again. The matter that motivates me is of some delicacy. For that reason, I have not shared my concerns with Lydia, who—good woman though she is—has not been blessed with a large measure of discretion. I did not formally request a visit, for fear of rejection. The importance of the matter demanded my best effort, and I determined that the most likely chance of success lay with an unannounced call. I did arrive just now with the intention of knocking at your door and requesting a quick word with you alone, so as not to antagonize Mr. Darcy needlessly. But I saw you here on the grounds and decided to approach you here, where it is quite private."

"Mr. Wickham, after a ragged beginning, we have learned to be frank with each other; at the very least, you can have no doubt about my ability to be frank with you. If you have come to request addi tional financial assistance, I can give every assurance that Mr. Darcy will remain deaf to all such entreaties. Given the state of relations between you and my husband, that must surely come as no great shock. As you are doubtless aware, I have endeavored to help Lydia by periodically sending her money that I saved out of my household budget; but I cannot increase such assistance at this time."

"Sister, you are right about my past dealings with your husband, but you mistake the reason for my visit. Both Lydia and I are grateful for your kind assistance, but I do not come with an extended hand. I come rather to solicit your aid in presenting to Mr. Darcy a matter of importance to him, but one that he might be tempted to dismiss, given our strained relations."

Wickham produced an envelope from his coat pocket. "If you would perform the kindness to give this letter to Mr. Darcy, impress upon him the earnest manner in which I delivered it, and entreat his prompt response, I would be much obliged."

"How very mysterious you are, Mr. Wickham!" exclaimed Elizabeth, refusing to accept the letter. "In the current circumstance, I find it impossible to honor your request. I cannot in good conscience promote something that I know so little about. First, divulge the contents of the letter; then, I shall decide whether to abet your cause."

Elizabeth paused and then added, "You know me well enough to respect my discretion; surely, I have proved that to you more than once. You also certainly understand that Mr. Darcy and I never allow secrets to divide us. Your secret is safe with me."

"I wholeheartedly believe that to be true, and you must understand that I intend no disrespect to you. I can only say that the matter I wish to bring to your husband's attention involves the late Mr. Darcy, and I have determined that, for the sake of courtesy, I must discuss the matter with your husband first."

"A secret concerning the late Mr. Darcy? Whatever can you mean? That is too vaporous an implication to provoke me; I am afraid that you must be more forthcoming."

"I am sorry that it is impossible for me to be substantive at this time, but you have my assurance that my information will be of the greatest interest to Mr. Darcy, as it directly concerns not only him but his sister, Georgiana. I am staying at the Lambton Inn for the next few days. Please emphasize to Mr. Darcy the importance of meeting me there this evening or the next."

"Involving both Darcy and Georgiana? Very well, Mr. Wickham. You have succeeded in sufficiently rousing my curiosity, and I shall deliver your letter. I give you fair warning, however, that Mr. Darcy is not likely to grant the meeting you so desperately seek."

Wickham smiled with perverse confidence as he bowed to her, gave her the letter, and kissed her hand. Elizabeth returned only a weak smile. Before she began walking back to the house, she watched him retreat to fetch his horse, jump onto the saddle in one fluid motion, and trot off toward Lambton.

Chapter 3 — Wickham's Letter

Elizabeth could well believe that Wickham would rather not meet her husband at Pemberley. In the neutral setting of the Lambton Inn, Wickham's inferior rank and character would not appear at such a stark disadvantage. He must have carefully thought out the chances and consequences of his scheme.

She entered her home and found an agitated Darcy preparing to leave in search of her. James and Jenny were running after him in the hall.

"Oh, there you are, Lizzy," said her husband. "James told me of the stranger. Did Wickham really dare show his face here?"

"Yes, it was rather a shock to encounter him. He has just departed for Lambton. Excuse me for a moment."

Elizabeth took the children over to the housekeeper. "Mrs. Reynolds, I understand that Mrs. Pearce is making marzipan in the kitchen. I'm sure James would like to shape some animal figures, and maybe he can teach Jenny how to do it, too. Does that sound agreeable, children?"

"Oh yes, Mama," cried James. "I want to make another hog's face, only better than last week's." He grabbed Jenny's hand and led her down the hall. The parents then moved to the privacy of the study.

Darcy looked worried. "What the devil did that scoundrel come round here for? It can only be to our detriment."

"I share the same fears and expressed them plainly to Wickham," replied Elizabeth. "He put me off, however, requesting only that I give you this letter and strongly urge you to respond to it."

Darcy carefully inspected the envelope. "I suspect that such poison ought not to be self-administered. I have a mind to toss it into the fire, unopened. Said he anything about its contents?"

"Only that it pertained to some hidden dealings of your late father, but his demeanor clearly implied some unsavory business."

"So Wickham is attempting to use my father's good name in his design? It is beyond belief that any human being could seek to malign a man who was the source of his prosperity and happiness! My father attended to Wickham's every need, excessively so, and this is how he honors my father's memory?"

Lizzy agreed, but added, "Wickham made particular mention that the letter had equal import for Georgiana. At first, I refused to accept the letter, but upon reconsideration, I felt you might want to ascertain whether Georgiana required protection in this matter."

Darcy acknowledged the implications of the situation, grateful for his wife's concern for Georgiana. He reluctantly broke the seal and began reading aloud:

Mr. Darcy,

My regard for family duty compels me to address you in this letter. As I grow older, I have increasingly come to value good family relations above all. Although I have much to regret about our mutual past, I realize that simple apology, no matter how sincere, would be woefully inadequate to redress the wrongs I have committed. It is my sincere hope, however, that you share my belief that it is never too late for family to replace discord with harmony.

Your excellent father, in the fair and generous manner with which he treated his entire household staff, made all who depended upon him feel like family. That he would deign to become godfather to me speaks to the close relationship that existed between our late fathers. For that intimacy, I shall be forever grateful.

I have come to realize that you, sir, have the same qualities of fairness and generosity that the late Mr. Darcy had. But it is not generosity toward myself that I now seek; rather, it is for an unknown member of your family. Let me state the matter plainly. I have in my possession strong evidence that your late father sired a son outside the marriage bond. Although such news will most likely precipitate disbelief and distress, my source of information is trustworthy. My sole reason for bringing this information to your attention is this: were the circumstances reversed and I had a lost half brother, I certainly would want to know. I expect that you share my sentiments.

I have spoken to no other about this, as such disclosure would be your rightful prerogative alone. I hope that you can now appreciate the pains I have taken to convey this information to you confidentially.

If you would consent to meet with me, this evening or the next, at the Lambton Inn, I will gladly show you the documentation that I possess.

Respectfully,
George Wickham

"How perfectly outrageous!" cried Elizabeth. "I did not think him this cold and calculating, to hide behind praise of family and your father's good name while simultaneously threatening to bring shame to his memory."

"Eternal hell is too cold a residence for that bastard," Darcy muttered as he began to reread the letter.

When he finished, he spoke somberly: "I am certain that Wickham intends to share this document with the world, but he will share it first with Georgiana, driven as he claims to be by strong familial considerations. That is, of course, unless I intercede with sufficient incentive to convince him to forget the matter."

"Blackmail, Darcy? Wickham has proved himself to be reckless and dishonest, but never did I imagine him capable of such malice and ingratitude as this!"

"It appears that I, too, have underestimated him."

"You give no credence, though, to his tale about your father having an illegitimate son?"

"It sounds improbable," replied Darcy thoughtfully. "By all appearances, my parents were devoted solely to each other. Yet if there had been such a child, my father certainly could have had reasons for wanting to maintain secrecy."

"What sort of document could Wickham possess?"

"A birth certificate perhaps."

"It would be an extremely good forgery, then, for he seems extraordinarily confident of his scheme. Wickham is no fool; surely, he must know the consequences of trifling with you, Darcy."

"Yes, that is what concerns me most. Why would Wickham put himself at such great risk—why would he confront his estranged brother-in-law—if his allegations were unfounded? No, he must be certain of the authenticity of his claims, and he plans to enrich himself accordingly."

Lizzy pondered the consequences. "Why should we have to make any response to Wickham at all, Darcy? We both know him too well; this must be some sort of trick. We are under no obligation to investigate his wild claims; we can, in good conscience, denounce them as false. Even if he were to make the matter public, you could censure him and disgrace him. Society knows what sort of fellow he is; and Georgiana certainly would disbelieve such a story."

Darcy pondered the matter for a few moments, finally speaking in resignation. "Wickham knows me too well. He is right. If there were the slightest chance that I had a half brother, I would want to know."

"You are determined to meet Wickham?"

"I see no other resolution. I shall procure the documentation and have it validated. If it is true, I shall find our new brother; if false, I shall have the scoundrel cast in chains."

"Will you go this evening, then?"

"Yes, directly after supper," answered Darcy. "It is best not to permit boils such as this to fester."

Chapter 4—The Meeting

Darcy rode his horse to Lambton at a deliberate pace, for he was by no means eager to meet the man who had proven to be such a constant thorn in his side. Darcy recited the tableau of troubles to himself: Wickham's dissipation at school, his attempted seduction of Georgiana when she was still very young, his lies to Elizabeth during Wickham's Meryton encampment, and his scandalous desertion of the army and elopement with Lydia.

The constant swirl of rumors concerning Wickham's gambling had also reached Darcy's ear. Unhappily, Wickham's professed regard for family, so lately acquired, had little practical application as far as his wife and children were concerned. Having long ago grown tired of playing benefactor, Darcy briefly entertained the small hope that Wickham's skill and luck with cards had somehow improved sufficiently to prevent his family's ruin; but he knew such a wish to be hollow. His brother-in-law had evidently sunk to such a desperate state that slander and blackmail were no longer beneath him. Darcy, agitated by anger and despair, nearly abandoned his mission, but his duty to family gave him the strength to press onward. He resolved to maintain his composure and conclude the sordid business as quickly as possible.

When Darcy arrived at the inn, the transition from brilliant evening sky to dim candlelight momentarily blinded him. Eventually, he discerned Wickham in the corner, befriending a nearly empty bottle of wine. On the vacant side of the small table stood a second glass of ruby port, which he had confidently poured for Darcy hours earlier. Darcy calmly walked to the table and stood before him without greeting. Wickham rose quickly and extended his hand, but his guest ignored it, so he simply reemployed it in gesture, motioning for Darcy to be seated and enjoy the glass of wine.

"I am glad that you have come, Mr. Darcy. It has been too long since our paths have crossed."

"A few more decades of separation could have been easily tolerated on my side, I assure you," responded Darcy. "Despite your dreams of family unity, this is not a social call, is it?"

Wickham was at a loss for an adequate response. Darcy continued, "Your letter mentioned that my father had two sons; I have come to inspect your proof for such an incredible assertion."

"Always to the point, aye, Mr. Darcy? No time for inquiries about health or happiness? Well, I trust there will be plenty of time for that after you accept the truth of my information."

Wickham reached into his waistcoat and produced a single sheet of paper. Darcy read the brief document aloud:

Sylvester Glennie
Baptized October 20, 1784
St. James parish, Clerkenwell, London
Mother: Ellen Glennie
Father: a gentleman
Robert Jegon, curate

"What?" shouted Darcy. "You consider this proof? This proves nothing!"

The outburst attracted the attention of the entire room. The pair remained silent until the ambient noise resumed. Darcy then spoke moderately but not less forcefully. "Wickham, you astonish me. I had expected a more artful attempt than this! This is merely the transcription of a baptismal record; and the name of the boy's father is completely absent. How can you maintain any hope of laying this at my father's door?"

Wickham, not intimidated, waited in silence for Darcy's storm of emotion to dissipate. Darcy began to suspect that the surprising weakness of the document might, perversely, be a point in favor of Wickham's case.

Wickham began, "There is much more to the story. Would you like to hear it?"

"By all means. I have not been entertained by a good fairy tale since early childhood."

"Well," continued Wickham, "you will notice that this document contains some unusual features. In the first place, the lack of the father's name indicates that the child is illegitimate. As a rule, the names of such children are not recorded in the parish register."

"Too obvious for words and signifies nothing; you must improvise better than that."

THE ROAD TO PEMBERLEY

"Second, the mother's full name is listed in place of the father's name. You must know that the parish custom is to list the father's full name, whereas only the first name of the mother is stated, and then only below the father's name."

"Yes," conceded Darcy, "that is unusual. What else?"

"Consider next the character of the gentleman. Most gentlemen who sire children out of wedlock take pains to separate themselves from the scandal. They would banish the child to an orphanage and pay handsomely to make the mother disappear rather than come forward and do right by mother and child. According to the document before us, this gentleman is worthy of the name. Evidently, he wished the world to know that the child entered the world as the son of a gentleman, and so enjoyed some advantage and protection. So concerned was he for the child's soul that he did not abandon mother and child, but persuaded the priest to administer the sacrament of baptism. It would seem probable that such a gentleman would provide financial assistance for the care of both mother and child. Your father was a gentleman of such caliber."

"Yes, such actions would not be out of character for my father, but conjectures are a far cry from proof! You invent an interesting story, Mr. Wickham, but important additional links are required. Who is the mother, for instance? What do you know of Ellen Glennie?"

"I know a little about her, but not where she is, or even if she is still living. She is of Scottish descent, of course, but she did not always use the name Glennie. She was a popular dancer on the London stage several decades ago, and she danced under the name Holly Doolittle. Have you never heard your father mention that name?"

"No, I have not. So you would have me believe that my father's love of theater gave him the incentive, and his frequent solo trips to

London gave him the opportunity, to woo dancers and sire children while his devoted wife waited at home? This tale grows more fanciful by the minute. Pray continue!"

"That is precisely what I am intimating, and it would remain mere speculation had I not more information." Wickham reached once more into his waistcoat pocket and handed over a card.

"What's this?" asked Darcy. He read the card:

Hugh Slithy and Henry Bandersnatch, Solicitors
Charing Cross Road at Oxford Street

Darcy grew concerned. "Should these names have some meaning for me?"

"They will," promised Wickham. "Shortly after the birth of Sylvester Glennie, your father transacted business with Slithy and Bandersnatch that involved the parents and child. You may wish to search the legal records of your late father to confirm that such a transaction took place shortly after the child was born."

"May I inquire how all this intelligence happened to come your way?" snapped Darcy.

"In due time, I shall be happy to answer, but it is impossible for me to do so now."

"Impossible? Why would you think that? Do you fear I would believe you any less now than I would in the future?"

"No, but to trust me further, you must first be convinced of the truth of what I have just laid before you."

Darcy frowned. "Have you met this Sylvester Glennie and know his character and whereabouts?"

"Yes."

"It is a great sadness, then, that you did not bring him here. I should very much like to meet my imaginary half brother."

"As you have indicated, Mr. Darcy, to have done so would have been pointless. You would have dismissed and humiliated him. No, it is best that you first convince yourself of the facts."

"Very well, assuming again the truth of the matter, what sort of man is my half brother? Does he in any way resemble my father?"

"It is indeed regrettable that I must defer all such questions. You have the name of the parish and the solicitors. From those sources, you should have no difficulty obtaining answers to all your questions and doubts."

"We finally come to the sticking point, Mr. Wickham. I do not understand the motive for your role in this whole business. What do you seek to gain for all your troubles?"

Wickham smiled insouciantly. "I thought my letter gave sufficient reason for my coming forward. You would have done no less in similar circumstances."

"You would have no objection to my refusing to offer compensation of any kind?"

"I expect nothing, sir. But if you were to reimburse my expenses for collecting this information, no one could think that unfair."

"Expenses only? And how much would that total be?"

"A mere fifty pounds."

"Only fifty? That is surprising! Should I expect this to be an installment for additional expenses down the road?"

"That hardly appears likely, Mr. Darcy, as I have given you all the information I have. It is you who will be performing the investigation from this point forward."

"No, Mr. Wickham, I do not believe you have given me all the information you possess. You have disclosed neither your sources nor the location of the elusive Sylvester Glennie. Presumably, that would entail considerable inconvenience and expense at some later date? How large a reimbursable item would that be, do you reckon?"

"I have included everything in the fifty pounds, Mr. Darcy. I will make no additional claims."

"What? Not a shilling more? Am I guaranteed that such an amount will result in your eternal contentment?"

"I can understand your reluctance to take my word at face value, Mr. Darcy, but that is all I shall ever ask. Naturally, when the happy day arrives and you are finally reunited with your half brother, should you, in your generosity, wish to offer further reward, I would not be so ungracious as to decline."

Darcy rose. "At last, we come to a complete understanding, Mr. Wickham. Perhaps you mean to get revenge on me by sending me off on this idle chase. But I warn you most earnestly: if there is no basis to what you have told me, I swear on the sacred graves of my parents that I shall have you yanked before the magistrate on charges of malicious slander, and you shall languish in prison until you rot."

Without waiting for a reply, Darcy withdrew five 10-pound notes and slammed them on the table.

"You can expect a letter as soon as I have completed my investigation," promised Darcy. He then turned and walked briskly out the door.

Chapter 5—Revelation

By the time Darcy returned to Pemberley, the sun had already marched over the distant hills, dragging behind it a blanket of darkness that covered the sleepy countryside. Little of nature's tranquility reached inside Pemberley—Wickham's sudden appearance and puzzling behavior had made Elizabeth uncharacteristically restless. After the children were put to bed, she sought escape by replaying chess games from the previous year's tournament.

She looked up at the sound of Darcy's footsteps. Elizabeth could sense from his tense demeanor that the meeting had not gone well. She went to the sideboard and poured two glasses of brandy.

"Here, William. You must be in need of some warmth and relaxation." They sipped at the brandy and then seated themselves in front of the fire. "Am I to understand that the meeting with Wickham was as unpleasant as we had feared?"

Darcy drank a second, more generous portion of brandy and stared at the dancing flames. "You have it right," he replied at length. "The meeting was one continuous vexation. Wickham was a study in evasiveness."

There followed a retelling of the evening's conversation and the nature of Wickham's proofs: the vaguely worded baptismal transcription and the solicitors' card.

"He produced a baptismal record that did not even list the name of the father? Is this the intricate trap he has prepared for us? What bald gibberish! You surely cannot believe a word of what he said?"

"During our meeting, I certainly did not. His ingratiating manner and insinuations kept me in a state of perpetual agitation and resentment; but as I traveled homeward, I was able to calm myself and ponder the matter disinterestedly. Wickham knows far more about this affair than he lets on. I believe that he speaks some component of the truth, and I am determined to discover precisely what it is."

"The solicitors that Wickham mentioned, Slithy and Bandersnatch, they were not your father's usual counsel?" asked Elizabeth.

"No, they were not, which at least should make it simple to validate that part of his story. Wickham suggested that I might find among my father's papers some record of transaction with that firm. But the hour is late and I am much too exhausted to begin now. I shall begin my search promptly in the morning."

The Darcys had another round of brandy before retiring for the evening. After a fitful start, a sound sleep finally overtook both of them.

Just after dawn, Elizabeth was awakened as her daughter ran, laughing, into the room and jumped into bed beside her. Jenny's nurse, hobbled by gout and unable to keep up with the two-year-old, soon limped into the room, apologizing for the disturbance; but the mother reassured her that nothing could be more pleasant than to be left alone with her daughter. Elizabeth and Jenny snuggled deeply into the bed and pulled the covers over them.

"So, my little piggy, you think it dandy to come squealing into the room and awaken your mother? How am I to remain beautiful if you always interrupt my sleep?" Elizabeth said and then laughed and tickled her gently on her sides.

Jenny only squealed louder. "Oh, Mama. I had such a good dream I have to tell you right away."

"A good dream?" Lizzy smiled. "Then it can only be about your parents."

"No, not you at all," said Jenny, pouting. "It was about me and James. I dreamed that we were in a boat on the pond, and then a big dragon swimmed to the boat, and then she tipped it over and we got all wet."

"That sounds more like an annoying dream. Did you like getting your clothes wet?"

"Oh, I was wearing only my nightshirt, so it was not so bad, and the dragon was a real friendly dragon, and when she licked my face it tickled so funny. Then she put us on her back and took us to shore. Then she dived back into the water and brought back some fish for Papa. But Papa thought James and I caught the fish, and we didn't tell him about Mimsy. That's what I call my pet dragon!"

Elizabeth hugged Jenny and kissed her forehead.

"I love playing tricks on Papa," Jenny said and giggled in delight.

"I love to play funny tricks on him, too. Come, let us get out of bed and find what awaits us at the breakfast table."

While Elizabeth dressed, she remembered Darcy's search for Wickham's document. She gave Jenny back to the nurse, and promised to join them at breakfast in a few moments. Elizabeth then stopped by the study to see how her husband's search was progressing. She found the strongbox opened and documents scattered all over the desk. Darcy was leaning back in his chair and reading a document.

"Come in, Lizzy. I have found the very invoice I have been searching for." Darcy handed it to her and she read aloud:

November 17, 1784
Received from Mr. Edward Darcy
Transference fee: £5
Signed: Henry Bandersnatch
Slithy and Bandersnatch, Solicitors

"Transference fee? Whatever can that mean?" she asked.

Darcy shared her wonder. "I have not the slightest idea, which doubtless was the intent of writing the invoice in such a vague manner. But Wickham has scored a hit; my father did transact business with the solicitors precisely as he asserted, and in the relevant time period, too. I marvel that Wickham knows of the existence of this invoice. Regardless, my next course of action will be to travel to London and learn the particulars."

"When do you expect to leave, William?"

"I would go now, but for our engagement today with Bingley and Jane; so I shall postpone my departure until tomorrow. I shall write the office of the solicitors and request that the documents be waiting upon my arrival."

Darcy promptly dispatched the letter. The appearance of the Bingleys in the early afternoon was particularly welcome, as it provided a much-needed diversion. Darcy and Elizabeth both thought it best to keep the affair secret until everything was resolved, so they engaged the Bingleys in conversation, cards, dinner, and walks, but breathed not a word of their troubles.

The day after the Bingleys departed, Darcy rode in a chaise and four to his London home, paused briefly to recuperate from the bumpy journey, and then set out for the office of his father's solicitor.

Slithy and Bandersnatch may have seen prosperous days, but the condition of the office suggested that it had been uncontaminated by commerce for several years. As soon as Darcy entered the dimly lit front room, the dusty odor provoked several violent sneezes. There were no clerks to be found—only a short, fat man sitting at his desk and squinting at the *Times*.

"Ah, Mr. Darcy," he said as he stood and extended his hand. "Mr. Jonathan Bandersnatch, at your service, sir."

"Thank you, Mr. Bandersnatch, but I was hoping to meet with a Mr. Henry Bandersnatch, the principal who signed this invoice." Darcy showed him the receipt.

"That was my late father, sir. He died more than twenty years ago, and when Mr. Slithy followed him not two years later, their combined practice passed to me. How may I be of assistance to you?"

"In my letter, I mentioned that you might possess other records pertaining to this transaction between my father and yours. Were you able to locate any?"

"No, Mr. Darcy. I am sorry to report that it was impossible to comply with your request. The matter in question is quite ancient. Records older than ten years are routinely sent to the archives—a warehouse not two streets away. Unfortunately, fourteen years ago a nearby brewery caught fire and destroyed many of the surrounding buildings, the warehouse included. I am afraid that all records pertaining to the case are irretrievable."

This news momentarily stunned Darcy. *All records destroyed? Why, then, would Wickham have sent me here? Surely Wickham must have been ignorant of this.*

"Tell me, Mr. Bandersnatch, has anyone else come here lately to inquire about these records?"

"Why, no one at all, sir. I was unaware of the existence of the transaction until I read your letter."

"Neither your father nor Mr. Slithy mentioned this matter?"

"Why would they, sir? I did not join the firm until five years before my father's passing, a full ten years after the transaction took place. The transaction was most likely quite ordinary; it would have been highly unusual for any transaction among thousands to merit discussion so long after it occurred."

"Thousands of cases?" noted Darcy. "I take it that business was quite a bit more brisk during the days of the founders."

"That is true, yes. Unfortunately, my health does not permit me to duplicate my father's success."

"This office had clerks then, I imagine. Are any clerks from that era still living?"

"Now that you mention it, this office had four clerks in the old days. One of them had gone on to his eternal reward in advance of my father. The second clerk left for a better position outside London, but that was before my time, and I have no knowledge of his whereabouts. The third one set sail for the colonies during my apprenticeship. The last one, Mr. Archibald Leach, retired about ten years ago, after the business of this office began to diminish. But I have not heard from him since, and cannot say for certain that he is still alive. But if you allow me a moment, I can consult my records and fetch his most recent address."

The solicitor disappeared into the back room for a few minutes and returned with a piece of paper. "Here you are, Mr. Darcy. The Vicarage Hotel is his last known residence."

Darcy shook the man's hand and thanked him for his time. Then he left directly in search of the hotel. Much to his surprise and relief, Darcy learned from the hotel clerk that Mr. Leach, a healthy septuagenarian in full possession of his wits, was still in residence. Although engaged in his daily perambulation of the neighborhood, he was expected to return presently.

Within a quarter hour, a well-dressed Mr. Leach walked in with his dog, Rintintoul, an old hound whose stiff facial expression appeared to perfectly complement the stiffness of its arthritic joints. Darcy greeted the amiable old man and patted his decrepit dog. After acquainting the man with the purpose of his call, Darcy suggested that they retreat to the Bag O'Nails pub next door, where the atmosphere was more conducive to conversation.

After they took possession of a corner table and the barmaid delivered ale and bitters, the conversation quickly turned from pleasantries to business. Darcy introduced the ancient invoice and the baptismal record, and explained the predicament of the destroyed files.

Mr. Leach's countenance brightened as he perused the document carefully. "Yes, I do recall the matter quite well. It was a most unusual case....Mr. Edward Darcy... I had forgotten your father's name....My facility for recollecting names was not good to begin with, and it has not improved in my dotage, but I do remember your father, a most generous man."

"What transaction took place?" asked Darcy. "To what does this 'transference fee' refer?"

"Yes, that is an odd sort of description." Leach quaffed more bitters and began his narrative. "Your father first came to our office for assistance in establishing a trust for a mother and child. I believe he meant to set aside a thousand pounds—a handsome sum, even to this day. Another clerk handled the preliminaries....I apologize, sir, his name escapes me at the moment. Well, your father and the clerk hit it off—Gregory! Ah yes, that was the clerk's Christian name.... A week later, your father returned to the office with both mother and son to conclude the transaction. I remember the woman very well indeed—as handsome a woman as one is likely to see in three lifetimes. A dancer she was; a most popular dancer."

"Holly Doolittle was her stage name."

"Yes, that's it. You have it exactly right, Mr. Darcy. Did your father tell you the story?"

"Not at all. My father kept the matter completely to himself. Please continue."

"The clerk was quite taken with the baby boy as soon as he saw him. It was obvious to everyone in the room that the mother had no real interest in the boy. She being a dancer and all, the baby was, no doubt, a constant nuisance. Then a remarkable event took place. Gregory told Mr. Darcy that after eight years of marriage, he and his wife had not been able to conceive a child. He offered to adopt the boy on the spot, if the boy's mother were inclined to part with him. Your father was touched by his sincerity and found the proposal agreeable. The mother refused at first, but your father saw the sticking point. He offered to give the trust money to her anyway, but she held out until he doubled the amount. Now, that was a most magnanimous gesture, and that is why the matter sticks out so clearly in my mind. Imagine spending an additional thousand pounds just to be sure that the boy could grow up in a family that wanted him."

"Yes," remarked Darcy, "such a display of generosity would have been in character for my late father. But I must be certain of one thing: to the best of your recollection, did my father ever declare that the son was his?"

"I cannot recall explicitly," answered the clerk. "All I can offer is my impression that everyone in the office seemed convinced that such was indeed the case."

"And the mother?" added Darcy. "Do you know what ever became of her?"

"No, I never saw or heard from her again. But as I said, she was a theater girl, and I had no time or taste for the stage back in those days. As for the clerk and the boy, all I know is that three months later I came to work to discover that the clerk had suddenly left the firm for a better position outside the city. No one seemed to know exactly where he had gone or what ever became of him."

Darcy sighed in resignation. His discovery of the identity of the child was a most disheartening development. Feelings of shock, anger, and bitterness had already run their course. He had first suspected the truth when he saw the date of Sylvester's baptism. He found further confirmation when he learned the Christian name of the clerk, and now at last all the pieces of the puzzle had fallen into place. Darcy downed the remainder of his ale.

"Mr. Leach, the clerk's name was Gregory Wickham, was it not? I will wager any amount that he had little affection for the name Sylvester, and so he had the boy rechristened George."

"Why, yes. Yes!" he cried in sudden recognition. "You have it correct on both counts! How in heaven's name do you happen to know that?"

Darcy then proceeded to tell Mr. Leach of the family steward, Mr. Gregory Wickham. All Darcy had previously known of the man's past was that he had been a law clerk prior to his arrival at Pemberley. Evidently, the late Mr. Darcy's favorable impression of the clerk, his desire to see the boy taken good care of, his wish to permanently remove the boy's mother from the scene, and his need for a new steward combined to produce a result that was beneficial for all parties. For the first time, it became clear to Darcy what had motivated his father to become godfather to George and to treat the Wickhams so generously. For their part, the Wickhams apparently had agreed to hold the circumstances of George's birth and adoption in perfect secrecy.

Further clarification was needed on one more point: "Mr. Leach, have you told this story to anyone else recently?"

The retired clerk emptied his glass and thought awhile. "Well, sir. I do occasionally like to reminisce about the old days at the office, and naturally the story of the rich man's generosity to the showgirl and the clerk is too interesting not to talk about. But I swear, even if I had been able to recall your father's name, I would never have mentioned it. I have always been a model of discretion."

Darcy smiled. He then described George Wickham and related how the whole investigation had begun from documents he had provided. "Was ever this man present when you told your story?" asked Darcy.

"No, sir. No such young man ever loitered about with my cronies. I certainly would have remembered the likes of him."

It appeared that Mr. Leach had exhausted his knowledge on the subject, so Darcy paid the bar tab and slipped a ten-pound note to Mr. Leach, thanking him most heartily for his time and valuable information. As he was about to leave the table, Darcy was struck by another possibility.

"Mr. Leach, have you always maintained residence at the Vicarage?"

"Indeed, I have, sir, for these past ten years at least, excepting a few months ago, when I had to seek temporary lodging for a fortnight whilst the Vicarage was undergoing renovation. Other than that, my residence there has been continuous. Why do you ask?"

"Permit one more impertinent question, please. Your temporary lodgings—did you happen to take room and board next door to the Moon and Sixpence pub on Wardour Street?"

"Mr. Darcy, you continue to astonish me. How did you know?"

"A most unfortunate guess," said Darcy grimly as he took his leave.

Darcy soon found himself on Wardour Street, knocking loudly on the boardinghouse door. A slightly disheveled woman of middle age greeted him pleasantly.

"You don't have to force your way in this time, Mr. Darcy. Please come in, sir. I've been expecting you."

"Mrs. Younge, I wish I could say that this is a pleasure."

Chapter 6—Entrapment

Mrs. Younge led Darcy into the modestly appointed middle room, and invited him to sit in the hardback chair by the heavily shaded window. Darcy had no patience for her display of hospitality, so he politely but firmly declined her offer of refreshment. The hostess poured tea for herself, sat down in the chair opposite him, and gazed at him expectantly.

"Mrs. Younge," he resolutely began, "you can have no doubt about the purpose of my call. I have just met with your former tenant Mr. Leach, who, I surmise, has unfortunately supplied you with information concerning my late father's private dealings. You probably wasted little time in transmitting this knowledge to Mr. Wickham. Madam, I am in no mood for evasion or deception. Despite my wish to minimize my demands upon your time, I am resolved to remain here until you have fully disclosed Wickham's information and intentions."

"Naturally, Mr. Darcy. I can readily understand what distress you must have suffered upon first learning about your half brother," she mockingly replied. "Such a shock must be most disagreeable to any man of honor. I promise, however, to do my best to satisfy your curiosity about the peculiar history of both your father and your brother. Where would you wish me to begin?"

"From the inception of the plot," he answered coldly. "I am hell-bent on finding out how Mr. Wickham intends to convince Georgiana and me that we should share our father with him."

Mrs. Younge smiled sunnily. "He first learned of his true parentage from me, via Mr. Leach, as you have rightly asserted. What a kindly and gregarious man Mr. Leach is! He liked nothing better than to take a place by the evening fire and discuss events of the day or reminisce about old times. About one week after his arrival, he told the intriguing tale of the wealthy gentleman who had dallied with a dance hall girl and sired a son illegitimately. I am certain Mr. Leach has told you the whole story about the boy's adoption by his fellow clerk and the clerk's subsequent disappearance. That unusual story set me to thinking. I knew the elder Wickham for a long time. Every year, he would accompany his family to London for a week's holiday, and they always secured lodgings at my establishment. I knew that prior to becoming Mr. Darcy's steward, Mr. Wickham had clerked for a London solicitor. After Mr. Leach had finished his story, I innocently inquired about the date of the event and other particulars. The proximity of the event to George Wickham's birthday, and Mr. Leach's subsequent mention of the clerk's Christian name, convinced me that the child could be no other than George Wickham. I immediately wrote a letter to Mr. Wickham, telling him of my discovery."

"That most certainly was months ago," observed Darcy. "What has Wickham been up to between then and now?"

"Mr. Wickham was on regimental maneuvers when my letter arrived, and he could not depart for London until a fortnight ago. He was most naturally curious about the development, so Wickham went straight to see Mr. Bandersnatch as soon as he came to London."

"And what degree of success did he achieve?" asked Darcy.

"Wickham discovered that the clerk's name was indeed Gregory Wickham, and he found out about the lost records, too—a most serious blow. Fortunately, he learned that the elder Wickham's records were still intact, as employee records were segregated from client records, and their small volume made archiving them unnecessary. Wickham paid Bandersnatch for the file and obtained his promise to keep the meeting confidential."

"Just one moment," Darcy interjected. "I knew of Wickham's involvement in this affair—because he boasted of it—before I entered the Bandersnatch office. What did Wickham intend to gain by this secrecy?"

"It was all part of his plan to secure your involvement. When Mr. Wickham learned the name of his true father and wished to be united with his newly discovered brother and sister, he had a severe obstacle to overcome, namely, your intense dislike for him. How was he ever to induce you to meet with him? And if the meeting did take place and he had attempted to confront you directly with the facts of your kinship, you would have either laughed it off or tossed him out without ceremony. No, we had to find a better way. We determined that there was only one hope for your impartial review of the evidence. Because it was impossible for us to convince you of the truth, you had to convince yourself. We had to find a way for you to conduct an independent inquiry. By giving you a little information to begin with, and by lending an air of mystery to the proceedings, Mr. Wickham hoped to pique your curiosity and so keep you engaged in the hunt. He needed the solicitor's cooperation because he wanted to stay out of your way until you had an opportunity to interview Mr. Leach, whom I trust you have found to be as sincere and convincing as I have."

Darcy nodded in spite of his suspicions. She had just confessed to manipulating him; he could not help but wonder if he were being manipulated still.

"Yes, Mr. Leach did appear trustworthy," remarked Darcy. "Given the thirty-year interval since the transaction took place, it would have been difficult for anyone to learn of this matter except from someone with the office of Bandersnatch. I have no doubt that the substance of the matter is correct, but I cannot express equal confidence in all particulars. Perhaps you can provide clarification. What else did Wickham learn from the files he obtained?"

Mrs. Younge hesitated for a moment before she spoke. "Very well, sir, I shall lay it out completely. You will see the documents soon enough, so there is no need to prolong the suspense. It is probably best for all parties that you not be surprised when your brother reveals the documents to you. Surprises have an unfortunate way of hindering reasoning and judgment and getting in the way of a fair outcome."

"Let us not talk of the outcome for the present," said Darcy tersely. "Tell me plainly, what remaining cards does Wickham hold?"

"Just two," answered Mrs. Younge. "In the first document, the mother, Ellen Glennie, forever rescinds all claims on the child in exchange for a pension of one hundred pounds, payable annually for the following twenty years. That was very wise of your father, if you ask me. He made sure she would keep her mouth shut. By the terms of the agreement, if she talked to anyone about what had happened, the pension would be stopped immediately, but the child would remain with the Wickhams. The parents and Mr. Wickham signed the document, as did the witnesses: the elder Bandersnatch and Mr. Leach."

"Mr. Leach recalled the correct amount of the settlement," observed Darcy. "What is the other document?"

"The second is a letter that your father wrote to Mr. Wickham shortly after the adoption took place. He thanked and congratulated Mr. Wickham for taking on the joys and responsibilities of raising a son. He also mentioned his need for a new steward, and offered the position to Mr. Wickham. To avoid arousing curiosity about the boy, he suggested that the Wickhams take some months to first establish normal family relations before moving to Pemberley."

Mrs. Young took another sip of tea, pausing for effect. "And now we come to the point that may interest you most, Mr. Darcy. In the same letter, your late father made an explicit promise to become the boy's godfather, thus hoping (how did he put it) 'to supply, in the role of godfather, the proper nurture and the advantages that the natural father otherwise would be unable to supply.' So you see, the late Mr. Darcy definitely acknowledged his fatherly responsibility toward George Wickham."

Darcy winced at her bluntness, but suppressed his desire to contest the issue. He reminded himself that he was there only to gather information; there would be ample time for disputation when he next met Wickham.

"And how, exactly, does the prodigal son hope to profit from this information?" inquired Darcy.

"I was just coming to that, sir. Your father also promised to increase the elder Wickham's salary by one hundred pounds annually, specifically to alleviate expenses for the boy's upbringing. He further declared that when the boy attained the age of five and twenty,

Miss Glennie's expired pension and Wickham's one hundred—pound supplement would be combined into a pension for George Wickham. Unfortunately for George Wickham, both his natural and his adoptive fathers died before he reached that age, and the promise was unfulfilled."

"Ah! So now I see Wickham's plan in all its fullness," exclaimed Darcy. "He intends to apply for an annual pension of hundreds of pounds! So much for Wickham's avowed satisfaction with fifty pounds."

"I beg your pardon, sir?"

"It is nothing that concerns you, I am certain!" said Darcy sharply, a little surprised that she knew nothing of Wickham's reimbursement.

"But Mr. Darcy," implored Mrs. Younge, "you can hardly blame Mr. Wickham for seeking to secure what is rightfully his. Who could not regard it as his natural birthright, after such an explicitly written promise; and what honest son would nullify such clear testimony of his father's will?"

Darcy refused to be drawn into an argument with Mrs. Younge. Instead, he sat in silence for a few moments to contemplate developments. Mrs. Younge sipped her tea and assumed a more relaxed posture, feeling secure that her appeal to his sense of justice had been successful.

"Mrs. Younge," said Darcy, "there appears to be only one person left in this whole business who can identify George Wickham's true father: Miss Ellen Glennie. Have you determined her whereabouts? Wickham has told me that he is uncertain if she is still alive."

"Yes, Mr. Wickham must have told you that to heighten your suspense. I began searching for her as soon as I learned her stage name: Holly Doolittle. After visiting one dance hall after another, following one blind close after another, I finally discovered an old friend of hers at the Palladium, and she told me where the mother could be found."

"Are you at liberty to share her address?" asked Darcy sardonically. "Perhaps we can settle this whole matter before the day's end."

"Oh, finding her will be no problem at all, Mr. Darcy, but obtaining the information you seek will be impossible. I am sorry, but Ellen Glennie succumbed to rheumatic fever five years ago, and now lies near the plum tree in the St. James cemetery."

"Yes, very sorry indeed....I can see that plainly," said Darcy and sighed. The person who was his best and last means of establishing the truth was in the grave.

"You can go and see for yourself, Mr. Darcy, if you cannot take my word for it."

Darcy rose slowly and prepared to take his leave. "I have every intention of verifying your information. As it appears that we have exhausted your supply of facts, we are now both free to resume our happy separate lives. I thank you, Mrs. Younge, for the forthright manner in which you shared your intelligence. I extend to you my earnest wish that you may be doubly successful in extracting from Mr. Wickham what he seeks to extract from me."

Mrs. Young curtsied and smiled in appreciation of the delicate articulation of his suppressed rage. "Do you intend to write Mr. Wickham soon and settle this matter, Mr. Darcy?" she asked as he retrieved his walking stick, which he had left by the door.

"Yes, in due time, Mrs. Younge, in due time. But first I wish to interview Holly Doolittle's friend at the Palladium. Whom should I inquire after?"

"Miss Elsie Callooh, sir, but I'm quite certain that she will be unable to add anything to what I have already told you."

Darcy nodded good day, and then walked briskly out the door toward his waiting carriage.

Chapter 7—Illumination

Elizabeth's letter awaited him on the foyer table of the Darcys' London home. He opened it eagerly.

> *William, my dear,*
>
> *Please write soon and tell me that your search has met with every imaginable success. You need not worry about any anxiety on my part, for I have been far too busy collecting barrels of tar and bales of feathers to ensure that when Wickham takes his final leave from Pemberley, he will ride in warm and comfortable luxury.*
>
> *Your lady in waiting,*
> *Elizabeth*

Darcy grinned as he placed the letter on the writing desk. He washed away the grime of the day, dressed in fresh clothes, and sat down to enjoy a solitary dinner of savory lamb and exquisite Bordeaux. Darcy felt sufficiently rejuvenated to reconsider the progress of his investigation. He wrote his beloved wife a detailed description of what he had learned and expressed dismay that an unfavorable resolution seemed to be imminent. He closed by restating his intention to see the matter through, having not yet given up hope of returning to Pemberley with better news a few days hence.

In late afternoon the following day, Darcy went to the Palladium Theater. After several false turns in the cluttered backstage hallways, he finally knocked on the door of Miss Elsie Callooh. A gracious woman of not more than five and forty greeted him. Darcy introduced himself and stated the purpose of his call. She expressed surprise at being approached twice within a fortnight to discuss Holly Doolittle, but she was pleased nonetheless. She admitted him to her dressing chamber and removed a pile of costumes from a chair to make accommodation. As there was less than an hour remaining before the next curtain call, she attended to preparations at her dressing table while she conversed. If Darcy felt any discomfort about the impropriety of the situation, her easy manner soon dispelled it. She loved to laugh and tell tales, especially those involving her dear lost friend.

Talking was indeed her forte—she had an amazing capacity for continuous, animated speech with little apparent need for drawing breath. Before Darcy even had the opportunity to inquire, he was treated to her entire early history with Ellen Glennie—their childhood friendship in Edinburgh, their early hardscrabble days in the Scottish theater circuit, and their running off together to London a few years later to escape the disapprobation of their families. He was about to inquire about the birth of Glennie's son when a calico cat jumped down, unannounced, from the armoire onto Darcy's shoulder and began swatting at a swaying curl of his hair. Darcy stiffened involuntarily at the shock; upon comprehending the situation, he burst into laughter.

"No, Reddy! No!" scolded Miss Callooh loudly. "Off his head, Red Queen. You do not belong on the gentleman. Come down at once!"

The cat showed no inclination toward obedience, but before the woman could walk over to retrieve her pet, Darcy picked up the cat and placed her on his lap.

"Please forgive Reddy, Mr. Darcy. She's a good cat, but a bit naughty. Perhaps that's why we get along so well."

Darcy pretended not to hear her overture. "Oh, there is no need for concern, ma'am; no harm at all was done." He stroked the cat gently, soon setting her purring. The lull in the conversation provided just the opening he wanted.

"Miss Callooh, what I desire most to learn are the particulars surrounding the birth of Miss Glennie's son, Sylvester. What can you tell me about the boy's father?"

"I can only repeat what I told Mrs. Younge a few weeks ago," she replied. "Holly entertained many gentlemen in her time, and most of them I have quite forgotten, but him I remember well. He was tall, dark haired, and only a wee bit out of trim, but not more so than your average man of means. Almost every weekend for about six months, the gentleman was her steady companion. He seemed to treat Holly well enough—the model of attention, really, always bringing her flowers and expensive presents; but sometimes he would act strangely silly, rather like a giddy overgrown schoolboy, and that used to annoy us all. Once he joined us after attending *A Midsummer Night's Dream* at the theatre down the block, and he brayed for several minutes straight, pretending to be an ass. Everyone found his performance convincing."

This portrait shocked Darcy and started him wondering. He had never seen his father act in such a ridiculous manner. He muttered to himself in disbelief.

"As for the gentleman's name," continued the actress, "I only knew him by his Christian name. Holly always called him Sir Edward."

Upon hearing his father's name, Darcy sagged into the chair. His fears had been realized. Surely, there could be little cause for him to further doubt the truth, but he wanted to learn the whole of it.

"Miss Callooh, permit me to ask frankly. Did Miss Doolittle ever express any doubts to you about the paternity of her child? Was she entertaining anyone else while Sir Edward was her escort?"

"No, Mr. Darcy, Holly was a good woman, she was. She entertained only one gentleman friend at a time, and she told me herself that Sir Edward was the father of the boy."

"How did Sir Edward receive the news?" asked Darcy. "It must have been an unwelcome surprise."

"Indeed, sir, so it was. As soon as he found out that she was with child, he left straightaway. I never laid eyes on him again after that."

"He disappeared?" Darcy could not hide his surprise. "But he stood by her and the child at the solicitors and provided for them both....Did Miss Doolittle ever tell you about what happened at the meeting?"

"No, she never did, but I assumed that Sir Edward was there. She said she badly wanted to tell me about the meeting, but the terms of the settlement demanded her complete silence on the matter. I only knew that she returned without the child, much to her satisfaction, as it was very difficult to care for a baby backstage. She simply said that a kindly couple had agreed to adopt the boy; that is all I know. I never pried for details. But I do know that she must have frightened Sir Edward considerably to make him appear with her at the solicitor's office."

Darcy slowly shook his head at the discrepancy between her description of Sir Edward and Mr. Leach's description of the same man. "How exactly did she manage to frighten him?" he asked.

"Well, sir, Holly was furious to be abandoned in her time of need. After a late performance one night, she passed out while descending some stairs. Sir Edward caught her, but not before she had severely injured her ankle and back, incapacitating her for months. She could never dance after that, so she became an actress instead. Several weeks after she was laid up, she discovered that she was with child. Sir Edward denied all responsibility. She laughed at him and quickly disabused him of that notion. He ran, the coward. After the child was born, Holly was low on funds, not having worked in the previous months. She had pawned all the jewelry given by her gentleman callers, and her friends helped out as best they could, but it was not enough. Holly was too proud to go back to her family for support, and things were turning a bit desperate. She decided to visit the offices of Slithy and Bandersnatch and had them write a letter to the gentleman, requesting a conference. The solicitors managed to convince Sir Edward that it would be in his best interests to live up to his new responsibilities."

"And so we arrive at the happy meeting where the boy was transferred to his new family," noted Darcy wearily, "and so it appears that I have reached the end of this promising road."

After some moments of agitated reflection, he began pacing the floor. He tightened his right hand into a fist and slammed it into his open left hand. "Damn!" he cried. "Damn these circumstances! If only there were some conclusive...some unique artifact of his among Miss Doolittle's effects that could once and for all prove the gentleman's identity."

The startled actress stopped primping by the mirror and turned to view him. They looked at each other in silence. She slowly broke into a broad smile. "That's it, Mr. Darcy! That's it!" she cried as she grabbed him in a smothering hug. The close proximity of her feather boa to his nose made it impossible for him to suppress a sneeze.

He recovered quickly. "What is it, Miss Callooh? What have you remembered?"

"His walking stick, Mr. Darcy. His fancy blackthorn walking stick!" she answered excitedly. "When Holly took her tumble, her ankle injury did not at first appear to be as grievous as it actually was. Sir Edward loaned her his walking stick to make it easier for her to hobble around. He never came back to retrieve it; I remember seeing it used as a prop in some of our productions."

Darcy's spirits picked up immediately. After trudging through a desert of lost hope, he had finally reached a small oasis. "What did the stick look like? What became of it?" he asked excitedly. "Is it still here?"

"Holly used to keep it right here, in this room. It was ever so exquisitely carved—it had a goose head as a handle." Elsie began looking about the room; Darcy eagerly joined in the search. "Holly and I shared this room during the last years of her life, and I distinctly remember seeing it...Hmm...I wonder what became of it...I remember! She gave it to Freddie!"

"Freddie?" asked Darcy.

"Frederick Eiesvor-Hil," she replied. "He was a dilettante who got his jollies by hanging around with the theater crowd. He was smitten with Holly's great beauty, and acted rather like a puppy. He would wait in the street outside her door, just so he could accompany her to the theater. Holly grew quite annoyed by his unceasing attentions and finally refused to have anything more to do with him. Then Freddie's mother put her foot down and threatened to cut off his inheritance if he persisted in squandering his life on such a futile endeavor. So he reluctantly kept his distance from Holly, ever the heartbroken bachelor, although he did attend every one of her opening performances. His flame for her never completely died; during her last year of her life, when she took ill, he returned to her side and devoted himself to her care. I recollect seeing him walk with that cane at her funeral."

"And what became of Freddie?" asked Darcy. "Do you know where I might contact him?"

"No, I don't have his address, if that's what you mean; but I do know where you might find him."

Darcy arched an eyebrow.

"I'll wager that he visits Holly's grave at least once a week, the poor lost soul. I've seen him there when I've had occasion to stop by."

"Miss Callooh, I cannot thank you enough for your assistance!" exclaimed Darcy, shaking her hand and smiling. But Elsie did not find this parsimonious display of thanks at all acceptable from the handsome young man. She gathered Darcy in another warm embrace.

A brief downpour had turned the streets to an unholy muddy mess, but his carriage eventually navigated the rutted streets to the cemetery. As Darcy alighted from the carriage, sunlight finally punched through the clouds, lending gravestones an instant adornment of sparkling liquid jewelry. Larks and cardinals sang cheerfully as he walked toward the plum tree in the far corner of the yard. He found a man sitting on a stone bench—his trench coat thoroughly soaked—and grasping a solitary rose, along with a fancy walking stick. Darcy introduced himself, splashed away the pooled water from the bench with his hand, and sat beside him. Freddie was eager to make the acquaintance of someone so familiar with his beloved Holly, and listened sympathetically to Darcy's tale about Holly's son and his predicament. After nearly an hour and a half, Freddie willingly swapped his cane for Darcy's inlaid gold-and-ivory walking stick. Darcy departed, sighing with relief. He could now return to Pemberley, satisfied that there could be no further doubt about the identity of Wickham's father.

Chapter 8—Confrontation

The perfect travel conditions created by cool breezes and overcast skies expedited Darcy's return to Pemberley. James and Jenny ran to greet him in the entrance hall, eager to discover what wonderful treats their father had brought home for them. Darcy lifted them both in his arms and gave each a kiss, but they squirmed with so much excitement that he quickly had to set them down and retrieve their presents from his travel bag. Although James was happy to receive a new wooden jigsaw puzzle depicting the Tower of London, he became ecstatic when presented with a large bag of chocolate-covered walnuts, raisins, and pecans. He immediately plopped down, cross-legged, on the marble floor. He found a walnut confection, his favorite, and let the delectable chocolate layer slowly melt on his tongue. Meanwhile, Jenny's eyes opened wide with wonder as Darcy pulled out her new toy, a funny little stuffed warthog. She instantly named it Nelle, kissed and hugged it in delight, and then ran off to introduce Nelle to the other stuffed animals in her room.

Elizabeth and Darcy laughed at their children's uninhibited displays of pleasure. After taking full advantage of the opportunity for a proper embrace and kisses, they retreated to the study to talk about Darcy's adventures in London. Elizabeth was both surprised and relieved to hear the latest developments. Eager for a resolution of the matter, Darcy penned a letter to Wickham, announcing the completion of his investigation, and extending an invitation to visit Pemberley at his earliest convenience.

Ten days later Wickham arrived from the North country. The butler admitted him into the library and offered brandy as an antidote to the rigors of his long journey. Wickham gratefully accepted the refreshment and busied himself with a recent edition of the *Times*. Darcy joined him three quarters of an hour later.

"Mr. Wickham," said Darcy brightly as he greeted his guest with extended hand. "Please forgive my delay. I had to attend to the needs of another guest in the drawing room."

Wickham took this unexpected display of good cheer as an encouraging sign. "Mr. Darcy, it is most pleasant to be in your good graces at last."

Darcy smiled while inviting him to be seated. "Mr. Wickham, I believe that I have fulfilled the terms of our verbal agreement. I have completed my investigation and have written to you, as promised. As you have already forsworn demands for any additional compensation, I can only assume that we both regard this meeting simply as a social call—so we can, as you put it, 'replace discord with harmony.'"

"Ah, Mr. Darcy. So your investigation led you to the same conclusion that I reached. That is indeed most gratifying to hear."

"Yes, indeed, Mr. Wickham. I am certain that I now share your full knowledge of our relationship," Darcy said enigmatically. He enjoyed seeing Wickham's confident expression briefly dimmed by a twitch of alarm and concern before he could recover with a slight grin.

"It is a wonder, is it not," said Wickham, "that we grew up together on these very grounds, all the while unaware that we were half brothers."

"A wonder, indeed," returned Darcy. "I certainly never knew that such a connection existed. I cannot thank you enough for the pains you took to make me aware of our genealogy. I particularly commend you for the ingenious way that you induced me to follow the path to true knowledge. I cannot imagine a better return for the fifty pounds that I paid for your reimbursement."

Wickham was unprepared for Darcy's conciliatory attitude. Expecting only bitterness and spite, his well-rehearsed plan was of no use to him. How was he to work on Darcy now? His silence and vacant look betrayed his confusion.

Darcy leaned back and smiled. "Well, Mr. Wickham, it appears that our reminiscences are concluded. You must excuse me, as I am wanted by my other guest. Perhaps some other day we can reprise old times and hoist a few mugs down at the Lambton Inn. Please relay our family's best wishes to Mrs. Wickham and the children."

Darcy's gambit focused Wickham's mind wonderfully. "Pardon me, Mr. Darcy, but there still remain a few matters to discuss—"

"You are mistaken, Mr. Wickham. Did you not declare in our most recent meeting that reimbursement for your expenses was all that you sought? Did you not assure me that you would never seek more? I have acknowledged our familial bond and thanked you for your efforts, so I do not know what could be left to discuss."

"You must surely recall," countered Wickham, "that I raised the possibility that you might wish to offer some reward once you were reunited with your half brother. Can you be so unfeeling that you deny the bonds of duty toward your brother?"

"Duty, Mr. Wickham? Yes, I find it easy to be unfeeling, for my previous advancements of money on your behalf have paid my duty to you in full."

"That is scandalous!" cried Wickham. "How can you be callous to me, your elder brother? If not for an accident of birth, our roles could be reversed. Imagine, you could now be imploring me for the same justice that I seek! Had I inherited the vast property and resources of our father, there is no way under heaven that I could live with a clear conscience while denying my brother his due!"

"Rightful due?" replied Darcy, his demeanor calm. "At the risk of sounding cold, Mr. Wickham, I must inform you that no rights of inheritance accrue to an illegitimate son, firstborn or not. As for your heartfelt profession of generosity were our places exchanged, I remain unconvinced and unmoved."

"Yes, my rightful due," protested Wickham. "Here, read for yourself how our father planned to provide for my annual pension." He reached into his waistcoat pocket and produced a letter from the late Mr. Darcy to his adoptive father.

Darcy examined the letter carefully. "Ah yes, Mrs. Younge did mention something about this letter during my meeting with her. Hmm...I see here that my father intended to provide you with a pension of two hundred pounds a year once you attained the age of five and twenty. That much is clear, and the signature certainly is my father's."

"Well?" asked Wickham. "You refuse to honor an explicit wish on the part of our father?"

After pretending to study the letter once again, Darcy finally allowed, "No, of course not. I just wanted to review this evidence for myself." He then calmly walked over to a cabinet, retrieved a document, and presented it to Wickham. "Here you are, Mr. Wickham—the final disposition of my father's will, which my solicitor has drawn up for this occasion. Please sign both copies and I shall pay the balance of the annuity at once."

Wickham read the document rapidly, with wonder at first, and then disbelief, and, finally, alarm. "What!" he exclaimed. "This is impossible! Am I to renounce all claims on my rightfully inherited pension for a paltry fifty pounds? I certainly shall not!"

"Not simply for fifty pounds," corrected Darcy. "I have made the assumption that you will live to the ripe age of five and seventy. Thus, for fifty years at two hundred pounds per year, the total comes to ten thousand pounds. Naturally, I have deducted the money that I already advanced to you, namely, the three thousand pounds that you received in lieu of a living, and the six thousand nine hundred pounds that I advanced to retire your gaming debts at the time of your marriage to Miss Lydia Bennet. The additional five hundred pounds you received at that time I regard as my wedding present to you and your bride. Having advanced fifty pounds for your expenses, that, sadly, leaves only fifty pounds to be paid from the original ten thousand pounds. If, on the other hand, you reckon that you are shortchanged by my estimate of your longevity, I am perfectly willing to begin payments of two hundred pounds a year once you have lived beyond the nine thousand nine hundred-fifty mark, which I calculate to be three months shy of seventy five years. Which payment plan do you prefer?"

"Neither plan is acceptable!" shouted Wickham. "The money you previously donated had nothing to do with my annuity. You can discharge our father's obligation only by paying me the full two hundred pounds a year, beginning from my twenty-fifth year. I shall only be content with ten thousand pounds at once."

Darcy glared at Wickham for several moments and said nothing. Wickham began to squirm, realizing that he played with a weak hand. At length, Darcy dropped his controlled demeanor, walked back to the cabinet, grabbed the blackthorn walking stick, and slammed it hard on the table.

"Let us end this false dance, Mr. Wickham. We both know that we have no common father. This walking stick belonged to your father, not mine!"

Wickham looked at Darcy incredulously.

"Please spare me a display of manufactured surprise," continued Darcy. "You have lied to me long enough."

Darcy rang for a servant and within moments one appeared. "You can tell Mrs. Darcy that I am ready now, Thomas." The servant acknowledged his master with a bow and departed.

"Mr. Wickham, as soon as I learned that this walking stick was given to Holly Doolittle by your father, your scheme was in ruins. I returned that same day to Mr. Bandersnatch and convinced him to disclose his knowledge of Mr. Wickham's file. Yes, I am certain you are surprised to learn that the cautious Mr. Bandersnatch took the time to copy all the important documents prior to handing them over to you. It seems that you have conveniently neglected to share with me the first letter that my father wrote to the late Mr. Wickham. I am certain that it could not have escaped your attention—my father clearly states that he is acting as a proxy for another gentleman, whose name he is not at liberty to disclose. But this walking stick identifies your true father just as surely as if his name had been included in that letter."

"I don't understand, Mr. Darcy. How does this walking stick come into play?"

Darcy explained the circumstances of Holly Doolittle's fall— how her gentleman friend had donated his walking stick for her assistance, and how that same man had disappeared upon learning that she was with child.

He then handed the walking stick to Wickham.

"Here, see this emblem carved just below the handle? Do you not recognize it from the livery that has often visited Pemberley? And if that is not sufficient, look at the initials carved on the under-side of the goose handle."

"LDB!" exclaimed Wickham, growing pale.

"Yes, LDB. Sir Lewis de Bourgh of Rosings Park," explained Darcy. "Sir Lewis died several years before my father, leaving his widow, Lady Catherine de Bourgh, and daughter, Anne de Bourgh."

The revelation left Wickham incapable of speech.

"For Sir Lewis to use the name of my father as cover for his own activities was unforgivably duplicitous," said Darcy. "I met your father many times as I was growing up. When I reached maturity, I could clearly discern that although he retained little affection for his wife, he had lost none of his fear. That was not entirely with-out reason, for she was quite formidable, but that by no means excuses his cowardly behavior toward your mother. I imagine that when your father found out about Miss Doolittle's condition, he was terrified that word about the affair might leak back to Lady Catherine, and he tried desperately to distance himself from the situation. Bandersnatch's letter must have thrown him into a panic, and he probably went running to my father for advice. My generous father most certainly offered to act as Sir Lewis's proxy."

Wickham was the picture of confusion. Although he knew from the undisclosed first letter that Mr. Darcy was not his real father, he was unprepared to look upon Sir Lewis de Bourgh in such a capacity. He saw his dream for riches quickly fading, with no time to improvise a different plan.

A disturbance could be heard in the far end of the hall, and Darcy calmly offered a suggestion. "Mr. Wickham, I recommend that you sign this agreement now, take your fifty pounds, and accept my best wishes for a long and happy life. Of course, you are free to take up the matter with Lady Catherine instead, or perhaps with your half sister, Anne. Your desperation for riches may tempt you in that direction, but I advise against it. You are certain to find Lady Catherine even less tractable than I am, and Anne de Bourgh has recently married the Earl of Nottingham, who is renowned for his quick temper and excellent marksmanship. Still, if you think my advice wrong-headed, you have only to wait a moment longer. Lady Catherine has been our guest for this past week, and she comes now to greet you."

Lady Catherine exploded through the door of the study. "Nephew," she cried to Darcy, "Elizabeth has informed me of a most revolting circumstance. I am utterly ashamed of you! Whatever possessed you to allow this wretch to pollute Pemberley? This is not to be endured! My only solace is that your dear parents are not alive to witness this degradation!"

Elizabeth, who trailed Darcy's aunt only slightly, was unsuccessful in hiding her amusement at Wickham's fear and bewilderment. Lady Catherine turned her attention to Wickham and looked him over disdainfully.

"So here is the infamous scoundrel who has shamed the Bennet family, who has polluted the shades of Pemberley, and who now spends his time in drunken dissipation! Now, what is it that you want of me, Mr. Wickham? Mrs. Darcy informs me that you seek my advice on some matter relating to pensions. That is a foolish thought indeed. Why anyone should wish to squander a pension on an ingrate such as yourself is beyond comprehension. It is most vexing."

Wickham could only stammer out a reply: "There has b-been a mis-mistake. There is no need for your advice, your ladyship. All uncertainties are resolved." He looked around the table and added, "Darcy, where is your pen?"

Darcy lifted his pen from its holder and handed it to him. Wickham quickly signed both copies of the agreement, bowed, and bolted with his copy and his fifty pounds. Lady Catherine could only gape in wonder at the laughter of her nephew and niece.

So distressing did Lady Catherine find her encounter with Wickham that she could not collect her composure sufficiently to permit the continuation of her stay. None of Darcy's entreaties could soften her resolve. Within two hours she was riding in her Barouche box back to the safe and uncontaminated confines of Rosings Park.

"How delicious an irony!" remarked Elizabeth. "Lady Catherine condemns Wickham for his pollution of Pemberley, all the while oblivious that her husband was the source!"

"Indeed," answered Darcy, grinning. "I cannot imagine a more just and fitting resolution."

"You are not disappointed, then, that you have lost a half brother?"

"Not at all," he answered. "I happily pass along that distinction to our cousin Anne. So my half-brother has now been converted to a half-cousin; but as you know very well, my dear, some relations cannot be too far removed!"

"Yes," said Lizzy smiling, "and whatever direction Wickham's shadow decides to take, it seems quite certain it will never augment the shades of Rosings Park!"

Darcy laughed as he took her arm and walked toward the dining room. After finishing the first truly relaxing dinner in over a fortnight, the family strolled leisurely along the path through the manicured gardens and tall grass, finally reaching the pond, where they took turns feeding the ducks and geese.

A View from the Valet
BY NACIE MACKEY

Nacie (Nadine) Mackey was born into a family of five girls, so it seemed natural for her to be drawn to the classic *Pride and Prejudice* as it involves a family of five daughters in Regency England. Eventually, her interest led her to write two sequels to the novel: *A Woman Worthy* and *Regard and Regulation*, both with Lulu Press. Needless to say, she was thrilled to have her short story, an alternative viewpoint of Mr. Darcy's role, be included in this anthology. Mackey and her husband live in Waverly, Iowa, along with their two cats.

Servants were a major part of Regency England, particularly for the classes described by Austen, but they were largely invisible, both in fiction and in reality, but that did not make them unimportant. Mackey gives some relevancy to Darcy's valet in "A View from the Valet."

Part 1

To be employed at an estate such as Pemberley, a well-trained servant was expected to become blind, deaf, and dumb. And, case in point, no matter the unusual behavior of his master, a valet must especially adhere to such inflexible standards.

Having retained the position of valet to Mr. Fitzwilliam Darcy since that gentleman's eighteenth birthday, Samuel Preston accepted these responsibilities without question. After all, had not his own father served as valet to the elder Mr. Darcy for nearly forty years?

Through pleasant times and hardships, Preston stood by without apparent judgment. Twice, Mr. Fitzwilliam had fallen violently in love. Twice, his valet remained stoically silent while every manner of oath and curse were uttered within the confines of the young gentleman's rooms at the conclusion of these same affairs.

Two years following the second of these, Mr. James Darcy passed on, his demise leading to a period of grief for the entire county. A lifetime of treating his family, staff, and tenants with respect and consideration caused his death to remain quite painful for many months.

However, from such a loss was born new hope for the future of Pemberley, it's sister estates, and all Darcy lands, for Mr. Fitzwilliam Darcy, at three and twenty, stepped into his formidable father's shoes with surprising ease. At least, this was what the majority of the household presumed.

Preston knew otherwise. The others on the staff did not see the weariness of his master's countenance as, through long hours, he pored over the numerous books and documents regarding the estate. They did not witness the dark circles beneath his eyes when he arose from a night of restless slumber. They did not suffer silently upon observing his extreme sense of loss for his father.

Eventually, though, these burdens were overcome. Mr. Fitzwilliam applied himself to his new role, accepted his somewhat heavy responsibilities, and even designated duties to others, so that he might obtain some much-needed rest.

For nearly three years thereafter, serenity reigned. Daily life became an easy routine. In the summer, they traveled to London; in winter, they returned to Derbyshire. Mr. Darcy's sister, Miss Georgiana, sometimes accompanied them, and sometimes did not. As she enjoyed the services of a tutor, a music master, a dressmaker, a dance instructor, and a lady's companion, she usually remained at their townhouse in London.

During the summer of Miss Georgiana's fifteenth birthday, however, something happened concerning her that affected Mr. Darcy deeply. The details were rather sketchy (the other servants' gossip was largely ignored by Preston, and he would never even consider inquiring into the matter), but they seemed to involve a certain Mr. George Wickham, recognized by all as the son of the Darcys' former steward.

Somehow, Mr. Wickham had followed the inarguably blameless Miss Darcy to their other summer home of Ramsgate, and very nearly had her convinced to elope with him. How they were discovered in time was anyone's guess. Preston was convinced of there being little Mr. Darcy did not know, or would eventually find out, and, of course, deal with in as gentlemanly a manner as possible. After that, she was left alone far less often; until, that is, the journey to Hertfordshire.

Mr. Darcy's closest confidant, Mr. Charles Bingley, was eager to set up a household of his own, as his father's estate had recently been settled. Finding himself a wealthy man at the age of four and twenty, Mr. Bingley had heard of a suitable property to be let in that southern county. Having been apprised of its scenic beauty and friendly citizens, he was desirous to inspect the place and requested the company of his friend while doing so.

Mr. Darcy was not quite so enthusiastic, but if Bingley wished his opinion, then he would grant it. Hertfordshire—the way that Preston was given to understand it, at least—was so quaint as to be boorish. The society there would have little idea of true manners or fashion. In short, they were nothing but barbarians and should be regarded as such. All of these opinions were freely expressed by Mr. Darcy during those times when Preston was at his service. Even on the very day of their arriving at Netherfield, as the estate was known, Mr. Darcy did not alter his opinion.

They remained there for several weeks. During that time, a subtle change seemed to come over his master. He no longer complained of the inferior society, and although not really improving in mood, he seemed to be in a permanent state of anticipation. Having witnessed him twice while in love, Preston suspected that this was again the case.

The difference, it appeared, was that the lady in question was actually a member of this "boorish" society, and, most amazing of all, she did not appear to return his regard.

Preston happened to learn all of this and more through Mr. Darcy's nightly muttered grievances. He learned that the lady's name was Miss Elizabeth Bennet, that she was from a large and uncouth family, and that she treated Mr. Darcy as though *he* were the barbarian. Even so, great pains were taken in his dress and grooming during that period, and the situation seemed to come to a head on the evening of Mr. Bingley's ball.

After assisting him into his most impressive evening coat, brushing the lint from it, and giving a final adjustment to his neckcloth, Preston was startled to hear Mr. Darcy's low, "And so, into the fray, eh, Preston?"

"Yes, sir," the valet replied, not knowing what else to say.

"This, then," Darcy continued, "is the price we pay for love. I only hope it does not destroy me in the process."

"No, sir."

With that, Mr. Darcy descended to the already arriving guests, leaving a circumspect Preston to await his return.

At two o'clock in the morning, the valet was dozing in a chair, still fully clothed, as his duties were far from over. He was awakened by his master's door closing rather deliberately in the next room.

Instantly, he was with him, but that gentleman did not wait for his assistance. Almost savagely, the neckcloth was torn off, with the coat, waistcoat, and shirt swiftly following. In this state of semi-undress, Mr. Darcy strode to the window and glared out into the darkness.

Under his breath he was muttering, "Mr. Wickham! Go on and accept Mr. Wickham's attentions, Miss Bennet, and see where it leads you. You shall make a worthy pair indeed. After witnessing the appalling behavior of your family tonight, I believe he might deserve a Bennet woman." Then his anger seemed to leave him, and laying his forehead against the window sash, he emitted a sort of moan. "God help me, I must leave this place. I can bear it no longer...."

Hardly daring to breathe, Preston stood silently, waiting for some order to follow. Finally, lifting his head only enough to be heard clearly, Mr. Darcy spoke again, "Preston, we are leaving tomorrow. We shall be escorting Mr. Bingley back to London."

"Yes, sir."

They did leave the following morning, and remained at the London house throughout the winter months. This was unusual, but Preston assumed it had something to do with Mr. Bingley or Miss Georgiana or possibly both. During that time, Mr. Darcy attended concerts and plays, yet entertained very little. His mood, while never exactly cheerful, had taken on a sort of stoic defensiveness. At this time, the only words said to his valet were perfunctory orders issued in a voice of disinterest.

In March, Mr. Darcy, along with his cousin, Colonel Richard Fitzwilliam, traveled to Kent, where Lady Catherine de Bourgh, Mr. Darcy's aunt, resided with her only daughter. No sooner had the trunks been brought up to Mr. Darcy's apartment than he appeared himself, a new resolve apparent on his countenance.

"Preston, I require my blue coat," he declared. With his voice lowered, he went on pensively, "She is here. What chance is this, I wonder? Has she altered? What will she say?"

He left thereafter with undisguised haste, and such was the way it continued to be for several weeks. Mr. Darcy would appear, dress or change his clothes accordingly, and disappear, always with that same odd expression on his face. There were times, even, when he almost seemed sanguine. At least, he did not scowl or frown as he had while in town. If Mr. Darcy were a man to hum, Preston believed he would have.

One day, however, this pleasant interval ended abruptly. Mr. Darcy had left unexpectedly during the late afternoon, and arrived back less than an hour later in a mood as black as his coat. Preston, having seen these tempers often enough to wish to avoid them, did not disturb his master, but remained near enough so that if he were needed, there should be no delay. From time to time, he peered around the door frame to make certain that all was well, and, despite his training, would find himself quite taken aback by the devastation he witnessed therein.

Mr. Darcy, seated at his desk, was either writing furiously, staring vacantly out the window, or cradling his head in his hands. None of these things alone would have been cause for alarm, but when interspersed with several muffled groans and a desperate posture, they did seem to communicate a certain type of personal torment for which there could be no consolation.

They returned to London the following day. Other than the order to pack his trunks, Mr. Darcy spoke not at all, and did not refer to his behavior the previous evening. But then his valet did not expect him to.

The remainder of that spring was spent in town with only an occasional excursion to Pemberley. These were always on matters of business, and if they promised to be of a brief duration, he would go alone, without his personal attendant.

Come summer, this changed once more. Mr. Darcy began to speak of returning to Pemberley with the intent of remaining there for some time. Tiring of London society—in fact, tiring of many things—he displayed a restlessness that only a change of scene could appease. Therefore, in July, they proceeded to Derbyshire.

From there, Mr. Darcy traveled back and forth between Pemberley and London, making the arrangements for Miss Georgiana and several guests to arrive at a later time. This constant movement seemed to suit him, and though still not a man at ease with himself, he did relax somewhat.

One warm afternoon, he appeared in his room, his face ashen and his demeanor shocked. "My God, Preston. She is here at Pemberley. What am I to do? What am I to say?"

At that particular moment, however, the expression on the valet's countenance easily rivaled that of his master. For the gentleman had entered with not only his shirttail draped outside his breeches, his coat hanging in odd fashion over his arm, and his hair damp and disheveled, but the demeanor of a man in complete and utter confusion.

"Sir, have you suffered an accident?"

"Never mind that now. Help me here, will you?" replied his master.

No sooner was Mr. Darcy set to rights than, standing before the looking glass, he straightened his shoulders and, with his eyes sparkling with an unfamiliar exhilaration, stated aloud, "This is my chance. If only I might..." But with that, he turned and left as abruptly as he had entered.

In the days following, he was as good-humored as he had ever been.

Once, without intending to do so, Preston actually glimpsed the object of Mr. Darcy's desire. As he went down to dinner in the servant's galley, he happened to pass Miss Georgiana and another young lady as they stood together discussing a portrait hanging in a downstairs hallway.

Miss Georgiana, in fact, called out to him, asking, "Preston, do you know when this likeness of my parents was painted? Miss Bennet was inquiring, but I must confess I cannot recollect."

After bowing, he replied as best he could, estimating the time to be twenty-five years earlier. With a smile, Miss Georgiana thanked him, and as he bowed again, he glanced at the aforementioned Miss Bennet. Discreetly, he appraised her.

His first impression was that she was quite pretty. Yet she did not resemble the ladies of town, who prided themselves on their slender and almost boyish figures, their feather-laden hairstyles, and the latest in fashionable dress. Although her countenance promised an unusual liveliness, she stood sedately while Miss Georgiana went on to explain the other portraits along that same wall.

He was murmuring "Excuse me" when the two ladies were joined by Mr. Darcy. Even as Preston left them, he sensed the increase of a certain repressed exhilaration within the small group. Mr. Darcy's expression might have been described as deeply enthralled or quietly rapturous.

Either way, there was no doubt that this young lady was the cause of his unrest throughout the past several months.

At dinner, Mrs. Reynolds, the housekeeper, prattled on about the lady in question; how she had appeared a few days earlier to tour the house with her friends, how it had come as a great surprise to Mrs. Reynolds when she claimed (albeit reluctantly) that she was acquainted with Mr. Darcy, and how she had stood near his portrait for quite a long time, studying it as though she were sorting through a puzzle.

"But," Mrs. Reynolds had added as she finally ran out of words, "I must say she seems a genteel, ladylike sort of person. You saw her abovestairs, Preston. What thought you of her?"

Although reluctant to give his opinion, he concurred with Mrs. Reynolds. Yes, she appeared to be both genteel and ladylike, but he would not say if he believed her to return Mr. Darcy's regard.

By now, of course, most of the servants knew of their master's current infatuation. Despite their well-practiced facade of impassivity while serving the family, they took a keen interest in all of their affairs, but especially those of the heart. After all, if either of the Darcys became betrothed, the future of the entire household could be affected. It stood to reason, then, that any hint of such an outcome brought forth much speculation and comparison of theory.

Despite all of their gossip, however, not one of them had a clue as to who this Miss Bennet was. Where was she born? Had she family? Was she wealthy in her own right, or destitute and therefore hoping to secure an advantageous match? She was attractive enough, but was she respectable, accomplished, and all that she ought to be?

When Preston attended to his master that evening, he thought that he had never witnessed such a smile of gratification upon that gentleman's countenance. As he helped him prepare for bed, Mr. Darcy murmured several times, "Who could have foreseen such a turn of events?" and, "Do I dare entertain hope?"

The following morning, he left with the very same expectant expression, his impatience to be gone causing him to quit his room before his boots were even properly shined. After all of this, Preston was somewhat astonished when he returned but an hour later, his manner no longer displaying the optimism it had earlier. Yet this was not simply the onset of one of his darker moods. No, there was more to it than that.

Sharply, he ordered his trunk packed and the coach readied to return to town at once. Then he began to pace. His face, while he did so, was a study of varying emotions: frustration, distaste, irritation, and, above all, deep and overwhelming concern. He said little, but upon their arrival at the London house, he adopted the habit of vanishing to places unknown, not returning until far into the night.

On one of these occasions, when Preston dutifully inquired if Mr. Darcy should need anything further, that gentleman shocked him when he replied shortly, "Yes. Sit down, Preston."

Uneasily, the valet sat in a chair as near the door as he could manage. Mr. Darcy was not having it. "No," he commanded. "Over here by the fire. That's it."

With great reluctance, Preston did so, seating himself rigidly in a chair opposite his master. Then, falling silent, he waited for whatever was to come. "Preston," began Mr. Darcy after a long moment of staring into the fire, "have you ever been in love?"

Stunned by both the question and that Mr. Darcy should ask something so very personal, he stammered, "I could not say, sir."

Smiling wryly at his servant, Mr. Darcy answered for him: "In other words, you have, but it is not for me to trouble myself with."

"Something like that, sir." Although his face had taken on a reddish hue, Preston kept his eyes focused upon the wall opposite him.

"Well, Preston. I know that you have been singularly loyal to me for ten years. I know, as well, that whatever we speak of here and now shall not leave this room."

"Yes, sir." Shifting awkwardly, the valet glanced toward the door, as though seeking escape.

"I am, as you have probably guessed, most hopelessly, and—God help me—irreversibly in love."

"I have suspected as much, sir."

"Have you?" Appearing to be more amused than offended, he paused; then he asked, "And do you know with whom?"

"It is not my place to say, sir." Again, he shifted.

"Just the same, you do know." Mr. Darcy leaned forward, urging his valet: "Say it, Preston."

"Miss Bennet, sir?" Preston ventured unwillingly.

"Miss Bennet," Mr. Darcy repeated, an expression of longing overtaking his features. "Miss Elizabeth Bennet, whose heart I would do anything to secure." Rising suddenly, he began to pace, muttering, "Is there nothing so torturous as unsettled love, I wonder? And now, when I have it within my power to grant her every happiness, I am bested by that wastrel, Wickham. Sometimes I believe that I shall never be rid of him." He turned to Preston and asked abruptly, "Do you recollect a companion retained last year for my sister? A Mrs. Younge?"

"I...Yes, I think so, sir."

"I would give every crown I own to find her. You do not, by any chance, have knowledge of her whereabouts?"

Preston swallowed uncomfortably. "I suspect I might, sir."

A new hope surfaced on his master's face. Reseating himself, he leaned forward expectantly and said, "Tell me where, man, and you shall have anything you desire."

"It is..." Preston cleared his throat, loath to proceed. "It is in a most disreputable part of town, sir. I would not recommend your going there. At least, not alone."

"If you can but direct me, I promise you I shall not go alone."

"It is on a street very near the docks," Preston said reluctantly. "It is called Leadhall. Her house is there."

"You are certain of this?"

"Yes," came the cheerless affirmation. "Quite certain, sir."

"Excellent." For the first time in more than a week, his careworn expression abated somewhat. Standing, he offered his hand to his valet. "I was not speaking idly, Preston. Tell me what it is you desire and, if at all possible, I shall grant it."

Preston, rising as well, accepted the proffered hand with discomfiture. After all, Mr. Darcy, although a gentleman of faultless refinement and manner, was at risk of crossing a line considered to be a constant. He, Samuel Preston, was a servant, not an equal—and never should that fact be disregarded.

When he did not answer immediately, Mr. Darcy repeated his supplication.

Finally, Preston, clearing his throat once again, found his voice. "If you please, sir, I should wish this whole matter simply to be forgotten."

After studying him for a moment, Mr. Darcy shook his head. "And that is all? I promise you, Preston, this chance may not arise again soon."

"Sir, I want for nothing. I have no need for more than I currently possess. I wish only to put this to rest. If you"—and here, he colored, lest he say too much—"find the contentment you seek with Miss Bennet, then that is all I could ever desire."

Silence filled the room. Finally, Mr. Darcy, with one eyebrow raised, said, "For this, I fear I am to remain most ignominiously in your debt. However," he added, a trace of a smile undermining his austere expression, "as at least partial repayment, perhaps I may refrain from asking how you happen to know of Mrs. Younge's location."

Meeting his eyes at last, Preston replied evenly, "Yes, sir. I thank you as well, sir."

Part 2

A valet (or, as Preston himself preferred, a gentleman's gentleman) lives out his existence providing whatever small satisfaction he can to his master through his own attentiveness and conscientious care. It was, therefore, an unexpected bonus for Samuel Preston to be able to do so outside the realm of his usual duties.

When supplying Mr. Darcy with the direction of Mrs. Younge, he'd had little idea that such information might be so vital to his master's future happiness. If he had, the knowledge would surely have frozen his lips together with profound trepidation.

As it was, the results of his reluctant disclosure were not immediately apparent. Mr. Darcy, still tense and preoccupied, did not confide any ensuing success or failure to him, and despite his personal curiosity, Preston could not fault him for it. The days following their "talk" passed, at least for the valet, with only slight variations to their master–servant routine.

Mr. Darcy continued to arise early, and other than reappearing for an occasional meal, returned only after many of the servants were already retired—excepting Preston, of course. And once those evening needs had been attended to, he would fall into bed with no more than two words to his dutiful attendant.

This, Preston knew, was as it should be. Indeed, as it must be. Still, he would occasionally catch himself wondering how Mrs. Younge's whereabouts might be of so much import to the eminent Mr. Darcy. The fact that he, Samuel Bard (his mother had held a certain sentimentality about poetry at the time of his birth) Preston, an unassuming servant, could offer any help whatsoever in the case, had been purely coincidental; but afterward, he'd been most grateful for the happy accident.

The facts of the matter were that the infamous Mrs. Younge, after being unceremoniously dismissed from the Darcy household, had removed herself to her sister's establishment in a less than impressive section of London. There, food, lodging, and even a particular type of female companionship were available (for a price) to idle sailors on shore leave.

Although Preston would not patronize such a place, there was a woman of his close acquaintance employed in the kitchen of that establishment. She, a Miss Clara Foster, spent many a backbreaking hour cooking vast quantities of stew, kneading and fashioning endless mounds of dough into loaves of bread, and laundering the linens from the abovestairs rooms.

How he came to be familiar with this humble individual, surprising as it might be to any who knew him, was not so very unusual. For, some years earlier, when both were yet between the ages of eight and eighteen, they had been quite good friends, sharing confidences as well as lessons in servitude from his own, dear parents. She was his cousin on his maternal side. Six months his junior, she had trained to be a lady's maid in much the same way as he had trained to be a valet.

But something had gone awry. Following ten years of faithfully serving the elderly woman by whom she had initially been engaged, that lady had suffered a seizure so severe as to render her no longer in need of such attention. Thereafter, the woman's nephew had employed her. He had turned out to be an empty-headed dandy whose youthful wife would not, or could not, be pleased. Three years of growing dissatisfaction on both sides finally led to Clara's services being terminated and then taken up by a widow of questionable reputation, a Mrs. Bates. This, as it so happened, was Mrs. Younge's elder sister.

Preston's consternation at Clara retaining this lowly position was severe, but he had nothing better to offer her. There was no appropriate situation available at any of the Darcy estates, or at least nothing he could request on his cousin's behalf.

In the few hours each week that he was not needed by Mr. Darcy, he would sometimes visit her, using the back door of the place so as not to be noticed, and often sneaking a few shillings into her apron pocket, despite her protests. It worried him to see how the work had aged her. Anyone meeting her would add at least five onto her thirty-two years.

Yet in spite of her red hands and care-worn face, she still retained the open, affectionate nature that had endeared her to him, even when they were both children.

"Worry not for me, Sam," she'd urged him recently when he scowled at Mrs. Bates's shrill voice in the front room. "I have prospects. Why, only yesterday, I heard a fellow mention a position in King's Cross that might be available very soon."

"Clara," he returned, unmollified, "it's always, 'Some fellow says,' or, 'Someone's heard.' Meanwhile, you've been here nigh on two years, and that's far too long. You're too fine a person for this."

"Perhaps not," she argued calmly. "Who can say what we're put on this earth for? Maybe I can do more good working here than if I were waiting on the queen herself."

And so he left her. Each occasion that he saw her became a heavier burden upon his conscience. Until he could promise her something better, however, he was helpless to alleviate her condition.

Mr. Darcy, after several weeks of almost frantic activity, at last settled down to a more reasonable schedule. Unfortunately, this alleviation of urgency did not mean any complacency on his part.

He began to relapse into the melancholia that filled Preston's heart with concern.

One morning after having been shaved, Mr. Darcy grimaced at his reflection in the mirror, an expression so rare as to cause his valet to scrutinize his master's face.

"Is something wrong, sir?" he inquired when no wound could be found. "I did not effect discomfort, I hope."

Ignoring the question, that gentleman announced, "I shall require a formal coat today, Preston. I am to attend a wedding."

"A wedding, sir?" the valet repeated, relieved that it was not he with whom Mr. Darcy was vexed. "A happy occasion, indeed." Carefully, he considered the array of frock coats hanging in the wardrobe. "Perhaps the blue?"

"Happy occasion!" was the scornful reply. "That remains to be seen. Yes, the blue is fine. As a matter of fact, Preston, you are acquainted with one of the party."

Pausing from brushing barely discernible lint from the coat, he questioned doubtfully, "Am I, sir?"

"I imagine you must recall Mr. George Wickham," his master went on, his voice thick with disgust. "He is to be the bridegroom."

"Indeed?" Moving to check the lay of the coattails, Preston kept his own voice inscrutable. "Should I recall the bride as well?"

At this, Mr. Darcy made a noise slightly resembling a laugh. "Not only have you never had the privilege of meeting her, Preston, it is likely you never will." Closing his eyes at some painful image, he murmured, "God help me. By this single act, I am linking his name with her family's forever, but...there is truly nothing else to be done...."

Tactfully turning away with the pretense of collecting his master's gloves, Preston was stung with pity. He did not understand what Mr. Darcy was speaking of, and never, so long as he lived, would he ever dare speak the words aloud, but at that moment, Mr. Darcy was pitiable.

In the evening, Mr. Darcy returned, his expression somewhat more relaxed than previously.

"I shall be dining out, Preston," he stated, tugging at the neck-cloth before the valet could do so.

"Yes, sir."

Mumbling to himself, Mr. Darcy stood before the mirror, try-ing to work through the stubborn knot placed there so many hours earlier. At last, he turned impatiently and allowed Preston to do his job.

"The Gardiners are fine, honorable people," the gentleman remarked after a moment, causing the valet to pause, although only infinitesimally, in his task.

"I cannot understand how..." he continued with evident mysti-fication, "although, I suppose it is hardly important. The Bennet sisters are all so very different themselves. The two eldest must have inherited their sense from someone...not their mother, surely. Their father...?" But here he stopped, pursing his lips thoughtfully.

The neckcloth conquered at last, Preston assisted him with the removal of his coat and shirt.

After splashing water on his face and drying it vigorously with the towel handed him, Mr. Darcy donned a clean shirt and waited while his servant tied a fresh neckcloth around the stiff collar.

"The question remains," he pondered just as a black evening coat was brought to him, "where am I to go from here? I have seem-ingly solved one problem, which hardly improves the prospect of the other. She will never know the effort I've expended, nor do I wish her to. Yet..." Here he sighed deeply. "But no, of all the sensibilities I would seek, it cannot be her gratitude. Dear God," he breathed, "how she haunts me still....How is one to recover from such an illness?"

As the question lacked any possibility of an answer, Preston gave none, but stepped back so that Mr. Darcy could survey his image in the mirror, and either approve the result or not.

However, the gentleman's attention was so engrossed by his private dilemma that he merely turned away dismissively. Picking up his hat from where it waited on the bureau, he hesitated long enough to muse aloud, "Perhaps the irony of this is that if she should discover my part in sealing her sister's fate, it may only encourage her to despise me further."

With that, he shook his head and quit the room.

⸻

Several weeks passed, with little change in the household. Preston remained concerned for his master, but, of course, could offer no words of comfort. He had no idea what event had occurred to check the blossoming relationship between Miss Elizabeth Bennet and Mr. Darcy. Obviously, it had something to do with that scoundrel Mr. Wickham—but what?

In spite of his usual avoidance of tittle-tattle, he found himself listening (while pretending not to— a difficult practice) as the other staff members exchanged idle gossip in the kitchen.

"I hear he compromised the young lady," Tilly, one of the upstairs maids, asserted on one such afternoon, her eyes round with delight.

"*I* hear," the cook, Mrs. Watson, returned in a conspiratorial whisper, "she was some wild thing who followed the militia around like a...well, you know what I mean."

"No!" Hattie, the parlormaid, gasped. "Mr. Wickham forced to marry one of those? Oh, the poor man!"

"Poor girl, you mean," Bert, the second footman, contradicted as he carried in a load of wood to stoke the fires. "That gentleman was bound to receive his just rewards sooner or later. After all of the unlucky servant girls he's ruined…"

"Bert!" his wife, Jenny the laundress, stopped him with a sideways glance at Tilly, who was just sixteen.

"What I don't understand," Mrs. Watson puzzled, "is why Mr. Darcy saw the need to step in. I thought we'd washed our hands of Mr. Wickham long ago."

"Maybe he felt sorry for the girl," Hattie suggested. "Maybe he knows her family…"

"Well, he is such a good, unselfish man. I'm sure he had his reasons," Jenny declared firmly.

But Mrs. Watson was far from satisfied. "Perhaps the father of the girl came to him for help," she mused. "There has to be a practical reason for it." Turning her gaze upon Preston, who was polishing a pair of riding boots, she asked, "What do you think, Preston? You see more of him than we do. Why would Mr. Darcy interfere in Mr. Wickham's affairs?"

"I'm sure he wouldn't confide in me, madam," Preston answered, rubbing harder at a smudge on the left boot toe.

"I heard her name was Benton or something like that," Hattie reported as Jenny handed her a bundle of clean linens to fold.

"Well, it hardly matters what her name was," put in Tilly brightly. "She is Mrs. Wickham now."

"Imagine being Mrs. Wickham," Jenny marveled, applying a heated flatiron to a dampened shirt.

"I always thought he was most handsome," said Hattie.

"What about what he did to poor Miss Georgiana?" Jenny chided her. "Why, the man's incorrigible."

Hattie frowned. "What exactly did he do? I don't recollect hearing any details...Just that he tried to take advantage of her position somehow..."

"And that is all any of us need to know," Jenny said firmly as the pressed shirt was replaced with another. "Mr. Wickham's always been out for whatever he can get, and fortunately, Mr. Darcy has trimmed his sails for him."

"Yet again," Mrs. Watson said and chuckled as she stood up to peek beneath a towel concealing a rising mound of bread dough. "So long as Mr. Darcy's around, Mr. Wickham doesn't stand a chance. Bert!" she called, "have you seen that lazy lout Nigel? I need those hares cleaned and dressed for supper, and he's made himself plenty scarce."

No, it was unlikely that Preston would ever discover the details of the affair, but he could at least be satisfied that his master had been in the right.

As summer waned, he fully expected Mr. Darcy to remove himself and Miss Georgiana to Derbyshire, but he heard nothing of such a plan. Instead, one afternoon, Preston was informed that a party of gentlemen would be organized to accompany Mr. Bingley to Hertfordshire for the hunting in that neighborhood, and that they would remain for several weeks.

Mr. Darcy did not mention an intent of seeing Miss Bennet while in the country. Although no hint was dropped, Preston could not help feeling that there was more than a single motive for the excursion. Netherfield appeared much as it had nearly a year earlier. Because Mr. Bingley's sisters were absent, it was far less inflexible in schedule.

Mr. Bingley's valet, Roster, was five or six years younger than himself, and seemed a friendly young man who did not mind advice from someone with greater experience. On the other hand, Underwood, the valet employed by Mr. Hurst (Mr. Bingley's brother-in-law), was somewhat older, more close-mouthed in company, and not much willing to exchange even pleasantries.

In the pursuit of sport, the gentlemen—Mr. Darcy, Mr. Bingley, and Mr. Hurst—fell into the habit of leaving the house each morning before full sun (accompanied by several baying hounds and enough servants to fetch the multiple kills), not to return until almost luncheon.

On the very first afternoon of their being in Hertfordshire, Mr. Darcy reluctantly submitted to escorting Mr. Bingley as he paid visits to several of his nearest neighbors. And because those neighbors were so pleased to have such distinguished guests, they could take their leave only after partaking of a substantial evening meal, followed by musical exhibitions given by any marriageable daughters of the household.

On the fourth day of this arrangement, Mr. Bingley must have suggested that they make their way to Longbourn, the Bennet home, for, as Preston assisted him in his usual morning routine, Mr. Darcy appeared to be in a state of no little distraction.

Several times he would begin to speak, and then stop himself before the sentence could go anywhere. All the while, he stared out the window at what appeared to be nothing of particular interest.

Finally, just as he was handed his hat and gloves, he said aloud, "In spite of the sense that I am entering the lion's den, every nerve, every thought is alive in anticipation of it." Then, with a bemused lift of one eyebrow, he added in a voice almost unintelligible, "There can be little doubt that I am the most shameless of frauds." Turning away, he gave his head a slight shake. "Yet any remorse I ought to feel is overcome by feelings far more powerful than that. Whether I am prepared or not, today may very well be the end of everything for me."

Later, Roster verified Preston's supposition.

"Mr. Bingley has said that he is eager to renew his acquaintance with Mr. and Mrs. Bennet," he supplied blithely.

"Oh?" Preston answered, looking up from a book on ancient Greece, which he had borrowed from the rather limited Netherfield library. "Then that was their destination this afternoon?"

"Oh yes," replied the younger man. "In fact, so far as I am aware, the Bennet estate was to be their only object today." He paused for a moment before confiding, "Mr. Bingley also anticipates meeting the eldest Miss Bennet again."

The most scrupulous part of Preston wanted to change the subject. But a tiny bit of him wished to be enlightened. "Have you had the pleasure of seeing Miss Bennet yourself?" he inquired in a nonchalant voice.

"Not near enough to address her, of course," was the quick reply. "Only from a very great distance. I recollect that I was able to admire their dancing together at the ball given here in November. From the servants' gallery, of course....My master has excellent taste, if I do say so myself."

"Have you any idea," Preston inquired, "why he did not make her an offer?"

"All I know is that we left the following morning in unseemly haste. Yet," he shrugged as he leafed with little interest through an ornately embossed volume of sonnets, "one does what is expected without comment....I had assumed, as taken with her as he appeared to be, he would return to Hertfordshire soon to do that very thing."

Rising from his chair, Preston tucked the book under his arm to read when he was alone. "Apparently, Mr. Bingley had his reasons."

Offering a bow of farewell to the younger man, he added, "Gentlemen such as Mr. Bingley and Mr. Darcy, who are fortunate enough to claim impeccable credentials, must consider any and all circumstances before undertaking matrimony."

"Which circumstances, pray?"

"As gentlemen of those very gentlemen, my dear sir, we shall probably never know."

When Mr. Darcy entered his apartment that evening, he said only, "We shall be returning to London tomorrow morning, Preston. I expect us to be gone by eight at the latest."

"Yes, sir." In spite of the impulse to inquire whether Mr. Darcy had again seen Miss Elizabeth Bennet (surely the event would have been inevitable; he'd spent the entire afternoon within the walls of her home), Preston resisted, as he knew he must.

Instead, he commenced packing the trunks, which had only just been unpacked a few days earlier.

Two days following their arrival in town, Mr. Darcy received an express from Mr. Bingley. Mr. Darcy happened to leave it lying open on his bedside table. Pretending to be replacing a spent candle there, Preston's eyes scanned the words with disgraceful curiosity.

My dear Darcy,

I must solicit your immediate congratulations. I have made the offer for Miss Bennet's hand and, by all that is most wonderful, she has accepted. What luck, what chance has deigned to favor me! Her father proved himself to be a splendid gentleman and granted his consent with no argument and very little embarrassment.

Believe me when I say that I count myself as the most fortunate of men. But will you not consider following me in the happy state of marriage, Darcy? Or are you no longer infatuated with her sister, as you were this summer? (Great God, I wish I could witness your

*expression as you read this, for I am certain you thought yourself
inscrutable in the matter.)*

*Alas, forgive me if I am sounding like an addled schoolboy, but
I fear I have suffered thus since my dearest Jane assured me of her
own unwavering regard.*

*I shall see you very soon, probably within the next week, for I
have much to arrange in town. I must entreat you, my friend, not to
mention this news to my sisters. I wish to take full pleasure in their
reactions when I speak to them myself.*

> *Until then, may God be with you,*
> *Charles Bingley*

Carefully replacing this missive in the position he had found it,
Preston considered its contents as he continued his daily tasks.

So Mr. Bingley and the eldest Miss Bennet were now betrothed.
Would Mr. Darcy, as his friend had so ecstatically suggested in the
letter, soon follow suit?

As that week progressed into the next, however, there was
no outward sign of his master's taking even a moment to ponder
such advice.

⸺•❖•⸺

Each day passed much as the one before, until one evening when the
eminent Lady Catherine de Bourgh and her daughter, Miss Anne
de Bourgh, came to call. Preston heard the details later in the staff
dining hall when Sarah, the maid attending her ladyship, related the
whole of it to the others.

"Apparently," Sarah shared excitedly, "milady was not pleased
with a young lady by the name of Miss Elizabeth Bennet....Have
you ever heard of her, Elsie?" she asked Mrs. Watson with breathless wonder.

As Mrs. Watson shook her head, Preston concentrated on his roast beef. Of course, no one in town would be aware of Miss Bennet's brief history with Mr. Darcy. Only himself, really. This realization filled him with a deep satisfaction that surprised him.

"In any case," Sarah was going on, "Lady Catherine was scolding... actually *scolding* Mr. Darcy to make him tell her what he obviously did not wish to. Lord, you should have seen his face. I think the man would have liked to bludgeon her with a poker."

"Sarah!" cried Peg, a kitchen maid. "Have a care!"

"I'm only telling you what I saw," she defended herself. "Do you want to hear or not?"

No one said anything, so she continued. "Lady Catherine was carrying on something awful, saying things like, 'This Bennet girl cannot be trusted,' and, 'Poor breeding will always tell.' And all the while, Mr. Darcy just sat and drank his wine without answering back two words! Well, I don't know who this Miss Bennet is, but it made me feel rather sorry for her just the same."

"What happened next?" breathed Peg.

"Well, Lady Catherine went on for quite a while in the same vein, until she said something that made Mr. Darcy look very different."

"Different, how?" asked Mrs. Watson skeptically in the very same moment that Bess, yet another maid, chimed in with, "What did she say, Sarah? Tell us!"

"She said..." Carefully, the girl worked on recalling every word. "She said that Miss Bennet refused, absolutely refused, to promise that she would not accept an offer from Mr. Darcy if he were to give it."

"An offer from Mr. Darcy!" repeated several of her listeners in open disbelief. "Mr. Darcy?"

"But pray," asked Peg, returning their attention to the former statement, "how did her saying such a thing affect him?"

"Yes, Sarah," said Mrs. Watson, frowning. "Why do you say he looked different after that?"

"I was watching him, out of the corner of my eye, of course, and I swear by all that is holy, he almost seemed to light up."

"Light up!" said Peg.

"Yes.…What I mean is, before, when she was speaking, he looked…well, dreadful really, but when she came to that point, he glanced at her real quick, and I thought he nearly smiled."

"Sarah," Mrs. Watson asked, "are you sure? You would not be reading more into it than what really happened, would you?"

"I swear it to be so, Elsie," replied Sarah, meeting the older woman's eyes.

A few moments of shocked silence followed, interrupted only when Sarah added almost timidly, "So what do you make of it? Do you think Mr. Darcy has intentions toward this Miss Bennet?"

"Obviously," Mrs. Watson acknowledged as she pushed herself away from the table, "none of us will likely know for sure until we've either been ordered to prepare the wedding dinner…or not."

After such an enlightening discussion, Preston was not surprised when Mr. Darcy announced their imminent return to Hertford-shire on the following afternoon.

"Lady Catherine has gone back to Rosings without the satisfaction she was seeking, yet her visit proved most useful to me," he mused aloud as Preston busied himself laying out his master's evening clothes. "I only pray that I am not acting prematurely.… Do I stand a chance at last? Can her disinclination mean anything at all? Or is she merely following the tenets of her own nature and refusing to be bullied? To consider the possibilities, only to have my hopes dashed once more, would be truly unbearable. Still…I must find out one way or the other, and that, I cannot do here." Glancing at Preston, he added with an expression of self-mockery, "You'll begin to believe me mad very soon, Preston. Indeed, I half-believe it myself these past months."

"Oh no, sir," Preston responded with practiced impassivity. "Would you prefer the vermilion waistcoat this evening?"

A flicker of a smile played at one corner of Mr. Darcy's mouth. "The vermilion will do….You are a study, Preston."

"Sir?"

"In other words," he elaborated, "you are not as insensible as you would wish me to believe."

Avoiding his master's gaze, Preston said only, "The wind has picked up, sir. Will you desire your greatcoat?"

And so they returned again to Netherfield. Mr. Bingley and his sisters were there to meet Mr. Darcy at the top of the driveway, and as Preston supervised the unloading of the trunks from the carriage boot, he heard the ladies' fervent greetings.

"Mr. Darcy, welcome!" cried Miss Caroline Bingley in an overly bright voice. "Have you heard the good news? My brother is to be married to Miss Bennet!"

"Of course he knows, Caroline," Mr. Bingley said as he stepped forward to shake his friend's hand. "Why, Darcy had as much to do with the happy outcome as anyone."

"What? What can you mean?" returned Miss Bingley, obviously astonished by this disclosure. "Mr. Darcy, pray, what does he mean?"

A moment of thick silence followed, during which the footmen conveying the trunks indoors were impatiently waiting for Preston to precede them, and so nothing more of the conversation could be heard.

During supper, Preston casually addressed Roster. "The household will soon have a new mistress, I understand," he remarked as he waited for his soup to cool.

Roster replied, "Yes. We are overjoyed at the prospect. Few young men deserve happiness as much as Mr. Bingley."

"Why do you say that?"

Roster answered, "Why, because it did not come easily to him—the engagement, I mean. There were several of his friends not convinced that the match was prudent."

"Were there?"

"Indeed. I do not know who these friends were, but Mr. Bingley, being a modest man himself, relied on them to guide him, and they refused to condone the union at first."

"What changed their minds, do you suppose?" Breaking a piece of bread up into the soup, Preston pretended an indifference to the answer.

"I could not guess, other than perhaps the lady's charm winning them over. She seems a very charming, pretty girl, after all."

"So I've heard. Are his sisters overjoyed as well, would you say?"

Reddening, Roster glanced around the table to see if anyone was listening. Then, ducking his head, he confessed, "They say they are to his face, but when they are by themselves, they put forth a very different view. It makes me feel rather bad for the lady. She can't know the mischief they are planning."

"What mischief?"

"I could not say exactly," Roster said and frowned. "But I understand they intend to make the turning over of the household as disorderly as possible."

Considering briefly the effect of such a scheme on a young bride, Preston pushed on: "Are Mr. Bingley's sisters to remain in residence at Netherfield, then?"

"For a time, I understand. Mr. and Mrs. Hurst are said to be returning to town after Christmas, but it is unclear whether Miss Bingley will follow their example. I suppose she shall be invited to remain if she so chooses."

"If they are successful in their scheme, I expect she will not be invited," Preston speculated.

"Perhaps, or perhaps they hope that the ensuing chaos will cause Miss Bingley to appear indispensable to the supervision of the staff," Roster suggested, his face wrinkled with distaste. "In any case, it makes me glad I see but little of her."

"But why would you suppose them to wish her such unhappiness at the very beginning of their wedded life?"

Accepting a plate of roasted pheasant and potatoes from Mrs. Maucker, the head cook, Roster thought the question over before answering. Finally, he said, "I think...I feel they look down upon the Bennets...I mean, all of the Bennet family. They make constant sport of the mother, whom I only vaguely remember from the ball. And there is another sister, the second eldest, whom they seem to despise without constraint."

Here, Preston straightened almost imperceptibly.

"Apparently," Roster continued, "she is a barbaric creature. At least, that is what I've been told by Miss Bingley's maid. She runs and plays like a child, and cares nothing of emulating the better class. They, Miss Bingley and Mrs. Hurst, are dreading having such a connection in the family."

"I suffered no such notion when I was fortunate enough to speak with her," Preston said stiffly. "She appeared to be most lady-like and intelligent."

"You spoke to her?" Roster turned to stare at him in disbelief. "Directly?"

"Well, not directly," the older valet corrected himself. "But my master's sister, Miss Georgiana Darcy, asked my opinion on some matter, and Miss Elizabeth Bennet was in attendance at the time. I was impressed with Miss Bennet's manner. I saw nothing barbaric about her at all."

This silenced Roster for several moments, until he asked in a very low voice, "So the other part of the gossip I heard—is that false as well?"

"What would that be?"

"That Mr. Darcy has been harboring feelings for her? Miss Elizabeth, I mean."

"That," Preston answered coolly, "I cannot comment on. Where have you heard such things?"

"Oh," was the determinedly offhand reply, "the staff overhear bits of the family's conversations and make the most of them. Much of the time, the rumor is false, but because of the frequency with which this rumor has been repeated, I am almost believing it myself." Glancing sideways at Preston, he added, "Miss Bingley, especially, seems concerned with the truth of it. Perhaps you could settle the matter once and for all, and the staff's gossip could be stopped."

"Why should it be stopped?" Preston inquired with a look that could only be described as sanguine. "Perhaps it is not simply a rumor, after all."

Preston regretted this breach of confidence almost immediately. Still, he knew that what he said at the table would be quickly routed through the household. And, in fact, when considering the subject of his master's ultimate happiness, he was counting on it.

Beneath the Greenwood Trees
BY MARILOU MARTINEAU

Marilou Martineau is a lifelong enthusiast of eighteenth and nineteenth century English and American culture and manners, and a collector of Regency antiques and original art. She has written numerous period fiction short stories for websites. She lives and works in Carson City, Nevada, with her husband, a teacher, and frequently visits her son, an illustration student, in San Francisco, California.

"Beneath the Greenwood Trees" is the only story in this anthology that concerns not only the imagined Darcy children, but Darcy himself as a child and the parallels between generations. It also is an excellent representation of growing up in Regency England.

❧❧

Chapter 1

The attics of Pemberley house were far larger than those of most great estates. The upper rooms had somewhat of a musty smell, although they looked clean enough. Cases and trunks from generations of Darcy families were placed about within; some concealing treasured possessions, long forgotten by the present owners of the place. Elizabeth Darcy had let herself through the door by using the keys she had been given upon taking up residence as the mistress of the manor. She had gone round to every room in the house, trying the locks, until she discovered that this particular key fit into the lock of an attic door.

A small stream of light shone through the undersize windows, yet there was enough light for Elizabeth to see her way through the trove of belongings. Given her curious nature, she was certain there would be no harm in opening a trunk or two and examining the contents. She was eager for a hint of her husband's family and of his childhood; she had always been curious to know what he had been like and how he had lived. He had admitted to being tall and gangly, or "all legs" as his mother had said of him, evident from the portrait of himself and his mother hanging in the library that had been painted during the early summer of his eleventh year.

Darcy had, at all times, been extraordinarily quiet on other aspects of his childhood and adolescence. Thus far, he had spoken mostly of Elizabeth, saying barely a word about himself, nary a story to satisfy Elizabeth's ardent interest. Elizabeth knew only that he had been left at the age of three and twenty with the duty of a great estate and the responsibility of a young sister to care for, as well as the loneliness of being a young man without the benefit or counsel of parents. She had never pressed him to tell her of his childhood, but now she was more curious than she had ever been before.

Elizabeth's fingers unfastened the latch on one of the trunks and she opened the lid. Within were stored three old morning gowns, which perhaps had once belonged to Darcy's mother. Elizabeth pulled one from its place and held it to her own frame. Even in its wrinkled state, it was three or four inches longer than would have fit her petite figure. She arched an eyebrow, understanding why Darcy was so tall. She closed the trunk and opened another, which had been placed far back in a corner beneath some old blankets.

Once opened, to Elizabeth's delight, she found it to contain a child's toys. There was an elaborately carved wooden horse and carriage, with working wheels and tiny leather harnesses, somewhat dried and stiff from the effects of time and use. She set the piece down and pushed it back and forth on the floorboards. Again, she peered into the trunk and found a small leather ball, a tin whistle, several small quills, and a leather bag. There were some folded clothes at the bottom, and she reached in and pulled out a pair of small shoes, a little blue waistcoat, and white breeches. She laughed at their small size and shook her head in disbelief that they would have ever fit her husband.

She happened to notice something beneath the clothing, and she reached in and pulled it from its resting place. It was a plainly carved piece of beech wood, resembling a sword. She was astonished to see such a thing made from such material, for certainly Darcy's father would have considered a beech tree a trespasser on his lands, worthy only of being chopped down. The initials FD were naively carved into the handle. Elizabeth held it in front of her, and then took a swipe through the air with it, pretending to wield it in battle. Elizabeth was sure Darcy would be able to tell her about its origin—whether he had made it or it had been the gift of a devoted servant to his master's child—and she hastily returned all the other items back to their hidden sanctuary and closed the lid to the trunk.

After dinner that evening, Elizabeth made haste to the library and eagerly sat in the chair beside the one Darcy always took up to read his newspaper from London. The publication came by post once weekly on Friday, and Darcy savored every word within, usually taking until Sunday to finish reading it. Elizabeth's eyes followed her husband as he went to the desk and picked up the newspaper, and then walked over to his chair, all the while skimming the articles on the front page. Methodically, he stood in front of his chair, turned about, and sat down, still occupied with his reading.

With a flurry of arms, legs, and newspaper, Darcy launched himself out of the chair. Something unfamiliar was beneath him. He quickly turned around to look at the seat, and Elizabeth tried her best not to laugh aloud at such a disorderly scene. Darcy's expression changed as he picked up the toy sword from his chair and held it before him.

"Say, there," he asked dubiously, "how is this come to be on the chair?"

Elizabeth laughed at the look of astonishment on his face. "I must admit that I went into an attic today and found that in an old trunk in a corner."

"What were you doing there, Elizabeth?" Darcy chided her.

"Searching for clues to your youth."

"For what purpose?" he asked disapprovingly. "You could have fallen."

Elizabeth sighed. "My dearest, I am with child, but I am not an invalid. Am I not to climb a few stairs? My dear husband refuses to allow me leave to do anything for myself, and I am oh so very bored."

Darcy sat back down in his chair and grinned in a boyish manner, "I thought this had been lost. Certainly cast out in the rubbish bin." He looked at Elizabeth, the grin still on his face. "It disappeared the summer that my aunt and uncle came for holiday at Pemberley with my cousins. I laid the blame on my eldest cousin, Edward, for taking it and burying it, repayment for the mischief Richard and I played on him that summer." Darcy took a swipe through the air with the toy weapon, "Odd, how I remember it being much larger."

"Pray, Fitzwilliam," Elizabeth teased, "I want to hear of it."

"And so you shall," he replied, "If you promise you will not go again into the attics. If you want something, you have only to ask Mrs. Reynolds and it will be brought down."

"Until I have gone through every article within?"

"If that is what you wish," Darcy said and chuckled. "I do not believe that there is any cause for reproach. Or perhaps I should look for myself first."

Although she would not have admitted to it aloud, Elizabeth had encountered some difficulty managing the steps to the attics. Her own adventures would, for now, have to wait until her child was delivered. For the time being, she would be quite content to listen to Darcy's stories of his youth. She sat back in her chair and placed her feet up on the ottoman, trying to find a comfortable position despite her awkward state of impending motherhood.

"Were you a knight—a defender of truth, justice, and distressed damsels?" Elizabeth eagerly looked to him for an answer.

"Hardly," he said and chortled. "I fancied myself as Robin of Loxley."

"Robin Hood!" she proclaimed with amusement. "You were a thief—you who are a man of means!"

"The Earl of Huntingdon—or Robin Hood, as he is commonly known—was a champion of what he believed was his right as a master of his property and as a free man" Darcy smiled at the thought of it. "There are some ruins not far to the east of the of the entrance to Pemberley Park. My cousins and I would run down to them and spend our days pretending to defend them from the Sheriff of Nottingham."

"I know them," Elizabeth declared. "I found them one day on an outing."

Darcy recited a child's ballad for her: "Now bold Robin Hood to the north would go, with valor and mickle might, with sword by his side, which oft had been try'd, to fight and recover his right."[1]

Chapter 2

"Who goes there?" a dark-haired boy called down from atop the rubble.

A fairer-haired boy replied, "'Tis I, Will Scarlett! I have come to pursue Robin the Hood!"

The darker boy jumped down from his perch atop an old pile of masonry rock, wielding a carved toy sword, and said, "No one sees Robin the Hood!"

The other boy put his hands on his hips, and gave a look of defeat. "How are we to play if no one can see you?"

"Of course, you can see me, Cousin," the boy said and sighed. "You are supposed to fight me for the right to join my band of men!"

Young Richard Fitzwilliam unsheathed his sword and pointed it at Master Fitzwilliam Darcy. "Very well, you—whoever you are. I shall not leave until I have bested all present and have earned the right to live amongst you!"

The two boys pushed and shoved, and clashed swords. The summer day was fine and the sun shone down on the battle scene, as the boys playfully fought each other until they could barely stand up because of exhaustion and laughter.

Yet another voice came from behind: "You there, you scurrilous pair. Prepare to meet your doom!"

The two younger boys stared, wide-eyed, at the intruder, and then looked at each other with broad grins. Yelling at the tops of

---

1 "Robin Hood and the Scotchman" from Francis James Child's *The English and Scottish Popular Ballads* (Child Ballad No. 130B).

their voices, they charged the taller boy, who held a toy sword in either hand and wore a wicked grin.

After battling for some time, young Richard charged the tall boy and stuck him in the ribs with the blunt point of his sword. "I have wounded you, you lecherous cur!"

"Nay, nay, you did not injure me at all."

"I say, Edward, he did so!" young Darcy complained.

"Oh, very well," Edward huffed, and he fell on the ground and rolled round, writhing in mock agony for some minutes.

"Edward!" Richard yelled. "How long does it take someone to perish, for heaven's sake?"

Edward stood up and looked down on his brother. "As long as I say it does!"

Richard stood his ground. "You never play fair—you fool!"

"Fool? Fool, you call me, and another thing—I am becoming bored with always having to play the evil character. Why do you not do it for a while, or are you afraid of being pummeled?"

"This is getting very tedious," young Darcy said and stomped over and stood between his two cousins. "Do you carry on like this all the time?"

Richard sheathed his sword and turned around to stomp back over to the ruins and sit down. "Only when we are breathing," he muttered.

"Well, stop it, or I shall tell your father," Darcy threatened.

There was no worse crime that could be committed by young boys than fighting each other. In their father's eyes, it was a punishable offense and simply was not tolerated. The three cousins sat atop the pile of stone quietly for a while, contemplating how they would draw to see who would have to be the villain.

"Hallo there!"

The three boys turned their heads in unison in the direction of the uninvited voice. A tallish boy trudged up the path with a littler boy, and the two came to a standstill, gawking up at the cousins.

"It is George Wickham," Darcy whispered to his cousins. "The steward's son."

"I do not give three figs who he is, as long as he is willing to be the villain." Edward jumped down from his perch atop the ruins and stood before young Wickham. "Do you want to join us?"

"Depends. What is it that you do?"

Young Darcy scrambled down from the rubble, followed closely by Richard. "We are in need of a Sheriff of Nottingham to battle our trio of men," Darcy replied.

Wickham smiled broadly. "Indeed. If you need a sheriff, I shall be your man."

"You there," Darcy said to the other boy. "You can be Sir Guy of Gisborne."

The other boy nodded enthusiastically. "What shall we do for weapons?" he asked.

"I shall be happy to lend you some of mine," Richard threw the boys a few pieces of his vast arsenal.

Darcy laid out the scene: "These ruins are your battlement, and you must come find us in the forest. 'Tis ordered by the king."

The cousins ran off into a stand of trees and waited for their adversaries to begin their search. Darcy and Richard climbed up into two of the trees and practiced their birdcalls, in case secret communications would be necessary.

"Quiet, you are going to give away our positions," Edward snarled in a whisper. "Besides, you sound like sickly pigeons!"

Edward ducked as a handful of the previous year's walnuts were hurled out of the tree and landed all about him. Darcy eagerly awaited the arrival of Wickham, or rather, the Sheriff of Nottingham. He had a score to settle with the boy, for it seemed that young Wickham was always getting Darcy into trouble with old Mr. Darcy.

Mr. Darcy had taken a liking to the son of his steward and young Wickham's easy manners and deportment. Mr. Darcy had also taken on the responsibilities of benefactor to young Wickham that spring, when Wickham's father had taken ill. Master Darcy, however, had learned to trust the steward's son only as far as he could toss him. There had been a few times during play that Wickham had led Darcy down a crooked path, only to deny it in the end, leaving young Darcy to take the blame and face his own father's disapprobation. As far as Master Darcy was concerned, it would be a pleasure to best the blackguard in battle.

While waiting, Darcy began to recite to himself one of the child ballads his father had taught him. The boy loved to sit in the library in the evenings, listening to his father tell him stories of long ago.

> *"Here is one of us for Will Scarlett,*
> *And another for Little John,*
> *And I my self for Robin Hood,*
> *Because he is stout and strong."*

> *So they fell to it hard and sore;*
> *It was on a midsummer's day;*
> *From eight o clock till two and past,*
> *They all shewed gallant play.*[2]

Before long, the enemy was in sight and the boys sprang down from the trees to defend their territory. It was all-out war for

---

2 "Robin Hood's Delight" from Francis James Child's *The English and Scottish Popular Ballads* (Child's Ballad No. 136).

upward of fifteen minutes. The odds were definitely in the merry men's favor; they outnumbered the villains, three to two. They were fortunate, in this instance, to have Edward on their side. He was a boy of fifteen, very tall and broad for his age. What he lacked in wit, he made up for in brawn, which he used to menace his younger brother and cousin.

He was no match for Richard and Darcy, however, when it came to imagination and slyness. He had learned to lament the times when they were all together, for he might find a live creature in his bed or wake up in the morning to discover that every pair of shoes he owned had been laced together and strung outside his window. All in all, he had a relatively good nature when it came to their teasing, and was even known to defend the younger boys against other boys.

When the battle had been waged and it was determined to be a victory on the side of truth and justice, the boys rested together beneath the trees.

Wickham grinned in the direction of young Darcy and said, "I heard your father say that you were to go to the assembly in Lambton tonight."

Darcy grimaced and said, "Good God, not an assembly!"

"What is wrong with an assembly, Wills?" Edward asked.

"You have to dance!" Darcy rolled his eyes in disgust. "I have no stomach for it at all. I would rather drink a bottle of castor oil than dance."

"You would *have* to dance if you drank a bottle of castor oil!" Richard laughed at his cousin, and the other boys laughed, too. Darcy frowned. He abhorred assemblies.

"Are there many pretty girls in town?" Edward inquired of Wickham; unaware of what a reliable source young Wickham truly was on that subject.

"Indeed, quite a few, and all are eager to dance. Occasionally, they will bestow on their partners an obliging kiss," Wickham ventured.

The rest of the boys looked like a bevy of owls as their eyes widened at Wickham's comments. Edward and Richard grinned together, as Darcy simply groaned at the thought of having to tolerate being slobbered upon by some nonsensical female, no doubt adorned in some shade of pink.

"I suppose it is our duty to dance with them, then," Edward replied. "I would not wish to disappoint them." He got up from his place beneath the tree and proceeded to walk back to the house. Wickham and his friend left as well, leaving Darcy and Richard under the trees.

"What do they see in them?" Darcy asked and sighed.

"In who? Girls?" Richard asked. "I suppose they are wanting to marry one day."

Darcy could only snarl, "I shall not marry a girl, unless I am sure she can arm wrestle."

"What has that got to do with it?" Richard asked and guffawed.

Darcy stood up and looked toward Pemberley house, "What else would a fellow do for amusement?"

Elizabeth laughed, shifting positions in the chair. "Well, my dear, you have not yet asked me to arm wrestle."

Darcy cleared his throat. "No, indeed." He noticed his wife's discomfort, and, making an attempt to avoid telling Elizabeth any more of his tale, said, "If you are ailing, Elizabeth, we can take this up at another time."

"Not likely, Mr. Darcy." Elizabeth's eyes squinted to show her displeasure, realizing her husband's ploy. "You shall not get out of this so easily." The housekeeper, Mrs. Reynolds, entered the library with a tray of tea and cake, and she set it down beside Elizabeth. "Thank you," Elizabeth said and smiled warmly at the servant. "Oh, husband," she said and sighed. "This child of yours likes to kick his heels at this very time each evening. Perhaps with such eager feet, he will find assemblies more agreeable than his father does, but for now he seems satisfied after having a little something sweet."

Elizabeth took a sip of tea prepared for her by Mrs. Reynolds, and a small bite of the cake. Then she lifted her chin resolutely. "Pray, continue."

Darcy smiled. "Where was I?"

"You were to attend an assembly in Lambton," she reminded him.

"Indeed, that regrettable event," he muttered.

Young Fitzwilliam Darcy stepped into his father's study and waited near the door. "Come in, Son," Mr. Darcy said to his eldest child. "And how go your adventures today?"

"Quite well," the boy replied quickly. "Papa, are we to go to an assembly tonight?"

A smile came to Mr. Darcy's face. "Indeed, Son, so it would seem. Your mother and your aunt have expressed a desire to attend such an event."

"Might I remain home?" the boy asked, slumping into a chair in front of the large study desk.

"No, you may not," Mr. Darcy said without hesitating. He knew his son disliked such social engagements, even at his tender age. Mr. Darcy and his wife had tried to do what they could to discourage the boy's taciturn bent, and they offered guidance when necessary.

"But Papa..." the boy began to protest.

"Fitzwilliam," Mr. Darcy said firmly, "summer is a time for families to participate in local society. It is a time for young men to put down their books and learn the refinements that will one day be required of them. You do not have to like it, my boy, but you do have to participate."

Mr. Darcy was a kind, patient father, but he was not always indulgent, and he expected his children to know their places within his household. A disappointed scowl began to emerge on young Darcy's face, until he thought better of any such display in the presence of his father.

"How will you know how to behave in society if you do not learn now?" Mr. Darcy inquired with a wink. "Besides, it is good to go while your cousins are present. They are very amiable young men, and you would do well to follow their examples."

"Truly?" the boy wondered at the statement. "But if I am already betrothed, why must I need to know these things at all?"

"Fitzwilliam," Mr. Darcy said as his eyes widened. "You must know it because I say you must; and as to the matter of a betrothal—I think it rubbish, my boy. You will choose your own wife." Mr. Darcy added beneath his breath, "And, I hope, one with a little life in her."

Young Darcy sighed, realizing he was losing a battle of wills with his father. It was a hopeless business, and he was fated to spend an evening bowing and affecting some sign of pleasure for the sake of young maids whose mothers pushed them toward the boys' general vicinity. He would loathe every excruciating moment of the whole affair.

Mr. Darcy stood up from his desk and put his hand upon his son's shoulder. "A country assembly provides good practice for the balls you shall attend in your future. You never know whom you will meet, Fitzwilliam. One day, you may meet the love of your life at just such an assembly."

The boy's shoulders slumped forward in subjugation. "I imagine not, Papa."

'Twas neither Rosamond nor Jane Shore,
Whose beauty was clear and bright,
That could surpass this country lass,
Beloved of lord and knight.

The Earl of Huntingdon, nobly born,
That came of noble blood,
To Marian went, with a good intent,
By the name of Robin Hood.

With kisses sweet their red lips meet,
For she and the earl did agree;
In every place, they kindly embrace,
With love and sweet unity.[3]

The Darcys and the Fitzwilliams entered the assembly room at Lambton to the great amazement of the other prestigious town folk. They were not often seen at assemblies, so this was indeed a distinguished occasion. Young Darcy moved off to the courtyard with the other boys, as their parents engaged in polite conversation before the dance. The children present held their own dance of sorts out on the courtyard, in the shadows of their parents. It was how one practiced proper etiquette at such functions and prepared to be ladies and gentlemen.

---

3 "Robin Hood and Maid Marian." Edited by Stephen Knight and Thomas H. Ohlgren, originally published in *Robin Hood and Other Outlaw Tales*, Kalamazoo, Michigan: Medieval Institute Publications, 1997.

Darcy and Richard stood in a corner and looked on as Edward boldly approached one young lady to ask for the favor of a dance. The young girl blushed and gladly accepted, knowing, even at her tender age, what an honor it was to be noticed by the eldest son of an earl.

The whole business made Darcy's stomach churn. His shyness and reserve did nothing to recommend him to others, and some of the children thought him conceited.

"Wills, do you see a girl who strikes your fancy?" Richard inquired with a grin.

Darcy glanced around the courtyard, shyly eyeing the young girls as they all giggled and blushed.

"They are laughing at us, Richard," Darcy whispered.

Richard smiled at his cousin, "They are not laughing, Wills, they are flirting." Darcy furrowed his brow as he attempted to digest his cousin's counsel. Richard put his hand on Darcy's shoulder. "Think of this as a game. Surely, if it is a game, you can overcome a little fright."

"Fright!" Darcy exclaimed. "You are wrong, Richard. Girls do not scare *me!*"

"Have it your way, Cousin. Look, there are two girls about our ages. I shall ask the one to dance and you shall ask the other."

"Which one, the right or the left?" Darcy inquired, as the butterflies in his stomach threatened to bring him to his knees.

"It does not matter—come on." Richard tugged on Darcy's coat sleeve.

"I beg your pardon," Richard said and bowed gallantly to the young ladies. "My name is Richard Fitzwilliam and this is my cousin, Fitzwilliam Darcy." Richard looked over at his cousin, who was standing and staring at the girls with a slight frown. He reached over and poked Darcy on the shoulder and Darcy bowed, as rehearsed. The girls curtsied and batted their eyelashes in a way that would have made their mothers proud.

"My name is Mary Chaney, and this is my friend, Annabelle Martin." Sweet Mary smiled at Richard, and Darcy let out a meager groan as Richard was overtaken by a rather comical grin.

"Will you do me the honor of dancing with me, Miss Mary?" Richard inquired.

Miss Chaney lowered her eyes and nodded her consent, much as a young lady ought. The young pair moved off in another direction, in polite conversation until the dance began. Darcy stood in front of Miss Annabelle Martin, alternating glances between her face and his own feet. Miss Martin was fair enough and not at all displeasing, but Darcy stammered and stuttered and his knees threatened to knock, nonetheless.

"Uh, if you are n-not otherwise engaged, will you do me the honor of a dance, Miss…Miss…"

"Martin," she coached him.

"Miss Martin. Yes, of course." Darcy wiped his sweaty palms on his coat.

"Yes, I thank you," she spoke politely and took Master Darcy's damp hand. Darcy was instantly grateful for the delicate gloves she wore.

The music began to play in the assembly hall, and the adults took their places along the line. The children formed two lines of their own, in imitation of their parents, and the dance began. Darcy moved as he had been taught by his mother and father; all the while praying to the Almighty that he would not miss a step or accidentally tread upon Miss Martin's delicate foot.

To his own satisfaction, Darcy made it through the set with hardly a misfortune, and he was quite pleased with the performance. When he escorted Miss Martin away from the dance floor, he noticed his cousins and friends were still engaged with their young ladies. Darcy looked at Miss Martin, wondering how a boy began a conversation with a girl.

"Do you attend Eton, Master Darcy?" Miss Martin asked.

"Yes, my cousins and I are all home on holiday for the summer."

Miss Martin nodded politely and awaited further conversation from young Master Darcy. The wheels turned in Darcy's mind as he strained to think of things to say. At length, he simply asked Miss Martin if she cared to take a turn with him and she accepted.

They walked along the back veranda and down the stone steps into a small park. Darcy mustered his courage and took a good look at Miss Annabelle Martin as she strolled a pace or two in front of him. She was not disagreeable to him, and she possessed fair skin and pretty dark curls that bounced when she walked. He supposed those to be the qualities of a young lady that should attract a young man, and he was quite impressed with himself that he had actually taken notice.

"What do you do for amusement during the summer, Master Darcy?" she said as she stopped under an oak tree and turned to face him.

Darcy was caught off guard as his gaze met with Miss Martin's large brown eyes. His eyes wandered down the bridge of her small nose, which was lightly freckled in a rather fine way. Her teeth were tolerable, he supposed, and she had a comforting smile.

"Um, well...I...I read, and we have gone riding. We have been lately at the old ruins near Bristol Cross. Sometimes we run into Lambton from Pemberley to play cricket on the green."

"I live near the green. Perhaps I shall see you there soon?"

"Per-Perhaps," Darcy stammered and blushed. Then the two stood for some time, with a rather lengthy pause between them.

Finally, Darcy managed to say, "I suppose we should be getting back to the assembly."

Miss Martin nodded and then turned when she heard her mother calling her name from the veranda. She quickly looked back at the handsome young man in front of her and before Darcy knew it, Miss Martin had placed a tender kiss on his unsuspecting lips, and then run back to the assembly room.

Young Darcy could barely move a muscle as he contemplated what had just happened to him. It seemed as if his heart had stopped beating. Practically every ounce of color had drained from his face, and his mouth had gone dry.

"Fitzwilliam!" Richard called out from the veranda. "Wills, where are you?"

Darcy turned around at the sound of his name, and on seeing that it was his cousin, called out, "Here! Down here!"

Richard came bounding down to the park, wondering what his cousin was doing out alone in the moonlight.

"Richard!" Darcy exclaimed as he began to panic. "That girl, she..."

"Hold a moment, sir!"

"What, my dear?"

Elizabeth was perturbed, "You mean to tell me that this girl was so forward as to kiss you?"

"Yes, quite."

"The little tart!" Elizabeth exclaimed under her breath. "Pray, who is she, Fitzwilliam? Does she still live in Lambton?"

Darcy chuckled as he realized Elizabeth's discomfort at the disclosure of his first kiss. She was not one to exhibit jealousy as a general rule. However, her emotions seemed to be more acute these days.

"Elizabeth, I was a man of eight and twenty when we married," Darcy playfully scolded her. "Did you expect me not to have been in the company of other women before we met?"

Elizabeth tried her best not to pout. "No, I cannot say that I did."

"Besides, Miss Annabelle Martin has long since taken the name of Mrs. Taylor. She married a man from Devonshire, and I have not seen her for many years." Darcy took Elizabeth's hand and placed a loving kiss on it. "Rumor has it that she has had at least six children in as much as ten years."

"I should not doubt it!" Elizabeth huffed and stiffly shifted her position in the chair.

Darcy glanced at Elizabeth, a sly grin on his face. "Perhaps you would wish me to stop for the evening, my dear?"

"Not at all!" she exclaimed. "That is, unless you are to inform me of any other young wenches who happened to make such advances on your person?"

"No, dear. I shall not tell you about *any* of the others," Darcy pretended to study the toy sword, awaiting his wife's reaction. Out of the corner of his eye, he saw her pick up her embroidery and begin to busy her hands and her mind with something constructive.

"Pray, continue," she said and sighed.

Chapter 3

There were outlaws, as 'tis well known,
And men of a noble blood;
And a many a time was their valour shown
In the forrest of merry Sherwood.

Upon a time it chanced so,
As Robin Hood would have it be,
They all three would a walking go,
Some pastimes for to see.[4]

As Richard and Darcy walked along the path toward the lake, they could hear Edward singing at the top of his voice. The boys stopped and hid behind a tree as they watched Edward cooling himself in Pemberley's lake, quite by himself, happily raising his voice in song.

They looked at each other and grinned, for Edward was indeed a sorry singer. Richard looked around and spied Edward's clothes atop a boulder beside another tree.

"Wills," Richard said in a low voice and then snickered. "He is stark naked! Look, there are his clothes."

Darcy began to giggle, but bit his lip for fear of Edward hearing them. "Do you think he will notice if his clothes turn up missing?"

"Not at all," Richard said and stifled a laugh. "Why would he need clothes on such a warm day?"

The boys crawled over to the rock, pulled off Edward's togs, and tucked them under their arms. As they hastily returned to the house, they could hear Edward's merry melodies wafting on the breeze.

As Edward pushed the food around on his plate, Fitzwilliam and Richard sat quietly, attempting to keep their faces from showing their guilt, though Edward's red cheeks made it very difficult.

"Well, Edward, I believe you have been taken in by one of the oldest tricks in the book." The earl looked at his son with a stealthy

---

4 "Robin Hood's Delight" from Francis James Child's *The English and Scottish Popular Ballads* (Child's Ballad No. 136).

grin upon his face. "It must have been one of the tenant children who took your clothes, for no son of mine would ever do anything so low." He eyed his younger son and pursed his lips.

Glancing at his own father, young Darcy met a look of disapproval. He lowered his eyes to his plate to hide his mirth and quietly ate the meal before him. Darcy nearly choked on his food as the earl recounted how Edward had been forced to make his way to the stables, quite in the buff, where he bribed a stable hand for a horse blanket to wrap himself in so he would be able to make his way into the house.

Young Richard let out a snicker at the story. "Do you find this amusing, Richard?" his father barked.

Richard gathered his faculties and snapped to attention. "No, sir, not at all."

"And you, Fitzwilliam?" Mr. Darcy inquired sternly of his own son. "You appear to be quite amused by your cousin's misfortune."

"No, sir, excepting that it does lend itself to a rather ridiculous picture," Young Darcy's grin turned into open laughter as Richard let out a brief guffaw.

"Mind your impertinence, young man," Mr. Darcy reprimanded his son. "The table is no place for foolishness. Perhaps a night spent in your room would be appropriate. Take yourself there now, straightaway."

"Yes, Father." Darcy got up from the table with his head bowed and quickly slipped from the room.

"You too, Richard, and do not let me catch you laughing at your brother's expense again," the earl snapped.

"Yes, sir." Richard followed his cousin's example and obediently left the room.

The earl turned to his brother-in-law with a purposeful look, which was returned by a meaningful twitch of Mr. Darcy's eyebrows before Edward could catch either gesture.

Side by side, Darcy and Richard headed for their rooms, grinning as they went. They both knew it would go better on them to take the easier punishment than be made to confess and suffer a worse one. Confinement to their rooms was not such a bad deal, as it also saved them from the wrath of Edward. They both had stowed a few good books in their rooms, for just such occasions.

It was Sunday and the morning was spent in church. This was torture for most boys, as it was expected that they would sit quietly and reflect for longer than they deemed tolerable. They had to listen to tedious sermons, droned on by vicars. The subject that week concerned the propriety of virtue.

Young Darcy sat next to his father in the family pew. He glanced around the church and happened to see Miss Annabelle Martin sitting across from him, with her parents. She gave him a shy smile as he caught her eye, and he looked back and smiled, too. Then he tried his best to pay attention to the sermon.

He thought perhaps he should feel some guilt at having compromised the girl, though as he contemplated it a while longer, he decided that the experience had not been wholly bad. In fact, he had rather enjoyed his first experience with the opposite sex, and besides, it had been she who had kissed him. He let his mind drift back to his present situation. He fidgeted in his seat as he thought of the battles to be waged and victories to be claimed down by the ruins.

Mr. Darcy looked down at his son and noticed his discontent. Though not unsympathetic to the discomfort of a hot, stuffy room, there was etiquette to be maintained. He reached down and put his hand on his son's knee, implying to the boy to remain on his best behavior.

Young Darcy knew the meaning of the press of his father's hand. His father was kind and loving, and not given to an ill temper, as were some he had seen. However, he had learned that it was not wise to test his father's patience too severely. From as much of a desire to please his father as to avoid any further gesture of correction, Fitzwilliam shifted once more and thereafter tried to emulate his father's still and composed posture.

Robin was a gentle boy,
And therewithal as bold;
To say he was his mother's joy,
It were a phrase too cold.

His hair upon his thoughtful brow
Came smoothly clipped, and sleek,
But ran into a curl somehow
Beside his merrier cheek.[5]

When the family arrived home, Darcy went upstairs and knocked on his mother's bedchamber door.

"Mama, may I come in?"

"Yes, Fitzwilliam. I would very much like to see you," Lady Anne's voice consoled him. His mother had taken to bed, for she had recently discovered she was with child, and she had begun to

---

5 "Robin Hood, A Child" by James Henry Leigh Hunt.

feel somewhat ill. The much-awaited news that a child was on the way had been a long time in coming for the Darcys, being as Fitzwilliam was already eleven. He really had no idea of the impact a baby would make on his life. He did not understand any of it, nor did he particularly care to.

"How do you feel, Mama?" he inquired.

"Well enough, under the circumstances. Are you and your cousins behaving yourselves? I do not wish to know that you are giving your father grief."

Fitzwilliam smiled mischievously and said, "Fairly well, Mama."

"You are not climbing trees and bashing one another with those sticks, are you?" his mother asked and raised her eyebrows questioningly.

"Mama, it is what boys do! If I am not allowed, there will be nothing left to do and the summer will be for naught!" Darcy protested.

"Fitzwilliam, I should not want any harm to come to you. You will surely hurt yourselves wielding those sticks and hanging like monkeys from the trees."

Darcy watched his mother shift position in bed and close her eyes as a wave of illness overtook her. "Are you certain you are well, Mama?"

"Yes, dear, it is only a little discomfort. It is endurable, as it is a sign that the baby is well enough."

"Your poor mama, Fitzwilliam," Elizabeth said and sighed. "I do know how she felt." Elizabeth lowered her feet from the stool and sat forward to stretch as much as she was able.

"Shall we walk for a bit, my love?" Darcy stood up and gave her his hand.

"Around the room will be sufficient, for I would not wish you to forget to continue your story," she said and smiled up at her husband.

"Somehow I think you will not let that happen."

Elizabeth stood up. "Ooh...there," she said. Grabbing Darcy's hand, she placed it on her belly. "There, do you feel the baby?" she said and giggled.

Darcy did feel the baby, poking and jabbing at him. "Does that hurt, my love?" he asked, looking a little squeamish but smiling nonetheless.

Elizabeth shook her head, "It mostly tickles, although sometimes the tyke gets a good shot in. It is, however, a very reassuring feeling."

Darcy's smile faded. He leaned over and kissed Elizabeth tenderly, as he whispered, "My dearest."

"What is the matter, Fitzwilliam?" she inquired.

Darcy shook his head. "Had I only known back then the things I know now, I would not have given my father grief. He must have been concerned about my mother, and about the baby. Instead of being allowed to attend to his obligations and worries, he had to contend with the antics of a spoiled boy." Darcy heaved a sigh as he thought of his father, but his smile reappeared as he felt his own child move once more against his hand, reassuring him that everything was well.

Chapter 4

Despite the looming threat of parental chastisement, Darcy and Richard continued to pull pranks on Edward. His irritation upon discovering their chicanery was too amusing to resist. For Richard, it was a matter of payback for Edward being the older brother. For Darcy, it was merely good sport.

Edward fancied himself a fearless hunter, for he had been on a hunt with his father and Mr. Darcy earlier that year. He delighted in tormenting the younger boys with the fact that he was of an age to be taken on such prestigious outings, while they were still infants, as he liked to call them. This caused great vexation for the younger boys.

During the summer months, bats had been known to hide in the attics of Pemberley house. That summer had been no different, and Mr. Darcy warned the children that if they saw any, they must tell him immediately, and never touch the creatures, for fear they would be bitten.

The younger boys delighted as Mr. Darcy told them this, especially when they saw Edward shiver in disgust at the thought of encountering such vermin. Later that night, when everyone was in bed, there was a knock on young Darcy's bedchamber door. He scurried from his bed and opened the door, and Richard stealthily slipped into the room.

"Wills, did you see? Edward is afraid of the bats!"

"I do not blame him, Richard. I have seen one and the sight of them makes your skin crawl." Darcy shook off the shiver that invaded his body.

Richard made a determined face. "Edward does not know that we fear them! I have an idea, but I need your help."

"Oh no!" Darcy resolutely shook his head. "I am not capturing any bats!"

Richard folded his arms across his chest. "I did not know you were such a coward, Wills!"

"A coward, me?" Darcy was incredulous. "Surely you are making a joke."

"Then you will help me?" Richard asked with glee.

Darcy nodded his head and then decided he would visit the library in the morning and restock his room with a few more good books. He had a feeling that when his father found out what they were up to, he would be spending more time in solitary.

The next morning, the boys were up early and stole out of the house before being missed. They ran down the lawn and stopped under a large pine tree, looking underneath for a pinecone that would be precisely the right size. Darcy picked up a perfect specimen and shoved it in the pocket of his coat.

After breakfast, the boys went to their rooms to gather their arsenal for play. Edward entered his bedchamber, followed by Darcy.

"What?" Edward said as he scowled at the younger boy.

Darcy shrugged. "Nothing. I thought today you could be Robin of Loxley."

"Really?" Edward said and grinned. He no sooner began to rejoice at his good fortune than Richard came running into his bedchamber, looking ghastly.

"Edward! There in my room!" Richard pointed hysterically.

Edward gasped. "What? What is it?"

"Something on the floor of my bedchamber!" Richard yelled. "You must go and fetch it!"

"I am not going to fetch it!" Edward screamed back. "It is probably a bat!"

Darcy stood behind Edward and nearly laughed at his older cousin's distress. "You are the oldest, and besides you are a fine hunter, or so you say," Darcy taunted him. "Richard and I are merely infants!"

"That is right! You *are* infants!" Edward said, sneering.

"Well, I am not afraid of a flying rodent!" Darcy went to Edward's bureau and found a small box on top of it. He emptied it of its contents and he opened the secretary drawer and took out a few sheets of paper.

"What are you doing?" Edward yelped as he watched his younger cousin.

"I am going to catch it in this box. I shall put the box over it, slide the paper underneath, and turn the whole thing over. Then I shall take the poor creature outside and let it go!"

Edward stood with his mouth open as he watched Darcy leave the room. Richard began to follow his younger cousin. "Richard! Where are you going?"

"I am going to help Wills catch the beasty," Richard said matter-of-factly.

"You are out of your minds!" Edward screeched.

"And you are fainthearted!" Richard lambasted his brother.

Edward was beside himself. He had boasted of his courage and daring to his younger sibling and cousin. Now here he was, standing idly by as the younger boys risked life and limb to rid the household of a scourge.

Darcy returned to Edward's room within a few minutes, with the box in his hand and the paper over it. "I got it!" he exclaimed with a grin.

"Nay, you are pulling my leg, you are!" Edward smiled. "There is nothing in that box."

"There is so!" Darcy protested. "Here, take a look!"

Darcy moved forward and slid the paper off the box a bit. Edward backed up and nearly fell on his backside in his haste to get away. "You are bluffing! There is nothing in that box!"

Darcy took the box and tilted it to the side. Edward heard something in the box scratching, and then bump the other side of the box. Edward's eyes opened wide and he started backing up farther and faster.

"Do you not want to see it, Edward?" Richard asked with a grin. "I saw it in my room. It is black and ugly, with big wings and fangs!" Richard imitated the creature the best he could.

"Uh...n-no...no..." Edward stammered, as the panic in him grew worse. "Get it *out* of here!"

Darcy moved the paper away from the box a little more and looked inside. "It looks harmless enough."

Edward became desperate. "Wills, take it away! It will surely bite you, and then you will be frothing at the mouth!"

"Not from a little thing like this!" Darcy grinned and pulled the paper from the box. He looked inside, and then with a jump, heaved the box up, letting its contents fly out in Edward's direction.

Edward shrieked and fell to the floor, and then quickly crawled out of the room, screaming at the tops of his lungs. The younger boys were overcome with delight as they fell onto Edward's bed in fits of laughter.

Richard ran over and picked up the pinecone from the floor and held it in the air. "Some great hunter he turned out to be! Afraid of a big, ugly pinecone!"

In summer time when leaves grow green
'Twas a seemly sight to see
How Robin Hood himselfe had drest
And all his yeomandrie.

He clad himselfe in scarlett red
His men in Lincoln green
And so prepares for London towne,
To shoot before the lovely queen.[6]

The boys had planned to run into Lambton that day to play cricket on the green. Young Wickham had told them a few of the boys from the village were organizing a game and all those willing and able were to be invited.

When they arrived at the green that morning, the scene looked like a knightly tournament, with young men waiting to show their expertise at sport, and young ladies lined up along the sides of the field to cheer on their favorites. Miss Mary Chaney was there, eager to see young Richard Fitzwilliam. Richard obliged the young lady, walking over to where she stood with her friends and taking a moment to play the flirting game, which he had tried to explain to Darcy after the assembly, but to no avail.

Darcy stood some ways back and watched his cousin's amiable nature with those of the opposite sex. It was no matter whether young Darcy wished to participate in this particular game; in his opinion, he would never have a talent for it. He noticed Miss Annabelle Martin amongst the girls, and for some reason he felt obliged to make sure she noticed his presence. Edward threw Darcy a ball, and Darcy began to make several practice bowls, while Edward took a few swings.

Darcy was convinced that there was no better way for a chap to be noticed by a girl, than while engaged in a little sport. Each time he bowled, he would steal a glance over in Miss Martin's direction, to make sure she was thoroughly impressed with the figure he cut

---

6 "Robin Hood and Queen Katherine" from Francis James Child's *The English and Scottish Popular Ballads* (Child's Ballad No. 145B).

on the playing field. Miss Martin watched and smiled as Master Darcy did his best to look impressive for her benefit. Darcy was annoyed, however, when young Wickham made his way over to the group of girls and began to monopolize their attentions.

Darcy bowled the ball again, and then looked over in Miss Martin's direction, only to see her laughing and her eyes sparkling at the amiable conversation of George Wickham. Edward hit the ball and it went flying in Darcy's direction.

"Look out, Wills!" Edward yelled, and Darcy fell to the ground just in time to avoid having his bell rung, much to his embarrassment.

When Darcy scrambled to his feet, he stormed over to where Wickham and Richard were entertaining the girls.

"Are we going to play this game?" he huffed. "Or are you going to lollygag all day?"

Darcy was selected the captain of one team and Robert Leyton the captain of the other. Young Leyton was a year older than Darcy, and the two boys were neighbors, although they did not play much together. Leyton's father and Mr. Darcy were not the best of friends, even though their estates bordered each other's. The Darcys and the Leytons had been involved in many land disputes throughout the years, going back as far as the boys' great-grandfathers. It seemed, in the opinion of the Darcys, that the Leytons were always making claim to Pemberley lands. The feud had been perpetuated throughout the years, but both boys knew little of the particulars, only that their families were not on good terms.

Wickham was chosen as umpire, much to the chagrin of both captains, for Wickham was known to make questionable calls. The teams were nominated, and play commenced near noon that day. The constable was taking his midday turn about Lambton when he stopped to watch the friendly play on the green. Seeing no problems, he decided to continue on, although he decided it best to come back by the green after some time.

Unbeknownst to Darcy and his cousins, there had been a match a fortnight earlier, which had turned into an all-out brawl. The constable was in no humor to see the same thing happen on this day, and he swore to himself that if there was any mischief, someone would face the consequences.

The midday sun beat down on the green, and after about an hour, most of the boys began to feel hot and testy. There were a few occasions when Darcy and Leyton argued over a call of Wickham's. However, Edward, Richard, and a few friends of Leyton's did their best to keep the peace.

A new boy walked onto the field for Leyton's side, and upon seeing this, Darcy ran over to Wickham.

"Who is he?" Darcy questioned in annoyance.

Leyton came out onto the field and said, "I am making a change in players!"

"You cannot do that!" Darcy looked at Wickham. "I say, he cannot do that! It is against the rules!"

"'Tis not!" exclaimed Leyton.

By now, the rest of the boys had gathered around as Leyton and Darcy argued the rules of the game.

"You nominated your players, and the rules state that you cannot make a change in the middle of the match without my consent!" Darcy huffed, quite put out by Leyton's audacity.

"Darcy," Wickham said as he smiled nervously, "give him your consent, so we can get back to the play."

Darcy began to waver in his determination to stick with the rules, especially because he was hot and tired. He made a move to give his consent when Leyton interrupted him.

"He will never consent! Like father, like son!" Leyton quipped.

Darcy frowned resentfully. "What is that supposed to mean?" Richard held onto Darcy's right arm and Edward held onto his left as the irritated boy tried to charge at his accuser.

"It means you are as unbending as a fence post," Leyton said and smirked.

Darcy screwed his face up in revulsion, but Richard and Edward kept their hold on him. Wickham quietly moved around the outer edge of the circle, careful to stay on the side of his benefactor's son, yet also near an escape route.

"At least *I* can win *and* play by the rules, instead of cheating by *moving* the fence posts!"

Leyton's face was red with anger as he came within inches of Darcy, shoving the boy's shoulder with the tips of his fingers, "You are stubborn and absurd."

"Here now, Leyton, there is no need—" But Edward was not allowed to finish, as he let go Darcy's arm to move Leyton's hand away. Darcy had heard enough.

With a quick jab to the belly, Darcy knocked the wind out of Leyton. A boy came flying across the line, intent on defending his captain from Darcy's attack, but knocked into Richard instead, sending them both to the ground.

Within a few moments, there were boys flying everywhere, knocking each other down and tumbling about in the grass. Girls were screaming at the horrifying scene, although in truth they thought it fairly good sport to watch the boys fussing and fighting.

There was a market at one corner of the green where local farmers sold their fruits and vegetables during the summer months. Wickham ran by one farmer's cart, trying to flee one of Leyton's supporters, but the other boy was too quick, as he reached out and caught Wickham by the coat, flinging him around.

Wickham reached behind into the farmer's cart and grasped a melon in his hands. He raised it above him and let it down hard upon the boy's head. Thankfully, the melon was extremely ripe and only succeeded in making the lad look like a salad. When he had cleared away the juice that was dripping down into his eyes, Wickham was gone. That did not much matter, though, as he grabbed two more melons and ran back to the fray. Soon boys were pulling out melons left and right, pelting one another in frenzied assault. The poor farmer tried his best to protect his crop, but every time he went to interfere, he was splattered with another of his own melons.

Darcy and Leyton were rolling around on the ground, punching and kicking each other, when Richard came up behind them with a melon.

"I say, break it up!" Richard yelled, but the boys kept punching and rolling. Richard waited until Leyton was on top of Darcy, and then let the melon crack onto Leyton's head. Darcy scrambled to his feet as Leyton rolled off, confused by the surprise attack.

"Thank you, Richard!" Darcy said and grinned.

"Do not mention it, Wills!" Richard said, laughing.

No sooner had they turned around to join the rest of the brawl than someone caught them by the scruffs of their collars.

"I never thought I would see it come to this!" bellowed the constable. He and some of his men gathered the boys that had not run off and took them back to the constable's office. They placed all the boys into a cell, including Darcy, his cousins, and Leyton. "Now, there will be no trouble out of you boys! Your parents will be notified of your whereabouts, and you shall remain here until they can fetch you!"

Darcy looked about the cell. There were battered and bruised boys everywhere, and each and every one of them was covered with melon pulp and seeds. Darcy made his way to one of the wooden benches and sat down with his head in his hands. He thought he might cry as he imagined the anger of his father and the grief of his mother upon hearing the news that he was incarcerated.

He looked up to see Edward and Richard looking much the same way. "Father will have our heads, or worse," Edward moaned.

"Edward, do not speak of it." Richard's heart pounded at the thought of their father's likely rebuke.

There was a commotion at the door, and every boy in the cell stood at attention, believing that his father was about to enter the room to claim him. You could hear a pin drop as a figure entered the room and came around the corner to peer into the cell.

The constable's keys jangled as he opened the lock and called out, "Robert Leyton, you are to go." Robert Leyton left the cell and stood next to the constable. Darcy saw Mr. Leyton come around the corner with a mortified look on his face. He grabbed the back of his son's collar and pulled him out of the room. Every boy in the cell jumped as they heard the front door slam and the driver of a carriage call out huskily to his team as the horses sped away.

It was not long before Mr. Darcy and the earl got word of their sons' whereabouts and drove to Lambton to fetch them. The earl came around the corner of the room and stood before the cell. His face was stone cold as he glared at his sons. Darcy had never seen Edward and Richard look so timid, or his uncle so furious.

The constable opened the cell door, and the earl growled, "Get into the carriage, both of you!" Both boys did as they were told, leaving Darcy still within the cell. The earl looked at his nephew, frowned, and then left the room. Darcy wiped the sweat from his palms, wondering where his father was as he turned around to look at the remaining boys.

"Darcy!" the constable's voice boomed through the silence, causing the boy to jump. Darcy turned to take leave, but froze where he stood, upon finding his father waiting for him, ominously silent.

"Come out, boy. Your father is waiting," the constable chastised him.

Darcy could not look up as he came to stand before his father and the constable.

"Mr. Darcy, sir," the constable started apologetically, "your son has never before been in trouble here. If it were not for...well, sir...if it were not for his part in this mess, I'd gladly have let him go without another word on the subject."

Darcy glanced up to find his father glaring at him, "Are you responsible for this scuffle, Fitzwilliam?"

Darcy searched his father's eyes, desperate to find any hint of leniency as he justified his involvement. "Papa, I had no choice! Leyton insulted me...our family..." The smoldering anger in his father's eyes told him his defense was useless. Hanging his head in dismay, Darcy admitted quietly, "So I hit him."

The constable cleared his throat before venturing tentatively, "Aye, sir, and there's more to the story, if you please."

Mr. Darcy frowned darkly as he pointed his son to a bench along the wall, "Fitzwilliam, sit yourself down. I will hear out the constable."

While trying to appear disinterested, Darcy strained to hear the conversation taking place across the room, but all he could hear were snatches of information.

"...came running for me...reluctant to say...said he'd be getting someone in trouble whom he'd rather not..."

"Where is he?"

"Sent him home, like a good lad...what else am I to think... Master Darcy standing in the middle of it all..."

"...lost the entire cartful?"

"That he did, sir. I cannot let your son..."

Unfortunately, as his father turned toward him, the last was pronounced with great clarity: "You have my assurance that he will be thoroughly punished. Please see that Mr. Landers receives this." Mr. Darcy took out his money clip and handed a five-pound note to the constable. "And please accept my apologies for the trouble you have endured."

Darcy stepped into the Fitzwilliam carriage and slipped quietly into the space next to his cousins as his father took his place beside the earl.

"Brother, Fitzwilliam has admitted to starting the fight," Mr. Darcy informed the earl sadly. "And according to young Wickham, Fitzwilliam was also the first to raid the farmer's cart."

Young Darcy exchanged wide-eyed looks of disbelief with Edward and Richard before sputtering an objection: "But Papa, I did not—I never—"

Edward, feeling the responsibility fell to him as the eldest among the boys, interrupted his cousin: "Father, it is not right— what Wickham told the constable."

"You are in no position to judge Wickham's actions," the earl growled, believing his son to be condemning the boy for telling on the others. "I want to hear nothing more from you—from either of you," the earl said, eyeing his sons sharply.

Mr. Darcy rapped the ceiling of the carriage with his walking stick, and the carriage began its silent journey to Pemberley.

Darcy and his father walked in the front doors of Pemberley house. Lady Anne was waiting for them in the hallway, and Darcy stood before her, trembling as he saw the grief on her face.

"Oh! Fitzwilliam, are you injured?" Lady Anne cried as she knelt down to her son, immediately using her handkerchief to wipe away the grime left by the dirt and pulp. The gentle strokes of her cloth revealed a small cut on his lip and a tenderness on his cheek. "My dear boy, you *are* injured," his mother pronounced with alarm as she scanned his person for other signs of injury.

Suddenly, Lady Anne turned ashen and teetered dangerously as she grasped for her husband's aid. Relying on the support of her husband's arms, Lady Anne fanned herself with her handkerchief until realizing it to also be a source of her distress. Casting it away from her, she fanned herself with her hand to rid her senses of the smell causing a consuming wave of nausea. "Mr. Darcy, that odor... I am unwell."

As he gently led his wife to a place to lie down, Mr. Darcy shot his son a stern look. "Get to your room, Fitzwilliam, and clean yourself up. I shall be up in a moment, and we shall have a talk."

Darcy let go the crumpled cloth of his shirt he had been worrying with his hands as he looked up at his father. "Talk" was most likely not the correct phrasing for what his father had in mind, but he would not argue the point. With one last look of concern for his mother, he did as he was told.

That night, young Darcy lay on his bed, smarting from the punishment his father had inflicted, while also dreading what was yet to come. What also stung was the lesson in human nature he had learned that day. He was angry with Robert Leyton for provoking his anger and speaking ill of his father. He was incredulous that George Wickham should implicate him when he had never been anything but forthright with him. He was upset that his father had taken the word of the constable and assumed his guilt without giving him a chance to explain. But mostly, young Darcy was disappointed in himself, for being the cause of such misery to his parents.

Elizabeth looked over at Darcy. "Melons?" she asked and laughed.

Darcy smiled slightly and nodded his head, "Indeed, it was quite a scene."

"How so like Wickham to behave in such a way, Fitzwilliam. It is a wonder you have tolerated him all these years. How did you know it was really he who owned the guilt?"

"Richard told me later, after the length of *his* punishment was fulfilled."

"Was your uncle severe?" Elizabeth asked.

"My uncle would not tolerate having felons for sons." He added, "Mention the Lambton honeydew affair if you want to see the colonel blanch."

"And you? Was your punishment indeed thorough?"

Darcy shifted unconsciously in his chair, remembering his father's words and the licks of the birch branch that had followed. *You are a* Darcy, *not some hooligan who goes brawling about. There will always be some windbag challenging you.* The now-grown Darcy smiled momentarily at his father's inadvertent admission of his opinion of the Leyton men. *Use your head, Fitzwilliam. Choose your battles carefully or you may wind up at the point of some fool's sword.* Darcy sighed as he admitted, "I was banned from the green for the remainder of the holiday."

Elizabeth pondered her husband's demeanor. For a moment, she thought that he looked just like that eleven year-old boy he once was. The blunt end of the sword he held had fallen to the floor as he contemplated some thought with a broodish push of his lower lip. "And?" she pressed, with unspoken mirth, wondering that there was not something more.

Darcy glanced at her uncomfortably before mumbling to the floor what had been the worst of his punishment, "And I had to apologize to Leyton the next day." Darcy's pout soon turned to a

wicked grin as he felt the satisfaction he had known then upon seeing the dark blue and green bruise consuming Master Leyton's
right eye. Darcy lifted the sword's point to an angle of inspection as
he murmured, "I swore to myself then I would never allow myself
to be humiliated by that person."

Elizabeth flushed and looked down at her needlework, realizing all the more acutely what her husband had forgiven about the
circumstances of her first meeting with Robert Leyton. After her
marriage to Darcy and her arrival at Pemberley, Elizabeth had been
headstrong and taken a curricle out alone one day to visit a neighbor. The horse had been stubborn and the curricle stuck fast in the
mud. It was Robert Leyton who had found her and returned her
home to her husband, but not without expressing a sardonic comment as to Darcy's aptitude as his wife's guardian.

"And you never told your father?" Elizabeth asked curiously, also
turning the discussion away from their querulous neighbor. "That
is, you never told him of Wickham's involvement?"

Darcy looked a little sad as he relaxed back into his chair, reflect-
ing, "He was a fair man, Elizabeth. He would have been grieved to
know he had believed less of his own son than his steward's son—
and made me suffer for it."

Chapter 5

Once their fathers deemed them sufficiently punished for the incident on the green, the boys were allowed to continue their pursuits
at the ruins. After breakfast one morning, young Darcy ran to his
room, grabbed the sword, and scurried down the stairs to catch up
with Edward and Richard. In his haste, he practically ran into his
mother in the gallery.

"Fitzwilliam!" she exclaimed. "Dearest, do be careful with that stick. You are surely going to hurt someone with it."

"Yes, Mama. I shall be back later, Mama!" Darcy assured her confidently as he continued on his way.

His mother watched him go, and hastily called after him, "And do not climb trees!"

When the boys reached the ruins, they drew sticks to see who would have to be the villain. Darcy, unfortunately, lost the draw and resigned himself to the odious task of portraying the Sheriff of Nottingham. He decided to fight fire with fire this time, so he ran into the wood and climbed a tree, lying in wait for the merry men.

When he saw Edward come bounding out from behind some brush, Darcy slipped his leg over the branch he was sitting on and jumped down to scare his cousin. His ploy worked and he did frighten his cousin. However, Darcy landed hard and fell backward as his feet hit the ground. He reached back and his arm became pinned between a rock and his body. He yelled out as he felt a sudden pain from the twisting of his arm.

Richard and Edward ran over to him, "Wills, are you hurt?"

Edward reached for Darcy's shoulder to help him up, but when he touched it, Darcy screamed out in pain, "No, no. Do not touch it!"

Edward ran back to Pemberley house for help, and Richard stayed with his cousin until the earl, Mr. Darcy, and a few household attendants came running. They carried Master Darcy back to the house, where Lady Anne was waiting to see her son.

"Mr. Darcy, Mr. Darcy, what has happened? Will he be well?" she exclaimed frantically.

"Yes, dear, he will be fine," her husband said in an attempt to console her.

Darcy looked at his mother as the attendants carried him up the stairs. She was worried beyond consolation, and he saw her grab his father's arm as she held Darcy's toy sword in her other hand.

"You know, my dear, that was the last time I remember seeing this," Darcy said as he looked at the toy sword.

Elizabeth gave a motherly smile. "She must have hidden it in the trunk in an attic, so that there would be no danger of you injuring yourself with it."

"I suppose you are right." Darcy sighed and then gave a chuckle. "All these years, I thought Edward took it. I owe him an apology, I think." Darcy looked over at his wife, and saw her fatigue. It was getting late and he had kept her from their bed and much-needed rest for too long with his stories of that summer long ago. "Elizabeth, you must go to bed now. I shall take you up, directly."

"Fitzwilliam, I am fine—really," she protested halfheartedly. "What happened during the rest of that summer?"

"There was not much more to it, really. I spent the rest of my holiday nursing my wrenched shoulder and arm. My uncle, aunt, and cousins left a few weeks later to return to London, and my father sent me with them to return to school. He had always taken me to London himself before then. I suppose his concern for my mother was too great to leave her alone."

Elizabeth noticed Darcy's happy countenance fall as he thought of that time. Was he melancholy? she wondered. But then, she saw his features harden into the taciturn man she knew him to be when he was resolved not to let the world inside his heart.

Darcy helped his wife up from the chair, and they slowly walked out of the library and above stairs to their chambers. Darcy left Elizabeth safely in the capable hands of her maid. "I shall return, my love. I will take a turn about the house." He kissed her and she smiled wearily, putting a hand to her back and one to her side as she thought of laying her growing body down in their comfortable bed.

Darcy walked out into the hallway with a candle and began his nightly inspection of the house. When he entered the library, he strode over and picked up the toy sword from the chair. He gave one last swipe through the air with it, and held up the candle to look at the large portrait of himself and his mother. He moved the candle to his right and illuminated a portrait of his father, painted around the same time, during his eleventh year.

"Father," Darcy said out loud, "why could you not have let me be a boy for just a little longer? Where is it written that a Darcy must be serious and reserved, when there is so much more to life?"

Darcy leaned against the desk for a time in quiet contemplation. He remembered how he had been unsure of his life after that summer. His sister had been born while he was at school, and she had become the child in the family. His father had encouraged him from then on to be a little more serious in his studies, and when he was home on holiday, his father insisted that he learn how to manage the estate and also learn about affairs of business. Not long after, Lady Anne became ill and left Mr. Darcy alone with his son and a small daughter. Fitzwilliam Darcy had felt the weight of the responsibilities pressing on his father—and his father's loneliness.

"How I wish you were here, Papa," Darcy whispered as he looked back up at the likeness of his father. "I have so many questions." Tears welled up in Darcy's eyes. "I fear I do not know how to be a father. That was always your part. I was contented to simply be your son."

Darcy breathed in deeply and collected his thoughts. He took one last look at the sword, and placed it in the top drawer of the library desk.

————◦•◦•◦————

Elizabeth and her young daughter, Hannah, walked along the path to the north of the house for some time, until they came to a clearing where the old ruins stood. They hid themselves safely behind a large tree and peered around it, quite unnoticed.

"Who goes there?" a tall, dark-haired man called down from atop the rubble.

"'Tis I, Will Scarlett! I have come to pursue Robin the Hood!" a thin, dark-haired boy yelled up, making his voice sound as big as he could.

The man climbed down from his perch atop an old pile of masonry rock, wielding a carved toy sword, and said, "No one sees Robin the Hood!"

"How are we to play, Papa, if no one can see you?" the boy said in defeat.

"Of course, you can see me, Andrew," Darcy said and chuckled. "You are supposed to fight me for the right to join the merry men."

"Oh," the boy replied, and then turned around and called out excitedly, "Christian! Christian! Make haste! Papa is going to challenge us to a battle!"

A very small boy came charging out from behind the bushes with a toy sword in his hand and a wicked grin upon his face. "Come down and battle me, Papa!"

Darcy brandished his toy sword and pretended to fight off the advances of his sons. He was laughing so hard he could barely catch his breath. Andrew stuck his father in the ribs with the blunt point of his sword, and Darcy writhed in mock agony and fell to the ground, much to the delight of the giggling boys.

"Get up, Papa! Shall we do it again?" Christian tugged on Darcy's sleeve. "I want to do it again!"

"Christian, I am not as young a man as I used to be. Shall we not rest here a moment?" Darcy smiled and the boys hurried over to where he sat on the ground and took their places at his side. Darcy wrapped his arms around his sons. "Shall I tell you more of Robin Hood?"

Elizabeth and her daughter laughed, but remained hidden behind the tree, listening to Mr. Darcy as he began to recite a child's ballad:

> *They are all gone to London court,*
> *Robin Hood, with all his train;*
> *He once was there a noble peer,*
> *And now he's there again.*

> *Many such pranks brave Robin played*
> *While he lived in the green wood:*
> *Now, my friends, attend, and hear an end*
> *Of honest Robin Hood.*[7]

---

7 "The King's Disguise, and Friendship with Robin Hood" from Francis James Child's *The English and Scottish Popular Ballads* (Child's Ballad No. 151)

Father of the Bride
BY LEWIS WHELCHEL

Lewis Whelchel was first introduced to Jane Austen in college by friends at UC Irvine in the mid-1980s. Since that time, *Pride and Prejudice* has been his favorite Austen tale. He started reading Jane Austen fan fiction in 2001 and began writing in 2003. His first full-length novel, *Rocks in the Stream*, was released in early 2011, and his second will appear later that year. He and his wife, Tracy, and their children still living at home, relocated to central Tennessee in 2010 at the invitation of his employer, and are enjoying the beautiful countryside very much.

Mr. Bennet is a favorite character of mine, and I wanted to include in this collection one story that focused on him. Welchel's "Father of the Bride" is that story.

☙❧

Chapter 1

"If you will thank me," [Mr. Darcy] replied [to Elizabeth], "let it be for yourself alone. That the wish of giving happiness to you might add force to the other inducements which led me on, I shall not attempt to deny. But your family owe me nothing. Much as I respect them, I believe, I thought only of you."

Elizabeth was too much embarrassed to say a word. After a short pause, her companion added, "You are too generous to trifle with me. If your feelings are still what they were last April, tell me so at once. My affections and wishes are unchanged, but one word from you will silence me on this subject forever."

Elizabeth, feeling all the more than common awkwardness and anxiety of his situation, now forced herself to speak; and immediately, though not very fluently, gave him to understand that her sentiments had undergone so material a change, since the period to which he alluded, as to make her receive with gratitude and pleasure his present assurances.

Pride and Prejudice, chapter 58

"My dear Lizzy, where can you have been walking to?" was a question which Elizabeth received from Jane as soon as she entered the room, and from all the others when they sat down to table. She had only to say in reply that they had wandered about till she was beyond her own knowledge. She colored as she spoke; but neither that, nor anything else, awakened a suspicion of the truth.

Pride and Prejudice, chapter 59

A suspicion of the truth was not awakened in anyone—except Mr. Bennet, who was determined to learn the cause of that blush. He looked sternly at Elizabeth. He finally caught her eye, but she turned away with a laugh.

Throughout dinner, Mr. Bennet kept a close eye on Elizabeth and her co-conspirator, Mr. Darcy. It seemed to him that Elizabeth and Mr. Darcy were exchanging frequent glances. Though never truly staring at each other, when their eyes did meet, it was plain that they were engaged in unspoken communication.

Mr. Darcy and Elizabeth never spoke, but sat so close that their shoulders frequently brushed against each other. For some reason, Mr. Bennet observed, Mr. Darcy ate only with his left hand and Elizabeth with her right. Their other hands remained out of sight, hidden by the tablecloth. He would bet the whole of Longbourn estate that those hands were touching.

Mr. Bennet knew his second daughter well. Ever since she could walk, she had wandered the countryside around Longbourn and Meryton. The older she grew, the farther she went. He knew that she had left late that morning in the company of Mr. Bingley, Mr. Darcy, Jane, and Kitty. He was also aware that Mr. Bingley and Jane had returned alone in the early afternoon, and Kitty not long thereafter. However, it was not until many hours later that Elizabeth and Mr. Darcy had come back.

Although they had been gone for a substantial period of time, Mr. Bennet was convinced that this was not because Elizabeth had gone beyond her own knowledge. That possibility was not a consideration. Something else had either held their attention or prevented their timely return. Either way, his daughter had been alone with Mr. Darcy, out in the countryside, for the majority of the day.

Mr. Bennet did not want to suspect his daughter of any...*what could he say...*misconduct...but her behavior at dinner with Mr. Darcy provoked questions he never would have imagined asking Elizabeth. It had been true of Lydia, though, and he would not dare venture an opinion of Kitty's...situation—but Elizabeth?

Determined to know what had happened, he excused himself from company and retired to the library. He knew it would be some time before the gentlemen left. Once they were gone, he would have a private conversation with Elizabeth.

Tea had been served and it was time for the gentlemen to leave. The acknowledged lovers exchanged handclasps and tender words. The unacknowledged lovers parted in silence, with longing in their eyes the only communication between them.

Mr. Bennet was out of his library the moment he heard the door close. Walking with as much ease as his agitated mind would allow, he crossed the hall to the drawing room. He found Elizabeth tidying up her needlework.

"Lizzy, will you come to my library? I would like to speak with you," said Mr. Bennet.

Elizabeth thought nothing of this request, as it was not un-usual for father and daughter to spend hours reading together or in conversation.

Mr. Bennet followed Elizabeth into the room and invited her to take a seat in front of his desk. He sat in the chair next to hers. After looking into her eyes for a moment with a glance she readily returned, he cleared his throat and began what he hoped would not be a distressing interview.

"Lizzy, did anything happen today about which I should know?" asked Mr. Bennet.

Elizabeth shifted in her seat. Mr. Bennet noticed her discomfiture with raised eyebrows.

"Happen?" she repeated.

"Yes, between you and Mr. Darcy."

"Well, we did all walk out today..." began Elizabeth. She could not continue. She could not meet her father's eyes.

"I am aware of that, Lizzy, but it occurred to me that you and Mr. Darcy were gone much longer than the others, and I was wondering...Lizzy, did you really walk so far that you did not know where you were?"

"As you know, Father, I do walk many places, and...well..." She hesitated.

"Well?" quizzed Mr. Bennet, urging her to continue.

"I confess, sir," said Elizabeth meekly, looking down at her clenched hands in her lap, "that we were not beyond my knowledge. I was not completely truthful. I hoped no one would notice. I should have known that you would. I am sorry."

"Dissembling is not a feature of your character, Lizzy. You do not do it well at all," said Mr. Bennet mildly.

Elizabeth smiled and looked up, grateful that her father was not truly angry with her. There would, however, be no escape from acknowledging the truth of her situation with Mr. Darcy.

"Sir, something did happen today, though it is not with me that you should speak."

"Oh, and with whom should I speak?"

Elizabeth paused under her father's unyielding stare. "With Mr. Darcy, sir," she said with a smile that seemed to Mr. Bennet to be directed inwardly rather than at himself.

"Will you tell me?" asked Mr. Bennet.

"I know you will not let me leave until I do," she said and laughed. "Very well. Today, Mr. Darcy asked me to marry him, and I accepted. We spoke of everything. It was not until we turned westward and the sun was low on the horizon that Mr. Darcy checked his pocket watch and realized that we had been gone far too long. But there had been so much to say. Oh, Father, I love him!"

"You *love* Mr. Darcy? I thought you hated him!" Mr. Bennet could not retain his seat. He stood and paced about the room. "Are you out of your senses to be accepting that man?

Elizabeth smiled tenderly at her father. "I know that in the beginning I did not always speak favorably of Mr. Darcy."

"Lizzy, is that what you call it? 'Favorably'? My dear, you taught half of Meryton to hate the man!" cried her father.

"I was wrong, so very wrong!" she protested. "I came to know him better when I was at Hunsford. He was staying with his aunt at Rosings Park, and we were with each other daily, and I saw him again in Derbyshire when I traveled there with my aunt and uncle, and I liked him so very much."

Mr. Bennet noticed a faraway look in her eyes.

"Lizzy, I know very little about what you did at Hunsford and nothing at all about Derbyshire," said Mr. Bennet.

"Mr. Darcy proposed marriage to me at Hunsford."

Mr. Bennet could not hide his surprise. "But—"

"I refused him," she answered, "because I did not know him then. Everything changed when I saw him and fell in love with him in Derbyshire. I loved him, and only news of Lydia's elopement could have taken me away from him."

"What do you mean, 'taken you away'?" Mr. Bennet was incredulous.

"I love him, Father," said Elizabeth unabashedly. "If he had asked me to stay with him at Pemberley, I would have, but we left before I had the chance to see him again."

Mr. Bennet asked the question that had been on his mind all afternoon.

"Have you…has he…I mean, have you been…" he cleared his throat. "Has he made any…advances toward you. I mean, have you been…*compromised* …in any way? Is there any reason—"

Elizabeth interrupted him with a gasp. "*No*, that has not happened."

Mr. Bennet took out a handkerchief and wiped the perspiration off his brow.

"You obviously feel a great deal for him, Lizzy," admitted Mr. Bennet, "but is he a good man?"

"He is the best man I know, Papa. He has the good opinion of all his servants and tenants at Pemberley. My Aunt Gardiner inquired of all her acquaintance in Lambton and the surrounding neighborhood, and he is held in high esteem. He is raising his younger sister, Miss Darcy, and you would never meet a more well-mannered, considerate young lady. She is a joy to be around, and I look forward with great anticipation to being her sister."

Her father frowned slightly.

"I know I did not speak well of him and that I accused him of pride, but, Father, he has no pride at all. The problem was me and the prejudices I had nurtured from the very beginning of our acquaintance."

"That is all well and good, Lizzy," said Mr. Bennet, "and I will give him credit for being a good brother, master, landlord, and neighbor, but that may mean nothing. Does he truly love you?"

"He does, Father. And you will love him nearly as much as I do when you get to know him. He is Mr. Bingley's closest friend, and I know your good opinion of Mr. Bingley," said Elizabeth.

"Why has he not sought my consent?" demanded Mr. Bennet.

"He wanted to approach you tonight, but I begged him to wait just one day until I could speak with you. I knew that you would be...surprised by the alteration in my feelings for him."

"Very well, Lizzy." Mr. Bennet pondered for a moment and determined to test her commitment. "I do not know if I trust your Mr. Darcy. What if I withhold my consent?"

Elizabeth was shocked and tears formed in her eyes.

"Papa, please do not put me in that situation! I love you both and you will love him, too. Please, Father! Please give us your blessing!"

Elizabeth buried her face in her hands and began to cry. Mr. Bennet watched her for a moment, regretting that he had provoked her. It had not been his intent to make her unhappy.

"Hush, Lizzy. All will be well." Mr. Bennet was resigned. Elizabeth would marry Mr. Darcy. "You know, Lizzy, it pains me to lose you."

Elizabeth looked up at her father. "You will not lose me, Papa. And I love him."

"Come here, child." Mr. Bennet stood pulled Elizabeth into his arms and kissed her forehead.

"I will give you my consent, Lizzy."

"Thank you, Papa."

"You run along to bed now. I look forward to seeing your Mr. Darcy tomorrow."

With a smile, Elizabeth rose and stepped to the door. Just as she took hold of the knob, her father called her back.

"Lizzy, it could be some weeks before you can be married." He cleared his throat. "I think it would be...inadvisable...for you and Mr. Darcy to be...to be alone...too much...together," stuttered Mr. Bennet.

"Can I not have a small ceremony scheduled in the shortest time?

"How short a time?" asked Mr. Bennet.

"Mr. Darcy can procure a license from town. We could marry within the week. But Mama—"

"You do not feel you need time to consider your feelings for him? You are certain in your decision to marry him?" asked Mr. Bennet.

"I am. Please, Papa, I know that my love for him seems to be a sudden thing. But I am convinced that it has been there—or at least developing—all along."

"Very well, Lizzie," Mr. Bennet said with a smile. "I have given you my consent, dearest, and I will give you my assistance. Lizzy, I promise that in five days you shall be Mr. Darcy's bride."

"*Five* days? You can do that for me? For us?"

Mr. Bennet nodded.

"Thank you, Papa! But what about Mama?" Elizabeth questioned. "She will insist on a large ceremony with all of Meryton there and—"

Mr. Bennet cut her off. "I will attend to her. Elizabeth. Five more days. Be patient, my child."

Chapter 2

The next morning, Mr. Bingley and Mr. Darcy arrived at Longbourn in such good time that none of the ladies were dressed for the day.

Mr. Bennet, however, was eager to speak with Mr. Darcy, so he went to the hall and welcomed the Netherfield gentlemen.

"Good morning, Son," said Mr. Bennet to Mr. Bingley.

Bingley laughed and wished Jane's father a good morning.

"And you are very welcome also, sir," Mr. Bennet said to Mr. Darcy as he took his hand. "I am pleased that you could come today, and so early, too."

"Uh…thank you, sir." Darcy was a little surprised at Mr. Bennet's warm greeting. "I am very happy to be here, Mr. Bennet," said Darcy. "I apologize that we are so early, as I see your daughters are not yet down. Bingley was eager to see Miss Bennet."

Mr. Bennet smiled. "And is that to say, Mr. Darcy, that you are not eager to see a Miss Bennet yourself?"

Bingley nudged Darcy with his elbow while Darcy looked at the floor, struggling to hide a momentary embarrassment.

"Well, I am happy, sir—"

"Mr. Darcy," interrupted Mr. Bennet, "I would like some private conversation with you, sir. If you will please excuse us, Mr. Bingley."

Mr. Bingley bowed his assent and Mr. Bennet led Darcy to the library.

Darcy had intended to arrange for a private interview with Mr. Bennet, but had imagined that it would take place in the evening. For now, he was eager to see Elizabeth again and renew all that they had said and felt the day before. He desperately wanted to see Elizabeth—alone, if possible—and be assured from her own lips that what she had told him yesterday was true—that she loved him. If even a moment of privacy could be attained, he would take her in his arms and kiss those lips again.

"Mr. Darcy, perhaps you would like to sit here," said Mr. Bennet, motioning to the chair Elizabeth had occupied the prior evening. Mr. Bennet moved behind his desk.

"I have asked you in here, Mr. Darcy, in order to establish the truth of a marvelous tale I heard yesterday evening."

"What tale, sir?"

"Elizabeth tells me that she is in love with a man whom she hates!"

Darcy's breath caught in his throat. "Sir?"

"Let me be frank, Mr. Darcy. From the very beginning of your acquaintance with my family, the only reports I have heard of you have been distressingly unfavorable. Indeed, if it were not for your close friendship with Mr. Bingley, my future son-in-law, you might not even be welcome at Longbourn."

Darcy could feel a cold perspiration form on his forehead. "I pray that you will accept my apologies, sir," began Darcy. "I know that I have behaved in a manner that could appear—"

"Let me see," interrupted Mr. Bennet. He was beginning to enjoy himself. "What was it that Elizabeth told me? Something shocking, offensive, and quite ungentlemanly."

"I do not understand——"

"Perhaps you will recognize these words, Mr. Darcy. I repeat them as Elizabeth herself related them to me: 'She is tolerable; but not handsome enough to tempt *me*.' Does that sound familiar to you?"

Darcy was stunned at hearing the cruelty of his own words. How often had he regretted saying them! How often had he feared that Elizabeth had overheard him! He had grown easy as time passed and she did not mention that awful occasion. He had begun to feel that she had not, after all, overheard him. To have it now mentioned, and by her father, was...horrible.

"Please let me apologize, Mr. Bennet," begged Darcy. "I did not know Elizabeth, and I was in a very ill humor. I wished to recall those words the instant they were spoken."

Darcy's discomfiture was evident and Mr. Bennet *almost* felt guilty for having thrust a dagger into Mr. Darcy's heart.

"Mr. Darcy," said Mr. Bennet, "you will be happy to know that Elizabeth has forgiven you, and if she can overlook the offense, then so can I."

Darcy was visibly relieved and managed to croak his thanks.

"In any case, Mr. Darcy, that is not the reason I asked to speak with you. You see, I am aware that you have some business with me. Perhaps you would like to begin?"

Darcy stood up and began to step away from his seat, as if escaping confinement.

"It is rather early, Mr. Darcy, but may I offer you a glass of port? You appear to me to be...uh...nervous." Mr. Bennet's eyes held a glint of amusement.

Darcy shook his head and resumed his seat, and summoning up what courage remained in him, began to speak.

"Mr. Bennet, you have me at a great disadvantage. I am in love with a woman who hated me, and through circumstances both propitious and fortunate, she now loves me and I have persuaded her to accept my offer of marriage."

"Ah, yes, persuasion. That is something I want to touch upon, but it can wait. I am fascinated, sir," said Mr. Bennet. "Please go on!"

"I have asked Elizabeth to marry me, and she has consented. I am now seeking *your* consent."

"That is very interesting, Mr. Darcy, but I am convinced that she hates you. How can I consent to a marriage based on such a feeling?"

"Mr. Bennet, I am quite certain that Elizabeth does not hate me. We have become good friends since our accidental meeting in Derbyshire. It is there that I won her affection and regard. I would have asked for her hand then, had not urgent family business arisen to take her away. You cannot imagine how I suffered when I learned she had left the country and I had not been able to see her."

"If you do feel as you say you do, then, yes, it must have been a difficult time for you."

Darcy was surprised to hear words of compassion from Mr. Bennet, and his failing hopes gained some life.

"I love Elizabeth very much, and we want your blessing to our union," said Darcy.

"And if I withhold my consent?" asked Mr. Bennet.

"You would disappoint and hurt your daughter." Darcy's head began to throb.

"That is a bold statement, sir."

"I am confident in my feelings for her and hers for me."

"*That* is a good basis for an understanding. I must be honest with you, Mr. Darcy. I had a private conversation with Elizabeth yesterday evening and she expressed a similar confidence in your feelings for her. She has spoken to me of your good qualities and has convinced me of your merit. It is not my intention to disappoint her, Mr. Darcy. Therefore, you have my consent to marry her..."

"Thank you, sir! I promise that I—"

Mr. Bennet continued his thought. "...but on my terms only."

Darcy's elation was quickly stifled.

"My daughter is impatient to marry."

"As am I, sir."

"Yes, well..." Mr. Bennet coughed. "Allow me, Mr. Darcy, to offer a suggestion. Elizabeth tells me that it is within your power to obtain a license to marry, and that you can do so in a short period of time. Is that correct?"

"Yes, sir, it is."

"I have heard a rumor that you are required in Derbyshire by the beginning of next week to attend to matters of your estate there," said Mr. Bennet.

"Excuse me?" said Darcy.

"I understand that you must leave Hertfordshire in just a few days."

"My plans were to remain at Netherfield until our wedding," declared Darcy.

"Mr. Darcy, I thought I understood that you were unable to remain long in Hertfordshire, and therefore a long engagement and a large ceremony were impossible. Is that not true?" said Mr. Bennet slyly.

"Well..." began Darcy hesitantly, "I believe...yes...I believe you are correct. I almost forgot. I must be at Pemberley next Monday. Since we have your consent, " he said bravely, "is there any hope of an early marriage that will make it possible for Elizabeth to accompany me?"

"Those are my thoughts exactly, Mr. Darcy."

"They are? I thank you." *What a relief!*

"I propose the following. I suggest that you leave this very day—this very hour—for town to obtain the marriage license. I recommend that you then find some reason to remain in town for three days. On the fourth, you will travel back to Netherfield, where you will have much to speak of with Mr. Bingley. On the fifth day, early in the morning, you will see Elizabeth at the altar of the Longbourn church."

"Mr. Bennet, I am indebted to your kindness and generosity. May I tell Elizabeth the good news?"

"That will be impossible, Mr. Darcy," said Mr. Bennet.

"I am certain she will be down by now. I have no doubt that—"

"Impossible, Mr. Darcy."

"Why is that, sir?" Darcy was annoyed.

"Because, sir, you have already left. I will extend your best wishes and warmest regards to my daughter. Indeed, as you have expressed to me your love for her, I will pass on that message as well, and relate the substance of our conversation. I assure you, Mr. Darcy, in five days she will be prepared to marry you. Five days, sir."

Darcy was speechless.

Mr. Bennet rose from his seat. "Let me see you to the door."

Chapter 3

Having heard that Mr. Darcy had already arrived at the house, Elizabeth readied herself quickly. She had passed a long night recalling the course of her relationship with Mr. Darcy. Whatever pain she may have suffered at the beginning of it was easily forgotten in the pleasure of his embrace and knowing that her future with him was secure.

Whatever the day would bring, Elizabeth knew that she would seek opportunities to be in his arms again.

Her father had promised that she would be Mr. Darcy's wife in five days. Five days! It seemed an eternity.

Elizabeth hurried down the stairs into the drawing room, fully expecting to see Mr. Darcy.

Entering the room, she was met not by Mr. Darcy, but by her sisters. And Mr. Bingley. And her father.

"Elizabeth, may I speak privately with you?"

"Of course, Father, but where is Mr. Darcy? I understood that he was here with Mr. Bingley."

At the mention of his name, Bingley bowed.

"Yes, it is he of whom I wish to speak," confessed Mr. Bennet.

Elizabeth gave him a questioning and confused look.

"Come with me into the garden, Elizabeth," said Mr. Bennet as he led the way to the door.

Elizabeth had no choice but to follow. Dark questions arose in her mind. Had Mr. Darcy not come? She had been expecting him. What did it mean that he was not there?

"Elizabeth," said Mr. Bennet softly, "I saw your Mr. Darcy this morning."

"But where is he?" cried Elizabeth in agitation.

"You were correct. Mr. Darcy arrived early this morning in company with Mr. Bingley. He and I had a conversation, during which time he asked for my consent to marry you."

"And?" pressed Elizabeth.

"Yesterday evening, I gave my consent to you. This morning, I gave my consent to Mr. Darcy, just as I told you I would."

"But where *is* he?" She was desperate to see him. She suddenly felt very alone and only Darcy's assurances of love would ease her mind.

"By now, he is on the road to London."

"To London! Father, what have you done?" Elizabeth was growing frantic. Her father was not being forthcoming with his information about Darcy, and if she understood correctly, it would appear that he had sent him away.

"I related to Mr. Darcy some of the details of our conversation last night. I told him that in five days you would be his. Today, he is traveling to London for the license. Business will keep him in town for three days. On the fourth, he will return to Netherfield and the company of his friends there, and the next day you will see him again early in the morning. He will be at the altar of the Longbourn church. I will accompany you to the church, escort you down the aisle, and give your hand to him. The pastor will solemnize your union, and thereafter you and he will be together."

"But could he not wait to see me?" asked Elizabeth, frowning.

Mr. Bennet looked away for a moment. "I told him," said her father, "to leave immediately. He will need to allow plenty of time to complete his errand, which is, of course, to obtain a marriage license."

"It does not take three days to obtain a license, nor does it take an entire day to travel between Hertfordshire and London. Why am I not to see him until then?" asked Elizabeth.

"I would not have anything unexpected—some bureaucratic hitch—delay your wedding."

"You sent him away!" cried Elizabeth.

Mr. Bennet blanched. It was one thing to confront Mr. Darcy. It was quite another to confront his daughter. "I can see how you might think so. And perhaps I did." He coughed. "Yes, I did. I sent Mr. Darcy away."

"Why? Why did he have to go?" Elizabeth asked. Her cheeks were flushed.

Her father sighed. "Young people can be...impulsive. Their emotions are often in an uproar. They may allow their...feelings and...sensations to overtake their good sense. Do you understand me, Elizabeth?"

Elizabeth sat heavily on a nearby bench. A tear escaped her eye.

"I shall dearly miss him, Father."

"I know you will, and it is right that you should feel so. In five days, Elizabeth, you and he will be together. Please be patient."

"Yes, Father," said Elizabeth.

Mr. Bennet said cheerfully, "Besides, how much time would you allow yourself for preparations for your wedding and imminent departure if you spent every moment with Mr. Darcy? You realize, of course, that there is much to do."

"Yes, that is true. In five days, I shall leave this place."

"There is one chore that must be completed before any of the others. We must announce your engagement to your mother. She will be elated—until she learns that she will have no time for lace, finery and an elaborate ceremony."

"Will she ever forgive me?"

"I will take the blame. After all, I—not you or Mr. Darcy— chose your wedding date."

Elizabeth laughed and took his arm. Father and daughter returned to the house to seek out its mistress and share what would be both welcome and unwelcome news.

Chapter 4

"Mrs. Bennet," said Hill, "Mr. Bennet would see you in his library."

"That is so like him, to just order me about." Mrs. Bennet was at her work in her dressing room. She was always resentful of interruptions, particularly by her husband.

"Very well, Mrs. Bennet. Shall I tell Mr. Bennet that you are unable to see him now?" asked Mrs. Hill, trying to hide a smile. This was a ritual in which she participated any time Mr. Bennet summoned his wife. It would end no differently this time than any other time.

"No, no. Please, do not say such a thing. Of course, I will go and see what my husband desires of me."

"Yes, ma'am," replied Mrs. Hill."

"Thank you, Hill. Well, I shall go see what Mr. Bennet is about now." And with that, Mrs. Bennet left her dressing room, descended the stairs, and crossed the hall to stand in front of the library. After a moment's hesitation, she knocked on the door.

"Come in, Mrs. Bennet!" called her husband.

She entered the library with her head held high. "And just how did you know it was me? It could have been anybody, you know!"

"I was expecting no one but you, my dear. Please do sit down," said Mr. Bennet as he pointed to the chair in front of his desk.

"Very well, Mr. Bennet. I am here. You have taken me from my work. Tell me what is so important."

Mr. Bennet looked over his shoulder. "Lizzy, please come here."

For the first time, Mrs. Bennet noticed that Elizabeth was also in the room. The young woman stepped out of the corner, walked to her father, and stood next to him near his desk. Mr. Bennet took her hand.

"Mrs. Bennet, I have some very good news. Actually, it is our daughter who has the news."

"Yes. Mama," Elizabeth said. "Mr. Darcy and I are to be married. Papa has already given his consent. I do hope that——"

"Mr. Darcy!" cried Mrs. Bennet. "You are to marry *Mr. Darcy?!*"

Mrs. Bennet rose and began to pace the room. Elizabeth's heart sank. Nevertheless, her mother's disapprobation would not shake Elizabeth's determination to marry Mr. Darcy. Nothing would!

"You are to marry Mr. Darcy," repeated Mrs. Bennet. "Lizzy, does he not have a house in town?" she asked.

"I believe so, Mama," answered Elizabeth hesitantly.

"And does he not keep more than one carriage?"

"Several, ma'am."

"And is not Pemberley a fine estate?"

"It is a beautiful place, Mama."

"Oh, Lizzy! I am so happy! You have no idea! Another daughter married. Oh, Jane has done so well! You have done so well! How much pin money shall you have? Oh, never mind that. A house in town. Carriages! A large estate in the country. It is as good as a lord!"

"Hardly that, Mama," said Elizabeth. "The Duke of Devonshire also resides in Derbyshire, and his income is much more than Mr. Darcy's. You must not say such things——"

"What do I care for a duke? Oh, Lizzy, I am so happy. Oh! Please excuse me, Mr. Bennet, I must immediately go into Meryton to tell the good news to——"

"Please, Mrs. Bennet. There is something else you should know," said Mr. Bennet.

"What else could I possibly wish to hear? This is such wonderful news. Oh, Lizzy, please do apologize to Mr. Darcy for my having disliked him, and Lizzy, what is his favorite dessert?"

Elizabeth laughed. "I believe it is treacle tart and custard, Mama."

"We shall have it this very evening. I am certain he will overlook my having disliked him. How could I possibly have imagined such a thing? How wonderful! First our dear Bingley and now our dear Darcy!"

"Mrs. Bennet, please!" cried Mr. Bennet.

"Yes, Mr. Bennet?"

"Mrs. Bennet, you should also know that this wedding will take place in the morning five days from now."

"How can that possibly be? Oh, Lizzy, you know that we must travel to London for your clothes. I have never trusted the modiste in Meryton ever since she…well, never mind. I shall send a note to my sister Gardiner. We will stay at her house while in town. I would expect that eight or nine weeks will be sufficient time—"

"Five days, Mrs. Bennet!"

"The young people do not know what they are about, you must see that!" answered Mrs. Bennet.

"I am pleased to see that we do agree on one thing. Yes, the young people do *not* know what they are about. Therefore, I have chosen their wedding date for them, and it will be in five days. I have promised them both, and I will fulfill my commitment."

"Mr. Bennet, I will speak with Mr. Darcy, and I am certain he will—"

"Indeed, Mrs. Bennet, I have had extensive conversations with both our daughter and Mr. Darcy, and I assure you that a long engagement is impossible." Mr. Bennet glanced over at Elizabeth, who was hiding a blush by adjusting her hair-pins.

"I am the bride's mother. Do I not have some voice in the matter?" asked Mrs. Bennet.

"Mrs. Bennet, you may have as much voice in your eldest daughter's wedding plans as she will allow, but you will have none in Elizabeth's. In five days, she will be Mrs. Darcy. Make what plans you can. Once the service is over, they will immediately leave for Pemberley. There will be no need to plan a wedding breakfast. Mr. Darcy must be in Derbyshire within a week's time, and he will not leave without his bride."

"No, I suppose that he would not wish to do that," Mrs. Bennet said slowly. "Leave without his new wife, that is. And his new wife will be our Lizzy." Her eyes sparkled. "Very well, then, Mr. Bennet., Mr. Darcy shall return for dinner and I will congratulate him then and let him know that I had been considering this very thing. What an excellent wife Lizzy will make him. I shall tell him I knew it all along!"

Mrs. Bennet ran from the room, unable to contain her joy, and gave orders in the kitchen for treacle tart and custard. Several hours later, she would learn that her future son-in-law was not to return to Hertfordshire until the very moment of his wedding.

Chapter 5

Clink.

Elizabeth awoke to the sound of small rocks glancing off her window. Looking outside, she could see the lawn, which was illuminated by a full moon...

Clink.

...And directly under the window was Mr. Darcy. Her heart skipped a beat when she saw him. Every feeling of love, longing, and desire she had for him burst to the surface, and she had to restrain herself from crying out.

She acknowledged Darcy with a wave and watched him walk off into the shadows. Pulling her robe over her nightgown, she crept down the stairs, avoiding the noisy steps, and stole out of the house.

The heavy latch of the door locked into place. Elizabeth paused, straining to hear any sound coming from the house. There was none. Her heart pounding with excitement, she ran around the front of the house to the side, where she expected to find Mr. Darcy.

Mr. Bennet was oblivious to time while reading a book, and his candle would often burn late into the night as he pursued his favorite occupation. Tonight, the subject had been a little dull, and as his candle burned low and then out, he fell asleep in his chair. It was the night before Elizabeth's wedding, and he was sorrowful at the thought of losing her.

It was not a rare thing for him to fall asleep reading, but it was rare—unique, really—for him to be awakened by the sound of the front door closing.

He looked toward the window as he rose from his chair, and was in time to see a blur of silk and dark curls rush by.

Mr. Bennet paused for a moment, chuckled to himself, and then retired to his bedchamber.

"Fitzwilliam, what are you doing here?" whispered Elizabeth as she was swept up into his arms.

"I could not go another hour without seeing you, Elizabeth. I had to come," replied Darcy.

"I am so glad you did. I missed you desperately."

"Elizabeth, I am sorry I left without a word, but your father—"

"I know. He told me everything. Please do not be angry with him."

"I am not angry. Not any longer," said Darcy.

Elizabeth answered with a smile as he caressed her cheek. "I have brought you a gift, my love," he said. He took a small black velvet bag with a drawstring from his pocket and gave it to her.

"Open it, Elizabeth."

Opening the bag, Elizabeth pulled out a sparkling necklace that seemed to reflect the beauty of the moon.

"Oh, Fitzwilliam, it is beautiful."

"The stones are sapphires, the color of a moonlit night. I hope you will wear this and remember this night when you do."

"I promise, Fitzwilliam. I will wear it and I will remember."

"Here, let me put it on you now."

Elizabeth offered him the necklace and turned her back to him. He brushed her hair to the side and placed it around her neck. She moved as if to turn around, but he prevented her when his lips touched her skin. Her body trembled in delight at his touch.

"In just a few hours, we will be married, Elizabeth."

"My father told me we are leaving for Pemberley directly from the church."

"Yes, if you concur."

"I desire nothing but to be alone with you, Fitzwilliam."

"We will be alone soon, my love. Let me accompany you back to the house. It is chilly and you should not be out here.

Elizabeth took Darcy's arm and they walked together to the door. There, they shared a lingering kiss. Breathless, Elizabeth leaned her head on his shoulder.

"You cannot know how lonely I was," he murmured. "Arranging for the license took no time at all, and I was left with three days in town to do nothing but think of you. Every waking hour, I was tortured with my aloneness."

Darcy kissed her again.

"I love you, Fitzwilliam."

"I do not want to leave you, Elizabeth, but I must."

"I know," said Elizabeth, "but I shall see you at church in no time at all, and I shall wear this necklace as a reminder of our first night together."

"Good night, my love."

The wedding of Elizabeth Bennet of Longbourn and Fitzwilliam Darcy of Pemberley was celebrated at the Longbourn church early in the morning. A few of the older ladies in attendance could not remember a service ever being held quite so early.

Despite the short notice, the church had been decorated with flowers, and the bride was dressed in a stunning white gown and adorned with a necklace of stones the color of a moonlit night.

After the ceremony, the company returned to Longbourn, where a sumptuous wedding breakfast was served. Although the absence of the bride and groom was questioned, it was agreed that the breakfast was the most superior affair in recent memory.

"I must say, Mr. Bennet," said his wife. She paused.

"Yes, Mrs. Bennet?" He waited patiently.

"I must say that the day has gone off remarkably well. The ceremony was spoken with all the solemnity and feeling that it deserved, And Mrs. Long said she had never seen as much food on a table in the course of her whole life. Mrs. Long is a splendid woman. And her two nieces are not *so* very plain."

"Indeed they are not, Mrs. Bennet, and you must confess that they are nice girls."

Mrs. Bennet did not seem to hear him. "Mr. Bennet, I am surprised that you allowed Mr. Darcy and Elizabeth to leave for Pemberley from the church and not attend the breakfast to receive the best wishes of their friends and family."

"My dear Mrs. Bennet, I could hardly prevent them."

"I suppose not," said Mrs. Bennet. "And Mr. Darcy is a very handsome man. What an excellent wife Lizzy will make him. I knew it all along!"

Pride and Prejudice Abridged
BY MARSHA ALTMAN

Marsha Altman exists more as a philosophical concept than an atom-based structure existing within the rules of time and space as we know it. She is the author of *The Darcys and the Bingleys*, *The Plight of the Darcy Brothers*, *Mr. Darcy's Great Escape*, *The Ballad of Grégoire Darcy*, and *Mr. Darcy is Also in This Title* (title and manuscript existence pending), and is the editor of this anthology. When not writing, she studies Talmud and paints Tibetan ritual art, preferably not at the same time. She does not own any cats.

Always leave 'em laughing.

☙❧

(Meryton assembly)

Darcy: She is tolerable; but not enough to tempt *me*.

Elizabeth: Excuse me!

Darcy *(remembering he's a gentleman)*: Excuse me. I did not realize you were listening in this relatively small ballroom, depending on the adaptation.

Elizabeth: I was.

Darcy: I really am sorry. *(Notices she's cute)* Listen, my friend dragged me to this, and I don't like assemblies, and I'm in a bad mood about this family thing. Can we start over?

Elizabeth: Hmm. What a reasonable thing to say. All right.

(Jane gets sick at Netherfield. Elizabeth goes to Netherfield, bumps elbows with Darcy.)

Elizabeth: So you are picky about the women you date, as is probably the thing a rich man with many fortune hunters on his coattail would be?

Darcy: Yes. I like intelligent women who read a lot. Do you read a lot?

Elizabeth: Yes.

Darcy: Awesome.

(Elizabeth meets Wickham.)

Wickham: ...And those are all the reasons that Darcy sucks.

Elizabeth: I'm tempted to believe you, man I just met and has no established reputation—as opposed to Mr. Darcy, whom I have known longer and is established to be a respectable gentleman—but I really feel like the horrible gossip you've just imparted to me, for no particular reason that I can see, should be verified by at least one other person.

Wickham: ...

Elizabeth: I know! Mr. Darcy wouldn't say anything good, but Mr. Bingley thinks the best of everyone. I'll ask him if he knows Wickham.

(At another meeting)

Elizabeth: Blah blah blah. Do you know Mr. Wickham?

Bingley: That guy? Oh, for the good of society, Darcy went out of his way to tell me what a devious man he was. He even told my sisters. Let me explain....

Elizabeth: Hmm. Wickham can't back up his story. Well, maybe I should take it with a grain—maybe a pound—of salt.

(After the Netherfield ball)

Miss Bingley: We must away to London at once!

Bingley: Why?

Miss Bingley: The Bennets are nothing more than scheming chits!

Bingley: Well, technically, they're gentry, and we're little more than middle class until I buy an estate. Darcy?

Darcy (*stops daydreaming about Elizabeth*): Their mother is detestable and their sisters little more.

Bingley: Well, am I marrying the hot, sweet girl I love or the mother? Or the sisters?

Darcy: Oh right. Yeah, um…let's give it another week or two. Until it gets really cold. You know.

(**Bingley** *gets the hint that* **Jane** *isn't timid and marries her.*)

Darcy: Well, have to run. Family stuff.

(*Kent*)

Elizabeth: Mr. Darcy!

Darcy: Miss Bennet!

Elizabeth: What are you doing here?

Darcy: You know how you have to hang around with annoying relatives during the holidays?

Elizabeth: Oh, right.

Colonel Fitzwilliam: And I'm his cousin! Darcy is so awesome. And dreamy.

Darcy: Shut up, plot device character who exists solely for us to have a reason to awkwardly flirt. (*To* **Elizabeth**) Marry me?

Elizabeth: Yes!

(*The double wedding*)

Vicar: Do you take—

Aunt Catherine: No! This cannot be! Darcy, you must marry your cousin, which I will remind first-time high school readers is an acceptable custom at this time period!

Darcy: Hmm. Maybe me *not* marrying her for the past five years hasn't been enough of a sign. Well, this is will be. I do.

Colonel Fitzwilliam: No! Jane!

Jane: Who are you?

Colonel Fitzwilliam: I'm the guy who's like Bingley, only less dorky and with no money to support you, whom many people think you should marry because I was cast well in the BBC miniseries!

Bingley: Hey! *I'm* a lovable dork.

Jane: And I've never even met this guy.

Elizabeth: And isn't the whole principle behind your character, aside from spreading good and bad gossip about Darcy, is that you need to marry rich?

Colonel Fitzwilliam: True love will show the way!

Darcy: I call Fuck with Canon. Anyone?

Bingley: Totally.

Jane: Who is this guy?

(Colonel Fitzwilliam is thrown out of the church, and everyone is married and lives happily ever after.)

Other Ulysses Press Books

The Ballad of Grégoire Darcy: Jane Austen's *Pride and Prejudice* Continues
Marsha Altman, $14.95
This riveting sequel to *Pride and Prejudice* captures Austen's style and wit, and brings old favorites and new characters to life. When Fitzwilliam Darcy discovers he has a long-lost illegitimate brother, he feels compelled to help his new sibling find a place in the world. Meanwhile, Elizabeth finds herself pulled into a web of commitments when her sister Mary Bennet finally falls in love.

Darcy's Passions: Pride and Prejudice Retold Through His Eyes
Regina Jeffers, $14.95
This novel presents Darcy as a man in turmoil. His duty to his family and estate demand he choose a woman of high social standing. But what his mind tells him to do and what his heart knows to be true are two different things. After rejecting Elizabeth, he soon discovers he's in love with her. But the independent Elizabeth rejects his marriage proposal. Devastated, he must search his soul and transform himself into the man she can love and respect.

Mr. Darcy Presents His Bride: A Sequel to Jane Austen's Pride & Prejudice
Helen Halstead, $14.95
When Elizabeth Bennet marries Mr. Darcy, she's thrown into the exciting world of London society. Elizabeth is drawn into a powerful clique for which intrigue is the stuff of life and rivalry the motive. Her success, it seems, can only come at the expense of good relations with her husband.

Darcy's Temptation: A Sequel to Jane Austen's Pride & Prejudice

Regina Jeffers, $14.95

By changing the narrator to Mr. Darcy, *Darcy's Temptation* presents new plot twists and fresh insights into the characters' personalities and motivations. Four months into the new marriage, all seems well when Elizabeth discovers she's pregnant. However, a family conflict that requires Darcy's personal attention arises because of Georgiana's involvement with an activist abolitionist. On his return journey from a meeting to address this issue, a much greater danger arises. Darcy is attacked on the road and, when left helpless from his injuries, he finds himself in the care of another woman.

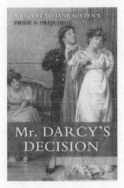

Mr. Darcy's Decision: A Sequel to Jane Austen's Pride & Prejudice

Juliette Shapiro $14.95

Mr. and Mrs. Fitzwilliam Darcy begin their married life blissfully, but it is not long before their tranquility is undermined by social enemies. Concern mounts with the sudden return of Elizabeth's sister Lydia. Alarming reports of seduction, blackmail and attempts to keep secret the news of another's confinement dampens even Elizabeth's high spirits.

To order these books call 800-377-2542 or 510-601-8301, fax 510-601-8307, e-mail ulysses@ulyssespress.com, or write to Ulysses Press, P.O. Box 3440, Berkeley, CA 94703. All retail orders are shipped free of charge. California residents must include sales tax. Allow two to three weeks for delivery.

Acknowledgments

I would like to thank the entire team at Ulysses Press: Keith, Bryce, Alice, Claire, Karma, and various people whom I'm sure had an unseen hand (from my perspective) in the creation of this anthology.

I would also like to give a special thanks to Victoria Claughton for creating the searchable Jane Austen fan fiction index, and therefore cutting down my work by about a thousand hours. She also provided help contacting authors I could not reach myself.

Finally, this could not have happened but for the inspiration from the great Jane Austen herself. In this book we are proud to honor her literary legacy in our own weird ways.